Other Titles by Cheryl Brooks

Cowboy Delight
Cowboy Heaven
Unbridled: Unlikely Lovers Book 1
Uninhibited: Unlikely Lovers Book 2
Undeniable: Unlikely Lovers Book 3
Unrivaled: Unlikely Lovers Book 4
The Cat Star Chronicles: Rebel
The Cat Star Chronicles: Wildcat
The Cat Star Chronicles: Stud
The Cat Star Chronicles: Virgin
The Cat Star Chronicles: Hero
The Cat Star Chronicles: Fugitive
The Cat Star Chronicles: Outcast
The Cat Star Chronicles: Rogue
The Cat Star Chronicles: Warrior
The Cat Star Chronicles: Slave
The Cat Star Chronicles Bundle: Slave, Warrior & Rogue
Sharing (Sextet Anthology)
Entanglements (Sextet Anthology)
Occupational Hazards (Sextet Anthology)
Mistletoe & Ménage (Sextet Anthology)
Dirty Dancing (Sextet Anthology)
Small, Medium, & Large (Sextet Presents)
The Lady Takes a Pair (Sextet Presents)
A Tale of Two Knights (Sextet Presents)
Midnight in Reno
If You Could Read My Mind (writing as Samantha R. Michael

UNLIKELY LOVERS

Unrivaled

CHERYL BROOKS

DERRYMANE PRESS

Derrymane
Press

Unrivaled
by Cheryl Brooks
Published by Derrymane Press
Copyright 2014. Cheryl Brooks.
Cover design by Dragonfly Press Design
Cover image by Shutterstock
ISBN 13: 978-0-9838081-9-0

For everyone who enjoys a bit of eye candy now and then...

ACKNOWLEDGEMENTS

My heartfelt thanks go out to:

My terrific critique partners, Sandy James and Nan Reinhardt.

My keen-eyed beta reader, Mellanie Szereto.

My pal and mentor in the self-publishing world, Marie Force.

My IRWA buddies for their support and encouragement.

My friends and family for their love and understanding.

I couldn't have done this without you!

Chapter 1

Nobody does it better…

৪৩৫

It was the day Leslie Wilkes turned fifty. No more pretensions of youth remained, regardless of the fact that her hair still had far more gold in it than silver. The aches and pains and the lines in her face were there to remind her, although in truth, they were no worse than they'd been the day before. It had been going on for more than twenty years now, this process of growing older—it wasn't something that had happened overnight. The unfortunate thing was that while her body had undoubtedly aged, her mind had not. She still felt thirty years old inside—perhaps even younger.

She could look upon the world with a more experienced eye, and when it came to matters pertaining to her work, honestly say, "I've been doing this for thirty years." But her heart was another story. It would still leap when she saw a man who intrigued her, and she still belted out love songs with as much feeling as she ever had—as long as no one else could hear her. On the surface, she was merely a middle-aged single parent trying to put her only son through college. But inside, she longed to run laughing through a meadow with a lover, have him pull her down on a bed of daisies, and make love to her beneath a midsummer sun.

Unfortunately, that kind of love was something she'd never experienced, although at one time, she'd thought she had a slim chance at it. She was thirty years old by then, and had almost given up believing that love would ever find her. Derrick McIntosh was tall and handsome, a strapping stallion of a man, but he was gone almost overnight, leaving her with the token of his affection that grew into her son—her dear, sweet Gabriel—who'd been her whole life ever since.

And now, even he was gone.

Gabe called and came home for holidays and such, but she was forced to admit that he truly was leaving her—bit by painful bit. Sometimes, she missed him so much it hurt. She'd hear an interesting news story or remember something funny that happened at work and want to share it with him. But he wasn't there. No one was—only silence, emptiness, and herself. She didn't even have a cat.

Change. Such an evil, insidious thing. It could be fought, but never vanquished—a strong, inexorable force that keeps pushing and nudging, often sweeping aside everything in its path. The best anyone could do was to adapt, which was what she was trying to do now that Gabe was gone.

She'd had to find something else to occupy the time spent away from work—though, in fact, she had less time to fill now that she was working extra days to pay his tuition.

Why did it seem like so much more? Had he really taken up that much of her time and energy? Probably not. He'd been slowly moving away from her for years now, becoming more independent and seeking less of her company—certainly needing less of her help.

Truth be told, she had more free time simply because he wasn't there. She had fewer dishes to wash, less laundry to do, and she rarely cooked anymore—fixing meals for one seemed pointless. The refrigerator was practically empty, and she washed any dishes as soon as she finished with them. Living alone gave her more time and more freedom. The trouble was, she had absolutely no idea what to do with it.

Since Gabe couldn't come home that weekend, her best friends Suzie Howell, Miranda York, and Angela Neely had insisted she go out to dinner with them to celebrate. Leslie looked forward to the event, but at the same time dreaded it.

They would only sit at the table talking about work, just as they always did. She enjoyed their company, but it would be nice to discuss something other than the crap they had to put up with at the hospital. Nothing had been the same since their small county hospital had been bought by an enormous for-profit healthcare company, and Leslie, for one, was sick of it. She wanted something else to occupy her thoughts. A diversion of sorts—anything to break the monotony of the daily grind.

She dressed warmly and set out for the restaurant, making sure she had her cell phone handy, knowing Suzie would be calling.

"Where are you?" she asked when Leslie answered the inevitable ring.

"On my way to the restaurant," Leslie replied. "We're supposed to be meeting there in ten minutes. Where else would I be?"

"I've got to stop by the fabric store and get some things. They're having a sale, and I don't want to miss it. It won't take long. It'll probably take an hour to get a table anyway. The Old Oaken Bucket game between IU and Purdue was this afternoon—it's probably just now letting out."

Suzie's strategy was admirable. Knowing that getting a table at a popular post-game restaurant in Bloomington would probably take forever, she'd come up with the best idea of them all. Leslie only wished she'd thought of it herself.

"We'll go ahead and get a table. We might even be sitting at it by the time you get there."

"Okay, I'll hurry," Suzie said. "See ya."

Leslie switched off her phone and tossed it on the passenger seat. Pulling into the parking lot at precisely six-thirty, her worst fears were realized. The place was packed, and the only empty parking space was next to an SUV that was parked so crookedly, she had to drive around the lot to approach it from the right direction. Hoping the other driver wouldn't take the rear end of her car with him when he left, she picked up her phone and called Angela.

"Hey, Angie, baby. Where are you?"

"Is that you that just pulled in?" Angela asked. "I'm right here on the porch."

Leslie glanced up and spotted Angela's feet through the railing and her hand waving over the top. "Yes, and if I'd just gotten my butt out of the car, I'd have seen you. Aren't you cold?"

"Not really," she replied. "I haven't been here very long. Miranda just called. She's on her way."

"Be there in a minute."

She switched off the phone and stuck it in her purse. Getting out of the car was a tight squeeze, but she managed to do it without either of the two vehicles exchanging any paint. As she walked around to the steps, she was struck by the incongruity of the weather and the tropical decorations. Outdoor tables on a white porch with electrically lit palm trees seemed wrong when the people milling around were all wearing coats and shivering.

Angela, on the other hand, wasn't even wearing a coat. Her flannel shirt seemed inadequate at best—although her long dark hair probably provided some warmth.

"Girl," Leslie exclaimed. "What are you doing out here without a coat?"

"I'm fine." She held up the pager. "Looks like a phone, doesn't it?"

"Yeah. What's the wait?"

"Forty-five minutes. I've been here for about five."

Leslie didn't think she would last that long outside on a bench—although being able to sit was a plus. "Did Suzie call you?"

"Not since this afternoon. Why?"

"She called me just now and said she's gone shopping."

"I'm not surprised," Angela said with a giggle. "Suzie's always late."

"No shit. That's part of her charm." With a shiver, she pulled her coat more closely around herself. "Are you sure you're not too cold?"

"No, but we can go in and stand around with all the kids if you like."

When they went inside, Leslie's first glimpse of the youthful clientele had her wishing they'd gone somewhere else.

God, this is making me feel old.

She was all for leaving when a waiter came over and announced that there were seats available at the bar to anyone over twenty-one. Not a single person took him up on the offer.

"Now I *really* feel old." She glanced at Angela. "Want to sit in the bar or wait?"

"I'd rather have a table," Angela said. With a wink, she added, "More room for the birthday cake."

"We'll wait then—but no cake," Leslie insisted. "Trust me, I feel bad enough as it is. I don't need a bunch of singing waiters to rub it in."

It's my birthday, and I'll do as I please.

"There'll be a band later. If we stick around long enough, we could request the birthday song. Any other night we could've done the karaoke version for you."

Leslie chuckled. "Yeah, right. I can really see you all getting up on stage."

"You never know. We might surprise you."

Since none of them had ever done anything of the kind—at least, not to Leslie's knowledge—she doubted they would start now.

A quick survey of the dining room revealed more of the tropical décor. The bar was situated off to one side near the bandstand and looked like a thatched hut. The bartender was a tall blond, bearded fellow with broad shoulders and a ready smile.

At least the scenery is nice…

When a perky waitress came over to take their drink order, Angela opted out.

Leslie hesitated, prompting the waitress to add, "I'm here to serve drinks to you people while you wait. It's my purpose in life."

Leslie considered it somewhat fatalistic to assume they'd be standing there long enough to order a drink, receive it, and possibly even finish it before they got a table.

Might as well… "Okay, then, bring me a Corona."

"Good choice." With a charming smile and a toss of her

ponytail, she headed off toward the bar.

Leslie wasn't sure she'd ever been that bouncy, even at the age of twenty—although it *had* been thirty years ago. There was a chance she'd simply forgotten it.

When the waitress returned with her beer, Leslie paid her five dollars for a three-dollar drink and took a long swallow, figuring she'd have plenty of time to metabolize the alcohol before she drove home—maybe even before they ordered dinner. She had just taken a suck on the lime and poked it into the bottle, thinking that perhaps they should've taken a seat at the bar after all, when the pager went off.

"Short forty-five minutes," Angela commented.

Angela was turning in the pager when Miranda came through the door, her long auburn hair fluffed as though she'd run all the way from Pemberton. "What'd I miss?"

"Not much," Leslie replied. "Just the wait and a beer."

"Perfect timing," Miranda said with a wink. "Where's Suzie?"

"Shopping," Angela and Leslie said in unison.

Miranda shrugged. "Figures."

The hostess led the way to their table, and Leslie was taking her seat when her gaze landed on a young man sitting at the bar in ragged jeans, a red T-shirt, and an Atlanta Braves cap worn backward. She'd never seen a cuter guy in her life.

Not even when I was twenty.

Even in profile, he was adorable, but when he happened to glance in her direction, their eyes met for an instant.

Suddenly, breathing became optional. A flush rose up her neck to her face, making her cheeks tingle, and her next heartbeat pumped heat into places she'd all but forgotten about.

Must be the beer.

When he glanced at the man sitting around the corner of the bar from him and grinned, Leslie's heart actually stopped for a second. Then she noticed that his friend had a full glass of something tall and frothy—not the sort of drink a man would usually order. It looked sort of…fruity, and given the large percentage of homosexuals in

Bloomington, it could've meant that he and his companion were a bit on the gay side.

Reminding herself that gay or straight didn't matter when it came to eye candy, she took another sip of her beer, which helped to settle her nerves. A little.

Their waitress, an attractive brunette with expressive brown eyes and a toothy smile, arrived, introducing herself as Tami. They ordered an appetizer and more drinks—Leslie opting for water since she clearly couldn't handle the beer. Tami was turning away when Leslie stole another peek at the guy at the bar as he took a sip from a drink that was mostly ice.

Her heart slid to her feet.

So much for that. He'll probably leave now. Damn...

A sudden impulse struck her. "Hold on a second," she said to Tami. Leaning closer, Leslie lowered her voice. "You see that cute little guy at the bar? The one with the red shirt and hat." When Tami nodded, she continued. "I want to buy him a drink, but I don't want him to know who sent it. He can have anything he wants, I just want him to sit there for a while longer. Today's my fiftieth birthday, and I want something nice to look at during dinner."

As co-conspirators went, Tami was a natural. With twinkling eyes and a mischievous grin, she gave Leslie a quick nod and headed off.

While Miranda smiled her approval, Angela giggled like a schoolgirl.

Leslie shot her a scowl. "Dammit, it's my birthday, and this'll give us something to talk about besides work."

Suzie would probably get a kick out of it, despite the fact that she considered Leslie's boy-watching tendency to be a bit silly.

Angela hadn't given up on finding another man, but it was something Suzie never mentioned, except when someone else brought up the subject—and then her usual response was that she didn't think about it.

Leslie, on the other hand, thought about it constantly, though it hadn't done her a lick of good. Still, a taste of eye candy on her birthday didn't seem like too much to ask.

"You tell her, Leslie," Miranda said. "There's no such thing as too young."

"Travis is only nine years younger than you," Angela pointed out. "*That* guy could be Leslie's son."

"Yes, but he *isn't* my son," Leslie insisted. "Which makes him fair game."

As long as I look and don't touch.

Suzie called again. "Have you gotten a table yet?"

"Yes," Leslie replied. "Where are you now?"

"I'm checking out. Don't order dinner without me."

At this rate, they could be eating dessert by the time Suzie arrived. "We'll wait for you, but hurry up."

"Where is she?" Angela asked.

"Checking out. Looks like we're going to be here for a while."

Thank God for eye candy.

Robin Thatcher stared at the waitress in disbelief. "Excuse me?"

"I said, someone wants to buy you a drink," she repeated. "What would you like?"

He glanced at his empty glass. He and his brother, Nick, had come to the bar with the intention of drowning their sorrows after IU's horrendous loss to Purdue. A free drink sounded pretty good. "Jack Daniels and Coke—but only if it's a woman who's buying." Robin had been hit on by gays before and wasn't interested—for a number of reasons, not the least of which being that he was straight.

"I'm not supposed to say who it's from, but I guess I can tell you that much. Yes, she's a woman. It's her birthday."

"And she's buying *me* a drink?"

The waitress, whose name pin identified her as Tami, shifted from one foot to the other. "Well, yeah. She just wants you to hang around for a while. She seems like a nice lady."

Not a nice *girl*, but a lady. For a second, Robin thought he knew who it might be.

No way. I couldn't get that lucky.

"Hey, how come she's not buying *me* a drink?" Nick grumbled.

Tami shrugged. "I guess she doesn't think you're as cute."

"She thinks I'm *cute*?" Robin echoed. "Geez, how old is she?"

"I probably shouldn't tell you that," Tami said. "Might give her away."

"Gotta at least be over twenty-one," Nick remarked.

He had a point. "Okay. I'll take the drink."

And fantasize about who might have sent it.

With a grin, Tami gave the order to the bartender. Robin watched her leave, hoping she'd report back to whoever ordered the drink. She didn't—unless she was lying about his admirer being a woman.

"She's probably a real dog," Nick said. "Otherwise, she'd let you know who she is."

"Maybe. Maybe not." If he'd been alone or with anyone but Nick, Robin might've pursued the matter. As it was, it seemed like a bad idea. Nick was always trying to fix him up with girls.

Too bad a *girl* wasn't what he wanted.

Chapter 2

Robin and Nick didn't see eye to eye on a lot of things—including the kind of women Robin should date. Sure, Robin was several years younger than his brother—and his youthful appearance did nothing to dispel the impression that, personality-wise, he was closer to seventeen than twenty-seven—but Nick never missed an opportunity to rag on Robin for his immaturity. Neither did anyone else. If he'd been told to grow up once, he'd been told a hundred times.

Still, Nick had taken Robin on as a partner in his construction business, which was possibly his way of making amends. He'd never done much to defend Robin when their mom's boyfriends got nasty.

As his friend George, the bartender, set the drink down on the bar, Nick raised his head and glanced around the room. "Don't see any chicks staring at you."

Robin was almost afraid to look in the direction he had earlier.

Show some courage, man.

Turning sideways, he spotted her just as she took a swig from a bottle of Corona. Their eyes met again for such a brief instant, he might've imagined it. She didn't smile, didn't wave—didn't do anything but swallow the beer and laugh at something one of the other women at the table said to her.

Damn.

She was fuckin' *beautiful*. Long blonde hair swept up in a clip at the back of her head. A low-cut sweater that displayed an absolutely fabulous pair of tits. His dick responded with a tingling surge at the thought of burying his face in the deep valley between them.

"See any likely candidates?" George asked.

"Not really." Robin honestly didn't care anymore. If some

chick wanted to buy him a drink, he wouldn't say no—but a *lady* had paid for that Jack and Coke. He wished he'd been sitting at a table facing her. That way he wouldn't have to turn around to stare.

If only he didn't have to leave when Nick did. Nick had left his car at Robin's house so they wouldn't have to park two vehicles at the stadium. Still, Robin lived close enough that he could run Nick home and come back. Maybe she would still be there.

He reminded himself again that the woman making his dick hard and the one who bought the drink weren't necessarily one and the same. Still, Tami had said it was her birthday. Someone might buy her a cake and sing to her...

Ordering it himself was an option, but he doubted Tami would do it. She'd seemed determined to protect the woman's identity. Maybe he would simply have to keep watching Tami and see where she went.

He spotted her at a nearby table, taking an order from a couple who appeared to be in their early twenties and very much in love. Another glance at the pretty mama in the sweater revealed another woman joining the party.

Birthday party?

Moments later, Tami approached that same table. He watched out of the corner of his eye as she crouched beside his dream woman and put a hand up, covering her mouth as she spoke.

She might as well have sent up a flare.

He saw no need to buy a birthday cake now. No, what he really needed to do was finish his drink, run Nick home, and come back before she left. With another person joining the group, they probably hadn't ordered dinner yet. He had time.

Unfortunately, Nick wasn't cooperating. He still had most of his pina colada left.

At least I'm drinking whiskey.

He'd already downed the last of his first drink before he'd noticed her, and now he had to drink another one before he could leave.

The one time I really need to be sober.

"Say hello to my sister Amy," George said, distracting him from his thoughts.

Robin turned around as a pretty brunette held out her arms, clearly anticipating a hug.

"Nice to meet you, Amy." Hopping off his barstool, he gave her a quick hug, hoping that would be the end of it.

Amy must've had other ideas. As he resumed his perch on the stool, she sidled up beside him. "What're you drinking?"

Was she the one? His hopes sank into oblivion. "Um, Jack and Coke."

"Ooh, my favorite." Picking up his drink, she took a long sip, nearly emptying the glass.

Guess I won't be getting drunk after all.

"Don't worry," she said. "I'll buy you another one."

"No need," Robin said quickly. "That was a freebie anyway."

George snickered. "Some dame bought him a drink—anonymously." He frowned at his sister. "Wasn't you, was it?"

With a sardonic smile, Amy shook her head. "Trust me, if I bought a guy a drink, I'd make sure he knew who was paying."

Robin had known George since their college days at IU, and he'd always liked him. He wasn't sure about Amy.

Not my type.

If he had a type, it was the gorgeous blonde who'd bought him that drink, rather than the pushy chick who'd gulped down most of it. He glanced at George. "Could you get me a glass of water? I need to sober up a little before I take Nick home."

Amy didn't seem to know how to take that, and neither did George. She backed off slightly, while George shot him a quizzical look. "Uh, sure thing, Rob."

As soon as George sat the glass in front of him, Robin drank it down and asked for another. A glance at his benefactress caught her slightly disappointed expression.

Damn. I hurt her feelings.

He sat there in a dejected daze, barely listening while Nick and George traded jibes. Apparently sensing his disinterest, Amy disappeared.

Time passed, and though Nick seemed to have no desire to leave yet, the water had its inevitable effect. Robin hopped off the barstool and headed for the restroom, stealing one more glimpse of that beautiful woman and wishing he had the guts to ask her if she was the one who thought he was cute.

Cute. Not handsome or sexy. Just cute. Still, cute was good—good enough to get him a free drink.

Too bad that was all it would get him.

ഔരു

"So, where's the guy?" Suzie asked as she settled into her seat.

"At the bar in the red shirt and cap," Miranda replied.

"Kinda cute," Suzie admitted after subjecting him to a cursory glance. "Way too young for you, though."

"I never said I was going home with him," Leslie chided. "I just want to look at him, that's all."

"You're crazy," Suzie said. "You know that, don't you?"

Leslie shrugged. "Maybe, but I'm having fun, and isn't that what you're supposed to do on your birthday?"

"I guess so—although I can think of better ways to have fun."

Leslie disagreed. She hadn't had this much fun—or felt such a strong reaction to a man—in ages.

She stole another peek at him, nearly getting caught when he turned toward her. Quickly averting her eyes, she picked up her Corona and took the last sip. She could read his T-shirt now. It had "PUCK FURDUE" written on it in big bold letters.

"Check out the shirt," she said in a low voice. "I'll bet he could tell us who won the game."

Angela allowed a casual glance to drift in his direction. "Maybe you should go ask him."

"Sure, and then he'd figure out I was the one who bought him that drink and I'd die of embarrassment."

"Maybe not," Miranda said. "You haven't exactly been sitting here batting your eyelashes at him."

Leslie grimaced. "You're right. He has no reason to suspect me at all." Not when he was probably expecting some hot chick to pop up and claim responsibility—maybe even the one who'd drunk most of it.

Angela's dark brown eyes lit up. "I know what you can do. When we leave, you should just walk past him and say 'you're welcome.'"

"Nice idea, but I wouldn't have the nerve." She'd already broken the cardinal rule of boy watching.

Look all you like, but never, ever make eye contact.

Actually speaking to him was out of the question.

Time to change the subject.

She paused, taking in Suzie's short, perfectly-coifed black hair, pink turtleneck sweater, matching gray and pink plaid jacket and slacks, and floating heart pendant. "You look nice, Suzie."

"Thanks. So do you," she said and directed her attention to her menu.

Tami returned a few minutes later to take their order, but the excitement had passed. Their entrees arrived and with the exception of Miranda's announcement that her sister, Tracy, was about to make her an aunt, they wound up talking about work while they ate.

Just like we always do.

Leslie had finished her last teriyaki chicken wing when she glanced at the bar and felt the blood drain from her face.

He was gone.

Shit. Needing a moment alone with her disappointment—not to mention a place to wash her sticky fingers—she excused herself and headed toward the restroom.

He'd seemed so lively and friendly. What would it be like to take that little bundle of energy home and—

Don't go there, Les. Such thoughts were pointless, except to remind her of what she couldn't have. She'd missed her chance. She was too old—and the birthday she was celebrating proved it.

Lost in her own dismal thoughts, she nearly ran into him as he came out of the men's room. Standing a good two inches shorter than her five-foot-seven, he smiled and muttered a sheepish apology as her gaze met his.

He had the biggest, most adorable brown eyes she'd ever seen in her life. Before she remembered why she shouldn't say a word to him, she gestured at his shirt. "Who won the game?"

He grimaced. "Purdue creamed us, forty-one to fourteen."

"That must have been painful."

"Yes, it was. That and practically freezing to death."

She let her gaze roam over him one more time. "You look pretty good for a frozen man. I'd never have guessed." The words were out of her mouth before she realized she might've given herself away.

Not seeming to make the connection, he simply laughed at her pathetic joke. "I'm thawed out now. Are you an IU fan?"

"Actually, I can go either way. I went to IU, but my son is a freshman at Purdue."

He gasped in mock horror. "How could you let him do that?"

She shrugged, chuckling. "Purdue was the logical choice for an engineer wannabe. I sure miss him, though."

"Is he your only kid?" A swift, downward glance accompanied his question, making Leslie wonder if she'd spilled teriyaki sauce on her slacks.

"Yeah. He doesn't make it home very often. I can't wait for the holidays."

"I'll bet you aren't the only one." His wink and subsequent grin hit her full force, sapping the strength from her knees.

My God, he's adorable.

"True." She took a hesitant step toward the ladies' room. "Um, thanks for the score. Better luck next year."

"Thanks." With another wink, he sauntered off.

Once inside the restroom, Leslie fanned herself furiously.

Damn! The little bugger is making me hot.

A quick glance in the mirror revealed bright pink cheeks and a blotchy flush that crept down her neck. Cursing herself for having been so damned obvious, she ran cold water over a paper towel and dabbed it on her cheeks in an effort to force the blood back down to her knees where it belonged. A similar attempt to make her neck appear more normal didn't help a bit.

Her heart was still pounding as she returned to their table. Given that a brief conversation with him had practically made her faint, she'd probably have a heart attack if he actually touched her.

How ironic. Then again, it served as a reminder that she was too old to be lusting after a man who was undoubtedly half her age.

Always the last to finish, Suzie still had a full plate. At this rate, they might actually be there long enough for the band to start playing. Leslie glanced at the bandstand, noting that no musicians were setting up as yet, but her eye candy's brother—who, according to Tami had been miffed that no one bought *him* a drink—had just downed the last of his drink.

Won't be long now.

Moments later, Tami sailed over with a thick wedge of chocolate cake, complete with a flaming candle.

"Happy Birthday!"

"Oh, you guys," Leslie said with a grimace. "Thanks, but I'm stuffed to the gills."

Suzie and Angela exchanged puzzled glances. Miranda shook her head in denial.

"We didn't order that," Suzie said.

"Oh, I know," Tami said. "But everyone gets a piece of cake for their birthday. On the house."

Leslie hated to be a party pooper, but the mere thought of being so much older than the man who had her bouncing off the walls made her never want to admit to another birthday again as long as she lived. Nevertheless, she made a wish and blew out the candle. In the next heartbeat, her wish was granted when their eyes met one last time as he and his brother shook hands with the bartender, clearly preparing to leave.

That's that.

"I don't suppose you could put that cake in a box for me, could you?"

"Oh, sure," Tami replied. "I'll be right back."

By the time Tami returned, the two men were donning their jackets. At that moment, Leslie couldn't think of a single cause for celebration. She put the cake in the box and closed the lid.

Angela nodded toward the bar. "Looks like they're leaving. Guess you won't get to say 'you're welcome' after all."

"Too bad," Suzie commented. "That would've been pretty funny."

Miranda opened her mouth as though about to say something, but snapped it shut, seeming to think better of it. She, of all people, understood the dangers of not speaking her mind to a man she found attractive. Then again, Miranda had known Travis pretty well. This guy was a total stranger.

The tiny demon perched on Leslie's shoulder urged her to run after him and give him the cake to make up for IU's loss to Purdue—not that mere cake could ever atone for such a trouncing. "It's okay. I wouldn't have had the nerve, anyway."

Nerve, hell. A full-blown panic attack was more likely. She was calmer now—able to breathe easily and be blissfully unaware of her heartbeat—but her rampant pulse had required medication to subdue it on more than one occasion. Thankfully, the most recent source of her anxiety was leaving the building.

Suzie finally finished her dinner and Tami brought them their checks. Scanning her bill, Leslie noted that the infamous Jack and Coke had cost her all of five bucks.

Worth every penny.

80CR

Robin was already convinced of the identity of his admirer, but the birthday cake clinched it. He just wished he could've gotten Nick out of there sooner without making his intentions too obvious. He was careful to adhere to the speed limit during the short drive to his house. Nick, however, seemed surprised to be dropped off at the end of the driveway.

"I just thought of something I need from the drugstore," Robin explained. "See you on Monday."

Fortunately, Nick didn't argue, and Robin drove back into town a little faster than he should have. He pulled into the parking lot just as the woman and her friends came out the door. A few more seconds, and he'd have missed them completely. He'd hoped to catch them at their table, maybe strike up a conversation and buy *her* a drink. What the hell was he going to do now? Follow her like a stalker?

He was about to jump out of his car and run over to her when he saw one of her friends pointing toward the bookstore in the strip mall. If they went to the bookstore, he'd have time. Maybe he could even bump into her there. He'd rather talk to her alone, but—

Damn. His heart took a dive as they each got in a different car. He didn't have any trouble deciding which one to follow, but he was relieved when they all drove across the wide lot to park closer to the bookstore. He waited until they went inside and then pulled into the space next to her car.

Now what?

Should he go inside or wait for her there? He knew that store. The shelves were so tall he wouldn't be able to spot her easily. If she left without him seeing her, he'd lose her forever.

"Okay, then," he muttered. "I'll wait right here."

Unfortunately, his truck hadn't warmed up much, and pretty soon, his teeth were chattering. Figuring he had time, he ran in and bought a cup of hot chocolate from the café and took it back outside.

Never having done anything like this in his life, he suspected that the chilly weather wasn't the only reason he was shaking. What on earth should he say to her? Would she scream or call the police? He wouldn't blame her if she did either of those things.

This is such a bad idea...

But if that was true, why was he still there?

∞↵↪

After driving over to the bookstore, Leslie and her pals spent the next hour cracking up continuously as they perused the erotic romance section and searched the magazine racks for pictures of nude men. Unfortunately, all they could find was gay porn, and even those magazines were sealed in plastic.

"It's not fair," Leslie complained. "They could've at least had a copy or two of *Playgirl*."

In the end, Suzie bought a bestseller, Miranda bought a book on horse training, Angela bought two erotic romance novels, and Leslie bought four. If she couldn't fool around with the boy at the bar, at least she would have something hot to read.

After saying goodnight to her buddies, Leslie stepped off the curb and headed out to her car. This might have been one of her more memorable birthdays, but it was also one of the colder ones. Shivering, she buttoned her coat against the biting wind, shoved her hands into the pockets, and walked out to her car, doing her best to avoid the icy patches on the pavement.

She had just unlocked her car when she heard a door open on the vehicle parked next to hers. She didn't think anything about it until she saw the red baseball cap. Then her heart slowed to a dull thud, like a hammer-stroke in her chest, as *he* got out of his truck.

Chapter 3

Any thoughts Leslie might have had about this being a coincidence were dispelled when their eyes met. He'd been sitting out there waiting for her—a circumstance that made it patently obvious he knew she'd been the one to buy that drink. Just how he knew it was a mystery. Surely Tami hadn't told him, but somehow, he knew. The knowledge was right there in his eyes.

If she'd been quick about it, she could've gotten into her car and closed the door before he could reach her. But his gaze locked onto hers with so much purpose and intent, she simply stood there, powerless to move. As he came around the car, her keys slipped from her nerveless fingers and fell to the pavement. He swooped down to retrieve them, then straightened up to his full height, his face mere inches from hers.

"Thanks for the drink." His even tone held no accusation or threat, but when she didn't reply, he added, "It *was* you, wasn't it?"

Leslie swallowed with difficulty as a hard shudder shook her chest. She hadn't expected this. Not in her wildest dreams.

"How did you know?" she asked.

Since she'd only done it for fun—and on the merest whim—the situation shouldn't have seemed quite so dramatic, but his compelling expression made it seem that way. Sure, he was cute and friendly, but at that moment, he was as serious as a heart attack.

"Aside from the bartender's sister, who denied doing it, you were the only woman who spoke to me all evening. And the waitress told me it was your birthday." He gestured toward the box on the front seat. "I saw the cake." He was still holding her keys, toying with them as they clinked together in his hand. "She said you just wanted to look—which was okay with me—but, be honest now. Is that really all you wanted to do?"

"Eye candy," she said, surprised that her voice sounded comparatively normal. "You were something nice to look at during dinner—sort of a birthday present to myself."

"Are you sure that's all it was? Absolutely sure?"

"W-what is it you want me to say?" Eye candy wasn't the only thing she wanted, but she couldn't say *that*.

Could she?

A ghost of a smile teased the corner of his mouth. "That you'd like to do a whole lot more than just look."

"And what if I do? Then what?"

His smile was slow and seductive. "I give you back your keys, and you follow me home."

Her already dry mouth turned to dust in the space of a heartbeat. "And if I don't?"

"Then I give you back your keys and you go home alone." His smile was disarming, but its heat melted her resolve. "And no, I won't follow you. I'm not *that* pushy. Just promise me one thing. Take my phone number. If you ever change your mind, call me. Anytime—day or night."

Somewhere in the back of her mind, two voices were duking it out. One was screaming that this was a total stranger whom she shouldn't trust for an instant, and the other was Humphrey Bogart telling her how much she would regret saying no.

"Oh, maybe not today, maybe not tomorrow, but soon, and for the rest of your life…"

With a deep sigh, she realized that this kid had probably never even heard of *Casablanca*, let alone actually seen it…

Something was wrong. He wasn't acting reasonably. No man his age could possibly care less whether she found him attractive or not, and he certainly wouldn't be giving out his phone number. It was surreal, like something out of the *Twilight Zone*—which was yet another reference he probably wouldn't understand.

"I don't suppose Tami told you which birthday I was celebrating, did she?" If not, this conversation or seduction or whatever it was would end just as soon as he figured out that, thanks to modern cosmetic science, she didn't appear to be quite as ancient as her chronological age would suggest.

He shook his head. "Doesn't matter."

"It's my fiftieth."

"*Still* doesn't matter."

"And you're all of, what, twenty—?"

"Seven," he replied. "Almost twenty-eight—in two weeks, as a matter of fact."

As if that made a difference. Either way, he was still more than twenty years her junior. Her only consolation was that he was older than Gabriel.

Obviously having no clue as to the nature of her thoughts, he leaned a tiny bit closer. "Wanna help me celebrate?"

Ignoring his question, she asked one of her own. "Why on earth would you want someone old enough to be your mother to follow you home and celebrate anything?"

The slow blink of his deep brown eyes was like that of a contented cat. "I've always liked older women. Ever since I was a kid, I always liked my friend's mothers better than their sisters. The younger ones don't interest me very much. Whereas you... well... you intrigue the hell out of me."

I'm intriguing? Seriously?

Her skepticism must have shown in her face, for he added, "You don't believe me, do you?"

"No, I don't." Her heart began skipping beats, and the deep breath she took didn't do much to settle it down. "Does that line ever actually *work* for you? What I mean is, how many older women have you managed to pick up with it?"

"Counting you? None so far. I'd never even thought of it until now." Tilting his head to the side, he gazed at her, his expression thoughtful. "I've been sitting out here wondering why a woman like you would find me attractive, and I couldn't come up with a reason that made any sense."

He must not be very bright if he couldn't figure that one out.

All he had to do was take a peek at himself in the nearest mirror. "B-because you're cute."

His dejected sigh somehow managed to make him seem more adorable than ever. "That's all?"

"I'm sure there's more to you than that. You appear to be very nice and friendly—everyone at the bar seemed to like you—you drink Jack and Coke, you have an older brother, and it's fairly obvious you're an IU fan. Other than that, what could I possibly know?"

"You know when my birthday is—which is more than I can say for a lot of people."

She had to laugh. "Yeah, like nearly a hundred percent of the world's population. I can count on one hand the number of people who can rattle off *my* birthday." Then it dawned on her that he happened to be one of them. "Which now also includes you."

He pounced on the idea like a cat on a mouse. "You see? We know that much about each other and we're still talking. There has to be a relationship in there somewhere."

There were two things wrong with his last statement. First of all, in Leslie's experience, men didn't voluntarily use the word "relationship" in a complete sentence. And second, that if he thought what they had was a relationship, he hadn't been in any good ones lately—perhaps ever. "You're looking for a *relationship*? That's funny, I thought you just wanted to get laid."

He seemed a bit hurt by that suggestion. "Sex is a relationship, isn't it?"

Despite her howl of glee, she was forced to admit he was right. Sex might not be lasting or terribly meaningful, but it did qualify as a relationship.

"I meant what I said about you being intriguing," he insisted. "I'd be willing to bet that what you read is fascinating too."

In all the excitement, Leslie had completely forgotten about the books in the bag dangling from her wrist. Four steamy erotic romance novels, when he was probably expecting Hemingway or Steinbeck. When he reached for the bag, she couldn't make a move to stop him.

Pulling out the books, he studied the covers.

"Damn." He closed his eyes and let his head fall back as though beseeching the heavens for assistance. "Puh-*leese*, follow me home. I can do better than this stuff. I promise."

"I dunno," she drawled. "Some of those are pretty hot."

"Maybe, but I can do it for real." He handed the books back to her along with her keys. "Come on, pretty mama." His voice was a deep, throaty whisper. "Follow me."

Smiling in a very disturbing fashion, he leaned even closer. She could almost feel the heat emanating from him, could almost imagine what it would be like to be in his arms, kissing him.

Oh, God...he's getting to me.

"Give me a chance to show you what a good boy I can be."

This time, she not only dropped her keys, but all of the books as well. Seeming to ignore her clumsiness, he leaned in and took the kiss before she had a chance to move away. Not that she was in any hurry to move or wanted any space between them. Nor could she protest that she didn't long to kiss him—that she hadn't been thinking about it all evening. Wondering how it would feel... How he would taste...

He deepened the kiss as he stepped around her, pinning her against the car. Pressing the entire length of his body against hers, he slid his arms around her in the most sensual embrace she'd ever been a party to—with or without a coat. Her head was swimming and, despite the weather, her body melted like a Hershey bar on a sidewalk in July.

Oh, yes, he was a *very* good boy. If this was any indication of how he could make her feel, she should definitely consider following him home.

His tongue teased her lips, politely asking for admittance. When she parted her lips, not only did he make her feel like hot chocolate, he also tasted like it. He must have gone to the café for something to keep him warm while he waited. Not coffee, not tea, but hot, creamy, sensuous, delicious chocolate...

Cupping the back of her head, he held her firmly, kissing her even more deeply.

I'm losing it...

Backing off slightly, he sucked her lower lip into his mouth and ran his tongue over her sensitive flesh. A low moan rose from somewhere deep inside her, and though she knew there were bound to be witnesses to this seduction, she simply didn't care.

"Come on, pretty mama." He speared his fingers through the hair at her temples, holding her head in his hands. "I want you. Now. Please... say you will. Say yes... say it... please..." His voice was a low murmur, and he filled in the pauses with hot kisses scattered over her face.

A moment later, she realized she was nodding. She could have been doing it herself, or perhaps he was doing it for her, but regardless of the cause, he took it as a yes. After planting another searing kiss squarely on her lips, he stooped to retrieve her books and keys. Pulling a pen from the breast pocket of his jacket, he scribbled something on the inside cover of one of the novels before putting them back in the bag and handing them to her.

"Follow me." The words were much more compelling than before—more of a command than a request—and impossible to ignore. "It's not far, and it's warm inside. You won't be sorry." With that, he took her hand and, moving her aside, opened the car door and held it for her. Leslie got in the car without a word.

He handed her the keys. "If you get lost, call me."

She sat there for a moment, eyes closed and breathing deeply.

I shouldn't do this. Shouldn't, shouldn't, shouldn't...

But her lips still tingled from his kiss. She could still taste him, still smell him—his scent, his leather jacket, and whatever else there was about him that made him unique. His own essence, perhaps. She heard him get in his truck and start the engine as she opened the book to see what he'd written.

Robin Thatcher.

Just the name and two phone numbers written beneath it.

Robin.

Yes, it suited him very well. He had a bit of the perky little bird about him, along with a touch of the mischievous Robin Hood—charming rich damsels out of their money to give to the poor, no doubt.

Was she one of the rich or one of the poor? She could've made an argument for both.

Leslie glanced over at him as she started her car and put it in gear. With an encouraging smile and a wave, he pulled away.

As he turned onto the highway, she was right behind him.

 80Q3

Robin checked his rear view mirror at least a hundred times. He'd made sure the traffic was clear enough for her to turn when he did—not that finding his house was difficult. One straight shot down the road and a right turn into his driveway would do it. She couldn't possibly get lost.

But she could *change her mind.*

He forced that thought aside. She'd come this far. Surely, she wouldn't chicken out now.

Robin knew what he was asking, the kind of risk she was taking. Hell, he could be a serial killer for all she knew. He still couldn't believe he'd actually succeeded—had convinced an apparently sensible woman to do something incredibly dangerous. She knew better than to trust a stranger.

How in the world had he done it?

Then again, she'd been the one to buy that drink. Perhaps he was the one in danger. Perhaps she was the serial killer who tossed out lures to lonely, unsuspecting young men...

She couldn't have known that about him—the lonely part, at least. And she'd seemed genuinely surprised that he'd found her out and waited for her.

No, *he* was the stalker, not her.

Shit.

The seductive persona he'd adopted had worked. She was actually following him home.

But could he maintain it?

Did he need to?

His heart and body had taken over, doing everything possible to convince her that he was precisely what she needed—not simply as eye candy, but as an honest-to-God lover. Spotting her lack of a wedding ring when he'd met her by the restroom had encouraged him to believe she was available. The fact that she was following him home proved it.

Maybe.

She might have been on the prowl for someone to cheat on her husband with, although he doubted that. After all, being married would've given her the perfect excuse to say no to him—or slap him silly. She hadn't done either of those things. She'd seemed—*what?*

Interested?

Aroused?

He'd been all of that and more. Holding her was only the beginning. Kissing her had been intoxicating—making his dick harder than it had ever been in his life. Actually fucking her would be heaven itself. On top of that, she was... fascinating. She hadn't said much, but she was like a book he couldn't wait to read.

His driveway was up ahead; he could already read the numbers on the mailbox. Signaling for the turn, he held his breath until he was halfway up the drive and her headlights gleamed in his mirrors.

Yes!

Even if she didn't stay all night, she knew where he lived. She could visit him anytime the spirit moved her. She had his phone numbers, too. She could call him whenever she liked, for any reason—or for no reason at all.

Robin hadn't had a woman in his life in forever. And she had all the makings of a perfect match.

He hoped she liked it kinky.

Chapter 4

I don't have to stay. I can leave anytime I want.

Perhaps that was why Robin wanted her to come to his place rather than follow Leslie to hers—giving her a way out if she got cold feet. She wouldn't have to ask him to leave her apartment, and he wouldn't know where she lived. All she had to do was get in her car and go. It was reassuring in a way, but by the same token, no one would know where she'd gone if she turned up missing. No one would ever find her at Robin's—or even begin to know where to look.

He was right about it not being far. In less than a mile, his turn signal flashed before he pulled into a driveway on the right. The large log house was set well back from the road, nestled beneath the shelter of several tall pines—rustic and somehow secluded from the surrounding houses and the highway. Once inside, it would seem as though they were miles from anyone or anywhere. Just the two of them.

Alone.

Smoke curled from the chimney into the crisp, clear sky, promising snug warmth within. Suddenly, Leslie felt colder than she could ever remember being. Her hands and feet were numb, and she shivered so hard her teeth chattered. The drive hadn't been long enough for her car to warm up, and, despite the sexual heat, she was freezing.

I'll only stay long enough to thaw out my feet.

After that, she would reevaluate the situation and make her choice. It was a good plan—if she could keep her wits about her long enough to carry it out.

With a deep, uneven breath, she got out of the car, only to be blasted by a gust of frigid air that swept across the yard from the street. A strange sound surrounded her, high-pitched and eerie, startling her until she realized it was simply the wind whistling through those enormous pines. She gazed upward at the swaying tree tops and the starry sky beyond.

Robin waited silently on the front porch, holding the door open. A lamp shone from within, welcoming her inside. She caught a glimpse of a vaulted ceiling and the unmistakable flicker of a fire.

"Don't forget your birthday cake," he said. "We'll have a party later. I'll even sing for you."

His ingenuous tone made her laugh, breaking the tension that kept her feet rooted firmly to the spot. *He's a nice boy*, she reminded herself. Everyone liked him. Hell, she'd liked him from across the room, and she'd never even met him. With those bracing thoughts in mind, she retrieved her cake and started for the house.

"Of course, if I'm gonna sing the birthday song, I'll have to know your name," he added. "Unless you want me to keep on calling you pretty mama."

"Pretty mama actually sounds kinda nice, but, if you must know, my name is Leslie."

"Hmm…let me see, now..." He sang the last line of the song, inserting her name. "Yeah, that fits."

"*Any* two-syllable name fits," she chided. "Robin would work just as well."

When she reached the porch, he took her hand and helped her up the steps. "Be here two weeks from now, and you can sing it for me."

"I wouldn't hold my breath," she warned. "Aside from the fact that I'm a lousy singer, I seriously doubt I'll be around two weeks from now."

"How come? Are you planning to go somewhere?"

"Yes," she replied, keeping her tone firm. "Home."

"But you could come back. You know where I live now. You can come back anytime."

Somehow she doubted he'd want her to come back after

tonight. She still didn't understand why he'd invited her in the first place. It seemed... odd, despite his professed penchant for older women.

"Come inside," he said. "Your hands are frozen. Haven't you ever heard of gloves?"

"Yes, I have. But, as I recall, *someone* had me so rattled I neglected to put them on."

His twinkling eyes were even more disarming than his smile. "Certainly not me. I've never gotten a woman rattled before in my life."

"Sure, you haven't," she mocked. "I'm guessing you've had plenty of practice."

He shook his head. "Not really."

She didn't believe that, either. Her eyes widened as she stepped across the threshold. "Wow. What a fabulous house."

He closed the door. "Thanks. My brother and I built it."

"Really? I'm impressed." She wasn't kidding. The place was absolutely breathtaking. "Is that what you do for a living? Build houses?"

He nodded. "Log homes mostly, but we do other kinds. Solar-powered, energy-efficient models—that sort of thing."

Walking to the center of the great room, she turned slowly, taking it all in. The décor had the same Northwest flavor as the pines—wooden furniture with hunter green and dark red fabrics. The to-die-for kitchen was on the right. Acres of oak cabinets lined the walls—more than enough room for all the stuff Leslie had squeezed into the miniscule amount of cabinet space in her apartment—along with a central island for the range and sink. A wrought-iron rack hung above the island, with comparatively few pans dangling from the hooks. Peering around the corner, she spotted a greenhouse window and a second oven that would have held a monster turkey with room to spare.

Her gaze drifted upward to the ceiling, complete with skylights, recessed lighting, and wooden beams running the full length of the room. Thick, earth-toned rugs were scattered about the hardwood floor, and a woodstove with a glass door sat near the rear wall, the flickering fire creating a cozy atmosphere. She felt as though she'd stumbled into a ski lodge or a Swiss chalet. There was even an eight-point buck mounted on the wall.

"I see why you wanted me to come to your place instead meeting me at mine. What I don't understand is why you don't have dozens of women leaping into your bed, demanding to become Mrs. Robin Thatcher. I'd kill for a kitchen like that."

He shrugged. "We bring potential clients here to show them the work we do, which is why it's kinda fancy. I'd never have picked out this stuff myself—and I didn't actually kill that deer. I bought it from a friend of mine on the advice of a decorator."

"At least you're honest. I still don't see why no one has snapped you up before this. Not that I'd marry someone on the basis of their house, but I don't see anything wrong with *you*, either."

"Just never found the right one, I guess." He shrugged again. "Still looking—which is why you're here."

"Taking me for a test drive, are you?" She wondered what type of car was best to compare herself with. An Edsel? A fifty-five Chevy? Or, *wouldn't you really rather have a Buick?*

Leslie could've sworn he blushed. "I wouldn't put it quite like that—although dating *is* kinda like shopping."

She huffed out a laugh. "Apparently, you have a fondness for antiques. Really Robin, I've been on the shelf for a long time. I'm a little past my freshness date, don't you think?"

His burst of laughter contained no trace of irony. "You aren't a loaf of bread."

"You're right. I'm a different sort of commodity—one that's far more perishable." Wandering over to the kitchen, she set her birthday cake on the counter, noting that there wasn't a dirty dish or a spot of any kind—anywhere. He was either the neatest man she'd ever met, or it truly was all for show. She ran a fingertip along the squeaky clean counter. "Do you ever actually cook anything in this kitchen?"

"Not much," he admitted. "The cleaning service was here

yesterday, so it's in better shape than usual."

"Thank God. I can't stand the thought of a bachelor having a cleaner kitchen than I do." Her place was a lot neater now that Gabe was at Purdue—which was one of the few advantages of living alone. "Mine's a bit more lived in—not that it was ever as nice as this."

"Probably more homey, though."

"Maybe—if an apartment kitchen can ever be considered homey. Of course, if you use this place as a model, it's a good thing you don't mess it up much." She was rapidly running out of conversation. Her feet were much warmer now, but she was becoming increasingly aware of her heart beating a little harder and faster than necessary. As nervous as she was, she thought it best to leave before her anxiety escalated. "I should probably go home now. You can have my cake if you like."

Robin was standing between her and the front door. "No."

"Oh… Well, if you don't want it, I'll take it with me."

"That's not what I meant," he said. "I don't want you to leave."

Leslie's shivers returned, having nothing to do with being cold. "I've seen your house and I should—"

"I didn't ask you to come here to show you the house. But if you want the complete tour, we need to keep going. You haven't seen the bedroom yet."

She shifted nervously from one foot to the other, debating whether to make a run for it. Unfortunately, it must have seemed as though her bladder was about to burst.

"Or the bathroom," he added, smiling.

"I'm sorry, Robin. This wasn't a very good idea. I thought I could do it, but, now… I don't know. I'm getting *really* nervous."

"I was doing better with you in the parking lot." He sounded chagrined. "Guess the drive over here gave you cold feet, huh?"

"Quite literally."

With a sniff, he stared down at the floor. "Okay." He blew out a sigh. "I can't keep you here if you don't want to stay."

Well, shit.

Either he'd caught a cold—or he was crying.

What the hell should I do now?

As she thought about him sitting in the parking lot waiting for her, getting chilled to the bone and probably catching pneumonia, she felt a sudden warmth flood her face. Then came that sinking feeling—the one she always felt whenever she realized she'd made a mistake. A *highly significant* mistake.

"You *were* doing better in the parking lot." Perhaps she wasn't the only one with chilly toes and a pounding heart. "What's different now? It's not just me, is it?"

"That performance took all the courage I had. I didn't think I'd have to do it again—at least, I hoped I wouldn't. To be honest, I'm surprised I was able to talk to you at all, let alone get you to follow me home."

So, he wasn't some cocky, confident fellow who picked up women in bars. The role of seducer had been much harder for him to play than she knew. Leslie didn't understand why whether she stayed or left would mean that much to him, but with that thought in mind, she simply couldn't bring herself to walk out on him—yet.

Taking a deep, fortifying breath, she did her best to ignore the pulse pounding in her ears, laid her purse on the kitchen counter, and took off her coat.

"Want some cake?" she asked. "There's enough here for both of us."

Robin's sigh of relief left him light-headed and breathless. "You're sure?" He couldn't believe he'd done it again.

"Yes, I'm sure."

"You don't want to call someone and tell them where you are?"

He'd racked his brains for a way to help her feel safe, and that was the best he could come up with.

She hesitated, pursing her lips. "Maybe. My heart can't take much more of the drama." Unzipping her purse, she took out her phone. After a few taps, she held it to her ear. "Hey, Angela. I'm staying with a friend tonight. I just wanted to let someone know where I am. His name is Robin Thatcher, and the address is…?" She glanced at Robin. He told her his address, and she repeated it over the phone. "I don't think there'll be any problems—it's not like I've got any pets that need feeding. Just keeping you informed. Oh, and if you don't mind, please don't tell Suzie where I am. There's a *reason* I called you instead of her." She switched off her phone.

"That went to voicemail, didn't it?"

"Yeah, but trust me, Angela always gets her messages."

"How come you don't want Suzie to know about me?"

"Because if she didn't show up at the door in the next twenty minutes, she'd be calling me constantly." She glanced at her phone. "Damn thing's nearly dead, anyway." She shrugged. "I've got a charger in my car. I'll get it later."

His dick twitched as her gaze swept over him.

"So, Robin. Are you gonna take off your coat off and stay a while?"

"What— Oh, yeah." Slipping out of his jacket, he tossed it over the back of a chair.

She aimed a pointed stare at his head. "Hat?"

He pulled it off. "Better?"

"Yes, but you've got hat hair." With only a second or two of hesitation, she came toward him to sift her fingers through his hair. "Nice," she murmured. "I love curly hair on a guy."

Robin closed his eyes as she continued to fluff his hair, her touch sending tiny tingles skittering down his neck and across his shoulders. "Mmm… feels good."

"Really?"

With another sigh, he opened his eyes. "You have no idea."

Narrowing her gaze, she studied him for a long moment. "You still seem different than before. I can't remember ever feeling quite as pursued or hunted by a man. It was a little scary, but arousing as all get-out." Her smile was softer now, not as brittle as it had been when she first arrived. No trembling of her lips, no hesitation. "Who *was* that guy trying to seduce me in the parking lot? Was it you, or some fictional character whose lines you borrowed for the evening?"

He smiled and leaned forward, resting his head against her shoulder. "It was me—the me I wish I could be most of the time. You know… older, more confident." Raising his head, he focused on her eyes and found understanding and compassion there. "Most of the time I act goofy around women. They always think I'm funny—and I have plenty of female friends—but none of them have ever looked at me the way you did. You made me feel like a man instead of a boy."

"But you *are* a man. You're not a kid, even though you might seem that way to someone my age. Trust me, that was no kid coming on to me out there. You had my bones turning to jelly."

"Yeah, I did, didn't I?" he said, pleased that she'd appreciated his efforts. "Want me to do it again?"

With a quiver of apparent delight, she dug her fingers into his hair, pulling his head forward to massage the back of his head. "Sweetheart, you can do that anytime you like, just as long as you let me return the favor now and then."

He glanced up at her. "What do you mean?"

She blinked hard as she sucked in a shuddering breath. "Dear God, you're cute—those big calf eyes, that innocent expression…" She shook her head as though trying to clear it. "What was the question?"

"You said you wanted to return the favor. What did you mean by that?"

"Oh, yeah—I meant that I like to be the one doing the seducing once in a while."

Being seduced by an older woman was the stuff of Robin's wet dreams. "Really?" he whispered. "Oh, wow."

She chuckled. "You're making me feel like Mrs. Robinson."

Hold on… What did I miss? "I don't get it. Is that your last name?"

Her eyes widened. "Oh, come on now. I know you're nowhere near as old as I am, but everyone's heard of Mrs. Robinson. The movie? The Simon and Garfunkel song?"

Robin had absolutely no idea what she was talking about.

"What movie?"

"*The Graduate*—you know, Dustin Hoffman and Anne Bancroft? Mrs. Robinson is the older woman who seduces the college graduate, and then he falls for her daughter."

"Nope," he replied, doing his best to tamp down his rising panic. Was this a test? Would she leave if he failed it? "Don't know that one."

"Please tell me you've at least heard of Dustin Hoffman." Her beseeching tone held a trace of desperation.

I've blown it. "I'm not sure…"

"What about *Meet the Fockers?* He was Mr. Focker."

The light bulb went on at last. *Thank God.* "Oh, yeah, the horny old guy."

"Right. He was the horny *young* guy in *The Graduate.*"

"Okay. Got it."

Even though he'd finally made the connection, her pained expression and the way her teeth tugged at her lower lip had him worried.

And she hasn't even set foot in the bedroom yet.

"Maybe we should rent some movies for you to watch," she said. "The best I can tell, your education has been woefully inadequate—although to be honest, I'm sure there are lots of things I can learn from you."

"Sounds fabulous."

A moment later, her expression grew thoughtful, and she took a step back, biting her thumbnail. "We have to be smart about this, Robin. If we jump in and then end up annoyed with each other's ignorance…" She paused, shaking her head. "I honestly don't see how it can work. There are too many years between us."

"Maybe." Although he hated to admit it, she was probably right. Still, he grasped at the only straw he could think of. "You get along with your son, don't you?"

"Yes, but he's grown up with me. He knows my history, my likes and dislikes, and I know his—up to a point. He doesn't know everything about me, just as I don't know everything about him."

"But you still love him, right?"

"He's my son." Her tone had softened, as though she intended to let him down gently. "Of course, I love him. But you and I... we're strangers, and we've lived through different times. Sure, we might have some fun together, but—"

"Can't we at least *try*?" His own voice threatened to crack, and he had to stop to swallow the lump in his throat. "You know... have some fun and see where it leads?"

She didn't answer right away, and when she finally spoke, she might've been talking to herself. She wasn't even looking at him anymore. "All I wanted was a little eye candy for my birthday. Didn't seem like too much to ask, but maybe it was." Her gaze shifted to meet his. "I'm sorry. I should leave."

"I really wish you wouldn't. I mean, I don't even know your last name. How would I ever find you again?"

She was silent for a long time, as though mulling over the entire situation, trying to make her next choice.

"Wilkes," she said at last. "My name is Leslie Wilkes." A tiny smile lifted the corner of her mouth. "Got milk?"

"I think so."

"Come on then," she said with a decisive nod. "Let's have my birthday party."

Chapter 5

Knowing that a bachelor's refrigerator could be a very scary place, Leslie opened the door somewhat gingerly. Expecting the worst, she was surprised to discover that it was not only clean, but practically empty—even more so than hers tended to be. The contents included a half-gallon of milk, a carton of orange juice, several liters of Coke, a six-pack of beer with two bottles missing, one package each of American cheese and salami, and a squeeze bottle of mayo. Not an egg or a stick of butter to be seen. Such a tiny amount of food inside an enormous stainless steel, professional-grade refrigerator would've offended any cook worth their salt.

There oughta be a law...

Having noted the barrenness of his cupboard, she wondered if he even had more than one glass for the milk. As it turned out, she needn't have worried. As she grabbed the milk, he selected two glasses from a nearby cabinet that matched only in the sense that they belonged in the same genre. One had Bugs Bunny on it while the other sported a picture of Yosemite Sam.

He is too cute for words.

After checking a few drawers, she managed to scrounge up a couple of plain forks rather than the Power Ranger variety she'd expected. He did, however, have a set of Teenage Mutant Ninja Turtle plates.

She couldn't help but grin. Even Gabe had outgrown the Turtles, and he'd loved those guys. Still, there were other explanations. "These plates look original. Are you a collector?"

He cleared his throat. "You could say that."

Robin took his seat at the table with an oddly contented smile as she poured the milk and divided the cake between them. She sat down and picked up her fork.

"Wait! I'll be right back." He scurried over to the woodstove, retrieving a box of matches from the mantelpiece. "We forgot to light the candle."

She put the candle back into her cake and waited while he struck the match. "Are you going to sing to me again?"

"I guess I should. Otherwise the candle will only be burning for about two seconds."

Following his rousing chorus of the birthday song, she made a wish—a different one this time—and blew out the candle. To the best of her recollection, her first wish that evening was the only one to ever be granted, and Robin had made it a reality before he ever left the restaurant. The odds against a second wish coming true were astronomical.

"This is really rich," Leslie remarked as she sampled the cake.

Robin dug into his with gusto. "Yeah. It's even got chocolate chips between the layers."

Too bad she couldn't share his enthusiasm. Her first mouthful seemed to get stuck about halfway down. She took a sip of milk. "If we'd stayed to eat it at the restaurant, we probably would have split it between the four of us."

He merely nodded and proceeded to polish off his portion in the time it took her to eat two more bites. It wasn't until he began eyeing her plate that she recalled that while she'd enjoyed a full dinner, he'd only had a couple of drinks at the bar.

If he wanted it, he could have it. She certainly didn't need the extra calories. "Want some more?"

"Um, yeah. If you don't want it…"

Scooping up a forkful of the gooey confection, she held it out to him, lowering the pitch of her voice in a feeble attempt to sound sexy. "Here you go, baby."

She could've sworn his pupils dilated as he leaned forward and opened his mouth. Closing his lips on the fork, he sucked the icing from the tines and savored it slowly, his unwavering gaze fixed on hers. If his expression of raw, naked lust was any indication, having her feed him cake was akin to getting a lap dance in a titty bar. No man had ever looked at her like that in her entire life—and she *liked* it.

She cleared her throat with an effort. "More?"

His slow nod made her wonder what else she could do to provoke that reaction. She sat for a moment trying to remember anything she might have heard or seen involving an older woman with a younger man—

What would Mrs. Robinson do?

She nearly laughed out loud at the thought, but it did give her an idea.

Rising from her chair, she took the plate with her and perched on the edge of the table, then leaned down, allowing the low neckline of her sweater to fall forward.

Robin took every bite of the cake she offered him before resting his head on the soft swell of her breasts, murmuring her name.

Setting the plate aside, she delved her fingers into his dark curls, cradling his head in her arms. Her nipples were so hard she could feel them, tight and tingling as he nuzzled them. His effect on her was heady, intoxicating, erotic, and baffling all at the same time. Her bones were already turning to mush—so much so that she had difficulty staying on the table.

He scooted his chair closer and pulled her down onto his lap.

She straddled him, feeling his heat through his clothing and hers as he tried to push her sweater up—unwittingly discovering exactly what it would take to trigger a panic attack.

"Oh, please, don't," she begged. "Not here, not in the light. I don't want you to see—"

Pulling her head down, he sealed her lips with his own, obliterating anything else she might have said. His hands crept up her back, unhooking her bra with one hand while cupping her head with the other. She twisted and squirmed, attempting to free herself, but his size was deceptive. She'd never have guessed he was that strong. In seconds, he had her bra undone and tugged at her sweater with both hands.

"Come on, pretty mama," he growled. "Let me see your tits."

"No," she gasped. "Please. I can't. I'm too old. You don't want—don't." She was babbling, pleading with him, but he did it anyway, removing her bra and sweater, leaving her fully exposed to his gaze.

Leslie had always been extremely shy about her breasts. They were okay in a bra with sturdy underwires, but without that support, they weren't exactly perky. Big perhaps, but they'd never been perky—not even when she was twenty years old. The rest of her body wasn't too bad—she did a lot of exercising to keep it in some semblance of order—but nothing short of a boob job could fix her particular problem.

Robin, however, didn't seem to notice and dove in face first, devouring them with his lips and tongue, wrapping one arm around her back while his other hand covered her left breast—or tried to.

"Oh, God," he said with a whimper. "I can't even get all of it in my hand." Although she wouldn't have thought it possible, this discovery seemed to turn him on even more.

Perky tits must not be a requirement.

Realizing he wasn't totally grossed out, she relaxed a little as thrills shot through her body, liquefying her core. He let go of her, pressing her back against the table. He didn't let up on her breasts for a second, giving them more attention than they'd had in years. Every now and then he would stop to catch his breath, gazing at them with awe before going back for more.

In a way it was almost funny. The part of her body she'd always considered to be the least attractive was the part he couldn't seem to get enough of. She suspected he would've kept it up all night if she hadn't gotten curious enough to pull *his* shirt off, which sent her own thoughts rampaging in an entirely different direction.

"Wow." She'd seen plenty of shirtless men—she'd even had sex with a few of them—but the sight of Robin without his shirt sent her over the edge.

His trim, muscular body got to her in a way that no big, brawny bodybuilder with six-pack abs ever had. She placed her hands on his chest with the same sort of stunned yet flaming desire he'd displayed while touching her. Tracing circles around his nipples, she let out a gasp as his pectoral muscles flexed beneath her fingers.

"Still want to turn out the light?" he drawled, leaning back in his chair to give her a better view. Cocking his head to one side, he gazed up at her with heavy-lidded eyes. "Just imagine what we'd be missing in the dark." He paused, letting his eyes roam over her bare skin, eliciting even more tingles. "I swear this is better than watching Indiana beat the shit out of Purdue."

She folded her arms across her chest in a self-conscious gesture.

"Oh, don't do that." He pulled her hands down. "Let me look." Sucking in a breath, he let it out with a throaty groan. "Man, those are absolutely *fabulous*. I've never seen tits like that before in my life."

His cock pulsed beneath her as he reached up and pulled the clip from her hair, allowing it to fall to her shoulders.

"Lean back and put your elbows on the table," he said. "Really show me your tits."

Although she did as he asked, she felt exposed, vulnerable.

"Lay your head back." Placing his hands at her waist, he slid them sensuously up to her chest, teasing her nipples before palming both breasts. "This is what I want to see when I fuck you. Promise me you'll never hide them from me again."

She replied with a nod, her throat too tight to speak.

"Good. Now I'll show you the rest of the house. Let me up."

Leslie did her best, but her legs refused to cooperate. "This is what happens when a guy turns you to jelly."

With a wink, Robin lifted her onto the table. A moment later, she was upside down over his shoulder, staring at the back pocket of his jeans. "Time for the rest of the tour."

Carrying her into another room, he laid her down on the bed, wasting no time covering her with his body and capturing her mouth with his. As before, he put a hand behind her head, holding her as though afraid she might try to escape. With his other hand splayed over her breast, he had her so effectively pinned down, she couldn't move at all. She seemed to have sunk into the mattress somehow and felt sort of… stuck. Reaching out a hand, she ran it over the sheets.

Flannel. She used flannel sheets on her own bed, but they'd never had that kind of effect. Panic rose in her chest as she tried to break off the kiss. When he didn't stop, a scream bubbled up in her throat, and she gave his shoulders a shove.

He pushed himself up on his hands.

"I can't move," she gasped. "I feel so trapped. Let me go."

To her surprise, he actually laughed—not a wicked, sadistic laugh, but one that was as disarming as his smile.

"Guess I should have warned you." Still chuckling, he rolled onto the bed beside her. "It's the bed. It's memory foam."

"What?" She sat up, feeling like she was climbing out of a hole.

"Memory foam," he repeated. Pressing down on the mattress, he left a hand print that remained for a few seconds. "It takes some getting used to, but once you do, you'll never want to sleep on anything else."

Leslie lay back down and flopped her arm out to the side. It landed with a thud that didn't rock the bed in the slightest. Lifting her hips, she dropped them down with as much force as she could muster. Her breasts jiggled, but that was about it.

He grinned. "Pretty neat, huh?"

"Well, yeah… I guess." She was still a bit doubtful. "It feels weird."

"Trust me, if you sleep on this thing enough, you'll get hooked and most of your aches and pains will disappear. Plus—" He paused, his eyes dancing with mischief. "—it's absolutely *fabulous* for fucking."

She had to laugh because he sounded like Gabe describing a new video game. "Is that what the salesman told you?"

He got up and went over to the nightstand. "Actually, a woman sold it to me. She didn't seem like the type to say something like that—not to me, anyway."

"Why not?"

"I dunno. She was young and sort of silly." Striking a match, he lit a candle in a glass jar. "Probably would've gotten the wrong idea if I'd asked her about it."

"She sounds more like the type to volunteer to help you break it in."

He blew out the match. "I doubt it. Now, if *you'd* been the one selling me a mattress, I might've said something different."

Ignoring that, she asked the next most pertinent question. "Obviously someone's been in it with you, or aren't you speaking from firsthand experience?"

"Yeah, I am." His sigh sounded weary, even jaded. "She liked the bed, the fuck, and the house, but she didn't like me."

"I find that hard to believe."

"Yeah, well, it's true." With a shrug, he continued in that same resigned tone. "It was the same complaint as always. She told me I needed to grow up."

"I take it she didn't like your dishes."

"No, she didn't. I don't know what girls expect from me, but this is just the way I am. I don't seem to be able to change." He lay down beside her, staring up at the ceiling. "All I've ever wanted is someone who'll love me, let me be myself, and let me love them back. I don't think that's too much to ask."

"You're talking about unconditional love," Leslie said gently. "That's hard to come by."

"Tell me about it." His voice was gruff. "That's why I haven't found anyone to be Mrs. Robin Thatcher."

At that point, he seemed to need consoling more than sex. Shifting onto her side, she held out both arms. "C'mere, babe."

He didn't hesitate. Cradling his head against her chest, she stroked his hair and trailed her fingernails over the smooth skin of his back. Holding him had a healing effect on her soul, making her realize how much she craved physical contact and how little of it she'd received in her lifetime. Hugging her son was wonderful and everything a mother could wish for, but holding Robin reached her on a unique level, triggering new responses. She could've lain with him like that all night and been satisfied.

He, however, had other ideas.

After a bit, he seemed to revive and began to nuzzle her breasts as though seeking a nipple to suck. For once in her life, Leslie was able to simply enjoy the sensations without worrying about what he might be thinking. Adrift on a sensuous cloud, she got so lost in the moment that when he gave each of her nipples a firm pinch, the pressure alone ignited an orgasm.

She was still coming down from her climax when he began to undress her the rest of the way. Too brain-fogged to protest even if she'd wanted to, she let him do it, no thoughts of shyness ever entering her head. When he stripped down to his skin, the sight of him was so shockingly male, so overwhelmingly arousing that she forgot everything—her age, her anxieties, even her own name.

Candlelight reflected off the smooth skin of his penis, accentuating every ridge and contour. As he gazed at her, his cock pulsed, pumping out a sparkling droplet that slid to the floor in a long, glistening strand. Did he have any idea how exotically beautiful he was? What the mere sight of him was doing to her?

She was still lying sideways across the bed when he spooned up against her back. Taking her in his arms, his caressing hands found her breasts, reminding her of what he'd said about wanting to be able to see them when he fucked her.

"Want me to turn over?"

"Mmm... no. I'll come too fast if I see them now," he murmured. "And I want this to take a very... long... time."

Pressing kisses on her neck and shoulders, he slid his hot, engorged penis between her thighs, teasing her clitoris with every stroke. Every feeling seemed enhanced—the heat of his chest against her back, the rough warmth of his hand splayed over her breast, the wet sweep of his tongue along her neck.

He eased back, altering the angle, his glans teasing her slit. "Do I need a condom?"

"Not unless you're carrying an incurable disease."

"I'm clean—got tested not long ago. Haven't been with anyone since, and I've always used condoms."

"But you don't want to use one now—or is it that you don't have any?"

"I've got some, but I'd really rather not…"

She believed him—trusted him—possibly because she didn't want him to use one, either. "Go ahead."

Her eyes widened as he slid inside, gently but firmly, until he'd buried himself to the hilt. He filled her completely, reaching deeply to find the sweet spots within, stroking them until she feared she would pass out from the overwhelming sensations.

The blankets were thrown back over the high footboard of the sleigh bed, leaving acres of soft, smooth flannel for her to stretch out across, and she used it all, sprawling with her arms outstretched and her head thrown back. The room was warm and quiet; the only sounds were his soft grunts of pleasure and the steady slap of his flesh against hers.

She pushed back against him, driving him in deeper, rotating his cock until she was seized with an orgasm even stronger than the first. Robin never faltered, pulling her hips against him, fucking her relentlessly and setting off wave after wave of mind-numbing ecstasy. Gripping the edge of the mattress, she held on for dear life.

"How many is that?"

She had no idea what he was talking about, but she knew she wasn't keeping track of anything. "I don't know, don't care—"

Suddenly, he was gone from inside her, rolling her onto her back as she cried out in anguish at his sudden departure. She needn't have worried. He soon filled her up again, facing her with her feet resting on his shoulders. His knees sank deeply into the mattress, allowing the perfect angle of entry. The foam held her in such a tight embrace she didn't slide away from him, enabling him to give her the most hard, solid fuck ever.

I think I'm gonna like this bed…

He picked up the pace, rutting hard and deep, pushing her knees forward and down, raising her hips to meet him thrust for thrust. When she came again with a deep, throaty cry, he slowed to a steady, rhythmic thud. A swift, upward glance caught him staring down at her breasts as they rocked with each stroke. In another instant, his body stiffened and his head snapped back. Holding his breath, he spurted so hard she could actually feel him filling her with his seed.

With a long exhale, Robin fell forward onto her chest, leaving his cock wedged inside her. Nuzzling her breasts, he seemed to doze, absently licking and kissing them off and on for a long time. Leslie had almost fallen asleep when he startled her awake.

"Wow. I never did that without a condom before. Absolutely *fabulous*."

Chapter 6

Leslie planted a kiss on the top of his head. "Just one of the perks of having a menopausal partner."

Robin had assumed she used some other kind of birth control. *Guess not.* "Really? I wouldn't have thought you were old enough— to be sure, that is. I mean, I've heard…"

She drew back in apparent surprise. "You're worried I might have a change-of-life baby?"

Me, a father?

Robin had been told to grow up so many times, he couldn't imagine anyone calling *him* Daddy. "Um, yeah. How likely is that?"

"Not very. I haven't had a period in three years—which is probably a good thing, considering I damn near died giving birth to the one baby I had."

His eyes widened. "Th–that's terrible. What happened? Or don't you like to talk about it."

She shrugged. "It may be ancient history, but it still affects me. They had to take me to surgery to stop the bleeding after Gabriel was born."

"Sounds scary."

"It was. I went under not knowing if I would ever wake up again. Gabriel's father wasn't around by then—he hit the road right after I told him I was pregnant—and I was so afraid Gabe would wind up being an orphan. I've been prone to panic attacks ever since."

That explained why she'd freaked out when he'd had her pinned to the bed. A trace of apprehension lingered in her eyes, and he chastised himself for putting it there. "I'm sorry I upset you earlier. I didn't mean to make you feel trapped."

"That's okay." Her gentle tone soothed his fears. "You couldn't have known. What you did wouldn't have bothered most women—it's just one of my weird little quirks. I didn't like not being able to move."

"I'll remember that," he promised. "If there's anything else you don't like, all you have to do is tell me. Okay?"

She smiled. "You make it sound like we'll be doing this again."

His heart took a dive, taking his jaw with it. "You mean we won't?" A one-night stand was unthinkable—certainly not what he'd ever intended—or hoped for. "You're not coming back? Ever?"

"I probably shouldn't," she said. "I'm much too old for you, Robin. This can't last, and you know it."

"How can you say that? Didn't you like it? What did I do wrong?"

"You didn't do anything wrong," she assured him. "I liked it all—loved it, in fact—but I don't see any future here. I've got more than twenty years on you. It might not seem like a big deal now, but when reality finally sinks in, one of us is going to panic—and it probably won't be me. You'll realize you've tied yourself to someone who will grow old long before you do."

"I don't care! Please, promise me you won't leave yet—at least stay until morning. That's happened to me so many times. I think I've finally found someone, and she's gone when I wake up."

Leslie was silent for a long moment.

Robin held his breath, waiting. He'd already begged, and if that didn't work—

"Okay," she finally said. "I promise I'll still be here in the morning. But that's *all* I can promise." Reaching up, she caressed his cheek. "Go to sleep now, babe."

His sigh of relief never made it past his lips. "Sleep? But we're not done yet."

"Not done? Geez, Robin. Your dick is getting soft, there's a puddle on the bed, and I've lost count of the number of orgasms you've given me. What else is there?"

"Like I said, I've never done that without a condom. There's something else I've always wanted to do. Would you mind?"

She eyed him with obvious suspicion. "This is gonna be kinky, isn't it?"

As kinky stuff went, Robin considered this one to be relatively tame. "I want you to sit on my face."

She blinked slowly, as though not quite believing what he'd said. "But I'm full of—"

"Yeah, I know, but I've always wanted to eat a pussy I've just fucked. I'd really appreciate it if you'd let me do that. I promise to make you come, and I'll fuck you again afterward. Please?"

She burst out laughing. "You have *got* to be kidding me."

He shook his head. "Nope. Perfectly serious."

"Damn... I've catered to some strange requests before, but that one takes the cake. Then again, I'd be an idiot to refuse." Clearing her throat, she shrugged. "Well, okay... if you insist..."

"Great!" Wasting no time, he crawled up to the head of the bed. Shoving the pillows aside, he stretched out on his back.

Moments later, Leslie sat up and turned around. The sight of her coming toward him on her hands and knees was one of the most fabulous things he'd ever seen, but when she sat back on her heels with her gaze aimed at his cock, he felt a twinge of alarm. Was she disappointed that it was lying limply on his thigh instead of standing straight up?

"Don't worry," he said. "It'll be hard again in a few minutes."

"That isn't the problem." Clearing her throat, she ran a hand through her hair. "Umm... which way do you want me to sit?"

"Facing the headboard," he replied. "I want to be able to see your tits while I do it."

"Of course you do," she said with a roll of her eyes. "How stupid of me to have forgotten." Placing her hands on the headboard, she positioned herself over him, then sank down until her creamy pussy hung tantalizingly above his lips. "You're sure about this?"

Robin didn't bother to reply. Grasping her thighs, he pulled her down hard, impaling her sweet pussy with his tongue.

"Evidently you are."

The blend of her juice and his cum was spicy and sweet, a deliciously heady combination that sent a surge of heat rushing to his groin. He licked her clean, inside and out, before latching onto her clit, taking the occasional peek at her awesome tits.

The sounds she made were like music to his ears, and he kept on licking, sucking, and fucking her with his tongue until he finally got what he'd been waiting for. Her sharp inhale, the stiffening of her body, the ecstatic cry that escaped her as she doubled over, narrowly missing the headboard.

"Oh, *yeah*," he groaned. "Now, scoot back and sit on my prick."

She threw a quick glance over her shoulder, although he could've told her not to bother. He was hard as a rock and ready to go. Not surprisingly, she seemed a little dazed, but she did what he told her to do without question.

She was so beautiful. Thick, golden hair fell in waves around her shoulders, and her full, rounded breasts were poised directly in his line of sight as she sat down and eased his cock inside her. Her pussy felt every bit as good wrapped around his dick as it had the first time.

Until she began to move.

Keeping him fully hilted, she slid him around inside her, rocking and rolling on his dick, pushing Robin closer to nirvana than he'd ever been in his life. Simply watching Leslie was a treat—enhanced by the fact that she didn't close her eyes. Her heavy-lidded gaze lingered on his face as though he was the sexiest, most desirable man in existence.

"Does that feel good, baby?" Her voice was languid, sultry.

With his climax rapidly escalating to detonation, he could only moan his reply.

She seemed pleased by that, swiveling her hips and rocking him even harder as her lips curved into a sensuous smile. When he reached the point of no return at last—his spine arching as his eyes rolled back in his head—his mouth fell open in astonishment at the incredible surge of ecstasy that flooded his being. But it was *her* softly uttered "Ohh…" he heard rather than his own.

Robin trailed his fingertips from her shoulders to her breasts, lightly touching her nipples before reaching up to cup her face in his palms. "That was better than anything I ever did in my whole life."

Leslie leaned down and kissed him, tasting of sex and chocolate.

"Happy Birthday, pretty mama," he whispered against her lips. "Welcome to your next—and best—fifty years."

If I don't die of a broken heart by morning.

Leslie had to smile at his optimistic estimate of her longevity. Another fifty years? Only one of her relatives had managed to live that long—her great-aunt Elnora, who'd spent the last fifteen years of her life deaf, blind, and incontinent in a nursing home. Her own mother hadn't made it to forty-eight.

Still, Robin had already managed to make this the best birthday she'd ever had. He might even be right about the rest of her life.

"Thanks, babe," she said. "Think you could sleep now?"

"Oh, yeah. Like a baby."

As she slid off him and went in search of a bathroom, she allowed herself to consider what might happen if she stayed with him.

Could she love him?

For that matter, could *he* love *her*?

She'd already pointed out the pitfalls of a relationship with someone twenty years his senior, and he'd denied having concerns about any of them.

He obviously thought it had a chance to work. She wasn't so sure—aside from the fact that they barely knew one another. It was too soon to make predictions and declarations—or even informed decisions. Her well-ordered mind issued dire warnings and advised caution, but her gut told her to go for it. Her heart seemed content with the turn of events, beating at a normal rate and rhythm, reminding her of the old adage that a heart wasn't worth a dime until it was given to someone else.

With those thoughts in mind, she chose a doorway at random,

found the switch, and flipped on the light.

The kitchen had been to die for.

The bathroom, on the other hand, was a religious experience.

The mirror that covered most of the opposite wall might've made the room seem larger than it truly was, but it was still huge. A Jacuzzi with seating for four sat in the center, and the shower could've easily accommodated a threesome. Astonished, she shifted her gaze shifted to an enormous oak vanity with a double sink, mirrored cabinets, and bright brass fixtures. Marble tile covered the floors and walls. Hunter green towels and rugs added color, as did the stained glass windows and shower door. Light from a ceiling fan worthy of Rick's place in *Casablanca* shone down on a toilet and a bidet.

She was so overwhelmed, she almost didn't make it there in time.

Afterward, her stunned expression still showed plainly in the beveled mirror as she washed her hands. Her hair was in wild disarray, and smudges of mascara made dark circles beneath her eyes.

I look like I've been fucked silly.

Leslie washed her face, then borrowed Robin's hairbrush and managed to arrange her hair in a slightly less pornographic style. Ordinarily, she would've drawn the line before using his toothbrush, but given some of the places he'd kissed her, she doubted he would mind.

Staring at her reflection, she tried to see herself from Robin's point of view and couldn't do it. No matter the angle, she still looked old enough to be his mother.

Maybe if I dyed my hair... and had a facelift and a tummy tuck.

She could see it now. One cosmetic surgery would lead to another and another until she looked like a freak. At least she could leave her breasts alone. As much as he enjoyed them in their current state, he might dump her if she got a boob job.

He likes me just the way I am.

Suddenly, her legs were as weak as noodles, and she nearly

collapsed on the chair by the vanity. Drawing her next breath with difficulty, she considered putting her head between her knees before she passed out from the shock. Robin was the most adorable man she'd ever seen, and he was willing to take her as is—without a major overhaul or modifications of any kind.

I don't believe it.

That wasn't too surprising. The entire evening was unbelievable. From the moment she'd spotted him sitting at the bar, she'd stepped into a dream—a surreal experience that couldn't possibly be true. Guys like Robin weren't normally attracted to older women. She should've been an anonymous face in the crowd, a non-entity sitting at a table, enjoying a night out with her friends, not going home with a man in a "PUCK FURDUE" T-shirt—and certainly not spending the night with him.

And yet, it had happened. This was real. The floor was cold beneath her bare feet, making her shudder from the chill. The cushioned chair was soft, but she'd landed on it crooked, so that the edge cut into her thigh. Blinking hard, she stood, holding the vanity for support. She took one step and then another. She brushed her hand over the light switch, plunging the room into darkness.

As her eyes adjusted, the candle he'd lit on the nightstand drew her back into the bedroom. Climbing in beside him, she pulled up the blankets, covering them both. His warmth surrounded her, just as the mattress had done.

Only this time she didn't feel confined.

With a soft sigh, he snuggled closer, resting his head in the hollow of her shoulder, his arm stealing its way around her waist.

She bit back a sob as she placed a tentative hand on his back. He was so warm, so alive, so real—his chest rising and falling, his breath tickling her breast.

Within moments, her awareness drifted into dreams.

৪০৫৪

Robin's eyes flew open. Leslie had rolled away from him during the night, but she was still there. He could hear her breathing and feel her heat.

And she packed some *serious* heat. A cautious fingertip on the middle of her back came back wet with sweat.

Hot flashes?

Maybe. She'd claimed to be menopausal, so that was to be expected. However, if she thought that was going to deter him, she had another think coming. He was about to show her just how little her being menopausal bothered him when his stomach let out a growl.

Breakfast. And he didn't have a damn thing to feed her except cold cereal. He'd seen her look of surprise when she'd opened his refrigerator. But an empty fridge was something he could fix. All he had to do was make a run to the store.

Ignoring his morning wood, he slipped out from beneath the covers and dressed quickly, grabbing the first shirt he touched when he opened his closet. Tiptoeing out to the kitchen, he glanced out the window.

"Holy shit."

While he and Leslie had been whooping it up in the sack, the weather had taken a turn for the worse. Two inches of snow already blanketed the ground, and it was still coming down heavily.

Her car was parked behind his truck. He'd have to move it. Hesitating, he gnawed his lip. Should he wake her and ask for her keys, or he should he find them himself? He doubted she would appreciate anyone rummaging through her purse. Thankfully, her coat gave a telltale jingle when he shook it. He dug his boots and his heaviest coat out of the front closet, donned his Braves cap, and was about to head out when it occurred to him that he should probably leave her a note. With any luck, he'd be back before she awoke, but after all the begging he'd done to get her to stay, she might be pissed if she woke up to an empty house.

Dashing off a quick note, he stuck it on the fridge.

Robin had only intended to move her car, but it handled the snow so well, he kept going.

He arrived at the grocery without mishap. However, after hearing another customer telling the cashier that six to eight inches were expected, he decided he should buy more than breakfast. He filled his cart—and subsequently the trunk of Leslie's car—then started for home.

Being snowed in for a week with Leslie sounded fabulous. She'd already given him the best fuck of his life—none of the others even came close. Despite what she'd said about eating sloppy seconds being kinky, he hoped she could keep an open mind about the other stuff. He'd do his best to return the favor—discover her fantasies and fulfill them.

That way she might not mind it so much when he asked her to spank him.

Chapter 7

Leslie awoke from a sound sleep with the uncanny realization that she was alone in the house. Climbing out of bed, she wrapped a sheet around her and padded barefoot out to the front room.

Although Robin was nowhere to be seen, he'd obviously put more wood in the stove. Orange flames curled around the new logs, filling the room with warmth.

A glance out the front window revealed two additional developments. First, her car was gone. And second, the ground was covered with at least four inches of snow. Huge, fluffy flakes continued to fall at an alarming rate, the tire tracks on the driveway already almost completely obscured.

"That's one way to keep me from leaving."

In less comfortable surroundings, these discoveries might have triggered a panic attack. However, despite being slightly pissed that he'd taken her car, she was still glowing from the night before. All she wanted now was a hot cup of tea, a huge breakfast, and Robin—preferably in that order.

Have to keep up my strength.

Returning to the bedroom, she dressed quickly, then went to see what she could scrounge up for breakfast.

She found her hair clip on the table and a note stuck to the fridge.

"Don't eat anything," it read. "I've gone to get breakfast."

So much for that.

After nosing around a bit, she concluded that the note had been intended to keep her informed rather than hungry. Aside from a box of Cocoa Puffs, there were no breakfast foods of any kind, and she simply wasn't in the mood for cold cereal. She could've made do with a bowl of oatmeal, but on a snowy morning after the most amazing sex ever, she craved a full breakfast of bacon, eggs, and toast. Bagels would also be a nice touch—or perhaps an English muffin.

Wondering what in the world he would bring home, she twisted her hair into a knot and clipped it in place.

The copper kettle on the woodstove was full of piping hot water, but if there was a single tea leaf in the house, she couldn't find it. In the end, she settled for hot chocolate and was sitting in a leather recliner sipping it from a mug that proclaimed "Builders Do It With Studs" when Robin came through the front door.

Stomping snow from his boots, he practically wiggled with enthusiasm. "Don't you just love snow?"

Her first impulse was to take him to task for running off with her car, but his excitement was such that she simply didn't have the heart to burst his bubble.

"Not really," she replied. "Makes it too hard to get to work."

"In *that* car? No way. That sucker will go through anything."

"It does pretty well as long as I don't have to plow through a drift," she admitted. "There's a lot to be said for front-wheel drive."

"No shit. I was only going to move it so I could get my truck out, but it handled the snow so well, I kept on going."

Leslie chose not to mention the dire consequences of possibly having wrecked her pride and joy, focusing instead on the numerous grocery bags dangling from his fingers. "I thought you went out to get breakfast. Looks more like you're stocking up for a blizzard."

"I *did* get breakfast," he said, scowling. "Oh, wait. I get it. You must've thought I was going to McDonald's or something. I went to the grocery." He finished on a note that made it seem as though shopping for groceries was a comparatively rare activity for him. "You *can* cook, can't you?"

"Yes, I can cook," she replied. "I take it you can't?"

He shrugged. "I never really learned how, so I usually eat out. Heating up a bowl of soup in the microwave is about the best I can do."

"And with a kitchen even Emeril would envy." *Go figure.*

"Who?"

"Never mind."

He set the bags on the table. "I didn't know what you'd like, so I bought lots of things. I got some stuff for lunch and dinner, too."

Evidently, he assumed she'd be staying for the rest of the day—possibly even all weekend if the snow continued—although he'd already proven she could probably make it home if she left immediately. Still, she could hardly wait to see what a guy who couldn't cook worth a darn might buy for dinner. Especially since he seemed to have bought everything anyone could possibly want for breakfast.

The fact that she could view this particular episode with a mellow eye was surprising. Ordinarily, she would've been pacing the floor, imagining all sorts of dire outcomes. Instead, she'd been able to sit down and enjoy a leisurely cup of cocoa.

This is so unlike me.

The fabulous sex was the only possible explanation, making her feel more relaxed than she'd been in ages. "Sounds good." She glanced out the window again. "The snow doesn't seem to be letting up."

Robin grinned. "They're calling for six to eight inches. We could be snowed in here for days and days."

"Really? I had no idea it was even supposed to snow, let alone that much." She shrugged. "Since I'm off until Tuesday, I didn't pay any attention to the forecast."

His eyes lit up. "You can stay until Tuesday? That's great!"

"I didn't say I'd be staying that long," she chided. "I only said I didn't have to go to work."

"Oh, right." The frown furrowing his brow was gone in the next instant. "I'd still hate for you to have to drive home in this mess."

Although his concern was undoubtedly genuine, Leslie wasn't fooled. The snow gave her the perfect excuse to stick around, and he obviously intended to play that card for all it was worth.

Not that she minded. She'd already decided she wasn't leaving yet, but watching his changing expressions was such a delight she couldn't resist the urge to tease. He didn't hold anything back, which was... refreshing.

"No worries," she said with a nonchalant shrug. "The road crews will have the main highways cleared as soon as it stops snowing. I should be able to get back to Pemberton without any trouble."

His eyes widened. "You have to go that far? Really? I figured you lived here in town."

She shook her head. "A trip to Bloomington is something of a treat for us Pembertonites." She gave him a wink. "Better restaurants."

He scowled at her for a long moment, then burst out laughing. "Okay, pretty mama. You can stop pulling my leg now."

"I'm sorry," she said between giggles. "If only teasing you wasn't so much fun."

With Gabe going off to college and all the changes at the hospital, her whole life had seemed like a melodrama lately, and turning fifty hadn't helped a bit. Robin, on the other hand, made her feel sort of giddy—not to mention sexy and desirable.

And she'd felt that way ever since buying him that drink.

The best five bucks I ever spent.

"I'm really glad you came here for your birthday." His emotions were painted clearly on his face. First gratitude, then mild surprise. "Just think what you'd have missed if you'd stayed home."

Or gone home last night.

If she'd paid attention to the rational side of her brain, she would've gone home. Instead, she'd followed Humphrey Bogart's advice.

Score one for Bogie.

Of course, actually listening to that voice in her head made her seem a little crazy. Perhaps she was. "Yeah. That was one of the best—no, *the* best—time I've ever had."

He gave her a wistful smile. "It doesn't have to end. We could have so much fun snowed in here together. The house Nick and I are building doesn't even have a roof yet, so I'll have several days off myself."

Time to let him off the hook.

She nodded at the groceries lying on the table. "If we're going to be stuck here that long, I certainly hope you got lots of tea."

"Sure did. I didn't know what you'd like, so I got coffee, too. I mostly drink Coke myself."

"No kidding," she drawled.

Having nothing better to do that morning, she'd counted the bottles—ten two-liter bottles and a 24-pack of cans—in that huge refrigerator with plenty of room to spare. The tea he'd brought was probably pretty standard fare. If she stuck around she'd have to educate him on her preferences, but not today. He'd done such a good job of winging it she hated to make him feel like he'd screwed up.

She peeked into the bags. "Hmm... Looks like we'll be having steaks and baked potatoes for dinner. And lunch will be..." She opened another bag. "Sandwiches with smoked ham and Havarti cheese?"

"Yeah. I asked the lady at the deli which cheese was a really good one. She didn't know what Havarti tasted like, but one of the customers told me it was really good, so I took her word for it."

"I agree. It's one of my favorites."

When she spotted the box of Earl Grey, she decided right then and there that he could drive her car anytime he wanted to. "God bless you." She gave him a hug and a kiss. "I've been dying for that."

"I thought it sounded interesting. Glad you like it." He said no more, but seemed terribly pleased with himself as he stowed the perishables in fridge. When he'd finished, he paused, peering at her from beneath his long, dark lashes. "Want breakfast now—or later?"

"Ooh, what a choice." Recalling how hot and bothered he'd gotten when she'd fed him cake the night before, she made a casual suggestion. "How about breakfast in bed?"

His lips curled into a smile. "Oh, yeah... But I want to stay here and watch you cook it. Then we'll *both* go back to bed."

She had no idea why watching her cook would be such a treat, but agreed without further comment. Robin rummaged around and found a non-stick frying pan that didn't look like it had ever been washed, let alone used. Some misinformed person must've given it to him, never suspecting he wouldn't have any use for it.

"Got an apron?"

A further search of the mostly empty drawers unearthed a black apron with "WILL GRILL FOR SEX" emblazoned on it in bold red letters—still in its original wrapping.

She was about to put on the apron when he stopped her. "Um… would you mind taking off your sweater?"

So that's why he wants to watch me cook. "The bra, too?"

His eyes lit up and his tongue slid sensuously over his lower lip. "Oh, *yeah*…"

Having hidden her breasts for so many years, Leslie couldn't believe she'd just volunteered to go topless.

First time for everything. "Hair up or down?"

"Up," he replied. "I like taking it down."

With a sly smile, she peeled off her sweater and unhooked the bra, turning away from him as she donned the apron. She didn't intend to let him see anything until after breakfast. Her growling stomach was bound to kill the mood—a risk she simply wasn't willing to take.

Gathering up the eggs, bacon, and the frying pan, she carried them over to the stove. She knew Robin couldn't see much of anything from the front, but when he pulled out a chair and sat with his back to the table, her left side—which included her largest asset—was directly in his line of sight. He stretched his legs out in her direction, making her wish she'd asked him to take something off, as well—preferably his pants. Somehow, she doubted he would refuse.

He was silent while she worked, and though she tried to focus on her task, her curiosity finally got the better of her. A sidelong glance revealed what had been keeping him occupied. His pants were unzipped, and he had his cock out, spreading his slick syrup over the gleaming head.

His eyes locked with hers. "When we go to bed, I want you to take off all your clothes and feed me."

Leslie glared at him with feigned indignation. "What about me? Don't I get any breakfast?"

"Of course you do. We'll share." Robin's cock pulsed at the thought of sharing *everything* with her. "You take a bite and then give one to me. Just like—" He stopped there.

I probably shouldn't tell her that yet.

"Just like what?" she prompted.

"Just like I've always wanted to do with a woman."

Her penetrating gaze displayed her doubt, and Robin had the strangest feeling she'd read his mind—perhaps even envisioning herself as the star of his fantasy.

If that was the case, she appeared to like the idea. With a gulp that could've meant almost anything, she transferred the bacon to a paper towel and started cracking eggs into the skillet. She put some bread in the toaster and pushed the lever down—yet another first. He'd never used that toaster for anything but Pop-Tarts.

"Damn. Almost forgot the tea." Snatching up a mug, she headed toward the woodstove, running her fingers through his hair as she passed by. After filling her mug, she returned, but this time she didn't mess with his hair. She leaned over and licked his dick.

He nearly came in her face.

"Mmm... slick and salty." She gave him a wink. "I'll have more of that later."

He stared at her, speechless, as she strolled back to the stove and gave the eggs a quick flip. What did a guy say to the goddess who'd just licked his cock?

She nodded toward the cabinet. "Better get a plate."

He gaped at her for another long moment before jumping to his feet. His pants dropped to his ankles and, suddenly, clothing became a superfluous annoyance. Toeing off his boots, he stepped out of his pants, yanked off his shirt, and threw it aside. Retrieving a plate, he stood beside her, doing his best to hold it steady while she piled on the eggs and bacon. When the toast popped up, she buttered it generously and added it to the stack.

She ran a hand over his ass and gave it a slap that sent a jet of pre-cum spurting from his slit. "Get your cute little butt back in bed." Taking a sip of her tea, she tore off some paper towels. "Lead on."

Robin made it to the bedroom in record time. He set the plate on the nightstand then arranged the pillows. Hopping into bed, he lay back against them.

She handed him the plate and proceeded to strip.

Granted, she wasn't wearing much, and her slacks and panties didn't take long to remove, but when she was down to nothing but the apron, Robin knew he'd never seen a more seductive vision in his life.

Until she took off the apron.

Raising her arms to pull it off over her head exposed her tits in a way that made him want to toss the plate away and feast on them instead.

"I'd drag that out longer, but I'm starving." Lounging beside him, she offered him the eggs, then alternated with him, bite for bite, holding the fork in one hand while caressing his cock with the other.

When he reached out to touch her, she stopped him. "Both hands on the plate, Robin. You have to wait until you're finished for your dessert."

Smiling slyly, she kept on feeding him, kissing him between mouthfuls and squeezing his dripping cock with her hand.

Not being able to touch her was rapidly driving him insane. By the time they'd finished eating and he reached for her breasts at last, his hands were shaking.

"*This* is what I want for dessert. I ate all of my breakfast, and now I want to suck your fabulous tits."

"You certainly have a way with words," she drawled. "Seems like I either have an orgasm or at the very least cream my jeans whenever you say something like that—if I'm wearing anything, that is. I've already made a wet spot on the bed. Hope you've got a washer and dryer."

"Trust me, washing sheets is not a problem."

Robin stroked the soft skin of her breasts, thumbing her firm nipples before sucking them into his mouth. Her contented sighs betrayed her pleasure, but his was so intense, he wasn't sure his dick could get any harder without rupturing something. Her skin was like satin beneath his tongue, and simply feeling the weight of her breasts in his hands made his balls ache.

Her fingers sifted through his hair. "How about doing that with your dick?"

She didn't have to ask him twice.

Pushing her back onto the bed, he slid the wet head of his penis over her engorged nipples, teasing them, soaking them with his juice. He moved over her, straddling her chest while sliding his cock between her big, soft tits, fucking them while holding them snugly around his dick.

She stared down at her chest. "Oh, God, that looks so incredible—the way the head sort of appears and disappears..." Lifting her head, she captured his dick with her lips on the forward stroke.

With a gasp, he gave an involuntary thrust, driving his cock further into her mouth. However, she didn't seem to mind, grabbing his ass and urging him to fuck even harder.

"You like that, don't you? Mmm... Suck my dick for me, pretty mama. Suck it *hard*."

She kept on until he was about to shoot his wad down her throat, then backed off to lick the shaft.

"Oh, yeah... I love the way you lick my dick."

His balls tingled as she teased his scrotum with the tip of her tongue. She'd been a damn good sport so far—hadn't refused a single request.

Might be worth a try...

Inching forward, he moved further up her body until his balls rested on her lips. "Wanna suck my nuts? I'd like to feel them in your mouth while you play with my dick."

Purring her approval, she bathed his scrotum with her tongue and then sucked each of his balls into her mouth in turn. Her purr escalated to a growl, and he felt her body curl up around him as though she'd had—

An orgasm? From sucking my balls?

A moment later, she let go of him and gasped, "Got any slippery stuff?"

Despite his state of near-delirium, he was back in seconds with a bottle of lubricant. Resuming his previous position, he dropped his nuts into her mouth and poured lube onto her palms. She laced her fingers together, creating a tight, slick channel for his cock, squeezing hard as she pumped up and down on his rod. Robin barely had time to register the fact that she'd fulfilled yet another of his fantasies when his balls tightened and he shot out an arc of cum that splattered the headboard.

"Impressive. But you might want to wipe that off before it dries."

Still dazed after coming harder than ever before, it took him a minute to realize what she was talking about. "What? Oh… right. The cleaning lady would probably freak out if she found it."

"Paybacks are hell." Her lips curved into a smile that belied her ominous tone, making her even more beautiful than ever—if that was possible. "She might retaliate by using your toothbrush to scrub it off."

Robin had kept one of his purchases a secret. A simple, ordinary item, it was the kind of thing that said it all—how much he'd enjoyed their time together and how much he hoped it would continue.

"Speaking of toothbrushes…" With a quick dismount, he landed on his back beside her. "I got you one."

Chapter 8

Leslie thanked him, although if Robin truly thought that a toothbrush was the only personal care item she might require, he had a lot to learn about fifty-year-old women. Hopefully, a previous girlfriend had left a bottle of body lotion behind, or Leslie's skin would probably crack right off her body.

After wiping her hands with a paper towel, she rolled over and rested her head on his shoulder, pulling the sheet up over them. She lay quietly, toying with the hair on his chest.

He sat up so suddenly, her head landed on the bed with a thud.

"I didn't get any sugar for your tea."

For once in her life, tea was the farthest thing from her mind. "That's okay, Robin." She gave him a placating pat. "I never put sugar in my tea."

He blew out a breath. "Thank God. I thought I'd fucked up. The last thing I want is for you to get pissed enough to leave."

She sat up, staring at him in disbelief. "Did you really think I'd get mad because you forgot to buy sugar?"

In the wake of his shrug, his shoulders sank even lower than they'd been before. "Women have left here with less provocation. You're the first one who didn't think I was weird."

That sounds interesting. "Weird? How so?"

"My... um... sexual requests. You don't seem to have minded any of them."

"Hey, at least you didn't ask me to stand on my head." She'd read enough erotic novels and letters to *Penthouse* not to have been too shocked by anything they'd done—yet. "You might offend me at some point. But not so far."

"Good. I'll be right back."

His apparent relief made her wary, but he returned with a freshly-washed penis and a cup of Earl Grey—rather than an armful of whips and chains.

"You're an angel." She accepted the tea, then arched a brow, listening. "Did you leave the water running?"

"I'm filling the Jacuzzi. It takes a while."

Being blessed with as many aches and pains as any woman her age, soaking in a Jacuzzi sounded like heaven. Still, she couldn't help wondering about all the kinky things he might want to do in a hot tub.

Robin didn't seem like the sadistic type—which might explain why the whips and chains notion hadn't triggered a panic attack. Granted, they'd done some stuff she'd only heard about, but nothing she'd truly objected to. Telling her what he wanted hadn't bothered her a bit, and the way he called her pretty mama was rather sweet.

It couldn't hurt to ask...

She took another sip of tea. "About your requests... You aren't into inflicting pain of any kind? Are you?"

He stopped dead in the act of climbing into bed, heightened color flooding his face and neck. "You don't think—"

"Just a question." She waved a dismissive hand. "Don't read too much into it. I just want to know if I should make my escape before the snow gets any deeper."

Leslie was grateful for his choice of mattresses—otherwise his abrupt push off the bed would have spilled scalding Earl Grey all over his favorite parts of her.

"No, don't leave. Please." He raked a hand through his curls with an air of desperation. "I'm not—I won't... Just... no."

"It's okay, babe. I'm not looking for a reason to bug out of here. I've had a wonderful time up to now, but I'm not willing to pay for it with my life."

He gaped at her like a hooked bass, not making a sound.

"You must understand why I'd be curious," she went on. "You keep telling me that women don't like you, but I've yet to see any reason not to want to stay here forever. I can't help wondering if maybe there's something about you that's a little... scary?"

If possible, he appeared to be even more aghast at this suggestion. "No, nothing like that. Believe me, hurting you is the last thing I'd ever want to do."

"That's good enough for me." She took another sip of the fragrant tea. "Besides, any guy who would bring home my favorite tea on a whim isn't someone I'd leave without a *very* good reason. End of subject."

He climbed into bed and lay down beside her, but seemed to have lost some of his sparkle.

That's my fault.

"Come here, babe. I'm sorry. I didn't mean to hurt your feelings." Enfolding him with her free arm, she kissed the top of his head. "I've never stumbled onto someone like you before. I'm generally not that lucky, so there has to be a catch somewhere."

Generally, hell. Who am I trying to kid?

She was *never* that lucky. Her son was one of the few men she'd ever known who hadn't turned out to be an asshole. Small wonder that she'd made no move to introduce herself when she'd spotted Robin at the bar. In her experience, men were far more likable *before* she got to know them.

She enjoyed sex and had an eye for a handsome man. Unfortunately, most of the men she'd dealt with had been arrogant, know-it-all bullies. Her body might crave them, but she didn't long for a closer relationship. Romance novel heroes were so much better—possibly because they'd been created by women who were as disillusioned as she was.

Was Robin truly different?

She doubted it. Her fifty years had taught her a few things—and not only that it was a long time to be alone.

Robin had never found the right girl, and she'd never found the right man. They were both misfits. Would they be better off together?

She set the teacup on the nightstand. Wrapping both arms around him, she held him close, blinking back tears.

I shouldn't be crying. Not when faced with the possibility that she'd finally found someone after so many years. Shouldn't she at least try to enjoy him while she had the chance?

If her previous track record was anything to go by, she would have a month at the most. She shouldn't be wasting a moment of it. Sliding down in the bed, she cupped his cheeks in her hands and gazed into his deep brown eyes.

What an adorable man. Despite his inherent sweetness, he was no less masculine.

"Please, don't cry," he whispered. "I don't want you to be unhappy."

"I don't want you to be unhappy, either." She did her best to smile. "And I'm not sad. Just kinda… scared."

"Same here. I'm afraid I'll do or say something that will ruin everything."

"Exactly."

Every moment they spent together was a test—an experiment to determine their compatibility. Unlike a blind date arranged by mutual friends or meeting through a dating service, they'd had no opportunity to learn about each other's background or personality beforehand. This was more about the feelings they evoked in one another.

He makes me want to fall in love.

Not cautiously or wisely, but passionately and completely, with no holds barred. Her heart ached to love him with as much tenderness as she loved her son and as much fervor as she'd wanted to love her son's father.

She'd never had that chance before. Not like this.

What Robin said about unconditional love made her wonder. Sure, he wanted it for himself, but would he let her love him like that? Would he place limits on her or repulse her as so many others had done?

As if in a dream, she scattered soft, loving kisses over his face. It had to be a dream because he didn't complain that she was smothering him.

Did he truly understand her needs?

Perhaps he did. He began kissing her in earnest before easing off, allowing her to take the lead.

She explored his body, leaving very little of it un-kissed as she memorized everything—from the swirling patterns of his chest hair to the arch of his brow and the way his toes curled when she kissed the soft skin where his thigh met his torso.

Not once did he give her the impression he wanted her to stop—not even when he got up to shut off the water when the Jacuzzi was full. When he returned, he slid into her embrace with a sigh, caressing her with his hands, just as she had caressed him with hers.

Give and take. Take and give.

The sense of joining, of finally belonging to someone was inexplicable. But the change was so profound she might have been a different person.

Before, she'd been alone and empty.

This new person wasn't.

Robin could've lain there for hours while she kissed him all over— and he would have—if he hadn't had other plans.

Taking her by the hand, he led her to the bathroom and into the hot, foaming water.

She sank into the tub with a sigh. "Damn, that feels good." Floating toward him, she encircled his neck with her arms, feathering his face and neck with kisses that made him shiver despite the heat.

"That feels even better."

"Glad you think so." Her eyelids drifted downward, her gaze directed toward his mouth. "You're such a kissable fellow." As if to prove it, she pressed her lips to his one more time—lingering, savoring.

His head was still spinning from her kisses when she reached for the soap. "How about a bath?"

He replied with a nod and was soon faced with the dilemma of which felt better on his skin—her soft, wet kisses or her hot, soapy hands.

She covered him with lather, tracing patterns through the suds with her fingertips. Raking her nails over his nipples sent even more heat rushing to his groin.

He leaned back against the side of the tub, thrusting his hips upward. "Wanna wash my dick?"

"Absolutely."

With a wicked smile, she trailed her fingers down his chest, skimming over his navel before delving beneath the water to grasp his penis. His cock twitched as she tickled the underside of his balls.

"Hmm… I think you need to stand up," she said. "Too hard to get it soapy underwater."

He rose slowly to his feet, his erection bobbing just above the surface.

She licked her lips. "Mmm… Hot, wet, and hard. Perfect."

Robin wanted to tell her how hot, wet, *soft*, and perfect she was, but the words became a groan as she began to wash his genitals. After massaging him to the brink of ecstasy, she paused to rinse the soap away.

"What a nice, clean cock," she purred. "So delightfully, deliciously sexy…"

Her quick wink was the last thing he saw before she sucked his dick into her mouth.

His eyes snapped shut and his knees threatened to give way as she stroked his shaft with her tongue. A pulse of his pelvic muscles sent out a jet of his juice, and she spread it all over him—from his slit to his nuts.

"Slick and salty. Mmm…"

Her hum of approval as she sucked his cockhead nearly sent him into orbit. He delved his fingers into her hair—an action intended to urge her on as much as it was to help him remain upright.

Gazing down at her, words sprang unbidden from his lips. "I still can't believe you're here. And you actually seem to like doing that—maybe even as much as I love sucking your tits."

She let go of him with a pop. "Adorable face, kissable lips, suckable dick, lickable balls... What more could I possibly want?"

At the moment, he'd have given her everything he had—whether she wanted it or not.

Is this what it's like to love someone?

Never having been in love, he had no idea. But she could've asked him for the moon and he'd have at least given some thought to how he might go about getting it for her.

Perhaps he could have a star named after her. He'd heard that was possible.

"Although, I believe I *would* like to wash your hair." With no further warning, she grabbed his hand and pulled him down into the water.

Despite all they'd done since she'd combed his hair with her fingers the night before, the sensuous effect of her touch hadn't diminished one iota. He sat there in a blissful daze while she lathered his hair, then rinsed it with her cupped hands.

Robin couldn't wait any longer. Hauling her into his arms, he kissed her, slipping his tongue past her lips and into the deep recesses of her mouth. His salty sauce mingled with her unique flavor was tasty, but he wanted more.

Sliding his legs between hers, he teased her clit with his cockhead, loving the way her expression softened, the way she clung to him, the way her lips formed a barely audible "Ohh..."

He eased her hips back and forth, allowing her delicate folds to glide, whisper soft, along the length of his shaft. While this was intended to be tantalizing and provocative from her perspective, his pleasure was such that he could scarcely keep from plunging into her. Lodging his cockhead in her slit at last, he pivoted her creamy pussy on the apex.

Feels even better than her lips on my dick.

"Good?" he murmured.

"You know it is. But I want you inside me."

Needing no further encouragement, he locked his eyes on hers and pulled her down on him with a splash, burying himself to the hilt.

Rewarded by her soft groan of pleasure and the passion in her gaze, he gripped the soft flesh of her hips, grinding her pussy around in circles and back and forth on his cock.

His own desire spiraled higher as her moans became continuous. Moments later, she fell forward with a cry, clutching his back as her body convulsed around him, squeezing his dick as tightly as if she held it in her fist.

Her orgasm ripped away the last shred of his control. Ramming into her repeatedly, he bounced her up out of the water until his own climax ignited. His mind went blank as his reflexes took over, filling her with his semen.

Leslie lay against him, her arms draped limply over his shoulders, her breath tickling his ear. "Oh, my..."

Smiling, he took her lovely face in his hands, kissing her again before lifting her onto the edge of the tub. "You ain't seen nothin' yet."

He leaned closer, nudging her legs apart. Sliding one finger into her creamy pussy, he found her G-spot, massaging it while licking her clit with a slow, circular motion.

Never having tried that technique before, he was unprepared for the speed and violence of her orgasm. With a climactic scream unlike anything he'd ever heard, she doubled over and fell into the water, taking him with her.

Quickly regaining his footing, Robin heaved her onto one of the seats. "Are you okay?"

She wiped the water from her face. "I'm fine. Just wasn't expecting anything quite that intense—although, you *did* warn me."

"True." Too bad no one had warned *him*.

Removing the clip from her hair, she shook her head, clearly oblivious to how hot she looked while doing it. "Where on earth did you learn all this stuff?"

Robin was reluctant to reveal his source, but he also knew she would figure it out eventually.

Best to be honest. "Remember when I flipped through one of your books while we were in the parking lot?"

"Yes, I do."

He grinned. "That was the part I read."

Chapter 9

Leslie's first instinct was to hide the books.

"Dunno how much more of that I can take," she said. "I'm not as young as I used to be."

Robin grinned. "Tell me that again twenty years from now, and maybe I'll believe it."

Such rigorous sexual activities probably weren't advisable for anyone over forty-five, let alone seventy. "Don't suppose you've ever seen a movie called *Cocoon*, have you?"

His blank expression didn't surprise her, nor did his negative reply.

Could've guessed that. "There's a scene where a guy has sex with an alien—joining, they called it. No actual physical contact, but this ball of light came out of her and hit him in the chest. He acted like he'd had a total-body orgasm."

"Your point?"

"Afterward, he said, and I quote, 'If this is foreplay, I'm a dead man.' That's how I feel."

With a burst of laughter, he pulled her into his embrace. "Trust me, that wasn't foreplay."

"I'm *so* relieved."

"Aw, come on, Leslie. You're tougher than that."

"Maybe. I'll let you know after my nap."

"Bath first." He lifted her face to his with a knuckle beneath her chin and kissed her. "I'm gonna wash you like you washed me."

"*Then* can I take a nap?"

He shook his head. "I got some body lotion for you, too. I'm gonna dry you off and slather you with it and rub it in 'til it's all gone. Might let you rest after that."

Had anyone ever done that for her? She doubted it. Surely she would've remembered it if anyone had... "I'll probably sleep for a week."

"Suits me." If he hadn't already made her an offer she couldn't refuse, his smile would've won her over completely. "Would you like that?"

She nodded, marveling that she still had that much control over her own muscles. Overall, she was nearing the wet rag stage.

He washed her like she'd bathed him, except that he spent an inordinate amount of time on her breasts. When he began shampooing her hair, she understood why he'd responded the way he had.

As he massaged her scalp with his strong fingers, she couldn't help comparing his technique to that of various hairdressers who'd washed her hair in the past. They had a tendency to scrub, scratching her head with long fingernails. Robin's nails were short, allowing him to use his fingertips, eliciting more sighs than she would've thought possible.

Afterward, he helped her out of the tub, enfolding her body in a thick, forest green towel.

She ran a finger down the center of his chest. "Don't I get to dry you off?"

"Maybe next time." Snatching up another towel, he quickly rubbed himself dry. "I'm taking care of *you* now." He pulled out the chair at the vanity. "Have a seat and I'll do your hair."

The last time she'd been in that chair, she'd nearly passed out from shock. Now, she was totally relaxed for an entirely different reason.

Snug and warm in the soft towel, she leaned back while his hands sifted through her hair. The flow of hot air from the dryer increased her drowsiness, relaxing her even further.

Glancing sideways at the mirror, all she could see of herself was the towel with her legs sticking out the bottom and her hair flowing out the top. Robin stood naked behind her. Her gaze roamed over his trim, muscular body, from the mop of curls on his head to the dark nest of pubic hair from which his relaxed penis and scrotum hung freely.

He put down the hairdryer and ran a brush through her hair, spreading it out over her shoulders. "How's that?"

Turning, she studied her reflection.

Robin had dried her blonde locks to a sensuous fullness. She seemed younger, more exotic—not her usual self at all. "Not bad."

He blew out a snort. "*I* think you're gorgeous."

"That's very sweet of you." She'd certainly never felt more beautiful. He, on the other hand, was one of the most appealing men she'd ever seen.

"You remind me of someone..." She paused, searching her memory. "I know...Michelangelo's *David.* Slightly different hairstyle, perhaps, but everything else..."

Blushing visibly, he couldn't have looked less like a marble statue. Still, he had a similar aura about him. "I'll take your word for it," he muttered.

"Something else you've never heard of?"

"I've heard of Michelangelo." He sounded a tad defensive.

She arched a brow, hoping the accompanying smile would take any sting out of her next question. "The artist or the Ninja Turtle?"

"Both. Just never seen *David*—at least, I don't think I have. I can do a computer search for it later. Right now, I have an incredibly beautiful woman to massage."

Incredibly beautiful?

He was certainly doing wonders for her self-image. Not bothering to argue, she held out a hand. "Do me."

Chuckling, he took her hand and kissed it before helping her to stand. "Don't worry. I'm gonna *do* you like you've never been *done* before."

"Promises, promises..."

Tucking her hand in the crook of his arm, Robin escorted her to the bedroom. "Lie down and close your eyes. I'll take care of the rest."

"I may fall asleep," she warned. Between the sex, the hot tub, and everything else he'd done, she was already halfway there.

"I'll take that as a compliment."

She did as he asked, wondering when she was going to be the one to take care of him. He hadn't mentioned it in his list of things he wanted from a woman, but somehow, she suspected it should've been in there somewhere. A man his age couldn't possibly want an older woman unless he needed mothering. Perhaps this was his way of setting the stage for her to reciprocate. The fact that he'd wanted her to feed him was a fairly reliable clue.

Still, as he squirted lotion onto his palms and rubbed his hands together, she found herself caring less and less about his motives. His warm hands on her back felt so shockingly good she had to stifle a gasp—an endeavor rendered pointless by her blissful sighs.

The professional massages she'd had were nothing like this— firm yet gentle, deft yet caring. His touch allowed her mind to drift into nothingness and melted her body even further into the cocooning mattress. He didn't even ask her to turn over when he was finished with her back, but rolled her over himself.

She'd assumed he would take the opportunity to stimulate her erogenous zones, but he didn't give her breasts or bottom any more attention than he did her arms and legs. Instead, he gave her one giant caress that soothed rather than enticed, encompassing her body with languid warmth, and reducing her to a state of relaxation so complete—

"Don't think I could move if the house was on fire," she murmured.

Kissing her cheek, he covered her with a blanket. "Sleep as long as you like. I'll be right here when you wake up."

80CR

Robin pulled on a pair of sweatpants and went out to the kitchen. Inhaling the lingering aromas of the breakfast Leslie had prepared, he tried to recall anything similar from his childhood, but that particular scent memory wasn't there. Mornings in the apartment where he grew up had smelled of beer and stale cigarette smoke rather than bacon and eggs.

Brushing those thoughts aside, he set about washing the dishes by hand—more out of habit than necessity since he'd picked up some dishwasher detergent that morning. The tiny smattering of plates he normally used had always made using the dishwasher somewhat ridiculous.

Afterward, he put more wood on the fire and picked up the clothing he'd left in the floor, then sat watching the flames until the fire burned hot enough to choke back the dampers.

He didn't mind that Leslie had fallen asleep. After all, she couldn't very well leave him unless she was awake. And he never wanted her to leave. She made him feel...

Loved?

Cared for?

He wasn't sure yet. But she reached a place inside him that no one else had ever come close to before.

The snow was still falling. He brought more wood in from the porch and set it by the stove. Normally, he spent days like this playing video games, but that activity didn't appeal to him now— didn't seem appropriate for some reason.

Then he remembered her books.

Donning his boots and jacket, he went out and retrieved them from her car. Once inside, he sat down on the couch to read. The first book he chose was the one he'd scribbled his name and phone numbers in. Staring at the words he'd written, he wondered if Leslie would've called him if she hadn't followed him home. For that matter, would she *ever* call him, or would she leave tomorrow and never contact him again?

There was a way around that. He glanced at her purse, still setting on the counter where she'd left it the night before. A quick check of her driver's license would provide him with her address— guaranteeing that he could at least find her again. Biting his lip, he fought with the urge, reminding himself that she was nothing at all like the other women he'd dated. No comparison whatsoever.

I can't do it. That would be cheating.

He had to make her *want* to come back, to freely share her life—as well as her address and phone number—with him. No coercion, no subterfuge.

She seemed happy with him—more so than any of the others ever had—but the age difference obviously had her bugged. For her to stay, she had to at least like him, and she had to like him for who he was. He couldn't pretend to be the sort of man he thought she might prefer. Sure, he could get some interesting ideas from her books, but those were only techniques to give her pleasure. They wouldn't make her like him—much less love him.

She had to do that all by herself.

Scary thought.

He was still contemplating this when the phone rang. The name on the caller ID didn't surprise him a bit.

"Hey, Nick. Guess we won't be working tomorrow, huh?"

"No—and probably not Tuesday, either," Nick replied. "Unless you want to go into the igloo business."

"Not much of a market for them around here."

"No shit." Nick seemed to hesitate. "Did you find what you needed at the store last night?"

If you only knew. "Sure did."

Robin had to press his lips together to keep from laughing. He had no intention of telling his brother about Leslie—not yet, anyway. He'd already heard all the reasons why he shouldn't want an older woman from Leslie. He certainly didn't need to hear it from Nick.

"Must've been important. After you dropped me off, you tore out of there like a bat out of hell."

"Did I? I don't remember."

"Yeah, you did. Are you snowed in?"

"Maybe," Robin replied. "I could get out if I had to."

"Better stay put. No point in tempting fate."

He rolled his eyes. "Don't worry. I will."

"Okay. If this snow doesn't melt off, I may not see you until Thursday. You're still coming over to Laura's for Thanksgiving, right?"

"Of course, I am. Wouldn't miss it." He'd much rather spend the day with Leslie, of course, but it was probably too soon to hope for that.

"Sounds good," Nick said. "I'll give you a call if the weather improves."

Robin switched off the phone. Nick was playing protective big brother again. Years ago, he would've appreciated the gesture, but not now.

Too little, too late.

℘℃

Leslie awoke from her nap with the aroma of potato chips filling her head.

Sour cream and onion.

Her eyes flew open when she heard the crunch. Robin lay beside her, propped up on a mound of pillows with a bag of potato chips on his stomach, reading one of her novels. Judging from the tent in the blanket over his groin, his choice of reading material must've been having the desired effect. The inevitable bottle of Coke sat on the nightstand.

"Have a nice nap?" he asked.

"Wonderful. I can't remember ever feeling more refreshed." She wasn't kidding, either. She hadn't slept that well in ages.

"I'm glad." With a wink, he added, "I've been trying to figure out how to fuck you without waking you up." He gestured with the book in his hand. "This isn't the only thing teasing my prick. Just watching you sleep and hearing you breathe makes me hot."

That's a first.

"If it's all the same to you, I'd prefer to be awake for that."

He grinned. "Same here." He held out a chip. "Hungry?"

"Oh, yeah—but not for chips. I'd like to have a dash of Robin's secret sauce first, if you don't mind."

She caught a fleeting glimpse of his self-satisfied smirk as she dove beneath the covers and went down on his slick penis. His cock pulsed, sending more of his salty syrup onto her tongue as she devoured him. She fondled his balls, teasing them, pulling the hairs as she sucked, delighting in the sounds he made and his sigh of ecstatic release when he spurted into her mouth.

Rolling her onto her back, he thrust his still-hard cock into her, fucking her with surprising vigor before collapsing on top of her in a boneless heap.

She sifted her fingers through his hair. "Had enough?"

"Oh, yeah… Totally fucked out."

"A little lunch will perk you up. After all, man does not live by Coke and chips alone." She paused, chuckling. "I don't suppose you brought home any oysters, did you?"

"To put lead in my pencil? Nope, didn't think of that—didn't think I'd need it. Maybe we could get some tomorrow."

"Does that mean you don't have to work?"

He nodded. "Nick called while you were asleep and said we'd probably take off until Thursday. It's supposed to turn colder tonight and snow more tomorrow."

The mere thought of going out in the cold made her shudder. "I'm glad I don't have to work for a couple of days. I really hate driving in snow." Snug and warm in Robin's bed, she was in another world when she was with him—no worries, no cares, and certainly no patients to take care of. Being with him was the closest thing to paradise she'd ever known. "Do you want me to stay until then?"

"Oh, please do," he urged. "Like I said before, I'd love to be snowed in here with you for days and weeks and months and—"

"I get the picture," she drawled. "I just hope we can get out again for more food or we'll starve to death. You don't exactly have a well-stocked larder."

"Larder?"

She waved a dismissive hand. "Old fashioned term—not used much these days. More of a *Little House on the Prairie* kind of word."

He looked up at her and grinned. "Had one when you were a

kid, did you?"

On impulse, she reached down and smacked him on the buns. "I'm not *that* old, smart ass."

To her surprise, his eyes flashed with a sudden explosion of lust. "Keep that up and we won't need oysters."

"Oh, God," she said with a groan. "Don't tell me you like being spanked. This is getting kinkier all the time."

"It's not that kinky," he protested. "One of the guys in that book you bought liked being *tied up* and spanked. That's a lot kinkier."

"You're kidding me, right?"

He held up a hand as though swearing an oath. "Honest to God."

"Damn. Wish they'd put that in the blurb."

"They couldn't put everything in the blurb. Those people are at it non-stop."

"Hmm… Sounds like fun, but doubt I could keep up the pace. I've never had this much sex in such a short length of time as it is. Of course, that's fiction. Real people can't do that." *Especially not at my age.*

"You can if you have multiple partners," he insisted. "The people in that book were doing everyone in town."

Evidently, she really should've hidden those books—perhaps even burned them. "At least we're limited to how much the two of us can take."

"I can keep going."

She shot him a scowl. "Thought you were fucked out."

"Right now, I am. But I'll be ready to go again after lunch." He gave his eyebrows a suggestive waggle. "I could leave the milk out so you'll fuss at me."

"And swat you on the ass with a dish towel?"

"Would you? Really?"

"To be perfectly honest, I'd much rather look at your ass than swat it."

Robin had such a cute, furry butt, she could probably work up a decent orgasm herself if she stared at it long enough. However, if he truly wanted swatting, she could do that, too.

Maybe. In her experience, men had no pain tolerance whatsoever.

Her stomach growled, reminding her yet again that it was way past lunchtime and so far, all she'd had to eat was semen.

Rolling him off her, she got up and gave him another smack on the buns. "It's time for lunch—that is, if you haven't already filled up on chips."

"Oh, I can still eat lunch." Judging from his salacious expression, he was thinking about having *her* for lunch instead of a sandwich. "I'm a growing boy, you know."

She snorted a laugh. "Growing boy, my foot. Someday, when you least expect it, your middle will start to thicken and pretty soon that cute little ass will be too big for your britches." She gave his bottom another firm pat before squeezing his butt cheek like a ripe peach.

"Not if you keep spanking it like that. I'll get enough exercise fucking you to make me really skinny, no matter how much I eat."

Something in his tone made her want to run, and he made a grab for her as she took off for the kitchen. She'd almost rounded the table when he caught her from behind. Making an immediate grab for her tits, he pulled her back against him and shoved his cock between her legs.

"But I need lunch," she protested, dissolving into helpless laughter. "I just sucked you off. You can't need more sex so soon. Whatever happened to being totally fucked out?"

"That was before you started hitting me on the ass. I can't help it."

He wasn't kidding. His cock felt more like a rolling pin between her thighs than the average erect penis.

"Just one more good, hard fuck," he begged. "Then we'll have lunch, I promise."

Leslie barely had time to nod before Robin spun her around, lifted her onto the table, and shoved her legs apart. His first wild thrust nearly detonated an orgasm, and his subsequent impalements soon had her screaming in ecstasy.

When he finally reached his own climax, his "Whoa, *momma...*" sounded as though it had come straight from his balls before bursting past his lips.

He came so hard, she actually felt his ejaculation. His hands gripped the edge of the table, and he gasped for air as his nuts spasmed against her bottom. Thrusting his hips forward, he rocked side to side, delving deeper than ever.

Leslie grasped his shoulders and pulled him down, capturing his mouth in a heated kiss. The altered angle popped his cock from her pussy, but that didn't stop him for a second.

Sliding backward, he licked her breasts before moving down to the apex of her thighs. After planting a searing kiss on her pussy lips, he stood upright, an unreadable expression on his face.

Stunned speechless, all Leslie could do was stare.

Robin wiped the sweat from his eyes and sucked in a breath. "Would you like mustard or mayo on your sandwich? I've got both."

Chapter 10

Leslie laughed so hard, Robin was afraid she would fall off the table.

"I can't believe you asked me that," she gasped between giggles. "And at such a time."

Chuckling, he helped her to stand, then gave her a hug. Making her laugh was even more fun than making her come.

Maybe.

"Hey, I promised you lunch after a good, hard fuck. What did you expect me to say?"

"I honestly don't know—but gee whiz, Robin. The earth moves and all you can say is 'mustard or mayo'?"

He gave her a cheeky grin, trying not to seem too pleased with himself, even though he was. Very pleased. "It *did* move, didn't it?"

"You're damn right it did. Remind me not to smack your buns unless I'm already in the mood to get nailed."

"Sorry—but I warned you."

"Yes, you did," she agreed. "But at the time, I didn't completely understand the effect. I know better now."

She might as well have sucker-punched him in the gut.

That's what I get for being cocky. "Does that mean you'll never do it again?"

"Of course, it doesn't, sweetie." She gave his ear a pinch that set off a wave of interesting tingles. "I just won't do it when I'm hungry or have something else I need to do."

Relief washed through him. He'd never been on such an emotional rollercoaster in his life. His heart might never be the same—but he was certainly enjoying the ride. "Gotcha. Let's eat."

He started toward the refrigerator.

"Umm… I don't suppose you have a robe I could borrow, do

you?" She crossed her arms over her breasts, shivering.

"Sure thing. Be right back."

He ran into the bedroom and after a quick search of the rear of his closet he found the robe Nick's wife, Trish, had given him for Christmas a few years ago. Robin had never actually worn it, but it would be perfect for Leslie. After putting on his sweatpants, he returned to the kitchen and helped her into the robe.

"Mmm… nice." She snuggled the thick, terry collar around her neck. The robe was a little tight across her chest—not that he minded—but seemed to fit her okay otherwise.

He pulled out a chair. "Have a seat. Since you made breakfast, I'll fix lunch."

"Sounds great. Sure you don't need any help?"

"Nope. I got this."

At least, he thought he did.

The lady he'd talked to at the store had made a suggestion that didn't sound too difficult—all he had to do was put the ham and cheese on a croissant with a little mayo and warm it up in the microwave.

However, when he gave Leslie a bite of her sandwich, he had to fight the urge to pat himself on the back.

Her reaction was, well… orgasmic.

"Mmm… You know, for a guy who claims not to cook very well, you sure did a bang-up job."

His face prickled with heat. Was he blushing because of her enjoyment or his own satisfaction at having earned her approval? "Glad you like it."

She gestured toward the sandwich in his hand. "I hope you aren't feeding that to me hoping I'll return the favor. You know what that does to you, and I'd like to get through at least one meal without stopping for sex."

This time, he knew precisely what caused him to blush.

Embarrassment.

"Sorry." He put the sandwich on a plate and handed it to her.

Setting the plate down, she fixed her gaze on him. "Mind telling me why my feeding you is such a turn-on?"

He shrugged, avoiding her eyes. "No reason. I just like it."

He knew why, of course, but he wasn't comfortable with the idea of getting into a deep, psychological discussion. Not yet, anyway.

Still, his feelings toward Leslie had altered several things. Having always longed to have a woman who would love him and take care of him, now that he'd found someone who might actually do it, he wanted to do everything for *her*—didn't want her to have to lift a finger.

Weird.

"Okay," she said. "Just curious."

He fixed his own lunch and sat down, only then realizing she didn't have anything to drink. "Would you like some more tea?"

"Sure, but you don't have to—"

"No trouble." Jumping up from his seat, he went and got the kettle from the woodstove, only to discover that the water wasn't hot enough to brew tea. He'd forgotten he'd filled it earlier. "Better warm this up in the kitchen. That's the trouble with keeping the kettle on the woodstove. Takes a long time to heat up unless the fire is burning really hot."

"Handy, though."

"Yeah." He set the kettle on the stovetop and turned on the burner. "That'll be ready in a minute. Do you need anything else?"

"No. I'm fine." She gestured toward the front window. "Looks like the snow's letting up. They'll have the roads clear soon."

A quick glance confirmed that the snow had diminished to flurries.

Damn.

"It's still pretty, though," she went on. "Between that and the décor, I feel like I'm in a ski lodge, waiting for the slopes to open."

"Really? Do you ski?"

"Used to. But that was a long time and a broken leg ago. I kinda lost my nerve after that."

"I don't blame you." Steam hissing from the kettle's spout

caught his eye. Hopping up, he fixed her a fresh cup of tea. If there was one thing he had in abundance, it was coffee mugs.

I might actually have a reason to use the dishwasher. Hopefully, it would still work after sitting idle for so long.

"I used to love to go skiing at Christmastime. They always had huge trees—real ones—in the lobby of the hotel where I used to stay." She smiled wistfully. "They probably have to use artificial trees now, what with fire regulations and all."

Robin had never seen a live tree in a public place in his life.

Leaning back in her chair, she gazed toward the ceiling. "You could put a really humongous tree in here."

"I could. But it seems kinda pointless when I'm the only one who'd see it—unless we show the house to someone. A huge tree might put some people off. Too much trouble."

She laughed. "I barely have the space, myself, but I do it anyway. Seems almost criminal not to have one in a place like this."

"Yeah, maybe," he conceded. "But, like I said, I've never seen the point, and I doubt I ever will. I always spend Christmas at Nick's house anyway. He's got a wife and kids and a tree and everything."

"Is that what you want?" she asked. "A wife and kids and a tree and everything?"

Robin had tried not to sound too forlorn, but apparently he hadn't succeeded. "Nick says I'm too much of a kid myself to ever have any of my own. Besides, you need a wife for that."

"Which is yet another reason why you shouldn't be picking up fifty-year-old women," she drawled. "There were all kinds of cute girls in that restaurant last night. I even saw you hug one of them. Why on earth would you choose to follow me?"

"That girl I hugged is the bartender's sister. He and I were at IU together. I think he was trying to fix me up with her, but I didn't like her much. Not sure she liked me, either. Besides, *you* were the one who bought me that drink. All *she* did was drink most of it."

"I noticed that. Kinda pissed me off."

"I thought so."

Her eyes widened. "You were *watching* me?

"Oh, yeah. I spotted you when you were being shown to your table. Couldn't take my eyes off you."

"Bullshit."

"It's true. I tried not to be too obvious about it—I couldn't believe my luck when I nearly ran into you. Then when I figured out you were the one who bought me that drink…" He shrugged. "I had to talk to you again—without Nick tagging along, which meant I had to take him home and come back. Came damn close to missing you."

"Good thing Suzie was late."

It took a moment for the implication to sink in. "Was that really a good thing?"

She glanced down at her cup, swallowing hard. "One of the best, actually. If you hadn't been waiting for me when I left the bookstore, I'd have gone home and read one of those books—would probably be sitting alone in my apartment, reading one of them right now." When her gaze met his, he could've sworn she was blinking back tears. "Instead, I've been having a marvelous time with you, and now I'm sipping tea and thinking about decorating Christmas trees and baking turkeys." Her voice dropped to a hoarse whisper. "A *very* good thing."

Damn. Leslie was every bit as lonely as he was. "I don't get it. Why doesn't a fabulous woman like you have a husband?"

She grimaced. "Not everyone thinks I'm fabulous, and I've yet to meet a man I could stand for more than a month. Some people are cut out to be single—whether they like it or not."

"Maybe you just had sense enough to wait for the right guy— you know, your perfect match?" Robin had already decided he wanted to be that man—and he wanted it more with each passing moment.

"Not sure there is such a thing. It might be that I'm simply the kind of controlling bitch men can't stand."

Controlling bitch? "You don't seem controlling to me."

"Wrong word, then. Bossy, perhaps."

He didn't consider either of those traits to be bad. In his opinion, in order to be bossy or controlling, a person at least had to give a damn. There was a lot to be said for that.

Sure beats being ignored.

He gathered up their empty plates, set them in the sink, and gave them a quick hit with the sprayer. "You don't boss *me* around."

"It doesn't seem that way to you because you actually like it when I smack your buns and tell you to get a move on."

"Sounds like we're perfect for each other."

She snorted a laugh. "Yeah, right. There's no such thing as perfect."

"I'm not kidding. I really mean it."

Leslie searched Robin's eyes for any trace of guile or humor and found only genuine warmth and absolute sincerity.

He was serious.

"Maybe we aren't a *completely* perfect match," he added. "But I believe we're damn close."

She stared at him for a long time, unable to think of a single thing to say. Beyond the confines of his beautiful home, there were people who would condemn the two of them with their last breath. The opinions of others shouldn't matter, but he had family and so did she.

What would Gabe think of his mother having a boyfriend who wasn't much older than he was? Robin had already indicated that his brother wouldn't approve—the fact that he'd gone to so much trouble to ditch Nick before approaching her spoke volumes.

And yet, if it really was true and they *were* a good fit, being together might be worth the disapproval.

What would it be like to live with Robin? To have someone to look after, someone to cook for, someone to love? Sure, the odds were against a successful relationship, but the potential rewards were astonishing.

You've known him for less than twenty-four hours. How can you possibly know anything?

The voice in her head was as relentless as it was reasonable.

"Where the hell is Bogie when I need him?" she muttered.

"Huh?"

"Humphrey Bogart. His line about regret in *Casablanca*. That's the reason I followed you home last night."

Instead of the blank stare she'd expected, he nodded. "'Maybe not today, maybe not tomorrow, but soon, and for the rest of your life?'" Amazingly, he understood what she meant. "I'm glad you listened to him."

"And I'm glad you've seen that movie."

He grinned. "It *is* a classic. I'm not a complete ignoramus when it comes to old movies."

"Thank God."

His grin became a mischievous smirk. "I may not be an ignoramus, but I do tend to be sort of forgetful." He nodded toward the countertop. "I left the milk out. You should spank my butt for that."

Wondered when we were gonna get back to that.

She was glad the mood had lightened a bit. If they were going to have fun together, they might as well get on with it—starting with the tease…

"So you did. However, I'm not sure it warrants corporal punishment. I should simply tell you to put the milk back in the fridge."

"And what if I say no?"

"I'll do it myself."

He scowled. "You're no fun at all."

"Takes less energy to put the milk away than it does to spank a full-grown man into submission."

She didn't have to look far to see where this conversation was headed. His quiver of anticipation and the bulge in his groin were clearly visible—as was the wet spot on his sweatpants. Somehow she didn't think he'd gotten it wet when he'd rinsed the dishes.

Maybe we really are a perfect match.

"S-submission?" He couldn't even say the word without a stammer.

"Oh, please. Don't tell me you're into *that* shit."

"Never thought of it that way, but I might be."

She rolled her eyes. "Great. Silly me, I left my whips and bustier at home. What was I thinking?"

"You don't really—" He broke off with a gulp.

For one fleeting moment, Leslie thought he might've ejaculated. "You didn't come without me, did you?"

"Uh… no, I didn't."

"Good. I'd *really* have to spank your butt for that."

"I was just picturing you in a bustier." His scorching gaze threatened to burn right through her robe. "You'd look absolutely *fabulous*."

"Really? I've never thought of myself as the dominatrix type."

With a slow, deliberate nod, he moved closer. "Trust me. You're a natural." Taking her hand, he pressed his lips to her palm.

Despite her apparent aptitude for domination, her body reacted like it had when he kissed her in the parking lot. The same sense of bone-melting surrender—minus the attack of nerves.

"I dunno, Robin. As a nurse, I have to do a lot of things to people that are pretty painful. I don't particularly enjoy doing it."

"Yeah, well, this is different."

There it was again—that lip-curling, bad-boy grin that completely destroyed her defenses. He was such an enigma. One minute he seemed lost and vulnerable—the next, he was seduction personified.

"How do you *do* that?" she whispered.

Still holding her hand, he pulled her to her feet. "Do what?"

"Become that other guy—like you did last night."

He shrugged. "Most people act differently when they think they might get laid."

"You have a point."

"Bring your tea," he said. "I think we need to continue this discussion on the couch."

Chapter 11

Robin tugged on her hand, but Leslie hung back. "What about the milk?"

Apparently, he'd found the right trigger. She might not give a damn if he didn't wash the dishes, but leaving the milk out was another matter. "Later."

"Robin." The trace of censure in her tone made his cock twitch.

"Make me," he taunted.

"Ooh, you little scamp. I ought to—" She stopped, her lips pursed and eyes narrowed with suspicion.

He wouldn't have thought it possible, but she looked sexier than ever. "What?"

"Never mind. You're manipulating me. You don't have to do that."

"I don't?"

"No. I'm game for whatever you want to do—unless you prefer to play it this way."

Did it make a difference? He wasn't sure. "I think you need to be mad at me."

"Robin, sweetheart, I don't *want* to be mad at you. Like I said, I'll play this however you like. Just tell me what you want. You've never been shy before."

"This is… kinkier."

"Just say it."

"Okay." He sucked in a breath. "I want you to spank me until I come."

For a very long, nerve-racking moment all she did was stare.

Wait for it…

"I believe I'd rather put the milk away myself," she finally said.

At least she wasn't calling him a pervert and running for the door. "Tell you what. If you'll do that for me, I'll take care of the milk—and anything else you want me to do. Anything at all."

"You make it sound like I'd be doing you a favor."

"Trust me, you'd be doing me a *huge* favor."

"Doesn't seem like it from my perspective. I'd much rather kiss you than spank you." She hesitated, her teeth pressed into her lower lip. "Are you sure it's even possible? My arm will probably give out before you get that far."

Robin shook his head. "I'd still like to try."

"Has anyone else ever—"

"You'd be the first."

"Oh, joy," Leslie drawled. "I take it this is a pet fantasy of yours?"

"Absolutely."

"I'm gonna have to come up with a real dilly for you to fulfill. Might take me a while."

"Does that mean you'll do it?"

"I guess so." She frowned. "I see now why you tried to piss me off. Helps to be in the right frame of mind."

He nodded toward the sofa. "Go have a seat. I'll be right with you."

Robin made quick work of putting the milk away, only then realizing he hadn't actually drunk any of it, and neither had she. He couldn't even remember why he'd gotten it out to begin with.

Must've been a subconscious thing.

He sat down beside her, then turned and lay on his back with his head in her lap.

Leaning over, she kissed his forehead. "This is more what I had in mind—sitting by the fire on a snowy afternoon, sipping tea and running my fingers through your hair."

"Is that one of your fantasies?"

"No—but it sure is nice."

Any other time, Robin would've agreed. Her touch was soothing and enticing at the same time.

Unfortunately, the anticipation had his dick shifting into overdrive.

Would his insatiable need for Leslie ever subside? Quite honestly, he hoped it never would. He'd spent his entire life looking for this kind of relationship—wanted to immerse himself in it and didn't really care if he drowned in the process. She was intoxicating, addicting, and, unlike a number of other things that shared those same traits, she was probably good for him.

He teased open her robe, trailing his fingers over her satiny skin. Moving closer, he rose up to take her nipple in his mouth, sucking it gently.

He understood why she didn't want to waste the energy whipping him into submission. This was a great way to spend an afternoon. She tasted good, smelled good, felt good. Her fingers in his hair relaxed him to the point of drowsiness—until he realized she was stroking his head the way she would pet a lapdog.

Robin wasn't sure he wanted to be a lapdog. He wanted more than a pat on the head. He wanted—well... maybe he *did* like the idea. Naked—wearing a collar and a leash...

The instantaneous surge of heat to his groin nearly doubled him over.

"You didn't come without me again, did you?" Her tone was light, teasing—like her touch.

He barely had enough breath in his lungs to speak. "Damn near."

"Kinda like I did when I was sucking your balls?"

Should he admit what he'd really been thinking about or let her believe what she wished? "Sort of—along with some other stuff."

"Can I assume you don't want to talk about that other stuff?"

The spanking issue was one thing. Those other things were *really* kinky. "Not yet. Wouldn't want you to freak out."

"I'm *already* a little freaked out."

"Believe it or not, so am I. Being here with you is giving me some pretty wild ideas."

"I know the feeling. I'm actually giving some thought to

smacking your ass." With a wicked chuckle, Leslie slid her hand into his pants. "But I'd rather grab your dick."

As her hand closed around his cock, his breath hissed in through his teeth. "Do whatever you like. I won't complain."

Not all of his juice had soaked into his sweats. Some of it was still on his cock, allowing her hand to glide the length of his shaft to his sac.

"Nice balls." She gave them a squeeze. "Not sure which I like best—them or your dick."

Shifting his attention to her other breast, he eased up over her—a move that put his junk within easy reach, along with his ass. "Not sure which of these *I* like best."

"I would've guessed the left one, but size isn't everything."

From his current position, he could enjoy them both—licking the right while the left pressed against his chest. Shifting his hips to the edge of the sofa allowed him to use his hands. He untied her belt and folded back each side of the robe, exposing her to his gaze. What was it about her tits that made him so crazy with lust? Simply holding her breast in his hand sent pre-cum gushing from his slit.

She ran her thumb over his cockhead. "Mmm… Love when you do that. Makes me want to suck your dick."

"Help me get rid of these pants, and you can suck it all you like."

She had them off him in seconds, but instead of sucking his cock, she slid her hand over his ass. "Mmm...nice and furry." Leaning sideways, she pressed her lips to his cockhead. "Every last bit of you is sweet and sexy—and impossible to resist." She sucked his dick into her mouth while still fondling his butt.

Nearly frantic with need, Robin wasn't sure which he wanted most. Did he want to come in her mouth because she sucked him or because she spanked him?

A moment later, he realized he didn't have to choose.

Leslie did both.

The first light smack caught him by surprise, but after the third she let go of him and sat up. "I'm afraid I'll bite you."

"Let's try it this way."

Moving closer, he lay across her lap and slipped his painfully stiff cock between her thighs. Her pussy was hot and wet against his prick, but best of all, his ass was right where it needed to be.

"Let me have it, Leslie. Hard as you can."

"Here goes..." The stinging slap she gave him made his balls jiggle.

"Oh, yeah. Just like that. Don't stop."

Despite his encouragement, she paused after several good licks. "I'm beginning to understand why women only stay with you for one night. This isn't an easy thing to do."

He slid his cockhead over her pussy lips, smiling as a pool of hot moisture greeted him. "Maybe not, but it sure is making your pussy wet."

She smacked him again—with a bit more vigor this time. "I'm not talking about whether I'm turned on or not—which, it pains me to admit, I am. The problem is that my hand is practically numb and my arm feels like it's about to fall off."

"How about if I turn around?"

"My right hand *is* stronger."

Robin stood up while Leslie scooted to the middle of the couch.

Her astonished gaze landed on his groin. "Damn. This really makes your dick hard, doesn't it?"

He chuckled. "I thought we'd already established that."

"Yes, but it seems to have increased exponentially. Maybe this spanking thing will work after all."

"Not if you can't keep it up."

"Guess I should consider that a challenge—or at least a testament to the strength of my right arm."

"I have great faith in that arm." With a wink and a nod, he lay down across her lap facing the opposite direction, once again inserting his cock between her legs. "Don't stop 'til I come."

"If I don't get there ahead of you. The way your dick keeps touching and yet not touching me is driving me absolutely insane."

He wiggled his hips. "Like that, you mean?"

"Oh, yeah… Just like that." She punctuated her sentence with the hardest slap on his ass yet.

"Nothing wrong with your right arm," he gasped. "Keep going."

Like a thrust of his cock into her hot pussy, the next blow doubled the tension in his body, forcing every other thought from his mind. Gripping the edge of the cushion, he held on as her rhythmic, measured cadence drove him upward, ever closer to the pinnacle of fulfillment. Never knowing where the next strike would land compounded the mystery, the submission, the unconditional surrender…

So close.

A moment later, she skipped a beat, her sharp inhale heralding the final impact that launched him into orgasm.

An unearthly cry erupted from his throat as his cock spurted between her legs. His eyes squeezed shut before opening on near blindness as his mind went blank. Even the stinging pain was gone, replaced by an ecstasy so intense, it engulfed him completely.

Leslie had barely registered the attainment of her goal when Robin tore himself away from her with a shout of triumph. Sinking to his knees, he pushed her legs apart and dove in face-first. His hot tongue found her clit, licking and sucking until she came—spasming hard against his mouth as she clutched the back of his head.

Sated and panting, she let go of him, and he hurled himself into her arms, covering her with wild, passionate kisses. She slid sideways and onto her back—had he pushed her, or had she simply collapsed? She had no idea, but seconds later, he embedded himself in her once again, fucking her with wild abandon.

"You liked that didn't you, Leslie? Your pussy was hot and wet and you came so fuckin' fast." He let out a sound that was somewhere between a growl and a snarl. "Next time, I want you to beat my ass until it's red and stinging and then roll me over and suck the cum out of my dick." He stopped long enough to slide his tongue down her throat in an invasive, possessive kiss. "I want you to be mine forever. Stay with me and fuck me all day and all night. Say you'll stay. Please, Leslie. Promise you won't ever leave me."

He went on and on—muttering, pleading, cajoling—until she lost track of everything—where she was, even who she was. All she heard was his voice telling her how much he wanted her and that only she could satisfy him. Her legs ached and her heart pounded, and still he went on, fucking relentlessly, occasionally leaning down to lick her tits as they rocked back and forth with the rhythm he set. Her entire body was on fire, searing her from within.

Finally, she came with a jolt.

Her orgasm seemed to drive him wilder still. "Help me. I can't—" The desperation in his voice was shockingly real. "Hit me. Please."

Drawing back a hand, she slapped his ass.

His body stiffened, and with a shuddering sigh, his back arched as he filled her with his essence.

No, she wouldn't leave him. She wanted to fall asleep with him and make love with him again when she woke up. She would be his lover, his slave, his wife—anything he needed her to be—as long as he wanted her like this. No one had ever wanted her as much, and she doubted anyone else ever would.

He was the one—the *only* one.

She'd simply been waiting all of her adult life for him to grow up.

No longer a boy, he was here with her now, his erection still wedged firmly inside her, his breath warm on her breast. Random thoughts drifted lazily through her mind, and as she marveled at the incredible odds against the two of them ever finding each other, he began to stir at last.

"One more thing," he murmured. "I left the milk out on purpose. You should whip my ass for that."

"Shhh…" At that point, she had neither the energy nor the desire to move a muscle.

"Or you'll what? Whip my ass?" He sounded much too eager.

"Oh, hell, no. I'm exhausted." Chuckling, she kissed the top of his head. "Besides, as much as you seem to like it, I should save that as a reward for when you've been extra good." She wasn't sure what constituted being "extra good"—although what he'd just done would probably rate a sound spanking.

"Smack my butt every day and being good won't be a problem."

Arching a brow, she let out a derisive snort. "I'll believe that when I see it."

He raised his head, his eyes round with surprise. "What? You think I'm lying?"

Her sarcastic rejoinder had been automatic—an ingrained response from having dealt with so many thoughtless males. Robin wasn't like the others. He didn't deserve that. "Sorry. In my experience, men don't often make good on their promises."

"You've known some real assholes, haven't you?"

"Sure have. Although you don't seem to belong in that category."

"I've been called a lot of things, but never that. Not to my face anyway."

How anyone could look into those big, brown eyes and call him anything but absolutely adorable was beyond her. Sure, he might like the kinky stuff, but he was damned cute about it. And he was by far the best lover Leslie had ever had.

"I'm not surprised. The best I can tell, you're a keeper—even if I *do* have to beat the shit out of you once in a while." She tried to ignore the irony of having to spank one of the few men of her acquaintance who didn't actually need it.

He grinned. "Think your arm will be okay?"

"Probably—as long as I don't tear a rotator cuff. I'm not so sure about my hand." She flexed her fingers. "I might have to invest in a paddle or a whip."

His smile broadened and his eyes took on a carnal gleam. "My birthday is in two weeks."

Despite her earlier doubts, Robin had made a believer out of her. She might have to rearrange her schedule, but she would be there to help him celebrate. "Guess I'd better go shopping."

"Should I make out a list?"

"Nah. Don't want to spoil the surprise."

This is gonna be so much fun...

Chapter 12

Leslie gaped at Robin in disbelief. "You want me to cook them *where?*"

"In the woodstove," he replied. "I have this rack that a friend of mine made for me. You let the fire burn down to coals, put the rack inside the stove, and use it like an oven or a grill."

"The steaks *and* the potatoes?"

He nodded. "The potatoes will probably take the longest. He said to wrap them in foil."

"Yes, but have you ever actually done this before?"

"Well, no," he admitted. "Sounds pretty easy, though."

"Lots of things sound easy in theory." *Like spanking a man until he comes in your lap.* Leslie gave her right shoulder a surreptitious roll.

Her gesture wasn't lost on Robin, whose laugh was reminiscent of Snidely Whiplash at his most wicked. "I'll take care of the fire. All you have to do is… whatever it is people do to steaks and potatoes to make them edible."

"Considering the only seasonings you have are salt and pepper, that shouldn't be too hard." Finding something to clean the cum off the couch had been more difficult. With no carpet or upholstery cleaner to be had, she'd wound up using dishwashing liquid.

"I have some garlic salt." He paused, frowning. "At least, I think I do."

He is just plain precious.

"I saw that," she said. "You know, after a while, that stuff tends to turn to concrete—although I might be able to pulverize it with a hammer."

He grinned. "Got plenty of hammers."

"I bet you do." She'd expected the hammers, but why he never even attempted to cook anything was downright weird. "I still don't get why you never actually use this kitchen. I mean, everybody has to eat, and most single men learn to prepare a few things out of necessity. I'm surprised your mother didn't teach—"

His stormy glare cut her off even before his words did. "The only thing my mother taught me was how to stay out of the way. I got yelled at every time I went near the fridge, and I wasn't allowed to *touch* the stove."

Knowing that men tended to get a bit testy when their mothers were criticized, Leslie deemed it best to keep her opinion of his mother to herself. "This is *your* house, Robin. No one can fuss at you for using your own kitchen."

Lowering his gaze toward the floor, he shrugged. "It's easier to eat out."

Leslie couldn't argue that point. She'd been doing the same thing ever since Gabe started college. "I suppose so." Still, given his guarded manner, there had to be more to it.

Better let that subject drop.

"Tell you what," she began. "If you'll get that rack set up and find me a hammer, I'll handle the rest."

Releasing a pent-up breath seemed to relax his entire body. "Sure thing."

After bringing her a hammer, Robin tended the stove while Leslie scrounged around the kitchen for whatever she could find— which, as she already knew, wasn't a whole lot.

Leslie was no shrink, but she suspected there was something unusual in his background that might explain some of his oddities. The fact that he didn't seem to want to talk about his family made her even more suspicious. How to broach the topic of family without upsetting him was something of a dilemma. There had to be some sort of common ground between them—some subtle way to get him talking.

Hmm…

As she wrapped the potatoes in foil, she used the only

conversational gambit she could think of. "My grandmother would've loved having a woodstove. Especially when she got older. She was always complaining about being cold."

"It does keep you warm, but it's a lot of work—even if you don't cut and split the wood yourself. You still have to carry in the logs and clean out the ashes. Might be tough for an older person."

"True, but Gran had a strong, pioneering spirit. She would've gotten a kick out of cooking on a woodstove. She was an awesome cook, too. Made the best fried pork chops you've ever tasted in your life." With a rueful smile, she added, "Mine have never been as good, even though I watched her make them a jillion times. Having my grandfather's pigs to work with probably helped."

"He was a farmer?"

"One of the best." She gestured toward the stove. "Is the fire ready?"

"Yeah."

Leslie handed him the potatoes and watched as he set them on the rack and closed the door. Instead of getting up as she'd expected, he remained on the floor, sitting cross-legged near the stove, idly picking fragments of firewood from the hearthrug.

"I never knew any of my grandparents," he said, still fiddling with the rug. "Most of them died before I was born. The rest died when I was a baby."

"Gabriel didn't know his, either. There are times I really hate his father for that."

He glanced up. "You mean his father's parents are still living?"

She didn't even know if Gabe's father was still alive, let alone his parents. Not that it mattered now. Gabe had stopped asking questions long ago.

"I have no idea. But it's possible." She winced. *Now might not be the best time to admit this.* "He was several years younger than me."

"You could do an online search. Might find them that way."

Apparently Robin didn't consider the age difference comment to be discussion-worthy. But at that moment, Leslie understood why he didn't want to talk about his folks. The subject was probably every bit as painful for him as it was for her, and she was already kicking herself for bringing it up.

"I'm not sure I want to know," she said. "Although it would nice if Gabe had some cousins. I was an only child, so there aren't any on my side. Oddly enough, both of my parents were only children, too."

"I take it your parents are dead?"

"Yeah." Cancer had taken them both—Gran, as well.

"Mine, too," he said. "I've got Nick and an older sister, Laura. We have some cousins, but they don't live around here. All the more reason why you and I need to stick together." He studied her for a moment. "I still don't get why you never married."

"There's a joke I use to explain that," she said. "Men are like bread in a bakery window. They look good and they taste good, but let them lie around for a few days and they tend to get stale."

To her surprise, he actually laughed. "Reminds me of your 'freshness date' comment. Do you compare everything to bread?"

"No, but if the analogy fits…"

"Some things really do last forever."

"Fruitcake?"

The slow wag of his head and his lazy grin warmed her from the inside out. "I was thinking about something a little less tangible."

"Oh? Like what?"

"The way I feel when I'm with you. I think I'll always feel that way."

She was almost afraid to ask him to describe that feeling—or give it a name. "It'll probably be gone in a week."

Needing something to occupy her trembling hands, she snatched up the hammer and gave the bottle of garlic salt a few gentle taps, hoping it didn't shatter the plastic. At least she wasn't panicking the way she normally did when forever was mentioned.

Forever had a way of turning out to be an incredibly short period of time.

"I doubt it." He gazed up at her from his seat on the floor. "You promised me a birthday present, remember? That means you'll be around for at least two weeks."

"True." She reminded herself that she was attempting to discover more about his past, not explore her own. Unfortunately, the best way to get him to open up was to take the lead. "You said you didn't understand why I never married. There are several reasons for that, but mostly it's because I have trouble getting close to people—especially men. They aren't all assholes, but they do like to be in charge, and I'm not very good at relinquishing control. I've been on my own too long."

He nodded slowly. "You panic when guys get too close."

Since Robin had already seen her panic a couple of times, there was no point in denying it. "Yeah. I start feeling like my whole life is being usurped and dominated. It freaks me out." Her attempted chuckle didn't quite make it off the ground. "Hearing all the shit my married friends have to put up with makes me feel lucky to be single—and I'm not alone. Of the four of us who were out celebrating my birthday, Miranda is the only one who has a husband, and they haven't been together very long. Suzie and Angela have both been divorced for years." She shrugged. "Too busy working and raising their kids to find a man, I guess." That was Leslie's standard excuse, albeit not the only one.

He grimaced. "Kids can be a problem when people start dating again, or remarry."

Now we're getting somewhere... "Firsthand experience?"

"Yeah." With a gulp, he surged to his feet. "Need help with anything?"

"Not really." Leslie didn't know a damn thing about his childhood, but she did know about Gabriel's. "Listen, if you're worried about how my son will react to us..." She hesitated. What was the correct term for what they'd been doing? A hookup? A fling or an affair? She settled for the simplest. "...being together, I'm honestly not sure. He's..." Pausing again, she recalled that Gabriel hadn't exactly taken a passive role in her relationships—or rather her breakups—with men. "He's sort of... protective."

Robin's shoulders slumped slightly, his eyes downcast. "I was afraid of that."

Moving closer, she raised his head with a finger beneath his chin. "He's run off several of my men friends—but only at my request. I don't believe he'll have any reason to chase *you* away."

Cocking his head, he aimed his soulful eyes at hers. "Big guy?"

"Um, yeah. But he only *looks* like a linebacker. He's more of a geek than a jock."

The quick flick of his brow hinted at his uncertainty.

"He won't hurt you, Robin." She leaned forward and kissed him. "I'm not saying he'll like the idea, but I'm pretty sure he'll understand."

At least she hoped he would. Gabe had never discouraged her from dating, but she'd never gone out with a man who was closer to *his* age than hers. He might feel differently about that. His approval wasn't strictly necessary, although he *was* her son and the only family she had. She hated to do anything that might alienate him.

Robin simply nodded and slipped his arms around her. "I'm not worried about whether he'll hurt me or not. I just don't want to lose you—and I don't want you to lose him, either. I know how much he means to you."

A fleeting pang shot through her chest, bringing tears to her eyes—not for herself, but for Robin. Sure, she might've only had her son to love. Robin, it seemed, didn't have anyone.

She hugged him close and patted his back. "No need to worry about that now—especially since it'll probably end up being a non-issue."

Robin wasn't sure what she meant by that.

A non-issue?

Was that because she wasn't thinking in terms of a lasting commitment, or because she didn't think her son would object? Or did she intend to keep their affair a secret?

Then he remembered the phone message she'd left for her friend. Leslie had told at least one person, but she'd also cautioned her not to tell anyone else.

He couldn't expect Leslie to stay with him forever. She had to go home at some point. He only had the two weeks until his birthday, and then he might not ever see her again.

Better make the most of the time I have—which shouldn't include crying on her shoulder.

Not that he was crying. He only felt like it. For some reason, she brought all of his emotions to the surface. He couldn't hide them behind a joke or a smile. Not with her.

Still, if she only considered this to be a vacation from her everyday life, he would make it the best vacation she'd ever had.

"Then I'll try not to think about it." He kissed her neck, enjoying her sigh and the way she quivered in his embrace. "Have a seat. I'll make you some tea."

"Sounds lovely."

She still hadn't told him any of her fantasies. She seemed to appreciate the things he'd done for her so far, but would she like more of the same or something different? For example, had she ever dreamed of being rich and famous? Perhaps she fantasized about being on a Mediterranean cruise. Did attentive Italian cabin stewards float her boat?

He wished she'd tell him what she wanted. His own imagination tended to be a little kinky. The cruise ship scenario already had him thinking about threesomes and foursomes. Would she like that? Would she prefer them one right after the other or all at the same time?

Robin certainly had no intention of asking anyone to help him out. Given the number of sex toys in his nightstand, he could at least *simulate* a threesome.

Keep it simple.

When her tea was ready, he set it on the table in front of her. Smiling her thanks, she arched her neck and stretched her shoulders back.

Her spine responded with an audible pop.

Aha...

With a knowing grin, he stood behind her and placed his hands on her shoulders. She was wearing slacks and that same low-cut sweater—not that she had much choice—still gorgeous, even without makeup or a fancy hairstyle. Dropping a kiss on the back of her neck, he began a slow massage—the kind that would make her moan with pleasure and turn to jelly in his hands.

Or so he hoped.

"Mmm…" She let her head fall forward, further exposing her neck. "Oh, yeah… Right… there, in the middle."

Robin probably could've found her sore spots without any prompting. The knots of tension were right there beneath his hands.

Working steadily, he kept his grip firm yet gentle, using technique rather than strength. He wanted her to feel pampered and special, not like she'd been put through a meat grinder.

He drank in the sight of her while kneading her muscles and stroking her skin, occasionally brushing her hair aside to rub her neck before spearing his fingers through it to massage her scalp. After several minutes, he realized he was enjoying himself— probably as much as she was. Once again, he was doing something for her, rather than asking her to do something for him.

But she *had* done something for him. He'd told her his fantasy and she'd fulfilled it. He was simply paying her back.

The give and take was happening again.

I'm getting used to it.

At some point, he suspected it would become automatic. He wasn't completely sure what that would mean, but he doubted it was a bad thing.

"Okay, sweetie," she said after a while. "If I get any more relaxed, I'll melt—speaking of which, we'd better check on those taters."

Robin kissed the back of her neck one more time before going over to the stove and slowly opening the door. "Well… they aren't on fire."

"Glad to hear it. If they still feel hard, turn them over. If they're soft, they're done."

Donning an oven mitt, Robin had to bite his lip to keep from laughing. "Sure you aren't talking about my dick?"

"The same rules apply."

He gave one of the potatoes a squeeze. "They're kinda soft, but they might need to cook a little longer. See what you think."

Leslie waved a dismissive hand. "Nah. I'll take your word for it. Just turn them over and make some room for the meat."

He did as she asked, but still wasn't sure if he'd done it right. "What if the potatoes don't get done at the same time as the steaks?"

"Then we'll cheat and nuke them in the microwave." Smiling, she patted his cheek. "No worries, Robin. As long as they aren't burnt to a crisp, it's all good."

He took a step back while she knelt down in front of the stove, astonished at how calm she was. Some of the worst disasters of Robin's life had occurred at mealtimes. Unlike his mother, Leslie wasn't stressed out. She seemed happy and content.

"You really don't mind doing the cooking, do you?"

"Are you kidding? I *love* to cook. Trust me, if Leslie is cooking, Leslie is happy. Thanksgiving is my favorite day of the year."

Robin could scarcely believe what he was hearing. "Better than Christmas?"

"Oh, yeah. No trees or presents to worry about. Just the heavenly aromas of turkey and dressing and pumpkin pie. Which reminds me, my turkey is still in the freezer." She pursed her lips, but only briefly. "No worries. I can always thaw it out in the sink. Wouldn't be the first time."

If I'd only had a mother like her...

Too bad kids didn't get to choose their families. He certainly wouldn't have chosen the people he'd wound up with, and he didn't want—or need—another mother now. His own mom had fucked him up enough.

No. He wanted Leslie as a friend and a lover—a companion he could feel comfortable with. Someone normal and sane, who acknowledged his existence and didn't fly off the handle at the slightest provocation.

Leslie glanced up at him and winked, clearly oblivious to the direction his thoughts had taken. "Of course, with you around to massage my feet, Christmas shopping won't be so bad."

"I'd be happy to take care of your feet. Anytime."

Then he realized what she'd said and how she'd said it. Not hypothetical or wishful, but a statement of fact.

Wow. And Christmas is several weeks away.

She poked the steaks with a fork, then flipped them over. "Most days at the hospital are even worse than Christmas shopping. A foot massage when I get home would probably have the same effect on me that spanking has for you."

"Orgasmic?"

"Oh, *yeah*."

Robin couldn't help chuckling. A foot massage might not be the ultimate sexual fantasy, but it was a start.

Chapter 13

"That was the best dinner I've had in ages—even if you wouldn't feed it to me."

Robin's sly smile and teasing tone proved he didn't hold a grudge for her refusal, but Leslie still didn't get why being fed was so important to him. It seemed... inefficient.

"My *not* feeding you probably improved the flavor—better to eat while the food's still hot, you know."

His smile took on an impish quality. "What? You mean we might've gotten sidetracked if you'd fed it to me?"

"You know we would have."

Robin had not only wanted her to feed him, he'd wanted to have a picnic on the floor by the fire. Leslie had nixed that idea and insisted that they dress for dinner, preferring to hold off on the fun and games until after they ate.

"There's a lot to be said for sexual tension," she added. "Besides, if we run the dishwasher now, we won't have to clean up later."

Hopping up from his chair, he began stacking the plates. "Don't like leaving things undone, do you?"

"Nope. I prefer a tidy kitchen—even if it means making my guy wait a bit."

He obviously had no intention of making *her* wait. A man with his pants on fire couldn't have moved faster.

"No need to rush, Robin." Night was falling and snow flurries still swirled outside the front window, but the house was warm and cozy, and she looked forward to a long, quiet evening by the fire. "We've got plenty of time."

"Can I help it if I'm anxious?" Never slackening his pace, he loaded the dishwasher in record time and added the detergent. "Sure hope this thing still works." Pressing the start button, he listened for a moment as the washer began to fill with water, then gave her a wink. "I'll be right back."

A few minutes later, he returned with what must've been every pillow, blanket, and cushion he possessed. After pitching them on the floor near the stove, he held out a beckoning hand. "C'mon over here, pretty mama. I need to work on your feet."

I'm gonna be so spoiled...

Robin had already done more for her in one day than any of her other boyfriends had done in a month.

Better make that a year—or two or three...

Nor had she ever been the object of such a determined pursuit—starting with the way he'd come on to her in the bookstore parking lot. It was... strange. Almost as if he was trying to win a bet...

And yet, she'd never met a man with less guile. True, he seemed to have secrets—deep-seated issues that affected his attitudes toward women—but most men hid their feelings. Robin didn't.

Stepping out of her shoes, Leslie sank into the deep pool of blankets—knowing it was only a matter of time before he had her naked again.

Robin left his sweatpants on, but elected to strip off his T-shirt before sitting down at her feet. After squirting lotion on his palms, he rubbed them together, then took her foot in his grasp.

Despite the blissful warmth of his hands on her skin, Leslie had no intention of closing her eyes—not when there was such incredible eye candy to be had. Allowing her gaze to roam at will, she delighted in the flex of his muscles and the light dusting of hair on his chest and forearms. Dark curls tumbled over his forehead, framing his face and those amazing eyes...

"Mmm... this is heavenly. I could lie here forever."

She wasn't kidding. Only being granted the sight of him and his touch would've pleased her for all eternity. He seemed ageless, somehow. Picturing him with lines on his face and gray in his hair wasn't too difficult, but even those changes didn't alter her feelings. Whatever it was, it went beyond age. Beyond time…

Her eyes drifted shut.

Robin pushed her slacks to her knees, massaging her calf muscles, kneading away her will to resist.

"Unzip your pants and raise your hips."

His voice seemed to come out of nowhere, but she obeyed it without question.

In another instant, he slipped off her slacks and laid them aside. "You aren't cold, are you?"

She shook her head in reply, her lips unable to form even that simplest of words.

"It's nice and warm here by the fire, isn't it?"

Rousing herself from her near stupor, she opened her eyes a slit. "Go ahead and say it."

"Say what?" The corner of his mouth quirked into a tiny grin.

"Don't go all innocent on me," she murmured. "You're dying to say 'I told you so'—and you know it."

"No point in that. Just making sure you're comfortable."

"If I was any more comfortable, I'd be asleep."

He seemed pleased, smiling to himself as he continued to work his way up her legs. "Want to turn over?"

"Sure." Letting him do her back had its appeal, but she was dying to return the favor. Slathering lotion all over his body sounded almost as good as sucking his dick.

Best not to mention that yet.

Leslie rolled onto her stomach, suppressing a chuckle when the first thing he did was remove her panties. She was in the process of deciding which was better—a foot massage or his hands on her ass—when he stopped to strip off his sweatpants. A moment later, he was on his knees, pressing his slick cockhead to her cheek.

"Sorry, but my dick is killing me."

"You must've read my mind."

She barely had to turn her head to take his penis in her mouth. Hot and wet, it oozed pre-cum onto her tongue. Salty, slippery, *delicious...*

Pushing him onto his back, she curled up between his legs with her head resting on his thigh. She'd never heard pre-cum touted as a moisturizer, but she certainly gave it a thorough, if somewhat subjective, field trial. Whether it made her look younger or not didn't matter; it certainly made her feel that way. She would've been happy to lie there licking and sucking him for days on end.

If Robin's sighs and moans were any indication, he would've let her—especially when she went for his balls. His juice leaked from his slit, forming a puddle in his groin. Sipping it up, she painted it on his scrotum with her tongue.

"Damn, that feels good." His voice was a hoarse whisper. "I'm gonna come if you keep that up."

"Isn't that the idea?"

He shook his head. "No. I want to fuck you... Want to fill you with cum and then eat your hot, creamy pussy."

Knowing that one glimpse of her tits would have him spewing in no time, Leslie rolled onto her side, facing away from him. "Have at it."

Robin spooned up behind her and slid right in, filling her with his hot, hard cock. Pumping in and out and side to side, he sent her mind soaring as her inner muscles contracted around him, gripping him like a vise.

"More," she urged. "Don't stop."

He took a deep breath and withdrew. "Forgive me, but there's something else I want to try. I'll be right back."

Oh, joy... Here come the whips and chains.

"I'll be right here—my empty body screaming for your cock."

He chuckled. "Just hold on. You'll love this—I hope."

Back in seconds, he rearranged the pillows and cushions, stacking them up in a pile. "Lay over this and get ready for the ride of your life."

"I've already had the ride of my life—several of them, in fact." Leslie had no idea how he could possibly top what he'd already done. Nonetheless, she climbed onto the pillows, feeling a bit silly with her butt sticking up in the air.

Wasting no time, Robin slid inside her once more.

Relieved that he hadn't fucked her ass—something she'd never considered to be even remotely comfortable before—she pushed back against him while he took up a steady rhythm.

He hadn't been at it long when she felt something cold and wet on her anus.

"Robin," she gasped. "I don't like—"

"Yes, you will," he said. "This will *not* hurt. I promise."

She held her breath as he slowly slid his fingertips over her tight hole, teasing and caressing it until she finally relaxed.

"Okay now?"

"Yeah," she whispered. "It feels good."

"I told you it would. You should learn to trust me."

"I do, I just never liked—" She broke off there, nearly choking on the memory of the excruciating pain.

"Having your ass reamed?"

She nodded. "It hurt like the devil the last time someone tried it—although he wasn't what you'd call gentle. I never let him touch me again."

"Which is why I'll never hurt you. Trust me."

Closing her eyes, she let her mind drift while Robin gave it to her with his dick and his hand. She jumped slightly when he added more lubricant and stroked her with something too smooth and cold to be a finger.

"What *is* that?"

"An anal plug," he replied. "Push back on it, and it'll go right in."

"What?"

"Trust me," he said again. "I won't hurt you."

He's never steered me wrong before…

One push really was all it took—and it didn't hurt a bit. In fact, it felt— "Incredible."

"Told you so." Using her anal sphincter as a pivoting point, he rotated the plug in a sweeping circle. "Okay?"

It was more than okay—just this side of nirvana, actually—but with her mouth hanging open, she couldn't voice her thoughts.

"I'm going to add one more thing, and if it's not the best ever, well..." His wicked chuckle hinted at what he was about to say. "You can beat the shit out of me."

Reaching around her with his free hand, he located her clitoris and took up a pattern of attack similar to what he was doing to her asshole. How he could do both and still fuck her was a testament to his coordination.

"I don't hear you complaining," he said.

She sighed.

"What was that?" He sounded much too pleased with himself—almost smug.

She moaned.

"I can't hear you," he teased in a sing-song voice.

She groaned.

"I *still* can't hear you."

Obnoxious brat...

"I'm gonna slap you in a minute," she grumbled.

Swallowed up by the great mother of all orgasms, she never got the chance. Her head snapped back as an inarticulate, strangled sound issued from her throat, followed by a deep-throated cry that sounded more animal than human.

She still had every intention of whipping his ass until he came all over the place—provided he hadn't come already. She had no idea—possibly because her brain had turned into pudding and everything below her waist was a mass of ecstatic nerve endings.

He truly had given her the ride of her life.

And she was about to return the favor.

Just as soon as I can move again.

Robin had about thirty seconds to pat himself on the back before Leslie took control, grinding her ass against his groin and squeezing his dick with her inner muscles so tightly it had to be deliberate.

"I'm gonna come *so* hard..."

"Ah, so you haven't come yet. Good."

Probably the only reason he hadn't already gone off like a bottle rocket was because he couldn't see her tits from his current vantage point. However, her ass had nearly done the job all by itself.

That and her pussy—not to mention everything else about her. Leslie was without a doubt the hottest woman he'd ever known. Simply being in the same room with her did more for his libido than anything—or any*one*—else ever had.

Abandoning his hold on her clit and the anal plug, he grabbed her by the hips and slammed into her with every ounce of strength he had left. He didn't even notice what happened to the plug, but when he stole a glance at her ass, it was gone.

After several hard thrusts, he gave up the fight and simply braced himself while Leslie fucked him into oblivion. He didn't have to actually *see* her tits to imagine the way they swayed back and forth as she rocked into him—her gorgeously lickable, suckable, fuckable tits...

His mind had touched briefly on the realization that her entire body was every bit as luscious as her breasts when his nuts contracted, sending jets of semen into her pussy with a force that left him gasping for air and seeing stars.

Thoughts crept back into his consciousness. His cock was still inside her, his body sprawled over hers.

She does that to me every single time.

But how? And why?

Was this what happened to a man when he fell in love? When he *made* love to his perfect match? The one. The only. The pinnacle?

Was it the same for her? Robin was almost afraid to find out, but at the same time, he needed to know.

Sitting back on his heels, he could only stare as his cum oozed from her slit. Simply seeing that made him want to go again. On impulse, he leaned forward to lick his cream from her pussy lips—sweet yet tangy when mixed with her juice. He teased her clit with the tip of his tongue, then thrust inside her so hard he could feel the stretch of the tendons in his neck.

Her soft "Mmm..." drove him on.

He'd been right about wanting to eat a pussy he'd just fucked. Tasting the evidence of the ultimate joy they'd given to one another made it seem more real—not simply a figment of his imagination or a fantasy that couldn't possibly be true.

"I'm beginning to understand the appeal of a threesome," she muttered.

Robin was glad she couldn't see his grin. If she thought *that* was good...

Rolling onto her back, Leslie gazed up at him through a wild tangle of blonde hair. "I heard that."

"Heard what? I didn't say anything."

"Maybe not, but you were sure thinking loud enough."

"Okay then. What was I thinking?"

"Something along the lines of 'baby, you ain't seen nuthin' yet.'"

"Isn't that a song?"

"Don't give me that innocent look—and don't try to change the subject." Scowling, she raked her hair back with her fingers. "Here I was, looking forward to a nice, quiet evening by the fire, and you—"

He winked. "Start one?"

"In a manner of speaking, yes. But what I was actually going to say was that you've turned me into a kinky slut. Anal plugs, spanking... What's next? Whipped cream? Whips and chains? Or are you prepping me for the friend who's waiting to join in on a threesome?"

Robin had no intention of sharing Leslie with anything that wasn't made out of plastic. Truth be told, he wasn't real crazy about sharing the limelight with a dildo, but he would do it if she wanted him to.

I'd do anything for her.

The thought struck him like a fastball to the head.

Heat flooded his face. "No friends" was all he managed to say at first. "But you liked that, didn't you?"

She nodded. "I'd be crazy not to. It's just that prior to meeting you, my sexual tastes were fairly conventional. You've broadened my horizons more in twenty-four hours than any other man has done in the past fifty years." She didn't look angry. She seemed... astonished. "Remember what you said about my next fifty years being the best?"

He replied with a nod.

"You might be right—that is, if today is anything to go by."

Sweet relief flooded through him, restoring his confidence. "Do I deserve a whipping?"

She snorted a laugh. "As a reward or a punishment?"

"I dunno. You tell me."

Her lips formed a thin line. "Do you really need to ask that question?"

"Maybe not, but I think I need to hear your answer." He held his breath.

"Okay, you cocky little punk," she growled. "It was wonderful, marvelous, fabulous, stupendous, the best, the top, the most, the greatest. Need I say more?"

Robin couldn't help but be pleased—even though he knew he hadn't pulled out all the stops yet. "Oh, but there *is* more. Lots more. Don't you get it, Leslie? I'll do anything to make you happy. Anything."

She stared at him for a long moment, her mouth agape. "Anything short of robbery, murder, and mayhem, I hope."

He frowned. "A few of the things we've already done are illegal in some states."

"True, but that's only if it's reported or someone catches you at it." Pursing her lips, she added, "Now that I think of it, I probably could've charged that one dude with sodomy."

The mere mention of the word made his ass tighten. "You wouldn't—"

"Oh, heavens, no," she said quickly. "Besides, you'd do it differently—just like you do everything else."

Hoping she meant that in a good way, he simply smiled.

She propped herself up on one elbow, her expression

thoughtful. "Looking back, I can't help but wonder if he wasn't *trying* to hurt me."

Robin knew that feeling all too well. "I've never understood why some people enjoy inflicting pain."

"Neither do I—which is yet another reason why I don't get the whole spanking thing. I mean, I don't mind doing it because you like it, but it isn't a turn-on for me—at least, not in itself. The only part I enjoy is the effect it has on you."

And it certainly had an effect. "Not a sadist at heart, are you?"

"No. I'd much rather play with your ass than spank it."

His butt tightened again. "I'd rather you didn't."

"No anal play for you?"

"Um, no. It's too… gay for guys to like that."

"Does that mean you *don't* like it or that you *shouldn't* like it?"

"Both," he replied. "Just don't care for it."

"But you like doing it to me?"

"Yeah, well, that's different."

She nodded slowly. "I suppose it is. Just so we're clear, I don't believe I'd enjoy being spanked."

"Wouldn't dream of it."

"One more thing that's been bugging me. Is there a whips and chains collection I should know about?"

"Nope," he replied. "Just a few toys. I've got a jelly pussy, some lubricants, and a cyberskin dildo that I bought thinking another girl might like it, along with the anal plug—neither of which have ever been used, by the way." Gifts for yet another girlfriend who didn't stick around.

"Cyberskin? That sounds interesting."

"It's supposed to feel like a real dick when you put lubricant on it." He shot her a sideways smile. "Remind me to use it on you when mine gets tired."

She chuckled. "By the time your dick gets tired, I'll probably be comatose."

"Can I help it if you turn me on harder than anyone? I'm not normally this enthusiastic."

"Really?" She drew back in surprise. "Same here. I mean, I've always enjoyed sex, but it was never like this. We must've been made for each other."

Leslie was kidding, of course, but Robin still liked the idea—aside from the fact that it helped explain why they'd both been unattached when they met. "I guess we were."

Smiling, she held out her hand. "Let's get some sleep. We've got the whole day tomorrow. We can build a snowman, have some hot chocolate, warm up in the Jacuzzi, nail each other, take a nap, have some lunch, nail each other again, have some dinner—you get the idea."

He grinned. "Just another day in paradise."

The first of many—if I'm lucky.

Chapter 14

After waking up at four in the morning, Leslie spent the next six hours puking her guts out. Granted, she'd never thrown up in such a nice toilet before. Still, it wasn't quite the sort of day she'd had planned.

If this is paradise, I want out.

Robin was very attentive despite her admonitions for him to keep his distance.

"I've already been exposed to every germ you could possibly be carrying," he said. "And even if I do catch it, I'm sure I'll live, so stop worrying and let me take care of you. Can I get you anything? Something from the drugstore maybe?"

She knew from experience that beyond cleaning up the mess or holding a cold washcloth to the afflicted person's forehead there wasn't a whole lot for him to do.

"This'll go away eventually. I just have to hang on and tough it out." She considered trying to go home to save him from any additional exposure, but between the vomiting and the snow, driving to Pemberton seemed an impossible task. "Dunno if I can make it to work tomorrow, though. Too bad I'm not more like Gabe. He'd throw up once and be done with it. Must be a guy thing—better immune system."

When the vomiting switched over to diarrhea later that afternoon, she admitted defeat. Her own phone was dead, so she borrowed Robin's and called the unit.

As luck would have it, Suzie answered.

"Where the hell have you been?" she demanded. "I've been trying to call you for two whole days. I was afraid you'd gotten stuck in a snowdrift or something."

Clearly, she hadn't tried calling Angela—either that or Angie had followed instructions and kept quiet.

"Sorry about that. My phone battery was getting low on Saturday night and I forgot to charge it," Leslie replied. "I didn't realize it was dead until just now. Listen, I've been sick as a dog all day. Could you ask Jeni to find someone to take my place tomorrow? I'll do it if I have to, but I don't think you'll want to get anywhere near me."

"You must have the intestinal virus that's going around. Stephanie had it yesterday, but she was able to work today." Suzie's tone suggested that Leslie should be able to do the same.

"Yeah, well, she's a lot younger than I am, so of course she'd be better at recovering from the creeping crud. I'll see how I feel in the morning, but right now, it's not looking too good."

"Okay, I'll tell Jeni, but would you mind explaining why the caller ID said Robin Thatcher when you called? Who the hell is that? A neighbor?"

Trust Suzie to be observant.

The very last thing Leslie felt like doing was admitting she'd gone home with the boy at the bar. "You haven't talked to Angela, have you?"

"No. I heard she called in sick today," Suzie reported. "Guess I'll be next."

"I hope not. I wouldn't wish this on anyone. I feel terrible." Considering the caller ID comment, further distraction was advisable. "Been busy?"

"Not too bad. One post-cath and a ruptured spleen." She paused. "You didn't answer my question. Who is Robin Thatcher?"

Leslie winced. "You should've been a detective."

"Yeah, right. I still can't believe you let your phone go dead. What did you do? Turn it off while you shacked up with that guy from the restaurant?"

The sudden urge to vomit would've made a reply impossible. Unfortunately, her stomach was behaving at the moment. "What makes you think I'd do that?"

"He was sitting in a truck next to your car when I left the bookstore. I'm sure it was the same guy."

Playing innocent was pointless now. *I should've called her and confessed to begin with.* As soon as Suzie saw Angela, it would all be over anyway.

"Leslie, did you hear me? Tell me the truth. You aren't really sick, are you?"

"Yes, Suzie, I really am sick—nausea, vomiting, diarrhea, and a low-grade fever." *Oh, what the hell...* "Ask Robin if you don't believe me. He's the one who's been mopping up the floor."

"Now I *know* you're lying. What's going on?"

"Talk to him." Leslie handed the phone to Robin and plopped back on the bed.

"Um, hello... Suzie?" He jerked the phone away from his ear, enabling Leslie to hear Suzie's exclamation from where she lay.

Groaning, she rolled onto her side hoping the mattress would swallow her up so she wouldn't have to listen to the interrogation. Oddly enough, she seemed to have sunk further into it than usual.

Probably my fever melting the foam.

"Yes, I was the guy in the bar," he said, nodding. "Puck Furdue... Red... Atlanta Braves... Not really. I just like the hat."

Leslie put a pillow over her head.

Unfortunately, she could still hear Robin's side of the conversation.

At least I can't hear Suzie.

"She's been here since Saturday night... What do you *think* we've been doing?" He laughed. "No, you probably don't. But she really is sick now... Yes, I do. Fifty... Almost twenty-eight... Yes, she probably is. That doesn't bother me a bit."

He was quiet for a while. God only knew what Suzie was saying to him. "No, I haven't met him. He's still at school, isn't he? ...Oh, I hope not—but we'll cross that bridge when we get to it. Listen, she really is too sick to work tomorrow. Can you find someone to cover for her? ... Call me back and let me know." He gave Leslie a nudge. "She wants to talk to you."

God help me. She held the phone to her ear. "Do you believe me now?"

"I guess so. Why didn't you tell me?"

"Because I was afraid you'd talk me out of it."

"You're right. I would've at least tried. What I can't figure out is how he knew you were the one who bought him that drink."

That part was easy enough to explain. "Our waitress told him it was my birthday. He saw the cake, and I spoke to him when I met him coming out of the restroom. Guess he put two and two together and—"

"He stalked you," she snapped. "Dammit, Leslie! What if he'd been some kind of creep?"

"Yeah, well, he's *not* a creep. I did the best I could to remain anonymous. How was I to know they give out free birthday cake at that restaurant? I'd never even been there before."

"I know that. What I can't understand is why you would trust him enough to go home with him."

Leslie hesitated. She wasn't stupid. She knew the dangers, and she'd done it anyway. She'd given herself some insurance when she'd called Angela, but she hadn't left that message until after she'd followed him home.

What *was* it about him?

Her gaze locked with his and her voice dropped to a whisper. "It was his eyes. He has the kindest, most sincere eyes I've ever seen."

Suzie's derisive snort nearly broke the spell. "*Sure* he does."

"I mean it. He's..." She hesitated again, knowing her friend would disagree. "Perfect."

"Don't be silly," Suzie said. "Nobody's perfect. You of all people should know that."

"But he *is*," Leslie insisted. "Honestly, I wouldn't change a thing."

"Not even his age?"

"Not even that."

Suzie sighed. "Okay. But please be careful, and try to get well.

Don't worry about tomorrow. I'll work for you. I need the overtime anyway."

"You always do. Thanks, Suzie. You're a peach." She switched off the phone.

"Did you really mean that?" Robin's eyes were misty with unshed tears.

"Every word."

He turned away for a moment, pressing his lips together and swallowing hard in a visible effort to control his emotions. "Following you was the smartest thing I've ever done. Even if your friends think I'm a creep."

"Hey, I'm the one who bought you that drink. If I'd truly wanted to remain anonymous, I wouldn't have said anything to you. I couldn't help myself—couldn't leave there without at least saying 'excuse me.'" She hesitated, fighting back tears as well as another poorly timed wave of nausea. "I could have said no—could've even called the police—anything but what I did, which was *exactly* what I wanted to do.

"I wanted you—enough to risk making a fool of myself. Even if this doesn't work out, I had one wonderful day with you, and even if I never get another, it was worth it." She choked back a surge of sickness. "I may be paying for it today, though." Struggling to get up from the bed, she pressed a hand to her lips.

"Whoa, shit." He helped her to stand. "We need to get you a bucket!"

She agreed, albeit silently. The bathroom seemed miles away, but thankfully, she made it in time. "This is really getting old."

Robin rinsed out a washcloth with cold water and pressed it to the back of her neck. "Wish I had a cot or something so you could camp out in here."

"Or a recliner."

"I *do* have one of those. I'll move it closer."

Leslie hadn't seen anything but a sofa and loveseat in the living room, neither of which appeared capable of reclining. "Where—"

"I have a gaming room—actually, it's another bedroom. There

are three altogether—and another bathroom. You must've missed them on the tour."

"Are you kidding? We never made it past the *first* bedroom."

He chuckled. "Sorry. My bad. I'll have to give you the full tour when you're feeling better. I've also got a couple of empty closets if you want to keep some stuff here."

"Oh, wow. Extra closet space—what a luxury." Having never made a habit of exploring other people's homes, Leslie hadn't ventured any further than necessary. Robin obviously wouldn't have minded, and just as obviously, he assumed she'd be coming back.

And she *wanted* to come back—often.

Now that Suzie and Angela both knew about him, the story was bound to spread. He wouldn't be her secret lover, which meant she could openly spend time with him. There would be no need to hide their relationship.

Unless she wanted to hide it from her son.

Something else to think about.

But not today. Gabe wasn't due home from Purdue until Wednesday night.

She'd think about that tomorrow.

છૅૄૹ

"You're sure you're well enough to drive?" Robin certainly had his doubts.

Leslie had spent the first part of the night in the recliner, and even though she'd improved enough to come to bed with him later on, she still didn't look very good. Pale and a bit haggard, she moved stiffly and yelped every time she laughed or coughed.

"I'm okay," she said. "Just very sore and kinda weak."

"I could stay home and take care of you if you need me to." The weather had warmed up considerably overnight, but even Nick hadn't seen any point in an early start. "I don't have to be at the site until ten or so anyway."

"I'll be fine. This isn't the first time I've had to nurse myself through an illness. But I believe I *will* stick around until you leave for work. That'll give the sun more time to melt the snow off my car."

"No worries there. I'll clean it off for you."

"Thank you, Robin. You're such a sweetie." She smiled at him with such gratitude, his face prickled with a blush.

He was pleased she was feeling better, but even more than that, he was flabbergasted by the realization that she'd actually spent three whole nights with him.

That's a first.

He reminded himself that it had taken a snowstorm and a bout of intestinal flu to keep her there. Would she have gone home after the first night if it hadn't been for the snow?

No. She could've made it to Pemberton easily enough. The snow hadn't been the only reason she stayed. She would be back.

Or he could go see *her*.

Would she tell him where she lived? Would he be welcome there? A few of her friends knew about him, but what about her neighbors or—more importantly—her son?

Here comes the tricky part.

"If you're feeling up to it," he began. "Maybe I could bring something over for dinner tonight. My treat."

He could almost see the wheels turning in her head. Was she debating whether it was a good idea to tell him where she lived, or was it simply a matter of what she thought she could eat?

"Not sure I could handle anything stronger than wonton soup," she finally said.

Robin did his best to gloss over his sense of relief. "No problem. Is there a Chinese restaurant in Pemberton? That way I could get it to you while it's still hot."

"Yeah. There's a pretty good one on Main Street." Her lips curled into a smile. "We don't *have* to go to Bloomington for decent take out."

An uneasy feeling rippled through him. What if she'd celebrated her birthday there?

Don't think about that now.

"I'm sure you don't." Swallowing his growing anxiety, he asked the toughest question yet. "Where do you live?"

She didn't hesitate. "In an apartment complex a few blocks from the hospital. I'll write down the address for you. It isn't hard to find."

As simple as that.

With a chuckle, she went on, "My apartment will probably seem cramped after spending so much time here at your place. It'll be good to get back home, though. No offense, but my clothes fit me better than yours do."

"What? Too tight across the chest?" His attempt at an innocent expression failed completely.

She nodded. "Among other things." This time, she *did* hesitate—moistening her lower lip with her tongue before sinking her teeth into it. "What you said about closet space... Did you really mean that?"

Robin somehow managed to control the urge to shout "Yes!" at the top of his lungs. "Absolutely. Bring over anything you like."

"I will—starting with a nightgown. I'm sure you won't think it necessary, but I've never liked sleeping in the nude."

If it would get her to sleep over, he didn't care if she wore a goose down parka to bed. "Just as long as you don't mind me taking it off now and then."

"I'm counting on it."

"Great! How about a cup of tea before I start shoveling snow?"

"Thank you. I'd love one."

He set about brewing the tea, mentally reviewed the things she might need. Body lotion and a toothbrush weren't enough. She would need a hairbrush and other items like shampoo and hairspray. Maybe he should buy her a nightgown, too—as a sort of welcoming present.

Then again, waiting until Christmas was probably advisable. He'd know more about what she liked by then.

Holy cow.

His friends were always grumbling about having to buy Christmas gifts for their girlfriends or wives. Robin, on the other hand, was tickled shitless at the prospect of buying all kinds of stuff for Leslie.

I need to start a list.

After getting her settled on the couch with her tea, he went out and cleaned off their vehicles. The snow was melting fast. Another hour and he wouldn't have needed to bother, but knowing how much she appreciated what he did for her made it worthwhile. Everything he did for her was worthwhile—unlike the way it had been with so many other women he'd known.

Nevertheless, he watched her pulling out of the driveway, wondering if he'd ever see her again. If he would wake up and find he'd dreamed it all.

Or if Nick would throw a monkey wrench into his plans.

Chapter 15

Robin arrived at the construction site, wishing he could've gone home with Leslie—particularly when he spotted Nick leaning against his truck reading a newspaper. Spending the day working with his brother wasn't nearly as much fun as hanging out with Leslie—even when she was sick.

Nick folded the paper and tossed it into his truck. "Sure glad we sealed that flooring before we left on Friday. This would've been a warped mess by now."

Which was yet another reason why Robin would've passed on this job. The previous winter had been mild enough, but this year, the weather had been completely unpredictable.

"What were you reading about?" Robin couldn't recall ever having seen Nick with a newspaper before.

"Wanted to see if there was anything more about the game. What a rout."

That was one game Robin didn't care to relive—along with most of the other bad news. Seemed like every time he spotted a headline, it was about some heinous crime. What Leslie had said about her boyfriend trying to hurt her came back to him. Considering that experience, the fact that she'd followed him home was even more surprising. Her friends would've tried to stop her. He was sure of that now. Just as sure as he was that Nick would've done the same to him—albeit for a different reason.

"No shit. Spend the weekend drowning your sorrows?"

"No point in that," Nick said. "Over and done with."

Robin nodded, feeling somewhat relieved. Nick had been known to overindulge with less provocation. For Trish's sake, Robin was glad he hadn't.

The rest of the crew arrived and they started to work. By lunchtime, he couldn't wait any longer. He simply had to talk to Leslie.

"You coming to lunch with us?" Nick asked as Robin started toward his own truck.

"Um, yeah. Just gotta make a phone call real quick."

The last thing he wanted was for his brother to overhear his conversation. Leslie was none of Nick's business anyway. He got in his truck and shut the door before punching up her number.

"Hey, Leslie," he said when she answered. "Feeling any better?"

"I think so," she replied. "I haven't been in the bathroom for at least two hours. I consider that progress."

"I'm glad to hear it. Still feel up to dinner tonight?" If she backed out, he would understand. Not that he liked the idea one little bit.

"Sure. But I should probably stick with soup. I've had some broth and juice and it's staying down okay. I'm still sore as hell. Can't seem to get warm, either." She drew a breath. "Am I allowed to say how much I miss you?"

"You can say anything you want." Especially since he'd been about to tell her the same thing. "I miss you, Leslie—miss my pretty mama and everything about her."

"You're so sweet." She sounded like she was about to cry. Her sniffle proved it. "Sorry. I didn't used to be quite so emotional. I think it's a hormonal thing—mood swings and such."

If only I had that excuse. Stoicism had never been his strong suit. "No need to apologize."

"Being sick makes it worse. Having someone—" Her voice broke on a quaver.

"Leslie? Are you sure you're okay?"

Her deep, uneven breaths were clearly audible. "Yeah. I'm okay. I just got to thinking about you and how good you are to me. I've never had that before. At least, not for a long time. I don't know how to act."

Robin knew the feeling. "You'll get used to it. I'll keep it up until you do—and even then I won't stop."

"I wish I could believe that. I mean, I do, but it's... hard."

She needs me as much as I need her. Wow.

The idea was astonishing, terrifying, and yet comforting at the same time. "I know. I won't let you down, Leslie. I promise."

"Did you—" She paused, clearing her throat. "—tell your brother... anything?"

"He didn't ask. But I'm going to have to tell him at some point."

"Listen, I don't want this to be a problem for you. I know you don't have a lot of family. I'd hate—"

"Leslie." Robin somehow managed to keep his voice steady when he wanted to shout out just how much of a problem she *wasn't*. "I'd rather have you. Trust me. I'd *much* rather have you."

Her sob nearly broke his heart. When she spoke again several moments later, she seemed to have regained some of her composure. "This is awful. I don't know why I'm acting this way. I'm usually so much... stronger. In charge... in control—not a weepy, spineless... whatever it is I'm being."

"It's called being human. Don't worry. I'll be there this evening. Just as soon as I can."

"Okay." She sniffed again. "You be careful."

"I will. And don't get all worked up about Nick. I can handle him."

"I'm sure you can."

Robin switched off his phone and leaned back against the headrest. For the first time in his life, he had someone depending on *him*. Leslie needed him—needed someone to lean on, a shoulder for her tears—even if it was only once in a while, when she was tired or sick.

That responsibility felt strange, but good.

Now all he had to do was be worthy of it.

෪ාඥ

Leslie stared at her phone, wishing it was a mirror so she could catch a glimpse of that weird woman who'd just been bawling over the airwaves.

Actually, her phone did have a mirror app, but it was too scary to use on a good day, illuminating every line, wrinkle, and pore. Dismissing the idea as bad for her mental health, she rolled over and set the phone on the nightstand.

She'd been happy to get home, to shower with her own soap, use her favorite lotion, don a comfy nightie, and crawl into her own bed. It wasn't as nice as Robin's bed, but she was used to it. What surprised her was how quickly she'd become accustomed to having him there beside her. After years of sleeping alone, he'd changed her in a matter of days.

Her one impulsive action had set the stage for a series of life-altering upheavals that had only just begun.

What on earth would Nick would say when he learned the identity—and age—of his brother's latest squeeze? What would his friends think?

They'll probably try to have him committed.

The fact that he'd had a woman spend the weekend wasn't such a big deal. The age difference was the kicker.

Leslie, on the other hand, had gone home with a strange man who was half her age. She would catch hell on both counts. The message to Angela had been easy enough. She'd simply stated the facts and hung up—no questions asked. The conversation with Suzie had gone pretty much the way she'd expected, but Gabriel? How would he react?

Should she call him and warn him? For that matter, should she call Angela?

No, Angie was sick too. She didn't need to be bothered with Leslie's escapade.

Escapade. What a word. A brash adventure, reckless, disregarding convention and her own good sense. She'd never done anything like that in her life.

Never broke down and cried for no apparent reason, either.

Still, she wouldn't have traded that weekend with Robin for all the Earl Grey in China. She'd never felt so cherished, so special, so loved…

Gabriel would understand that. Surely he wouldn't reject the idea out of hand. She'd raised him. He knew how alone she'd been, how many times she'd tried and failed to find someone to fill that void.

How in the world should she phrase it?

"Hey, Gabe. I've got a new boyfriend—and when I say boy, I do mean *boy*."

No. He wasn't a boy. He was in his late twenties, which made him a man by anyone's reckoning.

"Okay," she muttered. "So he's only nine years older than Gabe. Big deal."

But it *was* a big deal. That same age difference had been enough to make Miranda think twice about her chances with Travis. As the difference between the ages of a woman's son and her boyfriend, it was horrific. Not to mention the twenty-three years between fifty and twenty-seven.

"Better make that twenty-two," she chided herself. "He's about to have a birthday."

Groaning, she turned onto her other side, telling her brain in no uncertain terms to shut the fuck up.

Then she remembered the turkey.

Dragging herself out of bed, she transferred the bird from the freezer to the refrigerator, thanking God she hadn't left the Thanksgiving shopping until the last minute.

༄

Robin found the Chinese restaurant and Leslie's apartment without any trouble. He only wished the rest of his day had gone as smoothly—lunch, in particular. After once again bemoaning IU's loss to Purdue, Nick had told the crew the Jack and Coke story, and the day had gone downhill from there.

However, when Leslie came to the door wearing a scoop-necked, ankle-length flannel nightgown and her hair pinned up in a twist with sexy tendrils curling from her nape, his attitude improved considerably. She was even smiling.

"Feeling better?" he asked.

"Much. I might even try eating a fortune cookie. C'mon in."

He followed her into the kitchen and set the bags on the table. A quick assessment of his surroundings revealed why she'd liked his kitchen so much. Every square inch of countertop was in use. He'd never seen so many wooden spoons, skillets, and spatulas in his life. She'd been wrong about how homey an apartment kitchen could be. He could actually *feel* the love. And then, there was Leslie herself. "I could use some good fortune."

"Bad day?"

"Not entirely." Pulling her into his arms, he kissed her with all the emotion he possessed. Like a magic potion, her lips melted away all the irritations of the day. "I'm already seeing a definite improvement."

"Same here." Blinking rapidly, she took a step back, dashing a hand over her eyes. "I missed you like crazy. I didn't expect that."

Neither had he. "That's because you've been lying around feeling crappy all day. If you'd been busy, you wouldn't have noticed." Not that all the sawing and hammering he'd done that day had made a bit of difference in the way *he'd* felt. Her absence was like a toothache or a sore thumb—ever present and never quite sinking beneath his notice.

"Maybe." She didn't sound convinced. "So, did you tell Nick what you've been up to?"

"Um, yes—in a manner of speaking. He told the crew about how some chick bought me a drink."

"And?"

"I told them what happened after that. The guys didn't blame me a bit for going back to find you. Nick was pissed."

"Oh, Robin…" Her eyes were full of concern. Funny how he'd

never really noticed their color before—sort of a smoky blue.

"Not because I did it, but because I didn't tell him about it at the time." He blew out a snort. "That's Nick for you. Can't stand the thought that I could actually do something without consulting him first."

"He needs to get over that," Leslie said, her concern seeming to morph into annoyance. "Have you—what I mean is, have you ever thought about finding a different job? Or are you an actual partner in the business?"

"I'm a partner," Robin replied. "We tend to *consult* about everything. Just wish he'd leave my personal life out of it."

"I can see where you would." Opening the bag, she took out the container of soup. "What did he say when you told him which birthday I was celebrating?"

"I... um... didn't mention that part. Sorry to be such a wuss, but I'd taken enough shit from him already."

"Can't say I blame you," she said. "I'm still trying to figure out how to tell Gabe. I thought about calling him and telling him I was dating someone, but..." She shrugged.

"You wussed out."

"Yeah. I did." She shot him a grin. "We're such wimps."

"You are *anything* but a wimp." His dick twitched, reminding him that while he might be a wuss, his dick certainly wasn't. "You're strong, beautiful, loving, and kind. You're even sexy in flannel."

Chuckling, she patted his cheek. "Sorry I couldn't come up with something more exciting to wear for dinner. This is the warmest, most comfortable thing I own."

"I'm not complaining." *Especially since it looks pretty easy to remove.*

She took a few more packages out of the bag. "You must've been starving when you ordered all this."

"I thought you might feel more like eating later on, so I got the dinner for two."

"Maybe, but I'm going to try the soup first."

Robin didn't care what she ate, as long as she sat at the table with him. "It'll keep." He'd eaten enough leftover Chinese food to know that for a fact.

After getting out some plates and utensils, she motioned for him to sit. "This'll be the first time I've had anyone here for dinner since Gabe left for college."

"I've got you beat," he said as he pulled out a chair and sat down. "I haven't had company at my house in at least a year."

Meeting Leslie had certainly altered that trend. Not only did he want her to have dinner with him as often as she possibly could, he was all set for her to move in.

Be sensible now.

But he didn't *want* to be sensible. He'd gotten this far by throwing caution to the wind and saw no reason to stop now. He wanted to dive in headfirst and drown—in her life, her love, and her amazing self.

"*Had* me beat, you mean," she drawled. "I was there for three days."

"The three best days of my life."

"Even cleaning up my... um... accidents?"

"Even that."

"Sweet of you to say so." Smiling to herself, she picked up a spoon and stirred her soup. "Mmm... Smells great."

He started in on his own dinner. Still focused on her, he barely noticed what he ate. He even liked the way she held her spoon—the way her lips puckered when she blew on the hot liquid, the cautious manner in which she took the first sip...

Would he ever tire of her? He'd asked himself that before, and the answer was no. Hopefully, that would never change.

"Glad I'll be over this bug before Thursday." She shuddered. "I've never been sick on turkey day in my life—and I hope I never am."

There'd been plenty of times Robin had wished he'd been sick enough to stay home from his family's gathering. This year he considered faking an illness. Leslie's dinner was bound to be a damn sight better than anything Laura could cook. "I'm usually sick the day after."

"Too much of a good thing?"

"Not really."

She tilted her head, a puzzled frown wrinkling her brow. "Undercooked turkey?"

"More like *over*cooked turkey."

"Ah."

She went on eating her soup, leaving him to wonder whether he would be welcome at her house for dinner. She hadn't invited him, and she probably wouldn't—at least not before he'd met her son. No telling how *that* meeting would go. Having Nick ticked at him was one thing; he could live with that. If Leslie had to choose between her new boyfriend and her son, Robin had a feeling he would be the loser.

"My sister always has us over for Thanksgiving," he said. "Laura isn't much of a cook, but at least she tries."

"Those big dinners can be tough to pull off—especially if you're doing it all by yourself."

Beyond setting the table, he'd never offered to help Laura. Although she didn't appear to share their mother's aversion to having him hanging around in the kitchen, he had no desire to find out the hard way. "Does Gabriel help with the cooking?"

"He used to love stuffing the turkey." She laughed, shaking her head fondly. "Then his hands got too big to fit inside anything short of a twenty-five pounder. Gabe likes turkey—and it freezes well— but that's way too much for the two of us. My roasting pan can't even handle a bird that size—and neither can my oven."

Yet another reason why she'd liked his kitchen. An ox would probably fit inside that monster oven—and he'd never even turned it on.

He tried to imagine celebrating the holidays with Leslie at his house. What would that be like? She could bake as big a turkey as she liked. She could wear his apron and make the house smell like heaven.

This wasn't the first time he'd thought about it, but his reaction seemed to be getting stronger. An ache assailed his heart like nothing he'd ever felt before—nearly bringing tears to his eyes.

It was on the tip of his tongue to invite her and Gabriel over to his place. Only the fear that she wouldn't accept kept him quiet. So much hinged on her son and whether he could accept Robin as his mother's love interest—a son who tended to be protective...

"He's coming home tomorrow, right?"

"Yes, and I'll admit to being kinda nervous about that. Don't be surprised if he seems a little freaked out. Especially after that last guy. I said some things..." Pausing, she took another sip of her soup. "Let's just say he probably isn't expecting me to have a boyfriend of any kind, let alone one like you."

"Swore off men, did you?"

"Kinda. I made some comment about them only being useful as eye candy."

He chuckled. "And he wasn't offended by that?"

"He doesn't consider himself to be in the same category as the men I've dated." She blew out a long, slow breath. "Not sure *what* he'll think about you."

Neither am I. "Guess we'll just have to hope for the best."

"I guess we will."

After dinner, they curled up on the couch and watched a movie called *Moonstruck.* Robin had never seen it before, but he enjoyed the humor—and he certainly liked the premise. Maybe people really *could* fall in love and decide to marry in a matter of days. All it took was a super-sized moon.

He'd seen the moon, rising huge and full on the horizon during the drive to Pemberton. Even then, it made him feel lucky.

By the time the movie ended, he was toying with the idea of getting lucky in a different way. Pulling Leslie close, he kissed her cheek. "Don't suppose I could spend—"

Before he could even finish his question, the door banged open and a blond giant walked in lugging a duffle bag, a backpack, and a huge laundry basket piled high with clothes.

Staring first at Robin and then at Leslie, he said, "What's the matter, Mum? Did you miss me so much you went out and found another son?"

Chapter 16

"Looks like we're in for a bumpy night," Leslie muttered before getting up to relieve the guy—who Robin guessed was her son—of his laundry basket. "I didn't think you'd be home until Wednesday night."

"My classes were over today. Josh doesn't finish until tomorrow. I got a ride with someone else."

Robin rose from the couch, unsure of what to make of Gabriel, particularly since his lilting British accent had vanished. The fact that he was at least six-foot-five and could've passed for a vengeful angel or a Viking warrior was a secondary concern.

Raking a hand through his shoulder-length blond hair, Gabriel aimed a steely-eyed glare at Robin. "Obviously you weren't expecting me."

Considering the positions he could have caught them in, Robin was thankful he hadn't gotten any further in his seduction attempts. Still, there was no need to sugarcoat their relationship.

Might as well get it over with...

"Well, no," Leslie said. "But that's not a problem. I'm tickled to death to have you home a day early. Gabe, I'd like you to meet Robin Thatcher, my—"

"—boy toy." Robin grinned, extending a hand to Gabriel. "But don't tell anyone I said that."

"Wouldn't dream of it." Gabriel still seemed wary, but he *did* shake his hand. "Boy toy, huh?" He glanced at his mother, a tiny smile tugging the corner of his mouth. "You must've missed me a lot."

"Of course I did." She gave him a ruthless hug. "But Robin has nothing to do with that. I met him on my birthday."

"Sorry I had to miss the party." Slinging off his backpack, Gabriel dropped it on the floor beside his duffle bag. "Glad you didn't stay home and mope."

"No moping," Leslie said, crossing her heart. "I went to dinner and the bookstore with Suzie, Miranda, and Angela."

Gabriel peered at Robin. "And they introduced you two?"

The "boy toy" comment had been a gamble, but it seemed to have paid off. Gabriel was at least smiling. Sort of.

"Not exactly," Leslie said.

The ensuing silence was as deafening as it was lengthy. Robin was about to volunteer the details when Gabriel finally asked the question that had to have been first and foremost in his mind.

"Geez, Mom. How old *is* he?"

"Almost twenty-eight," she snapped. "And it's impolite to ask questions about someone who's standing right in front of you." Undaunted, she went on. "I spotted him sitting at the bar and thought he was cute, so I bought him a drink." Her gaze slid to Robin. "He's such a sweetie. You should see his house. It's absolutely beautiful."

"Do you mean to tell me you went home with a guy you picked up in a *bar*?"

Definitely an avenging angel.

Knowing that Gabriel had run off several of his mother's boyfriends, Robin couldn't help wondering if he'd be next—particularly in light of how they'd met. Still, honesty *was* the best policy...

"Yes, she did. I asked her to come over, and she followed me home." Taking a deep breath, he added, "That was on Saturday. We've been hanging out together ever since."

"Gabe." Leslie's tone was gentle. "Please don't make this any harder than it needs to be. I actually *like* Robin."

Gabriel didn't seem convinced. "You always like them in the beginning, but then they make you mad or scare you, and you dump them—or I have to run them off."

"I don't believe any of that will happen with Robin. He's... different."

"Yeah, right—about twenty years different. Most of your boyfriends have been older than you."

She paused for a moment. "That may have been my mistake." The fact that Gabe's father had been a few years her junior probably explained her hesitation. No doubt her son had the same thought. "So far, Robin and I are getting along quite well. Please, do me a favor and chill out. Okay?"

She'd drawn herself up to her full height, which wasn't anywhere near her son's, but Gabe must've been familiar with the gesture. The vengeful expression disappeared and he visibly relaxed.

"Yes, *Mother*." His growl was more teasing than angry. "Cool house, huh?"

"You wouldn't bump your head on *anything*."

"Really?" Gabe seemed genuinely taken with that idea. If he wondered why a guy Robin's size needed a place like that, he kept it to himself.

"Uh huh, and there's a Jacuzzi in the bathroom, big enough for several people."

"Four, actually," Robin put in. "It's supposed to hold six, but there are only four seats. I've never understood that."

Leslie shrugged. "The two in the middle have to stand up, I guess—or sit in someone's lap." She shot Robin a secretive little smile. "Actually, a stint in the Jacuzzi sounds pretty good right now. I still hurt all over."

Robin frowned. "I thought you were feeling better."

"You've been sick?" Gabe asked.

She waved a dismissive hand. "Just getting over a nasty case of the creeping crud. Robin's been taking care of me." Her grateful smile warmed him like a bonfire.

"Well, now, *there's* a new experience for you," Gabriel declared. "You're usually taking care of everyone else."

"Everyone?" Robin echoed.

Gabe nodded. "Her parents, grandparents, patients—and me, of course."

Robin knew her son was the only family Leslie had left. He

hadn't thought about her having to look after her older relatives, which was possibly another reason why she'd never married. Still, what surprised him most was the part about no one ever doing it for *her*.

"No one's *ever* done that for you? Not even your mother?" If so, he had a lot more in common with her than he'd suspected.

"He didn't mean it that way," she said. "My mother died from lung cancer at a fairly young age. I did some serious growing up when she got sick. After she died, I kept house for my dad before I went to college. About the time I graduated, my grandmother was diagnosed with breast cancer. My grandfather had died several years before that, and my father couldn't handle her, so I did it.

"When Gabe was born, I did the best I could—working nights so my neighbor's kid could stay with him while he slept. My father died from prostate cancer a few years ago."

Robin had learned more about Leslie in three minutes than he had in the past three days. But there were still some things he didn't understand. "How come it was just you doing all of that? Didn't you have anyone to help you?"

She shrugged. "I was the only child—and the only grandchild. God knows Gabriel's father wouldn't have helped me, even if he'd been around to do it. There wasn't anyone else."

"What about nursing homes or home health?"

"I went that route eventually—more for their safety than anything. I had to keep working, and as long as they were okay while I wasn't home, there wasn't a problem. Gabe helped out with my father quite a bit. I wasn't totally on my own that time."

She must've read the confusion in his eyes. "It wasn't as bad as it sounds. Those things didn't happen all at once—there was a long time in between." She glanced at her son. "Gabe teases me that once he's out on his own I won't know what to do with myself." She paused, grimacing. "I hate to admit it, but there *is* some truth in that."

Which explains why she was willing to follow me home.

"And he protects you from your ex-boyfriends?"

"He just made sure they understood they were no longer welcome."

He nodded slowly. "Like your father or an older brother might do." *Some* older brothers, anyway. How would his own life have turned out if he'd had *anyone* backing him up?

"Yeah," she agreed. "He's helped me out of some tight spots."

Tight spots? Oh, my God... Robin eyed Gabriel with increasing respect. "Sounds like you've been a good son."

She gave Gabe's chin a fond pinch. "The best."

"Yeah, well, you're the best *mom* ever." He hugged her like he really meant it—even lifting her feet off the floor.

There'd been times Robin would've given his soul for a hug like that. *This* was how families should be. Happy. Loving. Supportive.

Nothing like mine.

Leslie cleared her throat and wiped her eyes, hoping Gabe hadn't noticed the tears. "Enough about that. I want to hear all about your adventures at Purdue." Never one to say much on the phone, his calls had been brief, mostly concerning payment of fees and such.

"The classes are tough, the food is pretty good, and Josh and I are getting along great as roommates."

She stared at him, her mouth agape. "You're gone for months, and that's all you have to say?"

"Don't get to play video games as much as I'd like, but yeah. That pretty much sums it up."

"You're a gamer?" Robin asked.

Gabe snorted a laugh. "I was before I went to college."

"I can relate to that," Robin said. "Made up for it when I graduated—although I haven't played much lately." The look he shot Leslie spoke volumes. "I found something else to occupy my time."

Leslie knew exactly what Robin was referring to, but if Gabe had any suspicions, it didn't show. "I'm hoping to get caught up over the holidays," he said. "Speaking of which, I'd better get this stuff put away and get started."

"Holler if you need anything," Leslie said. "It's so nice to have you home."

"It's nice to *be* home. The food in the dining court is decent, but it isn't anywhere near as good as your cooking."

With that parting shot, Gabe picked up his bags and carried them into his room. Not surprisingly, he closed the door behind him.

She glanced at Robin. "That went rather well."

"A lot better than I expected." He hesitated, his expression solemn. "I'm sorry about your family. I mean, I knew they were gone. I just didn't know how hard it was for you."

Truth be told, she'd downplayed the horrors of those years. He didn't need to hear the gory details—especially since being with him helped her forget the pain of watching her loved ones suffer. She wasn't alone in that—nearly everyone outlived their parents—but when those older persons were the only family you had...

"That's all in the past now," she said, resuming her seat on the sofa. "I try not to dwell on it and only remember the good times."

Nodding, he sat down beside her, but his somber demeanor persisted. Was he trying to recall happy episodes from his own past? If so, he didn't seem to be finding many worth smiling about. Perhaps his history was even more dismal than hers.

He'd already made such a difference in her life. Did he know how much she cherished every cup of tea, every whispered endearment, and every caress? His own requests had been minor, especially when compared to what others had demanded of her—although it was a given that no one else had ever begged her to spank them.

Even when confronted with her scowling son, he hadn't been arrogant or defensive. He'd actually made a joke about it.

Boy toy? Seriously?

Robin had much more to offer than that. Not only to her, but to any woman, despite his protests to the contrary. He would go a long way toward filling up the empty spaces in her life. She only hoped she could do the same for him.

After a long silence, he cast a dubious glance toward the door to Gabe's bedroom. "You know him better than I do. Should I leave now?"

"I think you're safe. Gabe wouldn't hurt a fly, let alone another person. He only *looks* intimidating—which, I'll admit, can be very useful."

"Scared the shit out of me, and I knew what to expect—kinda. Although the British accent threw me at first. I wasn't sure who he was."

"Yeah, he does that—usually when he's saying something he's a little nervous about. Like he's hiding behind a different persona. He can do lots of different voices. He said something in Sean Connery's voice in a movie theater once, and I'll swear the woman in front of him turned around like she actually expected Sean to be sitting there. He does a damn good Gollum, too. I keep telling him he should be a voice actor instead of an engineer."

"If he'd come in calling you 'my preciousss...' I really would've freaked." He shuddered. "Someone that size with that voice..."

"No shit," she agreed. "He freaked a lot of people out when he hit puberty and grew two feet taller practically overnight. Before that, he was just this cute little blond kid who played video games all the time." She hesitated. Gabe was grown up enough to understand why Robin would want to spend the night, but he'd always been a bit squeamish about sex. "To answer to your question, it might be better if you didn't stay. I haven't seen him in months, and—"

"No problem. I'm not sure I'd want my mother's new boyfriend hanging around, either. But then, none of them were very nice to me when I was a kid."

"Your mother had boyfriends?" This was the first hint she'd had that his father hadn't been part of the family.

"Yes, and they were all assholes," he replied. "One of them used to beat the shit out of me whenever he got the chance. I was always pretty small. I'd have given a lot for a big brother like Gabriel."

Apparently Nick hadn't been much of a protector. "I take it Nick wasn't around to help you."

"Not much. He's a lot older than I am and was off with his buddies most of the time. I hung out with my friends as much as I could since it wasn't what you'd call pleasant around our house." Surprisingly, his tone lacked bitterness. "I was one of those 'accidental' babies. My mother made no secret of the fact that she didn't want to mess with another kid."

Leslie was horrified. "She *told* you that?"

"All the time. Remember what you said about only remembering the good things? I've tried to do that, but it's hard sometimes. I can't really blame Nick for anything. He was no match for the boyfriend, either."

Leslie had never understood how anyone could stoop so low as to beat up a child—or stand by and let it happen. "Didn't your mother try to stop him?"

"I'm not even sure she knew he'd done it. She broke up with him pretty quickly. I never knew why."

"I hope she had his ass thrown in jail."

"I doubt it. He went away. That's all I cared about."

"I don't think I'd have been quite so forgiving." She'd never been in a situation like that as a child, and she'd done her best to keep it from happening to her son. "I didn't date at all when Gabe was little. He meant too much to me to risk it."

Robin's mother apparently hadn't considered her son's safety to be important. Sure, he might be philosophical about it now, but he'd obviously wished for someone to come to his rescue.

"I tried dating when he was in high school," she went on. "Most of them turned out to be real losers. Of course, I wasn't what you'd call a prime article by then. It's not like I had to beat men off with a stick."

"You make it sound like I have lousy taste in women." He leaned closer. "I'd say you were more than prime myself."

Evidently he was in the mood for a lighter topic of discussion.

So was she.

"You say the nicest things. I wish—"

His breath on her ear sent a rush of tingles down her neck. "What do you wish?"

She certainly wasn't sorry Gabe had come home a day early, but his timing sucked. "I wish you didn't have to leave."

"Do I?"

"I don't know. Gabe's an adult, but I'm still not sure he'd understand."

"And *I'm* not sure he'd hear us."

"What—"

He put a finger to her lips. "Shh... Listen."

Gabe's snores were clearly audible from where they sat. Leslie stifled a laugh. "He must've conked out as soon he shut the door."

Robin pulled her into his embrace. "Does that mean I can stay a while longer?"

"I believe it does."

"Good." His whisper was so soft, Gabe could've been sitting across the room and he still wouldn't have heard him. "Because I don't think I can leave without telling you how beautiful you are and how much I want you."

"Keep talking," she murmured. "I love the things you say to me."

"The hot, sexy things?"

"Mmm, yeah. *Especially* those."

"Like how I love the way you suck my dick and then let me fuck you while you smack my ass?" A ragged breath hissed in through his teeth. "You drive me absolutely wild, Leslie. I don't think I can wait any longer. I want to feel your tits on my balls while you lie between my legs and play with my dick." His voice grew thicker and deeper with every word. "All I have to do is think about you and my dick gets so hard it hurts."

"I'm getting all wet and achy just listening to you," she admitted. "I think you've discovered my greatest weakness."

"I know your other weakness, too—but I can't do it right now, or Gabe might forget what you said about liking me and punch my lights out if he wakes up and walks in here."

"Oh, and what weakness might that be?" Her voice was practically a purr.

A flick of her earlobe with the tip of his tongue sent a thrill shooting from her neck to her core. Would he have the same effect on her twenty years from now? Somehow, she thought he might.

"All I have to do is stick my hot, wet wood in your face. You can't resist it, can you? You enjoy getting your face all wet and then sipping the syrup out of my cock. You like sucking my dick—almost as much as I like sucking your tits."

Those same breathless, melting sensations she'd felt the night they met enveloped her again. She wanted him—in the worst possible way.

Robin stood and held out his hand. "C'mon, pretty mama. Let's go have some fun."

Chapter 17

Thank God I'm feeling better now.

Leslie couldn't help smiling when she peeked in on Gabe as they passed by his room on the way to hers. Flat out on his back, snoring.

So much for quality time with his old mum.

Robin had his arms wrapped around her before the door to her room was fully closed. Her gown was gone in an instant, leaving her naked in his embrace. The fact that he was still fully dressed escalated her vulnerability to what should've been the panic level.

Only she wasn't panicking. With any other man, she would have been nervous or angry. With Robin, she could actually relax and enjoy herself. Breaking new ground with every encounter, he didn't trigger the usual reactions, allowing her fears to dissipate instead of compounding them.

Standing behind her, he devoured her breasts with his hands. "Light that candle for me. I love the glow of candlelight on your skin, the gleam in your eyes, and the sparkles in your hair." He kissed her neck and released her. "Go on. I'll wait."

A scented candle sat in a jar on the nightstand. She hadn't used it in years—didn't even remember who'd given it to her. Pulling off the lid, she searched the top drawer and found a tiny box of matches. She struck one, surprised they still worked.

Robin flipped off the light just as the flame caught and began to flicker.

With a carnal gleam in his eyes, he took her with an invasive, possessive kiss, his tongue delving deeply into her mouth as he removed the clip from her hair. Gripping her ass in his strong hands, he pulled her against his erection. "Get down on your knees and look at what you've done to me." He kissed her again, sucking her lower lip as though drawing sustenance from it. "Get my dick out and suck it. You know you want to."

Coming from Robin, those words were a welcome invitation to enjoy a hot, creamy delight. Anyone else would've gotten his face slapped.

Sliding down his body, she unbuttoned his jeans, exposing his stiff penis. Already gleaming with his slick sauce, she'd never seen anything more enticing. "Damn. You look good enough to eat."

"Then eat me." His cock pulsed, sending more syrup oozing from the slit.

She lapped it up, relishing the salty flavor. "Mmm... delicious."

"Take all you want." Cupping her cheek in one hand, he held his dick with the other, gliding his cockhead over her lips. "There's plenty more where that came from."

The pressure of his cock on her face brought a snarl of lust from her throat. She wanted to suck him until he came, wanted to feel him spurt into her mouth, longed to savor his sweet cream. Her core flooded with desperate need—an empty craving that only he could satisfy.

She yanked his jeans down to his knees, sliding her hands up the back of his legs to fondle his firm ass. Gripping his butt with both hands, she rocked him forward and back, urging him to fuck her mouth, doing her best to swallow him completely. His juice coated the back of her tongue, and she groaned around his cock as her body contracted in a gut-wrenching orgasm.

"I love when you do that." His hands were gentle, stroking her hair as he continued to glide in and out of her mouth. "Love watching you come. Love watching you suck me." He backed away, leaving her instantly bereft as his cock slipped from her lips. Pulling his penis up against his belly, he rubbed his scrotum on her face. "Lick my balls, Leslie... suck them... Oh, God... That's so fuckin' hot..."

Opening her mouth, she sucked in a testicle, cursing the illness that had robbed her of this special treat for two whole days. Was it her imagination, or was his effect on her even more powerful than before? She'd already made herself wait through dinner and a movie. Gabe's arrival had been welcome, but it was still an intrusion—keeping her from engaging in what was rapidly becoming her favorite pastime.

She teased his soft scrotal skin with her tongue, delighting in his wicked whispers and intimate sighs. Leaning her head back, she let his nuts drop into her open mouth. She urged him to move, gliding his balls in and out of her mouth—first one, and then the other.

"I can't take..." Spearing his fingers in her hair, he tilted her head back, pushing his dick down to point at her lips. "Please... Do it, Leslie. Suck my fuckin' dick before I lose my mind."

Without hesitation, she went down on him.

In the next instant, his stomach caved in and he gasped helplessly, his hips curling upward, forcing his cockhead against the roof of her mouth.

"Oh, yeah." The words burst from his lips as he ejaculated, filling her mouth with his sweet cum. "Don't swallow it. Let me kiss you first."

Pulling her to her feet, he fastened his soft, warm lips on hers. "Mmm... makes me hot all over again. You're so good to me... it's hard to believe." He blew out a sigh. "Damn. That was almost as good as being spanked."

Leslie chuckled. "I'm not sure I would've put it quite like that."

"I would," he insisted. "Favorite fantasy of mine."

"Ah."

His eyes locked with hers, curiosity lurking in their dark depths. "Don't you have any? Fantasies, I mean."

Robin had already fulfilled anything she'd ever daydreamed about simply by being there and not being a jerk. "Not sure I do. And even if I did, I bet you could top them without even trying."

"Sweet."

"I'm glad you think so. I can't help but wonder... Will the novelty wear off? When I've fulfilled all of your fantasies, will you lose interest?"

"No possible way," he drawled. "I'm always coming up with new ideas, and you've got my imagination working overtime. I might slow down in another forty years or so, but I'll never get tired of you."

"In forty years, provided I'm still alive, I'll be ninety. Somehow I don't think I'll be able to keep up with such a young whippersnapper."

He grinned. "You'll just have to tie me to the bed and have your wicked way with me."

She burst out laughing. "Sounds like something you'd put on a birthday card. 'At ninety, Myrtle was too old to catch Ralph anymore, so she took to tying him up whenever he lay down for a nap…'"

"Ooh…sounds *fabulous*."

"Sorry. Didn't mean to give you any more kinky ideas."

Sifting his fingers through her hair, his lips brushed hers. "You really think I'm kinky?"

Was being kinky a good thing or a bad thing? Not knowing how he felt, she opted for a diplomatic reply. "Let's just say you like some uncommon things—uncommon for me, anyway. I'm sure lots of people like the same stuff you do, but I'd be willing to bet they wouldn't want to do any of it with someone my age."

"Stupid fools. I'd settle for the ordinary stuff as long as I could do it with you." The sincerity in his eyes stole her breath. "I love you, Leslie. You know that, don't you?"

She'd waited fifty years to hear that from a man—and the same length of time to hear herself saying it in return. "I love you too, Robin." She kissed him lightly on the cheek. "You have no idea how much."

"I might." His voice was taut with emotion. "It's probably too soon to say it, but I can't help how I feel. I knew it the first moment I saw you."

Love at first sight?

She'd never believed it was possible, although she'd felt a

definite attraction when she first laid eyes on him. Maybe there really *was* such a thing. "Same here."

"We should celebrate," he said. "You know, pop open a bottle of champagne or something."

"Sounds great, but I have a better idea." She gave his belt a tug. "You'll need to undress so I can have your belt. I'll need it to tie you up properly. Too bad you're not wearing a tie..." Pursing her lips, she stepped back to study the rest of his attire. "Although I'm sure I can find something else that will work just as well."

He gave an audible gulp. "You mean it? You'd do that? Right now?"

"No time like the present—especially since I have something here that you don't have at your house."

"What's that?"

Her smile was slow and seductive. "A four-poster bed."

Holy shit.

Robin gaped at her for a long moment before springing into action. Pulling his shirt off over his head, he toed off his shoes and kicked them aside along with his jeans.

Actually, he *did* have a four-poster at his house. Leslie simply hadn't seen it yet.

Despite being sucked dry a few minutes before, his cock sprang to attention like a well-trained Marine.

"On the bed," she ordered. "Face down."

His breath caught in his throat. Much more of this and he'd come from pure animal excitement. "Okay."

"What did you say?" Her voice was crisp and authoritative, yet not loud enough to carry beyond the room. "Is that any way to answer me?"

"Yes, ma'am," he said, correcting himself. "I'm sorry, ma'am."

"That's better. Now, lie down and spread 'em."

Quivering with anticipation, he climbed onto her bed. Knowing that her gaze was probably glued to his ass had it tingling as though she'd actually smacked him.

"On your knees, head on the pillow."

Did she have any idea how hot it was to have his butt up in the air like that?

Maybe. He'd done it to her on the floor by the fire. It was sexy, seductive, and vulnerable—all at the same time.

She walked around to the foot of the bed. "Knees apart so I can see your balls."

Cool air flowed around his nuts, raising goose bumps on his scrotum. Was that her breath on his balls? Or was it simply because they were swaying in the breeze?

God, that sounds silly.

His cock dripped onto the bedspread. Shifting his head on the pillow, he watched Leslie rummaging through her closet—naked.

She had no idea how stunningly gorgeous she was. None. And she loved him—she'd even said it out loud. He hadn't quite wrapped his head around that yet. Not entirely. There were implications and—he hated to admit it—repercussions to that declaration he hadn't had time to explore. Not that any of those things would change his mind...

Moments later she returned with an assortment of belts and straps. His heart pounded as she buckled his ankles to the bedposts with leather belts, saving the softer restraints for his arms. His hands trembled as she looped the fabric around his wrists.

"You aren't afraid, are you?" she asked.

"No, ma'am." *More turned on than I've ever been in my life, but not scared—not one little bit...*

"If I get too rough, you can always yell for Gabriel."

As if. "Yes, ma'am, but I don't think I'll need to."

Maneuvering herself between his outstretched legs, she pressed a kiss on his ass. "Hmm... Wish I could've done this without getting you off your knees. Loved the view of your buns and danglers."

Not waiting for a reply, she went on, alternately kissing, licking, and nipping his skin. She obviously didn't intend to rough him up, but seemed bent on teasing him into insanity.

His breath quickened as her lips drifted toward his balls, then moved away again, seeking less erogenous zones. Grasping the straps in his fists, he strained against the restraints, biting his lip, trying to keep quiet, trying to stay sane…

Sweat broke out on his back, trickling down over his ribs. He'd figured out what her target was—that sensitive spot between his anus and his scrotum. She came tantalizingly close to it several times, always shifting away in the next instant. Down his leg and back, she skirted that same area again before moving on.

His skin tightened as her lips blazed a trail toward his neck. He held his breath, dying for her kiss, gulping down his disappointment when she stopped at the edge of his shoulder.

She moved back to his ass, catching the hair with her lips, tugging firmly enough for him to feel, but not hard enough to hurt. Adopting a random pattern, she found her way between his legs. Her breath on his scrotum signaled her intent before a nip at his scrotal hair lifted his balls off the bed.

"Ahhh…"

She released him so abruptly, his nuts bounced. "Did you say something?"

"No, ma'am," he gasped. "I didn't say anything."

"I'm sure I heard *something*." She sounded cross. "If we wake Gabriel, this is all over. You keep quiet."

"Yes, ma'am, I will. I'll be quiet." If she stopped now, he'd simply up and die.

"Have you anything else to say?"

"Yes, ma'am." His throat felt so tight, it was a wonder he could breathe, let alone talk. "I'm gonna come if you do that again."

"Are you asking me to continue or telling me to stop?"

"Neither one," he said carefully. "I just thought you should know that, ma'am."

"Okay, I heard you. Do you want me to make you come?"

He nodded vigorously. "Yes, ma'am, I do."

"I will," she said. "But not yet."

He did his best to stifle a groan, but she must've heard it because her own body responded, jack-knifing with what had to have been an incredibly powerful orgasm. Several moments passed before she spoke again. "I'll make you come, but not until you're inside me. Do you understand?"

"Yes, ma'am."

"I'm going to untie you now. Then I want you to turn onto your back."

Releasing the restraints, she rolled him over with a tug on the belt wrapped around his right ankle.

The wet spot on the satin bedspread was impossible to miss.

"You didn't come, did you?" she demanded.

"No, ma'am, I didn't. I swear."

As if she'd needed to ask. Swollen tighter than ever before, his cock was dark purple with a river of pre-cum flowing freely from the slit. Even his balls were wet.

She bound him to the bedposts again, leaving him flat on his back with his legs spread apart. Her hungry eyes swept his body from head to toe, lingering on his face before drifting to his groin.

Robin's balls contracted, pushing him perilously close to the edge.

Much more of this and I'll come in her face.

"Leslie, please…"

She shook her head slowly. "Not yet."

Blonde tresses framed her face and candlelight outlined the contours of her body—a body that smelled like flowers in rain—as she climbed onto the bed and crawled toward him.

This time, however, she didn't use her lips to tease him.

She used her nipples.

Hovering over his quivering flesh, she dragged her hard buds over his chest and down his legs, carefully avoiding his groin and face until he was sure he'd go mad.

Finally, she pressed her left breast to his mouth. "Suck it."

Her voice was so thick with lust, he barely recognized it. As her nipple slipped past his lips, his cock pulsed helplessly, sending more pre-cum pouring down his shaft.

She circled his cockhead with a fingertip. "Mmm… nice and

wet."

He groaned in desperate agony as she sat up, breaking the suction.

"I'm gonna sit on your prick," she said. "Try not to come too fast."

"I'll try." He could barely speak as tears of frustration slid from the corners of his eyes. "I don't know how long—"

"Shh..." she whispered. "It's okay, just hold on."

Bracing her hands on his chest, she mounted him, hissing in a breath as she slowly impaled herself with his dick. "So big, so hard, so hot..."

A deep, guttural growl curled up from his throat as she sank down on him, taking every inch of him inside her. Her slick inner muscles squeezed his cock, satisfying his need for her at last.

Rotating her hips, she circled his cockhead deep within her core, deluging him with wave upon wave of mind-altering sensations.

He arched his neck, pressing his head deeply into the pillow, and staring blindly at the headboard as he strained against the ropes that held him. Gulping in a breath, he held it, desperate to stave off his climax.

Not yet. Not... yet...

Suddenly, her body stiffened and her grip on his cock increased until she fell forward with a shudder.

"Do it, Robin," she gasped. "Do it *now*."

Still bound to the bed, he thrust upward, slamming into her with rampant fury, a deep, throaty growl accompanying each plunge.

But it wasn't enough.

He had to get his hands on her or die.

Unwinding the loops from his wrists, he freed himself, then pulled her down hard. Penetrating her completely, his body acted on instinct, unleashing an ejaculation that emptied his mind as well as his balls.

He lay beneath her, breathing heavily, until—finished, but not sated—he rolled her off him and sat up. Unbuckling the belts on his ankles, he pounced on her, burying his face between her legs.

Her entire body vibrated as he sucked her clit, launching her into orgasm so fast he could barely comprehend what had happened.

Crying out his name, she fisted her hands in his hair as her body convulsed around him.

Still, he didn't stop. Taking his sweet time, he licked her clean before finally collapsing beside her in a satisfied heap. With his head on her shoulder, he flung a possessive arm around her, drawing her close.

She kissed his forehead. "Honest to God, if you say 'mustard or mayo', you are in *so* much trouble…"

"Nope, wasn't going to say that." With a heartfelt sigh, he gave her a squeeze. "That was totally wicked, Leslie. Totally fuckin' *wicked*."

And he was never, *ever* letting her go.

Chapter 18

Leslie awoke the next morning feeling as though Christmas had come a month early. Robin was still snuggled up in the bed beside her, and if Gabe was awake, he wasn't making any noise. She had both of her guys under the same roof.

Had she ever been happier?

Probably not. For the first time in years, she could almost imagine being part of a family larger than two. With more siblings and cousins than they knew what to do with, most people probably took having a family for granted. They might not always be happy together—a circumstance that often made the bonds of friendship that much stronger—but when it came to celebrating the holidays, family ties usually won out.

The love she and Robin shared didn't change that. She would have Thanksgiving dinner with Gabe, and Robin would spend the day at his sister's house. It was too soon to claim him as family.

Yet.

She turned to find him watching her.

"I don't want to leave," he murmured, echoing her thoughts. "I want to stay here and do whatever it is you normally do on the day before Thanksgiving."

"Make a pumpkin pie, you mean?"

"Making pumpkin pie…" He said it with such reverence it might have been his fondest wish. "Now I *really* wish I didn't have to go to work."

"Ordinarily, I'd be scheduled to work today or tomorrow myself. This year, I actually have both days off—although I do have to work Friday and Saturday. I'm not much of a shopper, so I always work Black Friday to let the zealots have their fun."

He nodded. "Depending on the weather, Nick and I might work Friday since we missed Monday."

"Don'cha just hate it when work gets in the way?"

"Yeah. It took a birthday, a snowstorm, and you being sick for us to get to spend three days together."

"Don't forget the football game."

He chuckled. "How could I possibly forget that?" His gaze captured hers. "Must've been all the *fabulous* stuff that happened afterward."

"Except for the part about being sick. I could've done without that."

"I don't blame you."

Still, despite her misery, her illness had enabled her to see a different side of Robin—how gentle, caring, and thoughtful he could be. She would've learned how kind he was eventually, but that experience was a trial by fire—a test he'd passed with flying colors.

She glanced at the clock. "Got time for breakfast?"

"You bet." He hesitated, frowning. "That is, if you don't think Gabe will mind waking up and finding me here."

"Not unless you eat all the bacon."

He grinned. "I'll be sure and leave some for him."

Leslie gave him a quick kiss and got up. "Help yourself to the shower. I'll have breakfast ready by the time you're finished."

Dressing quickly, she was in the kitchen donning her apron when Gabe wandered in.

"Sorry I conked out on you last night." He wiped the sleep from his eyes. "I guess I didn't realize how little sleep I was actually getting. Then again, I slept through most of fall break."

"That's college for you," she said, giving him a hug. "Just wish you could've come home then."

He shrugged. "Not much point in that when you had to work the whole time."

"Yeah. I've already put in my request to have those days off next year." She shook her head in incredulity. "I couldn't believe waiting until May was too late."

"Lots of other nurses with kids in college?"

"Yeah." Being older than most of her coworkers, most of whom had had their children at a much younger age, she tended to forget that. *She* was the one who'd started late. "I've got your spring break off too. Not much I can do about Christmas, though." The hospital didn't allow requests off the week before, during, and after Christmas—but that was nothing new to her—or her son.

"We'll manage," he said. "We always do."

"True."

Leslie hated to think about all the juggling they'd had to do over the years. She'd had to miss so many of his school activities because of work, but he'd always understood. At least, he said he did.

Did he regret not having a father or any siblings?

Probably.

Then again, he hadn't particularly cared for any of the men she'd dated—some of whom had kids of their own.

She took eggs, bacon, and milk from the fridge. "I've got a new seasoning mix that is out of this world in an omelet. Want to try it?"

"Oh, yeah."

She smiled. "I've missed you so much."

"Same here." The hug he gave her left her breathless—or were those sobs rather than gasps for air?

Would he accept Robin? Or was having a father figure in his life something her son had given up on?

Father figure.

Even if he'd had hopes in that direction, Robin didn't exactly fit the stepfather stereotype.

Maybe that was a good thing.

"I, um, see that your—"

Leslie held her breath, half expecting him to say "boy toy."

"—uh, Robin, spent the night."

Thank you, God.

"Yeah." She turned on the griddle and began placing strips of bacon on it. "Does that bother you?"

"No. Believe it or not, I'm happy for you. I just wish I'd had some warning, that's all."

"I would've told you as soon as you got home. You must understand why I didn't tell you over the phone."

"Yeah. I get that—and if I hadn't come home last night, you would've had the chance. I'm sorry for the crack about you finding another son. It just... popped out."

"I don't think he minded. Considering what Suzie already said to him, he was probably expecting something similar."

Gabe grinned. He'd also known Suzie for a long time. "Ripped him a new one, did she?"

"Gave him a piece of her mind, anyway." She nodded toward the eggs. "Would you put some of those in a bowl, please? Six should be enough."

His sputter of protest had her rolling her eyes.

"Okay... make that eight," she said after an appraising glance at her son. "You *have* lost some weight."

"A bit," he agreed. "Sometimes I'm too tired to drag myself over to the dining hall—or I'm in the middle of something and can't stop."

"I can relate to that." She'd lost count of the number of times she'd gone down to the cafeteria for a tray and not gotten to eat any of it. "You can bring food back to your room, can't you?"

"Yeah. But I'm limited to how much I can carry. No fridge, either."

"I hadn't thought of that. Maybe we can get you one next semester."

"No, you've got enough expenses as it is. I'll manage. I'm not the first kid to go away to college without a refrigerator."

Leslie had been hoarding money for Gabriel's education for so long it was hard to believe the time had come to actually spend it. He'd worked several jobs as a teen, riding his bike to work rather than investing in a second car—yet another thing he'd been denied as a result of having been raised by a single mother.

Still, he was receiving a college education without going in debt up to his eyeballs to get it. Plenty of kids with two parents couldn't make that claim.

"Yes, but I don't want you to starve."

"Do I look like I'm starving?"

"Well, no," she admitted. "Actually, you look great." She washed her hands and got out the milk. "How about manning the bacon?"

"Sure." After cracking the last egg, he handed her the bowl, then picked up the tongs, clacking them together with a flourish. "I notice you haven't made the pie yet."

"*Now* I understand why you came home last night! You wanted to be here to smell it baking."

"Ye've caught me, lass," he said, lapsing into a Scottish brogue. "I cannae deny it."

"Yeah, well, you can make the cranberry sauce while I work on the pie."

"Geez, Mom. You make that sound like a punishment. I love watching the cranberries pop when they start to boil."

She smiled. "You always did."

It had always warmed her heart to know that, despite a few hardships, Gabe had fond memories of his childhood.

To hear Robin tell it, he didn't have many that were worth remembering.

His mother had actually told him she didn't want him.

Leslie couldn't understand that. She'd heard any number of women say how freaked out they would be if they were to conceive a child later in life, but to tell the child he was unwanted was horrific. Granted, Gabriel hadn't exactly been planned and raising him alone wasn't easy. But never, from the moment she discovered her pregnancy, had she not wanted him—not even when his father turned his back on them.

Blinking back tears, she put a dollop of butter in a skillet and turned on the burner. After adding milk and seasoning, she reached blindly for a whisk and began stirring the eggs.

"Uh, Mom, are you okay?" Gabe gave a nervous sort of laugh.

"I mean, what did those eggs ever do to you?"

She glanced at the bowl. Egg whites alone would've been close to the meringue stage by now and the butter was already sizzling and starting to brown.

"I'm fine. Just thinking about something... else." Not something she wanted to discuss with Gabe. Not yet anyway, and probably never. She poured the eggs into the skillet.

"Must've been something that made you mad."

"Kinda." Actually, she was furious. She'd been shocked when Robin first told her, but the more she thought about it, the angrier she got.

No point in that. The woman is already dead and gone.

That was all Leslie knew—only that his parents were both deceased—not the how or the why. They'd apparently split up not long after Robin was born—or conceived.

Yet another touchy subject, I'm sure.

The eggs were almost done when Robin entered the kitchen wearing jeans and a plain white T-shirt. One glance at him stole her breath. As cute as he was now, he must've been an absolutely adorable child. How any woman could've looked into those eyes and say she didn't want him...

"Damn, that smells good," he said.

"Careful," Gabe cautioned. "She's pissed about something."

"It's nothing to do with either of you." She was lying, of course, but this wasn't the time to discuss it. "Just... thinking."

A flicker of concern furrowed Robin's brow for an instant. "Anything I can do to help?"

She beamed a smile at him. "How about making toast?"

"Um, sure," he replied.

Robin hadn't been offering to help with the cooking—and he suspected she knew that. Nevertheless, he took two slices of bread from the loaf on the counter, popped them in the toaster, and pushed the lever down. "Anything else?"

"There's some grated cheese in the fridge. Could you get it for me?" She paused, brushing back a stray lock from her face. "Sorry, I just realized I didn't ask you what you wanted for breakfast. Is a cheese omelet okay?"

"Sounds great." As if he would refuse anything she would fix for him. No matter what it was, it was bound to be better than Cocoa Puffs. He found the cheese and set it on the counter beside the stove.

"Me Mum makes the best omelets in the world," Gabe declared. "Great scrambled eggs, too."

The British accent was back.

He must feel as weird about this as I do.

Robin had considered going home the night before to avoid this very scenario— which was awkward to say the least—but some things had to be dealt with head on, and his relationship with Gabriel was one of them. He knew firsthand what could happen when a child didn't get along with his mother's boyfriend, and even though he was in the boyfriend role this time, getting the shit beat out of him was still a possibility.

He glanced at Gabriel as he transferred the bacon onto some paper towels. He didn't seem violent, but as big as he was...

No. This was different.

Robin might be the smaller of the two, but he wasn't a kid. He was quick on his feet and stronger than most people gave him credit for. He could hold his own in a fight. He just hoped he wouldn't have to.

"Bacon's done," Gabe announced. "I'll get the plates."

The toast popped up. Robin put in two more bread slices and began buttering the toast. Gabe stepped up beside him and took a stack of plates from the upper cabinet.

The back of his neck prickled.

He wouldn't hurt a fly.

Leslie sprinkled cheese on the omelet and stuck it under the broiler. "Just need to melt the cheese real quick and we're all set."

The tea kettle whistled just as Robin was finishing up the toast. As she poured boiling water into a large teapot, he smiled to himself, wondering if she had any Coke. He hadn't noticed any in the fridge, but that didn't mean she didn't have a bottle or two stashed away somewhere.

Then again, perhaps it was time for him to develop a taste for Earl Grey, which was undoubtedly healthier than his usual fare. If only Coke hadn't always seemed like such a treat.

Because my mother would never let me have any.

His jaw went slack and his knees wobbled. Grateful for the support, he leaned against the counter for a moment. He hadn't thought about that in years—if, indeed, he ever had—and certainly not to analyze that preference.

Drawing in a fortifying breath, he regained his stance.

Definitely time to try some Earl Grey.

Robin took a seat beside Leslie at the small round table while Gabriel sat down in the chair to her right. He was about to pick up his fork when Leslie grabbed his hand. Then he noticed she'd taken Gabe's hand as well.

Bowing her head, she squeezed her eyes shut, biting her lower lip. Was she about to say a prayer? She'd never done that before. Perhaps it was something she only did when she was with Gabriel.

"I'm so glad to have both of you here." She smiled, but blinked rapidly as though fighting back tears. "This is just... perfect."

Robin thought it was pretty damn perfect too, but should he say so?

"Now, Mum," Gabriel began. "Don't be gettin' all mushy on us."

"Sorry. Can't help it." She let go of their hands and pressed her fingers to her mouth.

Gabe might've been uncomfortable enough to protest the mushiness with an accent, but he put a hand on her shoulder anyway. "This probably won't be the last time we have breakfast together."

She sniffed once, then nodded. "You're right. No need to get all weepy. Must be a menopausal hormone thing."

Gabe drew back, throwing his hands up like a shield. "Too much information!"

Chuckling, Robin picked up his fork. "What do you say we eat before the food gets cold?"

"Good idea," Gabe said. "Not sure I could stand any more hormone talk." He reached for his tea with a visible shudder. "So, are you going to have Thanksgiving with us?"

Robin couldn't decide whether he'd asked that as a means of changing the subject or if he truly expected Robin to join in the family festivities. Truth be told, he hadn't been invited. He cleared his throat. "I'm, uh, going over to my sister's house."

"Bet the food's not as good." Taking a bite of his omelet, Gabe smiled beatifically.

"I'm sure of it," Robin said.

"Maybe you could come over later," Leslie suggested. "For dessert."

Glancing up, he caught her eye and bit back a grin. The only thing he wanted for dessert was her—with whipped cream.

Gabe waved a hand. "Oh, yeah. Forgot to tell you. I'm going over to Dave's house tomorrow evening."

"Dave?" she echoed.

"He's the one who brought me home. Great guy—and one helluva gamer. He has some new games I want to try." His gaze touched briefly on Robin before returning to his mother. "I'm guessing you won't miss me quite as much as I thought you would."

This time, Robin didn't bother to hide his grin. "Probably not."

Any bad memories of holidays past would be overshadowed by this first Thanksgiving with Leslie—even though he wouldn't be spending the entire day with her. He certainly didn't begrudge her the time with her son. She needed that, and so did Gabriel—although perhaps not as much as he had when he was younger. Leslie's occasional puzzled expression proved how much he must've changed in the few short months he'd been away. No doubt Gabe felt the difference in himself as well.

Robin remembered that feeling. The college dorm was heaven compared to life at home—although he'd been living with Nick by that time, their mother having been killed in a car accident soon after he'd finished high school. The insurance money had paid for his education, and since Nick and Trish had kids of their own to worry about, he'd opted to live on campus.

Sometimes he still felt as though Nick was trying to make it up to him by taking on a parental role. He wished his brother wouldn't do that. He didn't need Nick to be his father any more than he needed Leslie to be his mom. He wanted a brother and a—

Wife.

If he and Leslie were to marry, how would he and Gabe relate to one another? As friends? As enemies?

"You gonna eat that?" Gabriel pointed at Robin's plate.

A quick glance revealed just how little he'd eaten. Apparently he couldn't think and eat at the same time. "Damn straight I am. Just because I'm not wolfing it down doesn't mean I don't want it. I'm… savoring it."

Grinning, Gabe gave Leslie a nudge. "D'you know something, Mum? I think I like him."

"I'm glad to hear it." Her smile showed more than a trace of relief. "So do I."

Chapter 19

Leslie felt like she'd somehow stepped into someone else's life. After "Dad" went off to work, she and "Junior" began the preparations for Thanksgiving dinner.

Too bad Dad isn't actually going to be here for that dinner.

The sweetness of Robin's goodbye kiss still lingered, along with the echo of his whispered, "See you tonight." It was... surreal. A week ago, she hadn't known he existed. And now...

Of course, she wasn't the only one with adjustments to make. Robin had to sort out how this relationship would affect him, which, given his relationship with his brother, might even be tougher than it was for Leslie. He'd hinted at all sorts of issues with Nick, although he seldom mentioned his sister. Then again, she was the eldest of the three. Perhaps he thought of her as more of an aunt than a sister.

Amazingly enough, Gabe seemed to be taking it in stride.

"Wish Robin was having dinner with us," he said as he took the bag of fresh cranberries from the fridge. "We've never had company on Thanksgiving, have we?"

"Not since your grandfather died."

"I meant boyfriends, Mom. Not family."

Slightly stunned, it took her a moment to reply. "You're right. We never have. Be nice to use more than two place settings of Gran's china, wouldn't it?"

Leslie could've served a football team on the number of dishes she'd inherited. Why her grandmother had needed two sets of china was beyond her.

Wishful thinking, perhaps.

"Speaking of which, I probably need to wash some plates—and iron the good tablecloth."

That linen tablecloth with its matching napkins was yet another heirloom that dated back to her grandparents' wedding. Never having seen the need for linen and fine china—or done much in the way of entertaining—Leslie used it exactly twice a year.

"Want me to get down the silver chest?"

As always, Gabe's offer drew a chuckle. Since she kept the silver above the kitchen cabinets, retrieving it allowed him the opportunity to utilize his superior height. "No need to rub it in."

"Can I help it if I can reach anything in this apartment without a ladder?"

"No. But you'd have a hard time changing a light bulb in Robin's place. With ceilings that high, I'm surprised he doesn't keep scaffolding in the pantry."

"He *is* kinda little."

She wasn't sure how to respond to that. In her opinion, Robin's size only added to his attractiveness. Gabriel, on the other hand, probably wouldn't appreciate the cuteness factor.

A pocket Adonis.

The epithet popped into her head unbidden—a carryover, no doubt, from all the historical romances she'd read.

Such a charming way of putting it.

"That isn't what I meant," she finally said. "He builds houses for a living—and builders use scaffolding."

"Got it. But he's still not very big."

"Compared to you, not many people are."

She'd sometimes wondered what it was like to be that tall—to look down at most people and to feel cramped in a house with ceilings of a standard height, seldom needing a ladder or even a stepstool.

Must be nice.

"You'd like to live there, wouldn't you?" he asked.

With a blink, she turned and stared. "Excuse me?"

"His house. You'd like to live there. Right?"

"I can't think of many people who wouldn't. The kitchen alone was enough to make me drool."

His expression had grown somber, thoughtful. "If it wasn't for me, you probably would—have a house like that, I mean."

Her mouth dropped open. "Have you lost your mind? Of course I wouldn't. Nurses don't make that kind of money. I'm not even sure Robin does. He said they use it as a sort of model home—they even have a service come in to clean it once a week—which makes me wonder if it isn't actually owned by the construction company."

Not owning it outright might explain why he never cooked anything there—perhaps even more so than his lack of culinary experience.

"Maybe. But if it weren't for me, you might have married someone with money. Someone who really could afford a house like that."

She gaped at him in total disbelief. "Who are you and what have you done with my son? Have I *ever* given you any reason to believe anything of the kind?"

"No, but it has occurred to me. You inherited some money when your father died, didn't you?"

"Not a lot, but I've kept it safe. I thought I might need it to help with your college expenses." Her eyes stung with tears. "Stuff like refrigerators and such."

"Never used it to buy anything for yourself, did you?"

"I didn't need anything. Truly."

"Mom. You know what I said about liking Robin?"

She nodded.

"I really do like him. And not because he's funny or because he plays video games—or even because he's closer to my age than he is yours. I like him because I think he'll be good for you. You've worked so hard... I mean, when was the last time you went out to a movie?"

"I don't need to go out to see a movie. For heaven's sake, we have cable—and all the stuff on the Internet. There are more movies than I ever have time to watch."

He arched a brow. "Really?"

"Yes, really." She shook her head, scowling. "I don't get this.

Are you upset with me for saving money to pay your tuition?"

"No, but there are some things you can't see until you back off a bit. I'm going to school with guys who'll owe thousands in student loans when they graduate—unless they're working and going to school at the same time, which means they won't finish as quickly. And yes, I had jobs in high school, and we saved most of the money I earned, but the bulk of it is coming from your work and your inheritance." He paused. "As I see it, you've spent the past twenty years on me. I'd rather you didn't spend the rest of your life the same way."

My next fifty years?

Robin had said something similar. Maybe it was finally time for her to live a little. To have fun. To have a real honest-to-God boyfriend she actually liked—one she adored and had fun with.

"I appreciate the sentiment, but parents are supposed to spend their life looking out for their children."

"Not entirely—and not forever."

He was right, of course. Part of the reason they'd been so close was that she didn't have anyone else. At least, not since her father's death. "You're really okay with this? Me and Robin, I mean?"

"I really am."

She threw her arms around him in a ruthless hug. "I knew there was a reason I loved you so much. You're such a *sensible* fellow."

"I am, indeed," he quipped. "Useful, too. You've probably worn out the stepladder since I've been gone."

"Haven't cooked much, either."

"Well, now that I'm home, you can cook all you like."

She chuckled. "Too bad we're not doing Thanksgiving at Robin's house. I could've baked a forty pound turkey with room to spare for a goose. It'd be a great place to celebrate Christmas, too—you could put a fifteen-foot pine in there with no trouble at all. The sad thing is he never has."

He gaped at her. "Never had a *tree*?"

"He says he never saw the point because he always goes to his brother's house."

Leslie caught herself before going into the whole "and he'll never have any kids of his own if he sticks with me" thing.

Too soon to be thinking that far into the future.

They might have decided they loved each other—as much as anyone could on such short acquaintance—but the whole forever thing was yet to be determined.

I'll stay as long as he wants me.

Then she would say goodbye with no regrets—not many anyway. She'd never been loved like that before and doubted she ever would be again. This love would be enough, even if it only lasted a week or a month.

Who am I kidding?

She wanted him, and she wanted him forever—no matter how selfish that wish might be.

"Geez, even Josh and I have a tree—although it *is* pretty tiny. We got it the last time we made a run to Walmart."

She patted his arm. "The operative word there is 'we.' Robin lives alone."

"No way. I'd have one even without Josh."

The vehemence of his response shouldn't have surprised her. But then, Gabriel had fond memories of Christmases past. She suspected that Robin didn't.

Still, where many people would've been bitter and resentful, Robin tended to be cheerful and friendly—a testament to his resilient spirit. Not that he'd emerged unscathed. He carried plenty of scars. They simply weren't visible on the surface.

Perhaps it was up to her to provide him with some better memories. Starting with the pie…

"Then let's get started. Remember how to make the cranberry sauce?"

Gabe chuckled. "Yeah. And even if I didn't, the recipe is on the bag."

"True."

Wish everything was that easy.

ಐೞ

Nick dumped a stack of lumber next to Robin's workbench. "Still hanging out with your new woman?"

Robin had been mulling over ways to break it to him gently and hadn't come up with much. "Oh, yeah. I–uh–met her son last night."

Nick shot him a scowl. "Her son? You didn't tell me she had a kid."

Oh, here we go again...

Robin shrugged and set a two-by-four on the miter saw. Making the cut gave him a little time to think. "Just the one."

"That can cause problems. Is the father around?"

"No. Not since he found out Leslie was pregnant."

"The bastard."

"Yeah, well, I wouldn't use that word around Leslie."

"I take it they weren't married."

Robin was about to reply when he realized that although he'd made that assumption, he honestly didn't know. He measured and marked the next board. "I'm not sure... but he's been gone for a long time."

"How long?"

The mental math was easy enough. He simply didn't want to say it, waiting until after he'd made another cut. "Close to twenty years. Gabriel's a freshman at Purdue."

Nick immediately began spitting expletives like brads from a nail gun. "Which means she's gotta be at least forty—unless she had the kid when she was fifteen."

Better multiply that by two.

"She was... older than that."

"Jesus Christ, Robin! I think you've finally gotten your shit together and you're dating a woman who's practically old enough to be your mother!"

If he only knew...

Nick had already run through the greater part of his repertoire of curse words, the only one left was—"Fuckin' pervert."

Robin had been called that so many times, the word had lost much of its impact. Several girls had said it to his face—or gone squealing to Nick, if he'd been the one to introduce them.

This was different.

Leslie was different.

Anger rose up in him, nearly squeezing out his ability to reason. He slammed a board onto the workbench when he would've preferred to slam it against Nick's head.

"Dating Leslie does *not* make me a pervert. She's a very nice lady and she's beautiful. I've only met him once, but her son seems like a great guy. I'd say I was more lucky than perverted."

Nick snorted with grim laughter. "You couldn't know either of them very well."

"I'm working on that," Robin snapped. "And for the last time, who I date is none of your damn business."

"Guess I should've tried to fix you up with my friends' mothers instead of their daughters, huh?"

His nasty tone made Robin itch to punch the smirk off his face. He marked the next cut, nearly breaking the pencil. "You shouldn't have tried to fix me up with anyone. I found the perfect woman on my own. Leslie's... wonderful. Great cook, too."

"I suppose you're having Thanksgiving dinner with her? Laura will be disappointed if you don't show—and so will Trish and the kids."

He hated when Nick played the guilt card.

Like I'm the one who has anything to feel guilty about.

"Don't worry. I'll be there. I'm going over to Leslie's place later on."

Still scowling, Nick simply nodded and stomped off.

If only Robin could be with Leslie right now. She was the kind of safe haven he'd never found before. Losing himself in a video game was similar—like the world couldn't touch him or hurt him.

Or call me a pervert.

Leslie made him feel safe and loved—perhaps the only person who ever had. If she didn't know that already, he would make sure she did. So many breakup songs were about guys who never said or showed how they felt about the women they loved. He refused to make that mistake. She was too important to lose—especially for such a ridiculous reason.

Letting Nick's opinion come between them was equally absurd. Given the choice between Leslie and his own family, Robin knew who he would choose.

And it sure as hell wasn't Nick.

ഇരു

By the end of the day, Robin was so anxious to see Leslie, he barely quashed the urge to drive straight to her apartment from the construction site instead of going home to clean up first. Vowing to take a change of clothes with him the next time, he took a quick shower before hitting the road for Pemberton.

Leslie came to the door in a ragged sweatshirt, faded jeans, a beat-up pair of running shoes, and no makeup—still managing to outshine every dream he'd ever had.

"Hi, sweetie." The subtle aroma of pumpkin pie combined with her own unique scent enveloped him, compounding the impact of her smile.

The cares of the day vanished as he pulled her into his arms and kissed her with all the love he could muster.

"You just missed Gabe," she murmured against his lips. "He went over to Josh's house to play some new game or other."

"And left you here all by yourself? Shame on him." His mischievous grin betrayed just how pleased he was to find her alone. "Have you had dinner?"

"Heavens, no," she replied. "Been too busy getting ready for tomorrow's feast."

"Good, because we're going out. Get your coat."

"Can I change my clothes first?"

"If you must, but be quick about it." He shot her a wink. "Although there's really no need. You look fabulous."

"Yeah, right," she drawled. "I'll hurry."

She returned a few minutes later—a little less ragged perhaps, but no less fabulous—and grabbed a coat from the rack by the door. "Where are we going?"

He shrugged. "You know this town better than I do. Where's the best place to go for dinner and a movie?"

"I'll tell you on the way." She slipped on her coat. "Right now, I'm so hungry I'd kill for a pizza."

"Hold on a sec." Plucking the clip from her hair, he stifled a groan as her soft blonde tresses slid to her shoulders.

Fabulous.

"Should I leave my hair down from now on?"

He shook his head and handed her the clip. "I like watching it fall."

"Sweet talker," she chided. "I'll bet you say that to all the girls."

"Nah, just you." Herding her out the door, he pulled it shut behind him. "I don't give a shit what anyone else does with her hair."

She paused on the landing, a funny little smile curving her lips. "How do you *do* that?"

"Do what?"

"Make casual, offhand remarks that get me right here." She pressed a fist to her chest.

He stared at her for a moment. Was this one of those times he should tell her how he felt? "I don't know *how*—but I do know *why*. I love you, Leslie. And I want to make sure you know that."

She gulped in a breath. "See? You did it again." Tipping her head to the side, she studied his face with curious eyes that seemed to see right through him. "I think it's the honesty. You said you love me—plain and simple, with no flowery speeches or poetic lines—and I believe you. Every single word."

"Is that so surprising?"

"When you've been burned by as many liars as I have, trust doesn't come easy. But you, I trust. Maybe that's why it's so easy to love you. I can't love anyone I don't trust—after all, I'm giving away my heart. You seem to understand what that really means."

She finished on a whisper, ducking her head and biting her lip, her cheeks suddenly rosy. Despite her apparent embarrassment, he was struck by her sincerity.

She was so beautiful—and not only in the physical sense. Love radiated from her like a sunbeam, and he felt honored to be able to see it. No doubt Gabriel had basked in her glow, but had anyone else beyond her small family circle ever experienced that joy?

He didn't think so.

"I *do* understand," he said. "Believe me, I understand."

Chapter 20

The pizza was hot and delicious, and the movie was exciting. However, all of that paled in comparison to the fun Leslie had feeding popcorn to Robin. She'd drawn the line against teasing him at the restaurant, but in a dark theater, he was fair game.

Halfway through the movie, he leaned over and whispered, "I'm not gonna be able to walk out of here if you don't stop."

"Getting too full?"

"In a manner of speaking."

"Good thing we're out of popcorn." Grinning, she folded the empty bag and set it on the seat beside her.

After a final scene loud enough to have masked Robin's climactic cry if he'd had one, they joined the throng filing out of the theater.

"That dude with the red hair was hot, even if he was the villain," Leslie commented as they entered the lobby. "Never cared much for redheads—or villains—before, but—"

Pulling her aside, Robin took her in his arms. "You're such a tease. First you get me so hot I can hardly sit still, and then you tell me you like redheads. What am I gonna do with you?"

She chuckled as his hungry gaze swept over her face before drifting downward to linger on her breasts. "I hope I don't have to tell you what to do with me, Robin. You should be able to figure that out for yourself."

He nodded. "I should take you home and fuck you senseless. Then you won't be thinking about redheads anymore, you'll be thinking about *me*." An impish smile curled his lips as his lids shuttered his dark, seductive eyes. "I want you thinking about me all the time—what my ass looks like when you spank me, what my cum tastes like, and how my cock feels in your pussy."

He paused, leaning so close his breath tickled her ear.

Tingles raced over her skin as her knees turned to jelly.

"*That's* what I want you to be thinking about. Not redheaded villains."

Sealing his lips over hers, he slid his tongue inside as though trying to purge her of all rational thought.

He nearly succeeded.

By the time her wits returned, they'd drawn a few stares. Was it the kiss, or the disparity in their ages?

Glancing around the lobby, she spotted two young men locked in a sensuous embrace. The tall blond ran his fingers continuously through the long dark locks of his shorter companion. No one gave them a second look, and she and Robin were at least different genders.

I need to develop a thicker hide.

There'd been a time when she would've been too nervous to go out with him. Fortunately, the new Leslie was more relaxed than the previous version. To be seen by someone she knew would've been tricky, but she wasn't ashamed of Robin or the way she felt about him. The questions in the eyes of others didn't bother her much— even if they *were* wondering what on earth she and Robin saw in each other.

She knew the answer to that question now. They were two sides of the same coin, and though they'd been minted in different years, they still matched.

Perfectly.

Taking Leslie by the hand, Robin led her out to the parking lot, debating his next move. Should he take her home and fuck her into a stupor or would it be best to let this "first date" pass without sex? Would she be disappointed if he didn't fuck her, or would she be afraid Gabe might stumble in on something he'd wish he hadn't seen?

Arriving at her apartment to find Gabriel and two of his friends in the living room engaged in a rousing video game battle eliminated any need for that discussion—and had him kicking himself for not taking her to Bloomington for dinner. They could've stopped at his place for a quickie before returning to Pemberton.

Not that a quickie was what he had in mind. He wanted a slow, sexy, sensuous evening, which was a far cry from some of their previous passionate encounters. Still, the kisses they'd shared in the parking lot had him primed and ready.

What *was* it about parking lots?

Doing his best to mask his disappointment, he gave her a reasonably chaste kiss at the door. "Guess I'll see you tomorrow night."

"Any idea what time?"

"No clue, but I'll be here as soon as I can."

She nodded. "Drive carefully."

Robin could've sworn she was blinking back tears.

Then he realized he was doing the same thing.

The drive back to Bloomington gave him ample time to think. After Nick's tirade that morning, he was looking forward to the festivities even less than usual. He liked his nieces and nephews, and he liked Laura and her husband. Trish was a nice woman too. Nick was the problem.

Somehow he didn't think he could trust his brother to keep his mouth shut about Leslie. Faking an illness seemed the best course of action, although he knew he'd have to face the music sooner or later.

He arrived home to a house that seemed more cavernous than usual and a bed that was ridiculously huge. He missed Leslie's scent, her warm presence—even the sound of her breathing. He hadn't slept alone since the night they met.

He'd known aching loneliness before, but nothing like the hollow emptiness he now felt. He missed her. Even knowing he would see her the next day didn't help much.

We belong together.

It was that simple.

After putting more wood on the fire, he went to bed but slept fitfully. Somewhere in the night, a dream startled him awake, his pounding heart proving that the dream hadn't been a pleasant one.

Dawn was breaking when he finally gave up on any further sleep. His footsteps on the way to the bathroom did nothing to disrupt the eerie silence, and he ran water in the sink, thankful for the sound, any sound—even the flushing of the toilet. An echo he'd never noticed before reverberated off the marble walls.

The kitchen was even worse. The memory of Leslie's presence haunted him like a ghost. He could almost see her, hear her voice, and feel her touch. Living alone had never spooked him before, but it did now.

She was right.

He needed someone to live with him in that enormous house.

He needed *her.*

࠾Ꭷ

Nick was ensconced in front of Laura and Jeff's big screen television when Robin arrived at his sister's house, but surged to his feet, smiling.

"Happy Thanksgiving! It's about time you got here." Rather than being rude or obnoxious, Nick seemed determined to be jovial.

Robin wasn't sure which he liked least.

Trish rushed in from the kitchen and gave Robin a hug. A trim redhead with abundant freckles and a ready smile, she'd always struck him as the perfect foil for Nick's swarthy scowls. "What's this I hear about you having a new girlfriend?"

He glanced at Nick, wondering just how much he'd told his wife.

A barely perceptible shake of his brother's head made it clear that Trish didn't know everything.

"Her name's Leslie," Robin said. "She's a nurse."

"Really? That's wonderful!" Trish seemed genuinely pleased. "When do we get to meet her?"

"Um, I'm not sure. My birthday, maybe?"

"That seems fitting since Robin met her on *her* birthday." Nick's cheerful demeanor was as annoying as it was false. Had he been warned to be pleasant?

After shaking hands with Jeff and receiving hugs from Laura and all his nieces and nephews, Robin watched the day pass by in a blur of parades, football games, and dinner with all the trimmings. Apparently Laura had started watching cooking shows, enabling her to perfect Thanksgiving dinner at long last.

He missed Leslie anyway.

৪৩৫৪

Having come from a long line of only children, Leslie's holiday memories revolved around celebrations with her parents and grandparents. She and Gabriel seemed to be continuing that tradition. She'd never been envious of people with huge families— she envied their discord even less—but families should grow and prosper rather than dwindle away as hers had done. For that reason, she hoped Gabriel would marry and have at least two children. Robin might have issues with his brother, but at least he had one.

Despite the lack of company, she and Gabriel had always enjoyed the holidays, and that she got a kick out of putting on a feast was a given. She busied herself with the preparations, enjoying the process as well as the enticing aromas—not to mention her son's presence.

Everything seemed to be in order as they sat down to dinner— the turkey was nicely browned, the dressing steaming hot, and the cranberry sauce perfectly jelled—but something was missing. And that "something" wasn't a large, boisterous family.

Robin was the missing ingredient.

Would he show up eventually? Or would he become so involved with his own family he forgot about her altogether? She wanted to call him to be sure, but hated to seem too anxious.

The idea that he was a replacement for Gabe was ridiculous. She wanted a husband, not another son. She'd leave having kids to

Gabriel—although she wasn't holding her breath for a grandchild. Being a bit of a geek and rather shy with girls, he hadn't dated much in high school. She'd hoped he would find someone at Purdue, and his chances were probably best while the mix of students was diverse and fewer had paired off. Was he making the most of that opportunity? Probably not—especially since he spent his leisure time playing video games with male friends.

She felt a surge of panic whenever she thought about him growing old alone. Had being the only son of a single mother affected his interactions with women? Without a father figure to advise and encourage him, was he less likely to date? Friends were important, but they couldn't replace family, and friends were usually contemporaries. Many of her elderly patients had spoken of the loss of their friends, and some had outlived their children. With a spouse, the odds were fairly even, and if she married Robin, she would almost certainly die before he did.

Unless he has an accident…

"Yo, Mom. Are you in there?"

She glanced up to find Gabriel eyeing her with concern. "Huh?"

"You've been staring at your plate for at least five minutes."

She flapped dismissive hand. "You're exaggerating."

"Maybe. But you're still awfully quiet. Is something wrong?"

"No." That much was true. Nothing was wrong, really. It was more a matter of something not being quite right. "I'm just… thinking."

"Uh huh. You've been doing a lot of that. Bet I can guess what you're thinking about. You wish Robin was here, don't you?"

"I suppose I do." For about the millionth time since noon, she stole a glance at the clock and then at the door.

"I can understand that. But would you please give it a rest and pass the gravy?"

Laughter bubbled up inside her. "Sorry." She handed him the gravy boat. "Funny thing, though. He told me he wanted me to think about him all the time—and I do, but not the way he meant. I'm starting to worry about him—almost as much as I worry about you. I keep thinking he's not coming—that he's changed his mind or had an accident or—well, you name it, and I've probably thought about it."

Gabe ladled a generous amount of gravy onto his turkey and dressing. "You've never felt like this with anyone else, have you?"

"I don't think so. It's uncanny how important he's become in such a short time. When you were born, that feeling of attachment—of being bonded to you—was automatic. This is similar. I've never felt so strongly about a man before. Just hope our relationship will last."

"You think it won't?"

She shrugged. "Who knows? I can't help believing he'll wake up and realize his mistake someday. No doubt I'll try to be philosophical, but the thought of losing him is just as scary as losing you would be. I try not to dwell on it, but anytime you go somewhere without me, I'm afraid I'll never see you again. I already feel that way about him."

Gabe nearly choked on a crescent roll. "So *that's* why I always have to call whenever I get wherever I'm going. I thought you were just keeping tabs on me."

"I *am* keeping tabs on you. I'm making sure you're still alive."

"Wish you'd told me that before. I used to resent it. I won't anymore." He opened his mouth as though intending to say something else, but stopped himself.

"And…"

He blew out a pent-up breath. "Just wanted to remind you that Dave is picking me up in a little while. I really hate to run out on you on Thanksgiving, but I know Robin was planning to come over, so you won't be here all by yourself. You're still okay with that, right?"

"Yes, but—"

"'Call me when you get there?'"

"Exactly."

"No problem. I'll be home sometime tomorrow."

She nodded. "I have to work anyway. Hanging around here by yourself couldn't be much fun. You might as well spend the time with your friends."

"Thanks, Mom. You're the best."

"Not really, although I *do* try."

As much as she'd tried not to smother Gabe, she would have to try even harder with Robin. Jealousy and possessiveness were relationship poison, and young men needed freedom far more than apron strings.

Even so, she missed Robin dreadfully, and he hadn't called her once.

I should spank his cute little butt for that.

Chapter 21

After Gabe went off to play video games with his buddies, Leslie put away the leftovers and cleaned the kitchen—which was what she usually did while trying to kill time. She had reached the last resort—cleaning the oven—when she finally heard Robin's knock.

Practically in tears when she opened the door, she fought the urge to fling herself into his arms.

"Is something wrong? Aren't you glad to see me?"

"What a silly question. Of course I'm glad to see you. Dying to see you, thrilled to see you—overwhelmed, in fact. Why do you ask?"

"Well, you aren't hugging me to death and covering me with kisses. Or are you holding back because Gabriel wouldn't like it?" Peeking inside, he whispered, "I think it's safe. I don't see him anywhere."

"That's because he isn't here. Dave picked him up right after dinner, and he's spending the night there. He didn't even have any pie before he left."

"Are you kidding me?" Robin peeled off his coat. "I'll have to eat it all before he comes back. That'll teach him. I'll bet you make a great pumpkin pie."

"I just follow the recipe on the can of pumpkin. No special touches or anything, but it *is* pretty good."

"It's bound to be better than what my sister makes. Although her cooking seemed better this time."

"Having the family all together is the most important thing anyway."

"I didn't really even want to be there for that—at least not this year. I've been trying to get away for hours. Nick and Jeff—that's

Laura's husband—couldn't understand why I didn't want to stay until all the games were over. They knew I had a new girlfriend, but they still thought football was more important." He paused for a moment. "Why are you smiling at me like that?"

"No reason." Actually, there were several. He'd not only referred to her as a girl, but he also considered her to be more important than football.

"Then stop smiling and kiss me. I've been dying for a kiss all day."

Not one to disappoint, she flung her arms around him and kissed him to pieces.

"That's better," he whispered against her lips. "I can't say I'm sorry Gabe isn't home, because I've had this fantasy running through my head all afternoon—and I can't do it with him here."

"Oh?" Leslie had indulged in a few fantasies of her own—none of which included an audience.

"You see, I've been thinking about this beautiful naked blonde with fabulous tits sitting in my lap feeding me pumpkin pie with lots and lots of whipped cream."

She shook her head, still mystified at this peculiar preference. "Someday you'll have to explain why my feeding you is such a turn-on. I don't mind doing it, but I don't understand the erotic nature of it."

He shrugged. "It's pretty simple, really. It means someone cares enough about you to make sure you get enough to eat."

"I get the caring aspect, but I've fed lots of patients in my day. I've never noticed any dicks getting hard—not that I've ever made a study of it."

"Everyone reacts differently, but even kissing started out as a form of feeding. Parents used to chew the food and then give it to their babies from their own mouths. That's why kissing is an expression of affection."

"Where on earth did you hear *that*?" Obviously, he'd spent time doing something besides building houses and drinking Jack and Coke.

He scratched his head. "I don't remember exactly—I probably saw it on TV—but it makes sense."

"Yes, but—"

"No need to think it to death. Just get naked and feed me some pie." His eyes took on a devilish gleam. "Unless you feel the need to spank me for making you wait."

"Actually, I've been giving that some thought. But now that you're here, I think I'd rather not."

"Oh, come on," he cajoled. "You don't have to beat the shit out of me, just a few good smacks on the ass. You can do it... Please?"

His pleading puppy-dog eyes were impossible to resist. If he ever figured that out, there'd be no living with him.

"I'll think about it," she grumbled. "I want you to be happy, and you want me to hurt you. I don't get that."

"But you *did* tie me up. That wasn't so hard, was it?"

"No, but if you'll recall, there was no pain involved. Teasing you was fun, and the sex was awesome. Hurting you is not something I enjoy. Dammit, Robin, I love you."

"And I love you. If you wanted me to tie you up or spank you or cover you with whipped cream, I'd do it to please you."

"What if I had a thing for cock piercings? Would you be willing to do that?"

Robin looked as if he'd tried to swallow a tuna—whole. "I'd... think about it. You don't *really* want me to do that, do you?"

"No. I prefer your cock without any embellishments whatsoever. I mean, why mess with perfection? But what if I did?"

"For you?" He shrugged. "I'd probably do it."

She eyed him skeptically. "Oh, sure. *Now* you can say that— after I've already admitted I don't want you to."

His lips curled into a smile. "Am I making you mad? Angry enough to smack me?"

Clearly, she was pitted against a much stronger, more determined will than her own.

"Yes, goddammit," she growled. "Get your cute little ass over there and bare it."

"Yes, ma'am," he said eagerly. "Over where?"

"There." She pointed toward the kitchen. "Bend over the kitchen table. I want to see if you really can come from being spanked. You know, the last time, you had your dick stuck between my legs. I think you got off more because of that than the actual spanking. I'm going to prove to you that a man cannot come from spanking alone."

He laughed. "Bet I can."

"Bet you can't."

"You're on. If I don't come, you don't ever have to spank me again."

"Fair enough. But if you do, how often do I have to do it?"

"Once a week?"

Her expression of sheer horror must've made him rethink that suggestion.

"Okay, not *that* much. After all, I've only gotten off that way once before. It might not work after the novelty wears off."

"Let's hope so. As foreplay or a touch of spice, it wouldn't be so bad, but—"

"What's the matter, Leslie?" he taunted. "Scared you'll have to spank me every Saturday night for the rest of your life?"

Her breath caught in her throat.

For the rest of my life?

There wasn't much she wouldn't do to keep him around forever. And she could always use a ping-pong paddle if her hand got tired.

She stiffened her spine. "I'm not a bit scared. Like I said, I don't believe you can do it."

"We'll see." Unbuckling his belt, he sauntered over to the table, then turned and dropped his jeans to his knees. His cock was already as stiff as a flagpole.

Whoa, shit. Maybe he really could do it after all…

"C'mere, pretty mama." He stroked his erection. "I've been very bad today. I drank beer and watched football, ate too much dry, nasty turkey, and left you here all alone. You need to slap some sense into me so I'll come here for dinner next year—here where the food's great and the company's even better." Pre-cum oozed from his slit in a long, shining strand. "Oops. Got a little joy juice on your nice, clean floor. I should be saving that up for you, not letting it drip all over the place. You should be very angry with me for wasting it." Toeing off his boots, he kicked them aside along with his jeans.

Actually, she *was* sort of angry. Not because he was wasting anything, but because she couldn't touch his dick, let alone lick the sauce from the head—not if she was going to prove he couldn't come simply from being spanked.

"Get your hands away from that dick, or the bet's off. You're messing up the experiment."

"Ooh, Leslie's *pissed.*" He slid a fingertip over his slick cockhead, taunting her even further. "Something tells me I'm about to get the ass-whipping of my life. Think of me as every punky kid, nasty prick, or arrogant asshole who ever made you mad or hurt you or scared you enough to make you want to beat the crap out of 'em."

There had been plenty of men like that in Leslie's life. The one standing before her in nothing but a shirt and socks wasn't one of them.

Maybe if I wasn't looking at his face...

"Turn around and bend over."

Unfortunately, she was almost as familiar with the back side of him as she was with the front. If she was going to pretend he was someone else, she'd have to close her eyes.

Pulling up his shirt, she placed a hand on an ass that was too darn cute to smack. How on earth had she managed to do it the last time? Closing her eyes, she did her best to imagine her last would-be boyfriend—that royal asshole she'd simply wanted to *kill*...

She started off slow, waiting for his response. His grunt of pleasure told her she was on the right track, but she stole a peek at him just to make sure. He gripped the edge of the table, not quite white-knuckled, but close. She took advantage of each stroke to feel the contours of his body and the soft hair that covered it.

I should be kissing these fabulous buns, not hitting them.

The prick she'd attempted to envision wasn't anything like Robin, nor was his butt anywhere near as cute. Closing her eyes again, she tried to picture someone else, but it didn't help. She was spanking her sweet Robin—and she didn't like it one little bit.

She tried again to focus on his response—listening to his groans and sighs.

No help.

"I need to look at you," she finally said. "I think it would be… better that way."

"Whatever you want," he gasped. "Just don't stop for long."

Pulling up a chair, she sat down. She could see him clearly now—his cock was purple and undoubtedly hard as steel. Plus, it was drooling again.

What a waste of joy juice.

Leslie had never heard pre-cum referred to in that manner, but she considered it wildly appropriate. She now faced an unexpected drawback to watching his reaction.

Not being allowed to lick or suck him was pure torture.

Her arm was already tired and her hand stung—before long, it would be numb. She was either going to have to switch arms or find something else to hit him with.

That he was enjoying it was fairly obvious. Perhaps he was right, and he really could come from being spanked. If so, Leslie would be doing this every Saturday night for the rest of her life. She would simply have to learn to like it. The first time had been a bit of a tease—his cock wedged between her thighs, barely touching her pussy in a tantalizing manner. This time, however, the only contact she had with him was her hand on his ass.

Perhaps focusing on how fabulous his buns felt was the best approach—the smooth skin, soft hair, and firm muscle. Either way, she needed to involve herself a bit more, if only to provide enough motivation to keep going. They hadn't discussed a time limit, and she was quite certain she couldn't keep it up all night.

What else could she do besides spank him?

The answer was so obvious, she almost laughed—but she

didn't.

She started talking.

"You've been so *bad*..." Adding the purring note to her voice was surprisingly easy. "I don't like having to have to do this, but you force me to. I have to keep you in line somehow. If you'd only be good, I wouldn't have to punish you. You misbehave on purpose, don't you?"

"Yes, ma'am," he gasped. "I do. I know I shouldn't, but—"

"But what?"

"Being spanked makes my prick hard. Is it wrong of me to like it?"

She switched from the purr to a stern tone. "*Very* wrong. I should keep doing it until you stop liking it. Until your ass gets so sore you can't take it anymore—or until your prick goes off by itself."

He tossed a smoldering glance over his shoulder. "Will you be mad at me when I come all over the place?"

"That depends... If I like the way you spurt—the way it looks and where it lands. You do a good job, and I might reward you and do it again sometime."

"Ha! You *do* like it, don't you? I knew you did. Keep going. I have to prove I wasn't lying."

Unfortunately, her arm felt like it was about to fall off. Switching sides, she tried spanking him left-handed, but was slightly uncoordinated at first.

She'd unwittingly placed herself on the horns of a dilemma. Although she hated to admit it, spanking him was making her so hot and wet she could hardly wait to fuck him. On the other hand, if she got him off, she'd have an even longer wait.

Unless he fucks me with a toy.

Robin had mentioned having a very realistic dildo in his collection. She'd been reluctant to confess it at the time, but she had one that was probably just like it. His dick was better, of course. The fake one wasn't hot, nor was it attached to *him*. Still, it couldn't hurt to tease him with the idea...

"I've got a nice toy for you to play with. When you're done here, I'll let you use it on me."

"What kind of toy?" Somehow, he managed to sound seductive.

"One that looks and feels a lot like your cock, only it doesn't taste very good. Maybe you could fuck me with it while I suck yours. That way I'd get two men for the price of one."

"As long as one of us is plastic," he said. "I'm not sharing you with anyone. You'll just have to be satisfied with me."

"Aha! I suspected you were a jealous, possessive little critter." For some strange reason, she liked that idea. "You want to keep me all to yourself and suck my tits, don't you?"

"You bet I do—and I want you to sit on my prick and feed me pumpkin pie."

"Hurry up, then. Come for me, babe. Come for your pretty mama."

He was close—very, very close. There had to be something she could say or do to send him over the edge before she lost the use of both her arms—which wouldn't be long now. Nearly exhausted, she was dying to stop hitting him and get naked. Her clothes were too tight, too confining, and much too *hot*...

Unbuttoning her sweater, she pulled it open and unhooked her bra—mentally patting herself on the back for having worn one that fastened in the front—and let her breasts spill out.

"I want you to come on my tits, babe. None of this on the floor crap. When you get ready to come, turn around and cover my chest with it. Then you can lick my cum-flavored tits."

As she smacked him one last time, his cock pulsed and he gulped in a breath. Spinning around to face her, he shot an arc of semen at her chest that probably would've hit her from across the table. After firing off three more rounds, he stepped close enough to smear the last drop onto her overheated skin.

Too much...

Her orgasm shook her so hard she fell forward against his thighs. Wrapping her arms around him for support, she trembled as Robin took her head in his hands, spearing his fingers through her hair.

"I told you I could do it." Only a faint glimmer of a gloat colored his voice. "Thanks, Leslie. I know that wasn't easy for you. I promise I won't ask you to do it very often, but from now on anything you want, you can have." The gloating note was more pronounced in his chuckle. "Although I'm guessing you got off on that too. Didn't you?"

Nodding, she let go of him and fell back against the chair. "I don't suppose you could put me to bed, could you? I've had it."

"But I haven't had any pie," he protested.

"Let me lie down for a while. You can have pie while I'm resting."

"But I want you to feed it to me." His persistence made her itch to smack him again.

Almost.

"Whatever happened to 'anything you want, you can have'? You *know* what happens when I feed you, and right now I need a break. I've been cooking all day, spent all evening cleaning up while I was waiting for *someone* to get here, and now I've worn myself out spanking you. That's what you get for hooking up with an older woman. I don't have your kind of energy. I have to pace myself."

Cupping her cheeks, he aimed her face toward his. The sincerity in his eyes brought tears to hers.

"I'm sorry. I know I'm being selfish. It's just that I've had to put up with my relatives all day instead of being here with you. I didn't think about you being so tired." He leaned forward and kissed her. "Come on. I'll put you to bed."

With that, he picked her up as though she were no heavier than a two-by-four and carried her to her room. Depositing her on the bed, he curled up beside her.

He's starting to make me feel bad.

However, that feeling was short-lived because while she may have forgotten her last set of instructions, he obviously hadn't.

He paused in mid-lick. "You don't mind if I do this, do you?"

"Help yourself," she murmured. "As long as you don't mind me snoozing a bit."

"No, I don't mind. Beggars can't be choosers." His voice brimmed with amusement before progressing to all-out laughter.

"What's so damn funny?"

"*You* are. You must figure I'm pretty self-assured to let me lick your tits when you have no intention of even trying to get in the mood."

"Correct me if I'm wrong, but I just spanked your butt—at your insistence. I'd say it takes a lot of self-assurance to admit to liking that sort of thing, let alone begging me to do it."

"True."

"You gotta love a man who knows what he likes. Some people can't make up their minds about anything. You, on the other hand, have some very definite ideas."

He grinned. "I do, don't I? I never thought of it that way. Right now, I have some very definite ideas about what I want to do once you've rested up a bit. So, why don't you lay back, relax and let me do my thing?"

"Go for it."

His "thing" turned out to be stripping off her clothes and giving her the most relaxing erotic massage imaginable. After licking the semen from her chest, he got a bottle of lotion from the nightstand and went to work. An ordinary massage probably would've put her to sleep, but in a very short time, he had her feeling like a new woman—a highly sensuous woman with extremely carnal ideas.

Massaging her breasts, he teased the nipples to hard peaks, turning her thoughts to feeding pie to a charming man with a hard, dripping cock that he planned to fuck her senseless with…

"You'll do anything to get what you want, won't you?" she murmured.

"Yes, ma'am. I'm relentless in my pursuit of Leslie—lovely Leslie, who'll spank me so hard I come all over her *fabulous* tits." He punctuated those words with firm strokes of his hands on her body. "You like it all—fulfilling every fantasy I've ever had. I'll do anything you want in return." His voice dropped to a rough whisper.

"We'll keep each other happy for a long, long time—feeding off each other's fantasies and deepest, darkest, most passionate desires."

"My, my... You certainly have a way with words."

"Any requests? I'm all yours." He paused, his eyes narrowing as a knowing smile curled his lips. "Oh, wait... Let me guess. You want to suck my dick."

"Am I that obvious?"

His smile broadened. "Oh, yeah. I know what turns you on, and my cock in your face is *numero uno* when it comes to making your pussy wet." He lay back on the sheets, stretching like a cat. "C'mere and suck my dick, pretty mama. Suck it all night if you want, but don't make me come—we'll save that for dessert."

Chapter 22

Leslie got up and positioned herself between Robin's open thighs, leaving him with serious doubts about his stamina—especially when she wrapped her arms around his hips and reached beneath him to fondle his ass.

"Not too sore, are you?" she asked.

Bending his knees, he planted his feet on the bed to allow her better access. "No way."

His butt still stung from her earlier efforts, but this felt marvelous. For that matter, everything she did felt terrific—simply because she was the one doing it. She massaged and caressed his skin while gliding her face along the length of his cock. Goose bumps tightened his scrotum as she skimmed the surface with the tip of her tongue.

"You have the most awesome dick." Her eyes drifted shut as she massaged her cheek with his cockhead. "I love the feel of it—in my hand, on my face, inside my body—*anywhere*. It's so hot and strong... as if all your desires are centered there—the lifeblood and essence of the man I love."

He laughed, wiggling his ass deeper into the mattress. "And here you thought *I* had a way with words."

"You bring out the eloquence in me—unlike most guys." Pausing, she licked a bead of pre-cum from his slit before spreading it down his shaft. "I mean, I love a good penis. Too bad so many of them are attached to four-star assholes."

"I'm glad you don't include me in that category."

"Wouldn't dream of it."

Reversing her position, she knelt alongside him. He could still see her sucking his dick, but her ass was now tantalizingly close.

Close enough to touch…

He ran his palms lightly over her butt cheeks, then slipped a hand between them, teasing her labia apart with his fingertips. She was so hot… so wet… He found her clit easily. The tight bud pulsed with each caress, reminding him of the other delights he had in store for her.

"This pussy needs fucking," he murmured. "Where's your toy?"

Tearing her lips away from his cock, she pointed a finger. "There. In the drawer."

Robin barely had time to register her reply before she went down on him again, sucking almost his entire length into her mouth. His head snapped back against the pillow as he clutched her succulent bottom, his fingers sinking into the soft flesh.

He allowed himself a few moments to drink in the sight of her as he savored the thrill of her lips and tongue on his cock. Then, teeth clenched in determination, he finally rolled sideways, only to find that she went with him, apparently unwilling to relinquish her hold on him for even a second. Rummaging in the drawer, he found the toy and a bottle of lubricant. Warming the dildo in his hands, he doused it with lube before slipping it inside her.

"Go easy with that thing," she warned. "It's a little longer than you are—which is about half an inch longer than it needs to be. I can't hold it all."

With a quiet chuckle, he withdrew it slightly before plunging it in again. "Are you saying my dick is a perfect fit?"

She sucked in a breath. "Yes, I am. Not too big, not too small. Just right."

Her back dipped down as she arched her neck, the altered angle of her hips giving him a better view of her pussy lips wrapped around the fake cock. His own dick pulsed in her hand, sending more juice oozing from his slit.

"Thick and long—" Her speech was interrupted by her deep-throated groan. "Enough to fill me completely while your balls tickle my buns."

"This thing has balls too." To prove his point, he bent the toy slightly, pressing the nuts against her skin.

"It's okay. Not nearly as awesome as yours, of course, but it'll do in a pinch."

He couldn't help but be pleased, even though he did have other talents. "Ah, but I'm the one wielding it."

And wield it, he did. A series of thrusts and parries soon had her moaning helplessly. Still clinging to his ass like a lifeline, she made one feeble attempt to suck his cock before collapsing onto his thigh.

"If you're through playing with my dick, I've got something else I'd like to do with it."

Her reply was more of a whimper than a word.

"I'll take that as a yes."

Robin somehow managed to curl away from her and get up on his knees while keeping the dildo in place. Positioning himself behind her, he reached for the lube. The sight of her ass in the air and those fabulous tits resting on the bed nearly made fucking her unnecessary. Following a brief tussle with his self control, he doused his dick and her anus, then began working her hole with his right hand while continuing to plunge the dildo into her with his left.

Raising her head, she tried, unsuccessfully, to peer at him over her shoulder. "How on earth are you doing that?"

"You didn't know I was ambidextrous, did you?"

"I do now—either that or you're the most coordinated man I've ever known. Bet you could pat your head and rub your stomach without any trouble at all."

"Sure can." He pressed his cockhead against her tight hole. "I'll prove it to you later, but right now, I need you to relax and take a deep breath. I'm coming in the back door."

It was all he could do not to take her with one plunge, but he knew better than to try it—experience had taught him that much. She'd done okay with the anal plug, but his dick was a helluva lot bigger than that. With more patience than he'd known he possessed, he finally made it inside—without hurting her or losing his grip on the toy.

"Okay, Leslie. If you've ever wondered what it's like to be fucked by two guys, now's your chance to find out."

He began to move inside her, first him, then the toy, and then the two together. Concentrating on the rhythm helped divert his mind from the incredible sensations as he fucked her tight hole. He was dying to look at her, but he knew he couldn't. Not if he wanted her to come first.

Squeezing his eyes shut, he did his best to think about something else—*anything* aside from what he was doing.

Leslie had never fantasized about a threesome, but she was beginning to wonder why she never had. The slight pain of entry was far outstripped by the ecstasy of withdrawal, which—when coupled with the dildo—bordered on nirvana.

With a brief, strangled apology, Robin came first. Abandoning the toy, he ground his cock into her ass, rotating his shaft deep inside her as he filled her with cum.

Moments later, her own orgasm detonated. Her knees slid straight out from under her, resulting in an abrupt withdrawal that sent her screaming into freefall.

"Are you okay?" He hovered over her, gently stroking her shoulder. "I didn't hurt you, did I?"

Judging from the sounds emanating from her throat, she probably should've been in pain, but she was so far from it, she couldn't even speak. Shaking her head in reply, she rolled onto her side, curling into a ball as the orgasm that wouldn't die shook her from head to toe.

Robin lay down behind her, molding his body to hers, holding her until her spasms finally subsided. His heated skin warmed her back, and she melted into his embrace, exhausted and completely sated. Snuggling against him, she wanted nothing more than to stay right where she was until morning.

Robin's stomach let out a growl loud enough to wake the dead.

She groaned in protest. "Oh, don't tell me you're hungry."

"Okay, I won't tell you. Is it okay if I raid the refrigerator?"

"Help yourself." No doubt he would want her to feed him. Perhaps she could do it lying down.

His stomach growled again. "I didn't eat much at Laura's house. The food was better than usual, but I saved room for your leftovers."

"Sweet of you to say that." Smiling, she stifled a yawn. "Go ahead and eat, babe. Just throw a blanket over me."

"I'll be right back."

She shivered at the loss of his warm body until he pulled the covers over her, tucking her in like he would a child. His kiss touched her cheek as she drifted off, delightful dreams already circling inside her head.

Wonder how long he'll let me sleep this time?

Not long. In less than ten minutes, Robin returned with a plateful of steaming Thanksgiving leftovers.

She peered up at him with a baleful eye. "Guess you want me to feed that to you, huh?"

"If it's not too much trouble—although it smells so good, I'll eat it myself if you're too slow."

"I'll try to shovel it in as fast as I can," she drawled, chuckling. "Just promise me I don't have to sit up."

"No problem. I've got this all figured out. Scoot back a little."

Despite her reluctance to move a muscle, she managed to make room for him. Robin set the plate on the bed and lay down on his side with his head propped up on one hand.

She glanced at the food, noting that he'd cut the turkey into bite-sized pieces. "I see you didn't skimp on the gravy."

Grinning, he handed her a fork. "I added more after I tasted it."

"Hmm… I hope you brought lots of napkins."

"Got that covered, too." He slid the plate closer until it was right beneath his chin. "If you miss, it'll land on the plate."

"Clever fellow." She scooped up a forkful of stuffing. "Say, ah."

Opening his mouth, he took the food she offered. His blissful expression as he chewed and swallowed it was enough to make any cook proud.

"Oh, wow… Even Laura would agree this is better than hers."

"Thanks, but please don't tell *her* that. She'll probably dislike me enough as it is."

"I doubt it," he said. "Nick's the only one pitching fits. Laura didn't seem to mind."

"I'm glad to hear it, but—wait a minute. *Fits?* As in more than one?"

He nodded. "He was actually pretty decent today—although I think Trish had something to do with that. Yesterday was awful."

She'd already heard about the discussion with the construction crew; apparently there'd been an additional episode he hadn't mentioned, despite having spent the previous evening with her. "Do you want to talk about it?"

"Might as well. You'll find out eventually." His jaw tightened in obvious annoyance. "After I let it slip that you had a son at Purdue, he called me a fuckin' pervert—among other things."

"Oh, Robin. I'm so sorry." Not that she was surprised. Although she hadn't actually met Nick, she doubted he was the type to mince words.

"Don't be. It's nothing to do with him anyway—and I told him so. This is my life, not his. One of these days he'll realize that."

"So he knows how old I am?"

He grimaced. "He figures you're at least forty."

"And you didn't tell him any differently?"

"No. I know I should have, but…" Heaving a sigh, he closed his eyes as though blocking out the memory. "He was already freaked out. I didn't want to make it any worse. I wasn't sure *what* to expect today."

She gave him a bite of turkey. "You said he seemed less…" She paused, searching for the right word, then realized there wasn't one. "…upset?"

"It was kinda creepy, really. He wasn't acting like himself. Too jolly, for one thing."

"You think his wife—that's Trish, right?—said something to

him?"

"Sure seemed that way. Wish she'd do that more often—although it must've worn off after a while. He never admitted it, but he kept coming up with reasons for me to stick around." He chuckled derisively. "He's usually not that subtle—always going on about how men should do whatever they damn well please and to hell with what women want. I don't know how Trish puts up with him."

Evidently Robin didn't subscribe to the same beliefs, or Leslie probably wouldn't feel quite so cherished. "You two sure turned out differently."

"Different upbringing, I guess." He shrugged. "When *he* was born, my mother actually *wanted* kids."

Leslie poked another forkful in his mouth, still unable to believe that a mother could want one child and not another. It seemed so heartless.

"Deep down, I'm sure she wanted you, too, Robin. She must've been very upset when she said she didn't."

Swallowing, he wiped his mouth with a napkin. "Most of the time she was. But you know how it is with kids. They take everything literally—especially when it's their own mother doing the talking—or the yelling."

"Which is why parents should watch what they say." She dunked a piece of turkey in a puddle of gravy while considering her own words. "Look, I'm not saying I don't believe you, and I'm not condoning what she did, but there had to be some other reason for her attitude besides not wanting another baby."

Nick might've been their mother's favorite, but he certainly couldn't have been the sweeter, more attractive child. Robin had inherited that particular gene. Nick had evidently been spoiled rotten.

"Maybe. I think—that is, no one's ever said—but she may have blamed me for my father's death. He died of a heart attack not long before I was born."

Aha! Now, we're getting somewhere.

Leslie had seen some strange reactions during her nursing career—many that defied explanation or logic. "Stress does strange things to people—although you'd think losing your father would make her want you even more. Besides, his death couldn't possibly be *your* fault."

"I don't know… maybe providing for another kid at that age was too much for him. Like I said, I've never been sure. God knows *she* never told me anything. Nick and Laura don't seem to want to talk about it, either."

"They might not know anything. Some parents aren't very open with their children."

"Mom was plenty open with *me*. Always telling me to get lost or shut up." He shrugged. "Then again, I was a little brat. Can't say I blame her much."

"That's very gracious of you." She somehow managed to keep her own opinion of his mother to herself. "But I'm guessing she shared at least part of the responsibility."

Receiving attention for bad behavior was sometimes better than no attention at all—which might explain the spanking preference.

He appeared to consider the idea, then shook his head. "It doesn't matter now. She's been gone for several years. I don't have to try to please her anymore. I never was any good at it anyway."

"I can't imagine any mother not being pleased with you. You're a very special guy." Tears stung her eyes, and she glanced away, struck with sudden shyness. "You certainly make *me* feel special."

"My pleasure."

She looked up to find him smiling at her. He was so adorable. "I don't know what I did to deserve you, but whatever it was, I'm awfully glad I did it."

Even if I don't get to keep you forever.

She left those words unspoken. The mood was already somber enough. Right now, she had so much to be thankful for she didn't even know where to begin.

"Me, too." His smile broadened to a grin. "It has to be something you did, because it sure as hell couldn't have been me."

"I doubt that. If nothing else, you've made me very happy." She waved the fork at the food. "Sorry. Your dinner's getting cold."

"No worries. It'll still be good."

She had just scooped up a forkful of potatoes and fed it to him when their eyes met and locked. Something was happening between them—something she couldn't recall ever having experienced before, unless it was when she first gazed into the eyes of her newborn son.

Robin's mother had clearly missed that step with him. How could anyone be so blind? How could anyone look into his big brown eyes and not love him? Not see the beautiful soul lurking behind his gaze?

She made a silent vow never to give him any reason to believe she didn't love him. Not even if he hurt her. Not even if he left her without saying goodbye.

Tears spilled down her face to fall lightly on the sheets.

His touch on her cheek was so soft she might have dreamed it. "Those don't look like happy tears."

"That's because they aren't," she whispered. "I'm crying for *you*, Robin. For all the love you should've had and didn't get."

She wanted to do more than cry. She wanted to hug him and kiss him and hold him and—

Feed him.

She understood what that meant to him now—the most basic means of showing someone how much you cared.

Making sure they didn't starve.

Brushing away her tears, she fed him until he couldn't hold any more.

Chapter 23

Robin was still asleep when Leslie awoke early the next morning. Since he and Nick were taking the weekend off, he could afford to sleep in.

Lucky guy.

She didn't have that luxury.

Still, she was pleased to have been granted the extra time to watch him while he slept, and she took comfort in his deep, unlabored breathing and his warm presence. With a whisper-soft touch, she combed the curls back from his face with her fingertips, inhaling his scent while she drank in the vision of him—the long dark lashes fanned out above his cheek, the arch of his brow, the angle of his jaw.

Stirring beneath her hand, he sighed in his sleep. His eyelids flickered, and his breaths became erratic.

He's dreaming.

The dim glow from the light she always left on in the kitchen enabled her to see myriad emotions sweep across his face. Was the dream good or bad? She couldn't tell. As soon as she detected a smile or a frown, it would change to something else.

Watching him as he sat on that barstool, laughing with his friends, she never would've guessed how much sadness lurked behind his smile—or how much passion. She'd been ignorant of his life and his dreams then. She'd only known that gazing at him made her feel good, just as it did now. He was food for her soul, and his very existence made her life complete. She wished him only good dreams and untroubled slumber for the rest of his days.

"Feeling better this morning?"

His rough, sleepy voice sent a thrill dancing over her skin. "I'm not tired anymore, if that's what you mean."

"No. I meant all the crying you did."

"That upset you, didn't it?"

He nodded. "I don't like seeing you cry."

"These menopausal mood swings make my emotions so unpredictable. One minute I'm up in the clouds, and the next I'm lower than the worms." Her wry smile was intended to lighten the mood rather than convey actual amusement. Thus far, she'd seen nothing funny about The Change. "See what you've gotten yourself into?"

She guessed his thoughts the moment his lips began to twitch.

"I didn't get *into* as much as I wanted to last night," he said. "You conked out on me."

"Sorry. Old women take naps—although I usually wake up raring to go."

"Glad to hear it." He skimmed a finger over her breast. "We, um, missed dessert last night."

"You said you were too full," she protested.

"That's because *someone* stuffed me with turkey and dressing."

"Anytime an emotional woman wields the fork, you run that risk. Perhaps you should feed yourself from now on."

"No way. I like what it does to my dick. I got up and washed it after you dozed off, but it was still hard when I fell asleep."

"That happen often?"

"Only when I fall asleep with you," he replied.

"Sweet." With a weary sigh, she pushed back the covers. "I guess this means you want me to get up and fix breakfast."

"You don't need to get up. What I want is already ready already."

"What?"

"Pumpkin pie, dummy."

"Who're you calling dummy?" she demanded. "You'd better watch your mouth or it might get smacked—no wait, you'd probably like that."

He shook his head, smiling. "I only like getting smacked on the ass."

"Hmm… something to remember when you're acting like a punk."

"I never act like a punk. In fact, I'll even fix breakfast." Kissing her cheek, he hopped out of bed. "Be right back. Don't go anywhere—or start without me."

"Wouldn't dream of it."

Damn, I like waking up with him…

She'd already turned over and snuggled under the covers when she realized the significance of his last admonition. Considering where he wanted her to sit while she fed him the pie, perhaps she *should've* gotten a head start.

He gave her one.

Within minutes, he returned with a plateful of pumpkin pie smothered in whipped cream. After sampling the pie, he stuck his cock in her face.

"Thought you could use an appetizer."

"I feel so used," she wailed in mock protest. "So manipulated, so cheap, so—"

"Aw, be quiet." His playful grin took any sting out of his words. "You know you love it."

"You've got me there. I *do* love it—way too much. Probably another menopause thing, or else there's something wrong with me."

"I'm not gonna complain—as long as you don't start crying again."

"But what if I do? Will you still love me?"

"Of course I will. It'd take more than a few tears to get rid of me. Now, suck my dick so we can have some pie."

She sighed. "I could *so* get used to this. I've never had this much favorable attention in my life."

"Me, either—and I've certainly never had this much fun. It's nice to feel… accepted? Does that sound right? I'm not afraid to tell you all the stuff about me that makes other people think I'm weird."

"You're not weird. Although I must admit you *do* look a bit strange at the moment."

He rubbed his cockhead on her cheek. "What? Never eaten pie in the nude before?"

"Can't say that I have." Turning her head, she licked the joy juice from his slit and smacked her lips. "You taste much better than pie."

"Then you must not have eaten any of this yet." He stabbed the pie with his fork and took another bite. "It's freakin' fabulous."

She snorted a laugh. "No need to butter me up. You've already got me right where you want me."

"Not exactly." He shot her a wink. "How's your pussy? Wet enough?"

Her shout of laughter drew a look of surprise.

"What's so funny?"

"You," she replied, still chuckling. "If you're not asking me whether I want mustard or mayo on my sandwich, you're asking how my pussy is."

He shot her a grin. "I only ask the important questions. I don't bother with the rest."

"Apparently."

"So, is it?"

She didn't have to check herself for wetness. The growing ache inside her was proof enough. "Yep. The cock syrup has had the desired effect. Want me in your lap?"

"You got it." He climbed onto the bed and handed her the plate. "Let me get comfortable first. Then you can sit on my prick."

Stacking up the pillows, he settled back against them, his cock standing as straight as a light pole. For all his casual talk, he'd evidently been anticipating this event a great deal. His dick looked even bigger than her toy. He held the plate while she got into position and slowly impaled herself with him.

What a way to start the day...

She had to lean forward to feed him, making his cock slide in and out with each forkful. He lay back with a blissful expression while she fed him tiny bites to make it last longer.

Dabbling his fingers in the whipped cream, he painted it on her breasts. "Saving some for later," he explained with a wink. "I've always enjoyed finger painting." He swirled his fingertips over her skin in playful fashion. "Although I've never finger painted like this. *Fabulous* fun."

She giggled helplessly as he tickled and teased her while she fed him the remainder of the pie with her fingers.

"Ooh, I just love these tits!" Cupping them in his hands, he dragged his fingertips from the base to the nipple on the underside.

A moment later, a different emotion flickered in his eyes and he slid his fingers to the nipple again and then back beneath her breasts.

Every trace of amusement vanished from his face as though he'd been sucker-punched in the gut.

"Leslie, what *is* this?" An ominous note colored his voice.

"What is *what*?"

"This." Taking her hand, he placed her fingers on the underside of her left breast. "Right *there*. Can you feel that?"

"I don't feel anything," she protested. "Not—"

Suddenly, she felt it. A firm, round nodule deep within the tissue. Not terribly painful, but most definitely there—most definitely and terrifyingly *there*. Blood drained from her face as though someone had pulled the stopper from her blood supply. She swayed sideways.

Robin wrestled her off him and laid her on the bed. "Are you okay?"

"Dammit, Robin," she whispered. "I had a mammogram two months ago. The report was negative. This *can't* be happening."

"You check them, don't you? Are you sure it's nothing you've ever felt before?"

"I don't think so."

She pressed her fingers over a spot that was already getting sore. Closing her eyes, she told herself it was probably nothing. A cyst, perhaps—certainly not the breast cancer that had killed her mother and grandmother.

She was conscientious about her health. She took vitamins, watched her fat intake, and exercised regularly. She didn't drink alcohol to excess, and she drank green tea for the antioxidant effect. God knew she'd never smoked. She *couldn't* have cancer. It simply wasn't possible.

The truth hit her with the impact of her own death knell. These past few days with Robin had simply been fate's last tease before serving her a backhanded turn. She'd had her glimpse of paradise. Now, her descent into hell had begun.

She'd seen it all before. The endless appointments, painful tests, and the life-shattering diagnosis, followed by treatments nearly as bad as the disease. Then came the eventual and inevitable painful, lingering death.

Survival rates were better now, but somehow, she couldn't see herself being spared—not after her entire family had been taken. Feeling hot and cold at the same time, she shuddered as a wave of sickness passed through her. She should call for an appointment this morning—unless the doctor's office was closed for the holiday. She might have to wait until Monday.

She didn't want to know—didn't want to hear Dr. Edlin tell her that her family history had caught up with her at last. That she would lose a breast—and probably Robin.

He wouldn't stay—not when half of what he loved about her the most was gone. She'd lose a breast and her lover in one fell swoop. She couldn't ask for his support, nor could she expect it. The prospect of dying wasn't half as terrible as the thought of having to go through it alone—of losing him—just when she'd finally found him.

Gabriel. He was the only family she had. They'd only had each other for so long. Surely she could survive long enough for him to finish college. But the money... Cancer treatment was expensive, and insurance didn't cover everything.

Life insurance. If she died, he'd have enough funds to finish his degree. But he wasn't ready to be on his own—at least, not entirely. That one thought was more horrifying than all the rest—the same thought that had nearly destroyed her sanity when he was born and she'd feared she wouldn't survive.

Where would he go? What would he do? He'd have no one to turn to. Her mind spun out of control as a surge of panic overwhelmed her. Fear unlike any she'd ever felt swallowed her up, freezing her solid.

She wasn't afraid for herself. She'd always known she would die. It was simply a matter of when. Gabe was the one she worried about—him… and Robin.

"Leslie? Leslie, say something. Can you hear me? Should I call an ambulance?" Robin's voice held all the concern and panic of a man watching a loved one die.

Perhaps she *was* dying. Sweat prickled her skin and she gulped air faster than her lungs could process it. Her feet and hands turned to ice as random thoughts ripped through her terrified brain.

I'm dying.

No, I'm already dead.

As inevitable as the sunrise of a new day, the how and when of her death had been determined at the moment of her conception, despite her futile efforts to prevent it. That time was *now*.

Robin said something. She saw his lips moving, but with cotton stuffed in her ears and a chainsaw buzzing in her head, she couldn't hear him.

She was breathing too fast and she knew it, but that didn't help. She had absolutely no control over anything—not her life, not her death, not her fate, and especially not her own body.

Dark spots wavered before her eyes, and her hands and feet tingled as her vision faded on the image of Robin's terrified face.

She wasn't dead. Robin knew that much. Dead people didn't breathe. Once she passed out, she began breathing normally again.

Thank God.

He ran into the kitchen and grabbed a cup. Filling it with water, he raced back to the bedroom, fighting the urge to simply throw it in her face.

She wouldn't thank him for getting the bed all wet—even though it was already smeared with whipped cream.

Think.

Darting into the bathroom, he found a washcloth and dunked it in the cup. Snatching up a towel, he returned to the bedroom.

He'd never been so scared in his life.

Well, maybe that one time—but that had been for his own life, not hers. Not Leslie's.

Even out cold she was beautiful. "Come on, Leslie. You just fainted, that's all. Wake up now. Wake up and tell me how much you love me."

He pressed the cloth to her face, wishing he'd thought to bring ice water. That would've worked faster. Then again, perhaps it was best to wake up slowly. Less of a shock that way...

Maybe. He just wanted her awake and talking to him.

She shivered. He poured more water onto the cloth dabbed it on her face. She still had whipped cream all over her chest. If he had to call an ambulance, she probably wouldn't thank him for leaving it there.

Tough to explain to the paramedics.

He wiped the cream off with the towel, then sponged her face again. "Come on, baby. Wake up."

Her eyelids twitched. "Gabe?"

"Gabe's not home yet. You fainted."

She giggled in an odd, feverish sort of way. "No shit. Where—? Oh. Right. Went to Dave's house, didn't he?"

"Yeah."

She laughed again. "I'm all... wet."

"You should be." The rush of relief nearly made *him* faint. "I doused you with cold water. Sorry."

"'Sokay," she muttered, slurring her words. "'S the perfect remedy." She paused, chuckling. "Damn... I sound like a drunk on a three-day binge." After several rapid blinks, her eyes finally stayed open.

"Are you okay now?"

She nodded. "I think so." She didn't sound convinced. "My brain feels like it's made of mud."

"Hmm… How about a cup of tea?"

"Perfect. Tea can cure anything." She paused, frowning. "Except breast cancer—although it's supposed to prevent it. I think we've disproven that claim."

Robin wasn't sure which part of that he should argue with first. "You don't know you have cancer."

"Not yet. But I bet I do. It's already killed everyone in my family. Now it's my turn."

He practically had to bite his tongue to keep from screaming at her to shut up. "You're not gonna die."

"Oh, but I will. Someday. It's only a matter of time."

"You could say that about anyone." He pulled the covers up over her. "I'll be right back. You'll feel better when you've had your tea."

And I'd feel better after a shot of Jack and Coke.

Chapter 24

I might have breast cancer, and I have to go to work.

The two seemed mutually exclusive somehow. For once, Leslie would've chosen going to work as the lesser of two evils.

How on earth could she waltz into the unit and make such an announcement? She didn't want to see her friends' faces when she told them.

Perhaps she wouldn't tell them at all.

As logic began to reassert itself, she realized that for the time being, all she had was a lump. She didn't have cancer—yet. She could hang on to that hope for as long as it took some surgeon to schedule a biopsy—some knife-happy butcher who probably took perverse pleasure in amputating things...

She gave herself a mental slap as Robin returned with a steaming mug of Earl Grey. He hadn't used her favorite cup, but he'd found the right tea.

My God, I'm going to miss him.

"Here you go, sweetheart." Bless his heart, he sounded so gentle and kind. "Drink this and then we'll take a shower. What time do you have to be at work?"

"Seven."

"Think you can do it?"

"Have to." With his help, she managed to sit up without keeling over again. "Besides, you were right. I don't know anything yet. I only have a lump."

"You'll see a doctor, right?" He sounded as if he thought she might not.

She shrugged. "Sure, but it'll probably take several weeks to get an appointment."

"Don't put it off. You need someone to take a look at that." From his tone, Leslie suspected that if she didn't make the appointment, he would—whether she liked it or not.

This was a side of Robin she hadn't seen before and had never suspected.

"Be sure and tell me when it is," he added. "Because I'm going with you."

Great.

Dr. Edlin had been her gynecologist since before Gabriel was born. He'd been fresh out of residency back then. Boyishly handsome and very kind, he'd held her hand while they put her under for the surgery after Gabe's birth. He hadn't changed much in more than twenty years and was still a bit shy. What in the world would he say when she introduced Robin as her significant other?

Probably recommend a psych consult for both of us.

Still, she had no real desire to talk Robin out of coming along. She wanted him with her when she heard the bad news.

And it would definitely be bad. She could kid herself into believing she would receive a clean bill of health, but deep down, she knew the odds were slim.

"Drink your tea," he urged. "I'll fix you something to eat. You need more than whipped cream—especially if you're going to work. We can take a shower after breakfast."

This was a new twist.

Robin cooking for *her*?

Then again, since he'd had pumpkin pie for breakfast, perhaps he'd heat up some turkey and put it on toast or something—not that she had much appetite. He could have given her almost anything and she wouldn't have cared.

He handed her a clean towel, and she dried her face before wiping away the remnants of whipped cream.

And we'd been having such a good time…

Too bad she'd gone and spoiled it. She wished she'd found the lump herself, sometime when she was alone and not having quite so much fun. Perhaps the contrast wouldn't have been as startling and she wouldn't have panicked.

Yeah, and maybe Hell will freeze over in mid-July.

Her reaction would've been the same, no matter the circumstances.

Telling Gabe would be the hardest part. If he didn't come home until after she left for work, she'd have more time to adjust. Perhaps by then she could phrase it better than a blatant, "I have breast cancer, kiddo. You might as well kiss me goodbye."

She thought it best not to tell him anything until she knew more. Sure, he might fuss at her later, but it would save him the needless worry now.

She leaned against the pile of pillows and sipped her tea. A glance at the clock informed her that she had an hour to get ready for work. After that, she would have to endure at least another twelve hours before she saw Robin again.

She was struck with an overwhelming desire to be married to him—to live together in the same house and to go to work knowing that he would be there when she got home. She hadn't felt that way about anyone in a very long time—maybe she never had. He would probably laugh if she told him that.

Might be best to keep it to myself.

Marriage was a far cry from being her boyfriend. He wouldn't want to be tied to someone nearly twice his age to begin with, let alone someone who would be lucky to live another five years.

She glanced up as Robin returned, her eyes widening in surprise. "Eggs? Really? I thought you didn't know how to cook."

"Geez, Leslie." He sat down on the edge of the bed. "I might not be able to make an omelet, but anybody can fry an egg."

"True." In addition to eggs and toast, he'd warmed up some leftover potato casserole. "Thanks, babe. You're so sweet to me."

"Yeah, well, you make it easy."

She smiled back at him, feeling a sudden urge to cry. "So do you." He'd brought enough for two, but never relinquished the fork. "You're feeding *me* now?"

He grinned. "Yeah. Do you mind?"

"Not at all."

He was such a sweetie. If only she could spend the next sixty years with him.

Sixty years.

What would he be like at ninety? He'd still be cute, of course—the kind of charming little old man that nurses actually enjoyed caring for. She could see him now, being wheeled around the nursing home by a pretty young aide, still wearing that red baseball cap. Oh, yes. He'd be adorable until the day he died, even if he lived to be a hundred.

"You keep looking at me and smiling," he said. "What are you thinking about?"

"You," she replied. "I was just thinking about what a cute little old man you'll be someday." Too bad she wouldn't live long enough to see him grow old.

Or Gabriel.

She caught herself before continuing any further along those lines. Giving up now was stupid. After all, she had some seriously good living left to do, and she needed to think positively. Robin had already welcomed her to her next, and best, fifty years. What if those words were prophetic and she truly *did* have another fifty years coming to her?

He chuckled. "I can see us now. We'll be the talk of the nursing home—me grabbing your ass whenever you go by with your walker, you licking my dick every chance you get."

"Sounds wonderful."

"It will be. Do you suppose my dick will still work when I'm that old?"

She shook her head, laughing. "I have a feeling it won't stop working until you stop breathing."

"You're probably right—as long as you're around anyway. It works better for you than it ever has for anyone else."

Leslie was a bit skeptical. Robin, however, seemed perfectly serious—even reflective.

"Why do you think that is?" she asked.

"Dunno." A frown furrowed his brow as he paused. With a shrug, he continued. "It just does. I can't explain it any better than that." The fork clattered as he dropped it onto the empty plate. "Ready for a shower?"

His abrupt change of subject piqued her curiosity, but since she really did need to get ready for work, she didn't press him any further. "Sure."

Robin took her hand and helped her up. Leslie headed off to the bathroom, and he set the empty dish in the kitchen sink before joining her. He still wasn't sure what to make of the morning's events, and as he stepped into the bathtub, he had to hold onto the towel rack to steady himself. Reviving her and fixing breakfast had given him something to do, but now that the adrenaline rush was over, he felt a bit shaky.

She'd seemed convinced that the lump was cancerous and truly thought she was going to die—soon. Given her age and family history, he couldn't blame her for having either of those thoughts.

But what she probably didn't know was that he had no intention of giving up so easily. Whatever it took to help keep her alive, he would do. He would be strong and stand by her through everything that lay ahead. Hell, he'd only just found her. He wasn't about to let it end.

Robin had known what he was getting into when he first approached her in the parking lot. He wasn't stupid. She had more than twenty years on him, and nobody lived forever—no matter how much others might wish it.

He wouldn't desert her—not even if it meant holding her hand while she took her last breath. He had to make sure she knew it, beyond a shadow of a doubt.

Leslie soaped up a washcloth and began washing her arm. "I can't remember the last time I showered with anyone—in *this* bathtub, anyway. Wish we had more time to really enjoy it."

Like the next sixty years.

He stood beneath the spray, letting the water rinse away his tears. "Yeah. Me, too. Here… give me that and I'll wash your back."

She didn't argue. Placing the soapy cloth in his outstretched hand, she turned her back to him. "No need for a scrub brush with you around, is there?"

The cheerful note in her voice sounded more than a little forced. He needed to say something, and he needed to say it now. "No. You won't need anything like that anymore." Moving closer, he took a gentle hold on her upper arms and pressed his lips to her shoulder. "I won't leave you, Leslie. I'll be here for you. Always. No matter what."

Bowing her head, she gulped in a breath, and then nodded. "Thank you," she whispered. "I'm just so worried about Gabe. I'm the only family he has."

"I'll be here for him if he needs help. Trust me, Leslie. I'd do anything for you."

Turning, she wrapped her arms around him and held him tightly, her body quivering with sobs. "I'm s–sorry. I know you don't like it when I cry."

"Forget about that. Cry all you like."

Because I'm crying too.

೮೦೧೩

Having acquired a boyfriend and a suspicious lump since she'd worked her last shift, Leslie drove to the hospital with a great deal of reluctance. Discussing Robin was one thing. Suzie already knew the details and had undoubtedly spread the word.

The lump was another matter entirely.

As she walked into the ICU, she spotted June sitting at the desk next to the monitors, pecking away at the computer.

Tall, slim, fortyish, and completely unflappable, June was also a bit of a perfectionist. Her charting was meticulous to begin with, and online charting had added hours to her shift. The new system hadn't helped a bit. With any luck, she'd be finished by lunchtime.

Glancing up, she swept a stray lock of straight brown hair

behind her ear and smiled. "Feeling better?"

Leslie set her purse on the desk and gaped at her for a long moment.

How could she possibly know?

Then she remembered calling in sick on Tuesday. So much had happened since then, she'd almost forgotten it. "Um... yeah. A little tired, though."

"Uh huh." June's sly smile spoke volumes.

"I see Suzie's been telling tales on me." Pulling up the sign-in link on the nearest laptop, Leslie clocked in.

June nodded. "Are you surprised?"

"Not a bit." Snatching up her purse, Leslie headed into the med room where Dana and Miranda were waiting to give report.

"Welcome to hell." Dana's bright smile and chipper tone clashed with Leslie's mood, which was becoming more morose with each passing second. Still, the pretty blonde would be a perfect match for Robin after Leslie was gone.

Perhaps I should introduce them before it's too late.

Shaking off her morbid thoughts, Leslie blew out a weary sigh. "Just this once, couldn't you have lied?"

Dana shook her head. "Besides, if what we've heard is true, you shouldn't be in a bad mood."

"But I was *sick*," Leslie protested. "Suzie didn't believe me, either—although she seemed happy for the overtime."

"We're not talking about *that* day," Dana said. "We're talking about your new boyfriend."

"He was a real hottie," Miranda said with a wink. "I'm surprised you can still walk."

To be honest, Leslie was a little surprised herself—and sex had nothing to do with it.

Suzie came in lugging her purse, a tote bag, and two sacks of groceries. After five years of living alone, she still hadn't broken the habit of shopping for a family of four. "I cleaned out my refrigerator, so we'll have plenty to eat today."

Leslie frowned. "Hmm... That reminds me. I forgot to bring

any Thanksgiving leftovers—not that Gabe will mind."

What if that was the last Thanksgiving dinner I'll ever cook for him?

Bowing her head, she bit her lip to keep from bursting into tears.

Not now. Not yet...

"If he's like most single guys, your new boyfriend probably won't mind, either."

Suzie's innocent smile didn't fool Leslie for a second, although it did divert her thoughts. "Just couldn't keep quiet, could you?"

"Are you kidding? That was much too good a story to keep secret. The whole hospital probably knows about it by now."

"Oh, great."

Suzie was right, of course. In a small hospital, gossip tended to spread like wildfire. Leslie sometimes longed for the anonymity of working in a huge facility, but their support system was unsurpassed. She worked with some truly wonderful people who were also her best friends. Any one of them would've shared their last dime.

"Well, *piss*," Lola exclaimed as she limped into the med room. "I just remembered the cafeteria is closed today. I forgot my lunch."

"Don't worry," Dana said. "Looks like Suzie's got plenty."

Lola peered into one of the bags. "Diet stuff, I hope. I've got to lose some weight. My knees are killing me." The tall, heavyset blonde had already had surgery on one knee, and it had taken so long to heal, she refused to have the other one done.

"Fruit," Suzie announced. "I've got lots of fruit—grapefruit, oranges, and bananas."

"I don't want fruit, goddammit. I want sex." Lola glowered at Leslie. "I hear you've been shacked up with some young stud all week. I don't suppose you'd consider sharing, would you?" Lola was working on husband number four, and he had a bad back.

"No way," Leslie replied. "I'll share anything but him."

"Guess I'll have a grapefruit, then," Lola said with a sigh.

Suzie held up a large banana. "Is that about the right size, Leslie?"

After giving it the onceover, Leslie concluded that while the banana was about the same thickness as Robin's dick, it wasn't as long or as straight. "Not quite."

Lola let out a whistle. "Way to go, Leslie."

Sofia, the monitor tech, returned from taking vital signs. Rail-thin with wavy black hair, she was the youngest of the group. "There you are, Leslie! Been having fun?"

I give up. "I assume you want details?"

"Oh, yeah." Sofia plopped down in the nearest chair. "My slug of a husband hasn't fucked me in a month. I want to hear everything."

Leslie had no intention of telling anyone *that* much. "Locations only. Starting with his house... the kitchen, the bedroom, the Jacuzzi, the middle of the living room floor, and the couch. Just the bedroom at my place, though."

Sofia counted it up on her fingers. "That's at least once a day not counting when you were sick, right?"

"Um... no," Leslie said. "Those are only the places, not the number of times."

"Spill it." Miranda was grinning like the Cheshire cat. Plenty of tales had circulated when she and Travis got together. Travis wasn't as young as Robin, but Leslie had gotten the impression that the frequency of their encounters was relatively high.

"On average, about three times a day."

Leslie cringed as Dana let out a squeal. "All I get are text messages from my boyfriend—thousands of them! I don't get any kind of daily activity—more like once a month—twice if I'm lucky. This month it'll be more, though, because I'm going on vacation."

Sofia frowned. "Why do you keep him around?"

"I keep asking myself that," Dana replied. "I think he only wants me for my car."

"Not much of a trade-off, is it?" In Leslie's opinion, Dana was pretty enough to be choosy in the extreme, and yet she always seemed to wind up with losers.

"Not really," Dana admitted. "He's such a pussy."

Sofia still seemed puzzled. "Then why do you think you're going to get so much more when you're on vacation?"

Dana laughed. "So no one will think he's a pussy."

"Yes, but how will we know if you don't tell us?" Miranda asked.

Dana's blush made her look like a blonde beet. "I–I'd better not say any more. He thinks I blab too much as it is."

Miranda snickered. "Doesn't sound like there's much to tell. Guess we'd better get on with report."

After grabbing a pad of paper from the shelf, Leslie was pulling up a chair when a male voice yelled, "Nurse!"

Dana rolled her eyes. "That's the guy in bed one. He's been yelling like that all night—can't keep track of his call light for more than a minute."

"Great," Leslie grumbled. "I am *so* not in the mood for a screamer."

Suzie giggled. "Seems like you'd be happy enough to put up with just about anything."

If Robin hadn't discovered the lump in her breast, that would have been true—but not today.

"What's the matter, Leslie?" June called out from the desk. "Not getting enough sleep?"

Leslie glanced up in time to catch her friend's provocative smile. Ordinarily, she would've responded in kind, but she had other things on her mind at the moment.

Apparently, it showed.

Suzie stopped giggling and fixed her with a piercing stare. "There's something else, isn't there?"

Knowing that Suzie was as persistent as she was perceptive, Leslie knew she would ferret out the truth eventually. "He found a lump in my breast this morning. It put a bit of a damper on things."

The ensuing silence was abrupt and complete.

June was the first to speak. "When was your last mammogram?"

"Two months ago," Leslie replied. "This thing is about the size of a pea. If it popped up in that length of time, I'm in big trouble."

"Unless it's a cyst," June cautioned. "Don't freak out just yet."

"I already have." Leslie shuddered as she recalled the horrible, sinking feeling and her subsequent meltdown. "On top of finding the lump, Robin had to deal with a full-blown panic attack. I actually fainted."

"Poor guy," Miranda said. "I bet that scared him almost as much as finding the lump."

"No shit," Dana agreed. "My boyfriend would've bailed on me right then and there."

"I'm sure he was scared," Leslie said slowly. "But he was still... wonderful. You wouldn't believe how sweet he is to me— both before and after he found the lump. No one has ever—" Her voice broke on a sob. Pressing her fist to her mouth, she closed her eyes, fighting for control. "He's simply the best."

Robin wouldn't bail on her. She believed that. Granted, she hadn't known him for very long, but he'd never disappointed her— not once—and she suspected he never would.

No. The question was, would *she* be the one to desert *him*?

Only time would tell.

Chapter 25

After a torrential rain ended his workday early, Robin spent Black Friday afternoon searching the Net for information on breast cancer diagnosis, treatment, and prognosis. What he found was encouraging. Most, though not all, cancers were hard and irregular in shape, and they usually weren't tender. He'd seen Leslie wince when he'd pushed harder on the lump, and to him, it felt more like a pea than a rock. Still, with cancer in her family, he could understand her fears.

He hoped he'd made it clear that *she* was the one he loved, and that her left breast didn't have a whole helluva lot to do with it. True, he took pleasure in the softness of her skin and the heavy feel of her breasts in his hands. He enjoyed sucking and nuzzling them, and if there was a better pillow, he had yet to lay his head on it. But they didn't make her the woman she was.

The woman I love.

If the worst happened and she had to have a mastectomy, there were reconstructive surgeries—implants and skin grafts to help restore a woman's self image as well as her body. Chemotherapy still evoked visions of hair loss and uncontrollable nausea, but even that wasn't the end, and he refused to see it as such. More than that, he refused to let *her* view it in that light.

The sky had already begun to darken before he realized the day was nearly gone. After stoking the fire in the woodstove, he started out for Pemberton, stopping to pick up a pizza on the way.

Since Leslie's shift ended at seven-thirty, Robin made a point to arrive at seven-forty. He would wait on her doorstep if he had to, but he didn't want to miss a second of the time he had to spend with her.

Gabriel answered his knock. Silhouetted in the doorway, his tall form blocked most of the light shining from the living room lamp. "Hi, Robin. Mom's still at work. Sometimes she doesn't get home until eight-thirty or nine. Depends on how busy they are."

"Guess I should've called." He held up the box. "Hungry?"

"Always." Gabe stepped back from the door and waved him inside. "You won't catch me turning away a guy with a pizza. I can eat one that size all by myself."

Unlike Robin, Leslie was accustomed to feeding a guy who was twice the size of practically everyone else.

Something else I'll have to get used to.

"Next time I'll bring two," Robin said, chuckling.

"Don't worry. We'll save some for Mom, although she doesn't always come home hungry. Sometimes she actually has time to eat at the hospital."

The roll of his eyes suggested that this was an unusual occurrence. Robin couldn't imagine working twelve hours without stopping for meals. But then building houses was rarely a matter of life and death.

Gabriel led the way to the kitchen, giving Robin an inkling of how Jack must've felt following the giant up the beanstalk.

"I've put a pretty good dent in it, but there's still plenty of stuff left over from yesterday." Grabbing some plates from the dishwasher, Gabe set them on the table. "I think Mom was kinda disappointed when Dave picked me up before dessert."

"She was, actually."

Gabe winced. "I was afraid of that—which is why I was glad you were coming over."

Judging from her son's casual demeanor, Leslie hadn't told him about the lump yet—unless Gabe hadn't grasped the seriousness of it. Somehow, Robin thought he would have.

"I was late getting here myself," Robin said. "She seemed a little... upset."

Gabe froze for a second, then frowned. "Came unglued, you mean?"

"Sort of," Robin admitted.

Nothing compared to this morning's episode.

Plopping down in a chair, Gabe took a slice of pizza from the box and ate it in three bites. "She does that sometimes—hyperventilates until she passes out. It's pretty scary. The weird thing is, I don't think she's ever done it at work, and the stuff she has to deal with there would make most people freak out." He heaved a sigh. "It's usually my fault."

"Oh?" Figuring he might not get a second chance, Robin put two slices of pizza on his plate.

"Yeah. She worries about me. I used to get irritated with her—always wanting to know where I was, what I was doing, who I was with—that sort of thing." Another pizza slice vanished. "I think I understand now."

Robin certainly hoped he did. He'd have given a lot for anyone—his mother in particular—to give a damn about *him* while he was growing up. Gabriel was luckier than he knew. "It's because she cares about you."

Gabe nodded. "I'm sure she explained that to me before. I just never actually heard it until yesterday." Fixing Robin with a rather pointed gaze, he added, "She also cares about *you*."

"Think I should keep her posted on where I am and what I'm doing?"

"Not exactly, but she's starting to worry about you the way she worries about me." The next piece of pizza went down more slowly. "You might consider calling her more often."

Never having had a girlfriend who expected frequent phone calls, Robin wasn't in the habit of checking in with anyone. Once again, no one had ever cared enough to want him to. Apparently, Leslie did.

What a concept.

"I'll do that—don't want to be a bother, though."

"She won't see it that way," Gabe said. "Trust me on that one. She needs... reassurance. I know she seems pretty tough, but she isn't. Not really."

"I'll be careful with her," Robin promised.

They ate in silence after that, Gabriel concentrating on the food while Robin focused on the food for thought he'd been given.

A simple phone call from Laura's house would've helped to allay Leslie's concerns. He could've told her how miserable he was and how much he looked forward to seeing her. She probably would've enjoyed hearing that.

He reached for more pizza—only to discover that only one small slice remained, along with a sliver of pepperoni and a few stray olives.

Gabe's chagrined expression was downright comical. "Think we should order another one for Mom?"

"Not unless you've eaten all the turkey."

"Nope. There's plenty of that left."

"Any pie?"

Gabe winced. "Sorry, mate. I'd be lyin' if I said there was." This time, his accent sounded more Australian than British. "How about a round of Halo before me Mum gets home?"

"You're on."

Leslie drove up to her apartment, relieved to see Robin's truck parked by the curb. After the initial ribbing about her new boyfriend followed by the breast cancer discussion, the shit had hit the fan, and she was exhausted—mentally and physically. All she wanted to do was to curl up with him and relax.

Or at least try to. She had a sneaking suspicion she wouldn't be able to relax completely for a long time to come.

"Hey, Mom," Gabe called out as she unlocked the door and stepped inside. "We're in here."

Following her son's voice to his room, she peeked around the corner. Gabe and Robin both looked up and grinned.

"Robin plays a mean game of Halo."

"I'm not surprised," she said. "You two probably have a lot in common. He's got quite a collection of Ninja Turtle dinnerware."

"No shit?" Gabe turned toward Robin. "I loved those guys."

"Same here," Robin said. "Who was your favorite?"

"Michelangelo." Gabe didn't add the "Well, duh," but he might as well have.

Robin nodded. "Mine, too. He was the best."

She couldn't help but be pleased that her son and her lover got along so well—at least as far as video games and the Ninja Turtles were concerned. Particularly since Gabe hadn't approved of any of the others.

Come to think of it, neither did I.

"Have you two had dinner?" she asked.

"Yeah," Gabe replied. "Robin brought pizza, but we ate most of it. I hope you aren't too hungry."

"Not really," she said. "And if I am, there's always turkey."

"Dunno why I didn't think of that before," Robin said. "Too used to eating out to check the fridge for leftovers, I guess."

"I don't cook as much as I used to," she admitted. "Until today, there wouldn't have been much to find."

Unlike my left breast.

What he'd found there might've been small but it was still stupendously significant.

Despite a busy shift, she'd had to fight the compulsion to check her breast every five minutes. Her other compulsion was a thought rather than an action—she couldn't stop wondering if Robin would feel differently toward her knowing the lump was there. Would he be afraid he'd hurt her or be turned off by the notion that she might be harboring a cancerous growth? Being the larger of the two, it was, after all, the breast he seemed to like best. Would they end up being the same size after a lumpectomy and radiation? She refused to let herself even *think* about a radical mastectomy anymore—*much* too depressing.

She left the guys to their game and went to change out of her scrubs, wishing she could down a bottle of tequila to banish the constant worry from her mind. She was beginning to realize why some people committed suicide rather than face the outcome. It wasn't so much the prospect of death or suffering as it was the incessant, irrational thinking—the inability to escape from her own mind.

In the end, she ate the last of the pizza and then curled up on the couch in her favorite flannel pajamas with a cup of tea.

Robin wandered in a bit later and sat down beside her with a dejected air. "He beat me."

"I'm not surprised. He's had plenty of practice."

"So have I. You never saw my game room, did you? I've got some stuff Gabe would flip out over, and there's even more of it in the basement. It's pretty nice down there—there's even a wet bar—not that I entertain much."

"Don't know why you'd need a bar anyway," she said. "Most people hang out in the kitchen at parties."

"True." He leaned in for a kiss that was even more effective than a bottle of tequila at driving away her morose imaginings. "How'd it go today?" He combed her hair back with his fingers. "I was worried about you."

"Not too bad—busy, though. I'm more tired than anything."

"I'm not surprised. You were up pretty early this morning." He hesitated. "I take it Gabe still doesn't know."

She shook her head. "I'm not going to tell him anything—at least, not until I know something definite." With any luck, there wouldn't be anything to tell.

Yeah, right.

"I can understand that, but I did some research today. What I found wasn't all bad."

"I probably heard the same things from the hospital gang. I'm still going to wait, though. Gabe needs to focus on his education—not worry about whether I'll live to see him graduate."

"You need to stop worrying about that yourself."

"I'm trying, but I can't seem to get my brain to shut up. Know any cures for that?"

His wicked chuckle made his idea of a "cure" quite plain. "I believe I do. But if you're too tired…"

"I hope I'm never too tired for *that*."

"But you do look tired. If I was any kind of decent boyfriend,

I'd put you to bed right now."

"Oh, really?" She noticed he hadn't said what he'd do once he put her there.

"Absolutely. My pretty mama needs her rest."

Somehow, she didn't think "rest" was on the agenda. "True—and I *do* have to go to work in the morning."

"All the more reason to get you to bed early." His voice dropped to an intimate rumble as he tangled his fingers in her hair. "I missed you today. If I'd known where to find you, I would've joined you for lunch."

She blew out a derisive snort. "My lunch break consisted of gulping down a banana while I was charting—which takes forever on this new system. The old one was bad enough."

Robin was nothing if not supportive. "Need to relieve your frustrations?"

She knew exactly what he meant. Too bad she didn't have the energy. "Like spanking someone?"

"Oh, yeah…"

"Maybe. But like I've said before, you aren't the one I'm annoyed with. I'm not even sure who *is* responsible. All I know is, one of these days they're going to have to hire someone else to take care of the patients because the nurses will be too busy charting."

"That bad, huh?"

She nodded. "It's getting there. A lot has changed since I graduated from nursing school—and not all of those changes were for the better." Yawning, she stretched until the joints in her back popped. "But enough about that. Unless I miss my guess, your dick is hard, and I can't think of anything I'd rather do right now than lie down and let you nail me with it."

"No spanking?" He sounded terribly disappointed.

"Could we use that as a sort of foreplay thing—you know, something to get you in the mood instead of spanking you until my arm goes numb?"

"You mean like the way your pussy gets wet when I put my hard, dripping cock in your face?"

"Um… yeah. Something like that."

With a blink, he cleared his throat. "Well, just so you know, all this talk has me about to pop out of my pants."

"Thank God." She started to get up, but paused as a new idea occurred to her—a new way to tease… "Although now that you mention it, I *had* thought about tying you up again, but since my dominatrix outfit hasn't arrived yet…"

His eyes lit up like roman candles. "No shit? You actually ordered one?"

"No, but with a reaction like that, perhaps I should."

"Ooh, yeah… You'd look great in a black leather bustier—the kind that supports your tits from underneath but doesn't cover them up."

Evidently, he'd given this matter some thought.

So had she—not that she had any idea what he was talking about. "Yeah, right. That'll look terrific after a mastectomy."

Robin's growl was clearly intended as a warning rather than anything of a sexual nature. "*Leslie…*"

"Sorry. I can't help it. Maybe I should slap myself every time I think shit like that."

"Nah. You'd just wind up with bruises. Then Gabe would think I beat you up, and he'd pound me into dust."

A tiny chuckle escaped her. "He'd *never* think that."

"Maybe not, but— Wait! I've got it! You could drape a strip of black satin over your shoulder—sort of like wearing a patch over one eye. *Very* sexy."

She burst out laughing. "If you say so. Honestly, I don't see myself as the dominatrix type even with two boobs, let alone one."

"Yeah, well, I think you're a natural. If you don't believe me, take a look at my dick." He reached for his zipper, bringing her peal of laughter to a screeching halt.

"Not in the living room. Gabe likes you, but I doubt if he likes you *that* much."

"True." He hopped to his feet and held out a hand. "C'mon, pretty mama. My dick can't take much more of this."

"You don't like having to wait, do you?"

He shook his head. "When it comes to wanting you, waiting is pure torture."

"That's one of the nicest things anyone's ever said to me—might even top the list." Placing her hand in his, she gave him a wink as he helped her to stand. "I'll meet you in my bedroom. Be ready for me."

"But what—"

"Shh..." She pressed a finger to his lips. "Just thought of something kinky."

Something guaranteed to make her forget just about anything.

For a while, anyway.

Completely engrossed in a video game, Gabriel never even looked up as Robin tiptoed past his door on the way to Leslie's room.

"Be ready," she'd said. Did that mean naked?

Probably. Once inside, he yanked off his shirt and stripped off his jeans so fast his dick bounced. He still had no idea what she was up to. The only place she could've gone was the kitchen, but what could she possibly—

A spatula. Perfect for smacking his ass. His cock surged with anticipation.

Moments later, Leslie entered. Closing the door behind her, she nodded her approval. "Nice."

No spatula. In fact, she didn't have anything in her hands—at least, not that he could see. His heart sank. "What's your kinky idea?"

"This." She held up a long piece of string.

His eyes widened. "W–what are you gonna do with that?"

Moving closer, she reached down and cupped his balls. "You seemed to like being tied up. I have an idea that tying a string around a guy's balls will make him come to heel like a well-trained Doberman. Bet it would make his cock really hard, too."

Robin was already about to explode as it was. "Probably."

She tied a slipknot in the string and looped it around his nuts.

Her eyes locked on his as she tightened the noose. "Not too tight, is it?"

He shook his head. "Feels pretty good, actually."

"Let's see how well you walk on a leash." She gave a tiny tug, leaving Robin with no choice but to follow. "Very good." She patted his head. "Now you need to learn how to stand tied to a post without getting yourself all tangled up in the leash."

Gulping in a breath, he clenched his teeth and followed her to the bed.

She tied the string to the bedpost. "Let's see how well you stand still when I paddle your butt."

Holy shit. "You've got a paddle?"

"Nope. I brought this." Reaching under her shirt, she extracted a rubber spatula from the pocket of her pajama bottoms. "Had to hide it in case Gabe saw me walk by. Not gonna wear out my hand on you this time."

A breath hissed in through his teeth. "What happens if I come?"

"Then I'll spank you until your dick is ready to go again."

"Promises, promises…"

"I'd rather you didn't come right away, though," she added. "So I won't spank you very much."

Given that his dick already felt like a Luger with a hair trigger, it probably wouldn't take a whole lot.

Three stinging smacks had him teetering on the point of no return. He held onto the bedpost, gritting his teeth. "One more and I'll come," he warned.

"Well, now," she purred. "We can't have that, can we? Especially since I'm in the mood for a good, hard fuck."

When she slipped out of her pajamas, Robin was surprised he didn't come simply from watching her. His cock pulsed as she untied the string from the bedpost.

"On the bed. Now." She punctuated that directive with a slap on his ass.

Robin scooped her up and practically threw her on the bed. He hadn't followed her instructions correctly, but at the moment, he didn't give a shit. Climbing on top of her, he kissed her, sliding his tongue deeply into her mouth.

"Fuck me, Robin," she whispered against his lips. "Fuck me harder than you've ever fucked anyone in your life. Make me forget *everything.*"

He knew what she was asking and why—and he was more than willing to comply. Spreading her legs, he entered her with one swift stroke.

Her initial gasp was followed by cries of passion so loud Robin was afraid Gabriel might hear them. Apparently, Leslie had the same thought and clapped her hand over her mouth, stifling her screams. As close as he'd been to climax only a few seconds before, he was amazed he was able to keep going, especially after her strangled, "Don't stop" nearly put him over the edge.

His persistence paid off as she came with a sharp exhale and an internal contraction that sucked him in farther than ever. Two thrusts later, the universe expanded like the second coming of the Big Bang.

He could barely feel his own body. Awareness returned slowly—first his breathing, then the heat where their skin touched. Where he'd seemed weightless before, he was now conscious of the pressure his body exerted upon hers. Lacking the strength to lift himself, all he could do was roll to the side.

He stared at the ceiling. Had he been successful? Had she forgotten her troubles for even an instant?

Turning toward her, he was immediately rewarded by the blissful smile curving her lips.

Content in the silence, he let his mind drift at will—touching lightly on her warm presence, listening to her soft, even breathing, feeling the beat of his own heart.

Her sigh broke the spell as she snuggled closer, resting her head in the hollow of his shoulder. "Was that what you had in mind?"

A chuckle rippled through him. "I've never had anything like *that* in my mind in my entire life."

"Me, either—but then, my imagination has never been quite so inspired." She trailed her fingertips through the hair on his chest—a caress as loving as a kiss.

"You certainly inspire me," she went on. "I mean, a simple piece of cotton string—the kind I used to truss up the turkey—and a spatula?" Giggling, she gave his nipple a tweak. "Still think I need a bustier to play dominatrix?"

He lifted her face to his with a knuckle beneath her chin, delighted to see the twinkle had returned to her eyes.

"No way." He kissed her, long and deep. "Like I said, you're a natural."

Chapter 26

Gabriel left for Purdue on Sunday night. Robin left for work bright and early Monday morning. An hour later, Leslie called Dr. Edlin's office.

The receptionist was sympathetic, if not terribly helpful. "The earliest opening we have is the twenty-seventh at ten thirty. We can call you if we have a cancellation."

Leslie figured that with her luck, the only opening they'd have would be when she was scheduled to work. "Okay. Let's do the twenty-seventh."

She hung up the phone, suspecting that it would ring any minute, and it wouldn't be anyone from the doctor's office.

Fifteen minutes later, Robin called.

Right on cue...

He didn't even bother to say hello. "Did you call the doctor?"

"Yes, I did."

"And?"

"I have an appointment on the twenty-seventh."

She could almost hear his jaw drop. "No way. That's practically a whole month! Can't they bump someone else? This is important."

"They said they'd call if they had a cancellation. At least I don't have to wait until January or February. And before you ask, seeing a different doctor would take even longer." Despite her intention to remain philosophical and reasonable, deep down, she wanted to scream in frustration.

"I don't believe it," he snapped. "Early diagnosis and treatment is *vital*."

That he was saying this to someone who'd been in nursing for thirty years was a testament to his anxiety level.

"I know, but it is what it is. At least I can get through Christmas without having to schedule... anything." She hesitated to say surgery—although God knew it was first and foremost in her mind. "The unit's holiday schedule was hammered out several months ago. I'm off Christmas Day, but I have to work Christmas Eve. Getting someone to replace me would be impossible."

His snort indicated just how little he cared about scheduling issues. "They'd find someone if you were in the hospital, wouldn't they?"

"Probably, but I'm not going to *be* in the hospital then, except in a professional capacity." Taking a deep breath, she tried to at least *sound* calm. "It'll be okay, Robin. Don't worry."

"Yeah, right. Like telling me not to worry will actually do any good."

"Same here, but we have to do the best we can."

"Okay. I'll try. But it sure as hell won't be easy." He blew out a breath. "There's something else that won't be easy. I... um... have a favor to ask."

"Oh?"

"On Thanksgiving, when Nick was being so creepily nice, Trish asked when they'd get to meet you, and stupid me, I said my birthday. Apparently, Laura's decided it would be a terrific idea to throw a party for me on Saturday night, and you're invited."

"You don't sound very pleased about it," she observed.

"I'm not. Between the two of them, Laura and Nick have asked practically everyone I know. The question is—will *you* be there?"

Leslie's initial inclination was to refuse outright. Robin's first meeting with Gabriel had gone better than she ever could've imagined, but she doubted a get together with *his* family would turn out quite as well.

"Nick still doesn't know exactly how old I am, does he?"

"Well, no," he admitted. "But most women won't tell you their age. Why should you be any different?"

"Because I *am* different, that's why. They'll take one look at me and—"

"But you don't *look* fifty," he protested. "Trust me, you don't."

"It doesn't matter, Robin. They'll know. Besides, how old are Nick and Laura?"

"Nick's thirty-eight and Laura is forty."

Great. I've even got ten years on his older sister. "Damn, you really were the baby of the family."

"No shit. Don't change the subject. Will you be there?"

The glance she gave the calendar only confirmed what she already knew. "I have to work Saturday. What time's the party?"

"Eight o'clock at Laura's house. I'll give you directions."

Obviously, this was important to him. "Okay, but if Nick calls either of us a pervert, I'm outta there—and you're coming with me."

"Fair enough," he agreed. "It's nice to know you've got my back."

She smiled. "Your back, your front, both sides, along with your top and bottom. Speaking of parties, I assume I'm expected to bring a gift. Any suggestions?"

"You, of course. What else could I possibly want?"

"Sweet." Obviously, she would have to buy two gifts. His real present and one that was politically correct enough for a family gathering. *An IU sweatshirt, perhaps.* "Never mind, I'll think of something."

"You don't have to get me anything," he said. "Seriously. I just want you to be there."

"I will be—although I might be a little late. See you tonight?"

"You bet."

In the end, Leslie did buy him two presents. One wrapped in red foil, and the other in blue tissue paper. This was one time she really couldn't afford a mix-up.

Shopping had helped to divert her mind from her health concerns—particularly while perusing the merchandise in an adult toy shop she'd discovered, but even they didn't have what she wanted. In desperation, she wound up at a farm supply store where she discovered exactly the right items.

Perfect.

She didn't tell the clerk she planned to use the stuff on her boyfriend.

৪৩৫

Saturday evening, she changed out of her scrubs before she left the hospital and drove straight to Laura's house wishing that Robin was there with her. She'd been fighting a growing sense of panic all day, and it didn't improve as she approached the front door alone. He said he'd told everyone that she would be late, but she had no idea what else he'd said to them. Either way, they'd probably all drop their teeth when they saw her—that is, if any of them wore dentures. Somehow, she suspected she would be the oldest person present.

She tried all the usual techniques for staving off panic, even considering taking a Xanax, but she dismissed that as cowardly.

They're just people. Just plain, ordinary people.

What she hadn't expected was that there would be so many of them. She walked through the open door into a sea of unfamiliar faces. Since Robin's family was relatively small, most of the people present had to be his friends. Had he told them who she was or that they were dating? Perhaps he would only refer to her as a friend. Being quizzed about their relationship by so many strangers—no matter how friendly—was something she wasn't quite ready for.

Robin dashed over to plant a kiss squarely on her lips. That kiss did nothing to dispel her fears, nor did it allay any suspicions that they were more than mere friends.

"Thank God you're here," he murmured. "I just want to get this over with and go home."

She'd seen him off and on during the week, and though they'd enjoyed several pleasant evenings together, she'd sensed his underlying current of anxiety. She'd assumed it was due to the lump he'd found in her breast rather than any misgivings about the party.

Now, she wasn't so sure.

He introduced her by name, rather than relationship, and after pointing out his brother and sister, he deposited her gift on the table along with all the others. "Can I get you a drink?"

She replied with an absent nod, all the while searching the room for a good hiding place. Her gaze landed on an empty seat in the corner, partially obscured by a Norfolk pine in a huge Aztec-style pot.

"I'll be over there," she said, pointing to the chair.

His smile was undoubtedly meant to reassure her, but she'd never felt so out of place in her life. Not only was she clearly the oldest person there, everyone else seemed to know each other and were all laughing and talking among themselves. She withdrew into the corner, wishing she'd followed her instincts and refused the invitation.

"I feel like Methuselah at a christening," she whispered when Robin brought her a drink.

"Don't be silly. You're the most beautiful woman here," he said. "Hell, Laura looks older than you—and she's not the only one."

"I doubt that." She took the glass he offered her, which was filled with a frothy pink punch of some kind. "What's in this?"

"Rum, I think," he replied. "Would you rather have something else?"

"No. Rum is good." Tequila would've been better.

Glad I didn't take that Xanax.

He shot her a sly wink and then left as someone called out his name.

Leslie sipped her drink.

Definitely rum.

She was already shaking like a leaf, but the liquid courage enabled her to glance around the room. She spotted a woman seated nearby who looked to be a little older than the others. Nick's wife, Trish, perhaps?

Leslie didn't have the opportunity to find out, because at that moment, Laura came waltzing out of the kitchen with a fully-lit cake. She was joined by the rest of the party in singing "The Birthday Song." One male voice rang out above the others, sounding a more than a little slurred and about a half-beat behind. The song ended, and Robin blew out the candles.

"Time for the birthday spanking!"

To Leslie's horror, she realized whose voice that had been. *Nick.*

Nick's eyes swept the room before landing on Leslie in her secluded corner. "Let's let Leslie do it."

Her stricken expression must have been obvious to everyone in the room. Nick drew back in a poor imitation of mock surprise.

"You mean he hasn't asked you to spank him yet? Honest to God, he's run off every girl I ever fixed him up with. They've all come back accusin' me of introducin' them to a pervert." He paused, swaying as though barely able to remain standing. "But maybe an old girl like you enjoys havin' a little boy to spank."

Nick started toward her. Although his gait was obviously that of a drunkard, no one made a move to stop him or shut him up. As shocked as Leslie was, she could only assume that everyone else was too stupefied to react. Robin looked as though he'd been hit over the head with a two-by-four.

"C'mon," Nick urged. "Let's see you do it."

The woman Leslie had assumed was Trish was the first to speak. "Now, Nick, you be quiet. Nobody wants to—"

"No, I wanna see it!" Nick waved his wife aside. "I wanna see what makes him so goddamned hot after this fuckin' grandma. I mean, she's not bad lookin', and she's got big tits, but there must be something else."

Leslie could barely hear above the pounding of her heart. Her vision narrowed, as though she was seeing him through a tunnel. In another minute, she'd be hyperventilating.

Cocking his head, Nick squinted at his brother's ashen countenance, then turned back to Leslie. "Did he tell ya why he likes bein' spanked?" Not waiting for her reply, he plunged ahead. "It was the only attention he ever got from a mother who didn't want him."

"Will someone please shut him up?" Leslie's voice came out with a croak.

A man took a step toward him, but Nick raised his fist.

"Back off, asshole." He focused on Leslie again. "Speaking of assholes, better steer clear of Robin's, Grandma. One of our dear, sweet mother's boyfriends figured out he liked bein' spanked. Thought rape would be a better punishment."

Somehow, Leslie was on her feet without remembering how she'd gotten there. Her legs were like two chunks of lead as she started toward the door. She looked over at Robin and called out his name.

Nick grabbed her arm and spun her around to face him. "Don' leave now. You haven't heard the bes' part. Ya wanna know why she named him Robin? 'Cause she said he was robbin' her of her freedom. Didn't want another baby after Dad died—even tried to get an abortion." He looked her up and down, his eyes filled with scorn. "You just don' get it, do ya, Grandma? He doesn't want you in *spite* of the fact that you're old enough to be his mother. He wants you *because* of it—the fuckin' pervert."

Suddenly, Leslie wasn't scared or anxious or nervous anymore.

She was *pissed*.

Snatching her arm from his grasp, she slapped Nick across the face with every last ounce of her strength. With a determined stride, she continued on toward the door, yanking it open and then slamming it shut behind her without so much as a backward glance.

She was halfway to her car before she remembered something.

Robin. I forgot Robin.

In her anger, she'd essentially left Robin behind to be torn apart by the wolves.

No. She'd called his name. She was sure she had. He should've followed her. They'd agreed—*If Nick calls either of us a pervert, we're outta there.*

But he hadn't come with her. He'd stayed behind to face the questioning glances and furtive whispers.

Leslie wanted to wipe every memory in that room clean of the events of the past ten minutes. She didn't want anyone to know those things about Robin.

No one except me.

It all made sense to her now. All the things he'd wanted from her—to be loved and accepted as he was—and to let him love her in return. He wasn't sick or perverted. It wasn't his fault he'd never received that kind of love from his mother—or anyone else for that matter.

Until now. Leslie had given him love, and he'd returned it tenfold.

Spinning on her heel, she opened the door and stormed inside just as Robin delivered a right upper-cut to his brother's jaw. As Nick dropped to his knees, Robin hit him again. "And that one's for Leslie."

Nick dissolved into tears. "I deserved that. I never helped you— never tried to protect you. Oh, God." His voice was a low moan. "I can still hear the screams."

Leslie stood silently in the doorway, waiting for the scene to play out, but it was already over.

Robin turned toward her and, unbelievably, smiled. "Sorry you had to see that, Leslie." His voice held no trace of anger or fear— only regret. "And I'm sorry I didn't shut him up sooner. He had no right to talk to you that way—I was just too dumbfounded to move."

"You did great," she whispered. "I–I shouldn't have left without you. That was… cowardly of me."

"No way." He pulled her into his arms. "You haven't got a cowardly bone in your body."

She kissed him hard on the cheek. "Come on. Let's get out of here. We can sort this out later—sometime when Nick is sober and there isn't such a crowd." She paused, grimacing. "No, that's cowardly of me too."

Nick sat in a pathetic, sobbing huddle on the floor. He might not remember anything anyone said to him, but a piece of her mind was definitely in order.

"Let's get a few things straight," she began. "I love your brother, which means I'm probably gonna have to put up with *you.* But if I ever hear you say another word like that to Robin or about

Robin, believe me, I will make you regret the day you were born."
Gulping in a breath, she glanced up at the sea of stunned faces and
attempted a smile and a softer tone. "Good night, everyone. It was
very nice meeting all of you."

A heartbeat later, the room erupted in a resounding cheer,
proving that Leslie wasn't the only one who had issues with Nick.
She and Robin might've been leaving him to the wolves, but at the
time, she simply didn't give a shit.

Chapter 27

Robin stepped outside, inhaling the crisp night air. He'd never once hit his brother—or anyone else. He still didn't know how he felt about it, whether Nick had it coming or not.

"I'm parked by the street," Leslie said. "Where's your truck?" On the surface, she seemed as brisk and practical as always, but the slight tremor in her voice betrayed her.

"Doesn't matter," he replied. "I can get it tomorrow."

She started down the steps, but stopped suddenly. "You don't even have a coat! Aren't you cold?"

Shaking his head, he put his arm around her waist and steered her along the brick-paved path to the street. "I'm fine."

"Honestly?" Judging by her concerned expression, she wasn't only referring to the temperature.

"Yeah. I'm okay." With a shock, he realized he truly *was* okay. In fact, he felt better than he had in a very long time. "I needed to get that off my chest—and so did Nick. Just wish he'd saved it for another time."

"No shit. I can't believe he said all that in front of your friends."

"Me, either—but then, Laura said he'd been drinking all day. I guess he and Trish had a fight or something."

"That's no excuse." She shuddered, pulling up her coat collar. "I'm not sure I could ever face any of those people after a scene like that."

"I dunno," he drawled. "I thought you handled it pretty well—better than I did, anyway. You were awesome."

"So were you—once you got started." Leslie clicked the remote to unlock the car before handing him the keys. "I was doing a lot better then than I am now. My hands are shaking. Would you mind driving?"

"Not at all." After helping her into the passenger side, he closed her door and slid into the driver's seat. "You know something? I'm actually glad that happened the way it did. I've managed to forget lots of things, but one thing I *do* remember is wishing Nick had stood up for me—just once—the way Gabriel did for you." He started the engine and adjusted the mirrors. "Obviously, he wishes he had too."

"Maybe." She buckled her seat belt then brushed a lock of hair from her face. "He sure picked a strange way of showing it. I've never felt very kindly toward any of the drunks I've had to take care of. I don't think I'll ever warm up to him."

Robin certainly couldn't blame her for that. He eased the car away from the curb. "Where to?"

"Your house," she replied. "I think we need some quality time in the Jacuzzi."

"*Fabulous* idea." The mental image of Leslie naked in the Jacuzzi banished every other thought from his head—except one. "I'll take that birthday spanking when we get there."

She stared at him, her mouth agape. "Well, shit. I hoped hearing all that crap about your mother and her boyfriend would change your mind."

"Nope. Call it weird or kinky or perverted if you want to, but I like it, and I probably always will."

"My right arm will never be the same," she lamented. "Too bad you aren't a massage therapist."

"I promise to go easy on you. Only once a week—remember?"

"Yeah. I remember. On Saturdays." She heaved a sigh. "I hate to say it, but this is Saturday."

He grinned. "I know. In return for the spanking, I'll let you suck my dick all night and into the morning if you like."

"You've almost got me convinced. Keep talking."

"Imagine my hard, pulsating penis—in your mouth, dripping down your throat, coming on your tits. My balls in your hands, my cock in your pussy. Don't you think a spanking is worth that privilege?"

"Oh, so now it's a *privilege*." Robin could almost hear the eye roll in her voice. "Next thing you know, it'll be an honor."

Flipping on the turn signal, he changed lanes. "I *do* have a pretty nice dick."

"Nice, hell. It's fucking *awesome*."

Robin couldn't help but be pleased. "Glad you like it." He was also glad they were able to lighten up a bit.

Too much drama for one night.

"Okay," she said after a moment's pause. "You win—after all, it *is* your birthday." For the first time that evening, her laughter contained genuine amusement. "Which means I only have to hit you twenty-eight times."

He smacked the steering wheel. "Damn. I knew there had to be a catch."

"You forget, I've dealt with young men before."

"Yes, but—hey… wait a minute. We had a bet, and you lost, so you *have* to do it. Which reminds me… what did we say would happen if *I* lost the bet?"

"That I'd never have to spank you again. Trust me, I remember that part quite well. I still can't figure out why I tried so hard to make you come."

"Temporary insanity?" he suggested.

"That'd be my guess."

"I'll have to think of some other punishment for you if you welsh on the bet—like maybe doing double duty the next week? We could get to the point where you'd be doing it every day."

There was no mistaking her cringe, but she was still smiling. "You wouldn't hold me to that, would you? I mean, even if you lost the bet to begin with, I'd have done it once in a while."

"You would have, wouldn't you?"

She nodded. "Absolutely."

For once, he was thankful for a red light. Stopping at the intersection, he cupped the back of her head and pulled her toward him for a kiss that made his dick tingle. "That's because you love me so much, right?"

"You got it." She glanced up. "The light's green. Better hurry. If we don't get home before midnight, it won't be Saturday anymore—and you know what *that* means."

Her ominous tone had him stomping the gas pedal before he bothered to check the dashboard clock. "Geez, Leslie. It's only nine-thirty."

"Yes, but you still might want to step on it. I'm anxious to give you your other present."

"My *other* present?"

"The one I couldn't let you open in front of the family."

"Sounds kinky."

"It is. Keep driving."

ℰℭ

They made it to Robin's house in record time, which didn't allow Leslie much opportunity to mull over the evening's events. Once again, his resilient nature amazed her. To be able to bounce back so quickly—especially after the sordid scene they'd left behind—spoke volumes for the kind of man he was. For him to have come through it all with nothing more than a touch of Peter Pan syndrome and a spanking fetish was truly remarkable.

In a way, his mother was lucky to have died before Leslie had the chance to rip the selfish bitch a new one. Doubtless, such an action would've been cathartic, but probably not in anyone's best interest.

No, the best she could do for Robin was to stay alive and well. Considering how much she loved him—and how much he loved *her*—dying before she was at least eighty was simply not an option. She had two young men she loved very much, and she was determined to beat this thing.

If only she knew what she was up against! A cyst posed no threat, but the odds were against it being anything that benign.

"We're home." His announcement startled her out of her reverie as he made the turn into his driveway.

Home.

Tears pricked her eyes as he brought the car to a halt. She'd like to be able to call his house her home—and him her husband—someday. But for that to happen, she had to at least be alive.

Robin hopped out of the car and came around to open the door for her. "Feeling better now?"

"A bit." Accepting his offer of assistance, she placed her cold, trembling hand in his, which was surprisingly warm and steady. "Still a little… shaken—which is stupid considering you're the one who should be shook up, not me. I'm still having a hard time believing your own brother could actually stand there and tell everyone and their mother's brother that you were raped. It's–it's… horrific."

"To be honest, I'm surprised he hasn't blabbed about it before tonight. I've seen him that drunk a few other times. Trust me, it's never pretty." Still holding her hand, he laced his fingers though hers—a gesture as intimate as it was soothing.

"I can't imagine it would be." And that wasn't the only thing she couldn't imagine. His reaction to the night's events still mystified her. "You said you were glad it happened the way it did. I don't get that."

"You know how much you dread having everyone discover your deepest, darkest secret?"

"Not sure I have any, but yeah, I know what you mean."

"I don't have to think about it anymore. It's out in the open—sort of like a homosexual coming out of the closet."

She arched a brow. "Are you trying to tell me something?"

He laughed. "I'm not gay, if that's what you mean. It's hard to explain, but I feel… free." After a pause, he added, "Maybe Nick will be free too—and maybe he'll stop trying to run my life."

"Let's hope so," she said with fervor. "I hate it when people tell me what to do—like I'm six years old and haven't got the sense God gave a goose."

A wry smile touched his lips as he raised her hand to kiss it. "I can't imagine anyone telling you what to do."

"Trust me, it happens—in fact, you should be telling me what to do right now, instead of standing out here in the cold without a coat." Popping open the trunk, she retrieved his present, then slammed the lid shut. "Let's get inside where it's warm."

The fire in the woodstove had burned down to embers in his absence, but Robin added more wood and got it going again. Leslie settled on the couch near the stove, surrounded by warmth and contentment.

I could get used to this.

Nevertheless, she studied him closely as he took a seat beside her. "Are you sure you're okay? Do you want to talk more about what happened?"

"Not really," he replied. "At least, not yet. I think I need some time to... I don't know… distance myself from it a little."

"Put it in the proper perspective, you mean?"

"Something like that. It's too raw right now. At the moment, I feel okay, but that might change. I'd like to just leave it be for a while. You and I are both facing some serious shit—your future and my past. All we can do now is drive ourselves crazy worrying about it. What you said about needing some quality time in the Jacuzzi was spot on."

"A diversion?"

"Yeah." He nodded toward the present in her lap. "I hope what you've got in that box is one helluva diversion."

"I believe it is." She handed him the package. "Happy Birthday, sweetie."

His troubles seemingly forgotten, he tore off the wrapping paper with all the excitement of a child on Christmas morning and lifted the lid. "Holy shit. What *is* all this stuff?"

"It's sort of a BDSM beginner's kit. The store-bought one didn't have much in it—just some restraints and a blindfold. It's there in the bottom of the box. I added the other things."

"You've obviously given this some thought." He held up a

black leather dog collar, complete with studs and a matching leash. "Where on earth did you find this?"

She rolled her eyes. "The pet shop? Trust me, they come in all sizes."

He laughed. "I thought they might have come from an adult toy store."

"Nope, they're the real thing. Now this," she said with a trace of guilt as she held up a long piece of flat, rubber tubing, "I 'borrowed' from the hospital."

"What is it?"

"It's a Penrose drain. They're used in surgery, but they also make great tourniquets for starting IVs. I was thinking I could wrap it around your dick—you know, to make it harder?"

"Like I need *that*," he said with a snort. "I'm already hard enough to drive nails."

And I'm already wet enough for your nail to slide right in.

"I know that," she said. "It's just a bondage thing. I wasn't sure about that one, actually."

"I dunno. I think I like the idea." He held up a braided leather quirt. "Ooh, now this is *really* kinky. Don't tell me you got that at an adult toy store."

"Nope. I found it in the tack shop at the farm bureau co-op. It's a western style whip—the kind you'd use on a horse."

He slapped it on his palm. "Damn. You could raise welts with this thing."

"That's why I got this other one." She pulled out another whip that looked like a horse's tail on a stick. "It's actually intended to brush the flies off of your horse." She gave it a swish. "See? It's made of horsehair, so it'll tickle rather than hurt. I could blindfold you and tie you to the bed and then tease you with it."

"Sounds *fabulous*—but you did pretty well using your lips the last time."

She gave him a wink. "You liked that, did you?"

"Oh, yeah. You can do it again *anytime*." He pulled out a length of silky black cord with a tassel on the end. "And this?"

"You seemed to like having that string tied around your balls. This is a fancier version. The tassel will hang down between your legs."

He nodded his approval. "*Very* kinky. And this is the one you bought from the adult toy shop?" He held up the "official" bondage kit.

"Yes, but after I got it home, I decided it was kinda cheesy and cheap, so I got the other stuff. I don't think those restraints will hold you—not the way you were pulling on them the last time. I'm thinking of ordering some better ones to give you for Christmas." She stole a glance at him. "So... do you like it?"

He gave her a swift kiss on the cheek. "Absolutely. In fact, it's the best present I ever got in my life—especially since it's from you."

"You're such a sweetie." She ruffled his hair. "Want to try some of it tonight?"

"Hmm... Maybe the collar and leash. I could be your slave boy that you're taking to the Jacuzzi for a bath—and his weekly spanking."

A thrill shot through her, delaying the intake of her next breath by at least ten seconds.

Robin must've noticed, for he pounced on her, grinning from ear to ear. "You're starting to like this stuff, aren't you?"

She cleared her throat with an effort. "I don't think I'd want to do it with anyone else—but I just got this mental picture of you—"

"Doing what?"

"Standing in the Jacuzzi wearing the collar and bending over so I could smack your buns." Her words came out in a rush and she sucked in a breath. "*Very* sexy."

"You'll probably need to bring the whip. I might get... unruly." He waggled his brow. "Might even try to fuck my mistress."

"You're a bad, bad boy," she admonished. "Keep that shit up and you might get more than twenty-eight licks."

"That's the idea." Robin was already irresistible, but his cocky smirk had Leslie creaming her jeans. "So... should I strip now or do you want to do it?"

Her throat tightened as a surge of something—lust, desire, need—ripped through her. She couldn't pinpoint the moment when kinky sex had begun to appeal to her—although it could have been that that sex of any kind with Robin was appealing. "How about if I put your collar on and then undress you?"

"Sounds *fabulous*."

Robin quivered with excitement as she buckled the collar around his neck.

Not too loose, not too tight.

Her core, on the other hand, tightened rather painfully. Gulping in a breath, she did her best to regain control—of herself as well as the situation. If anyone had told her three weeks ago that she'd practically have an orgasm from putting a collar on a man she was about to spank, she'd have had them committed.

But then, three weeks ago, she hadn't met Robin.

Snapping on the leash, she pulled him to his feet.

"C'mon, slave boy. It's time for your bath."

Chapter 28

Robin's main concern as Leslie led him into the bathroom was how soon he would be released from the confines of his jeans. If he had to keep them on much longer, his dick would develop a permanent kink.

"Go turn on the water, and then come back down here," she instructed. "I need to get you out of those clothes."

Thank God.

When he returned, she tied his leash to the towel rack. The surge of blood to his groin pushed him near the screaming point.

My dick will never be the same.

With excruciating slowness, she unbuttoned his shirt. "Have you been a good boy today?"

He gulped in a breath as she peeled his shirt off over his shoulders.

Skimming her palms down to his waist, she had his belt buckle undone in seconds. "Tell the truth, now."

"I've been bad," he said. "I hit my brother."

"And why did you do that?" Unzipping his fly, she let his jeans fall to his knees, then slid her hands into his briefs and pushed them down. Released at last, his cock sprang up in an instantaneous salute.

"He said some very bad things about you. He deserved it."

"Hmm... That makes it difficult to determine your punishment." Her voice had taken on a seductive yet authoritative tone that was driving him completely insane. "Is there anything else you should be punished for?"

His cock was already drooling as she knelt down to untie his shoes. It was right there in front of her face, but she didn't lick it or touch it at all. He racked his brain, trying to come up with something else he'd done that might require punishment. He couldn't think of a single thing—unless he invented some sort of infraction, which was a punishable deed in and of itself.

When in doubt, tell the truth.

"No, ma'am."

"Good boy." She patted his thigh before removing his shoes and socks. "I have the best, most handsome slave boy in the world."

Stepping out of his pants left him entirely naked except for the collar and leash—perhaps the most erotic experience of his life. But then, every encounter with Leslie was better than the one before. "Thank you, ma'am."

On her knees right in front of him, she shuddered as she gazed upward. A droplet of fluid welled up from his painfully engorged cock and began to fall.

She caught it on her tongue. "Keep it coming."

His cock pulsed of its own accord, giving her another sip.

"More."

Leaning closer, she allowed his penis to slip past her lips into the hot recesses of her mouth. Her tongue massaged the underside, ratcheting the tension up yet another notch. A few seconds more, and he would come in her mouth.

An instant before he reached the point of no return, she backed off. "You have the most delectable cock I've ever had the honor and privilege of sucking. So good... so big... so fucking awesome..." She pulled the leash loose from the towel rack and used it to bring him to his knees. "Lie down on your side."

The marble floor was cold, but he voiced no complaints. Arching his back, he squeezed his thighs together, forcing his balls forward. His cock was sticking straight out, but she went for his nuts, licking the skin until his scrotum was completely wet. Her sharp inhale was his only warning as she sucked a testicle into her mouth. His cock rested against her shoulder, drooling on her sweater.

She didn't seem to mind a soppy sweater any more than he minded the cold floor—especially when she reached up to stroke his dick. Rotating her palm over the slick head, she slid her hand down the shaft to the base. "Fuck my hand."

His penis seemed to have a will of its own, thrusting against her slick, grasping fingers. She sucked his other ball into her mouth, gliding the underside of her tongue over it.

A deep groan escaped him as his reflexes took over.

The first spurt of semen shot between her fingers, and she cupped her hand around his cockhead, catching the rest as she drove her face further into his groin. Her low moan reverberated through his entire body, prolonging his climax until he was sure every last drop of cum had been squeezed from his balls.

Releasing him, she sat up and ran her cum-slick hand the full length of his dick and back again. Her fingers circled his sensitive flesh, and he quivered as she scraped the semen from his skin.

Using the leash, she pulled his head toward her lap, then held her hand to his lips. "You did very well and deserve a reward."

"Thank you, ma'am." Robin barely had enough breath left to speak.

"Don't swallow it yet," she said as he licked the cum from her fingers. "Kiss me first."

Rising up to meet her lips, he surrendered completely, allowing her tongue to invade his mouth. He should've been sated, but with her kiss, renewed passion curled in his belly.

"You're such a good boy," she murmured. "What other reward would you enjoy?"

"You're too kind, ma'am," he protested. "I don't deserve anything more." He gazed into the depths of her eyes, knowing she knew perfectly well what he wanted.

"But *I* say you do." Her eyes narrowed with suspicion. "Are you disagreeing with me?"

He nodded vigorously. "I believe I am. You should whip me for that."

"Perhaps I should... or perhaps not. We'll see. At the moment, it's time for your bath."

He'd forgotten that the water was still running. Fortunately, it hadn't run over the side.

That would've given her a terrific reason to paddle my ass.

"You may undress me," she said in a lofty tone, "so that I may join you in the bath."

"Shall I bathe you?"

Leslie caught herself before giggling like a school girl. The formal speech patterns they'd adopted were unnatural to the point of being downright comical.

A glance at Robin proved he'd also seen the humor. His lips twitched.

"Why are you smiling like that?" Although she did her best to sound severe, she'd completely lost her grip on the role she was playing. When she dissolved into helpless laughter, he laughed right along with her, earning him a slap on the butt.

"Quiet!" She might've been shouting at him, but she still couldn't keep a straight face. "Oh, what the hell... Just take off my damn clothes and get your cute little ass in the tub."

"Yes, ma'am," he said, still chuckling. "Are you gonna whip me for laughing at you?"

"I should," she snapped. "You disrespectful little brat."

He pulled her sweater off over her head. "Mmm... Let's have a look at those fabulous tits."

"Go for it, babe. They're all yours." The parts that weren't cancerous, anyway. She shoved the thought aside like an annoying earworm. Unfortunately, like most earworms, it refused to be squelched.

Another month and I'll know.

Robin unhooked her bra and let her breasts spill into his hands. Leaning down, he took a nipple into his mouth. "I love sucking your tits—probably as much as you like sucking my dick."

Would he still love them when there was only one? She hoped she would never be faced with the need to know the answer to that question, but she couldn't get it out of her head.

She needed a distraction, and she needed it *now.*

"That's saying a lot," she said. "How about taking off the rest of my clothes before I get mad and paddle your furry little behind?"

The look he shot her was packed with raw, naked lust. "You *should* spank me, you know—I've been a very bad boy."

"Oh, I'll do it, all right. You've pissed me off now."

Stripping off the rest of her clothes, she led him to the tub, wishing she'd gotten a different kind of whip to drive him on ahead of her. The mental image alone was enough to make her forget everything but his bare buns, which were almost at eye level when he climbed the step to the tub.

You wanted a distraction, you got a distraction.

"Stop right there," she said as he started to put one foot into the foaming water. "I'll be right back."

She hurried into the other room and got the leather quirt. She would have to be very careful with it, but figured she could gauge the strength of her lashes by his reaction.

Robin's eyes widened when he spotted the whip.

"Bend over, slave boy. Your punishment is about to begin." As he complied with her instructions, she swung the whip gently, making the slightest contact with his bare skin. "Harder, softer, or just right?"

"Harder," he replied. "I want it harder."

She hit him with a little more force the next time, but it still wasn't enough for him.

"Harder, please."

She knew it had to sting, but it still didn't satisfy him.

"More, please," he begged. "Whip my ass. Make it hurt, just a little more."

She was already hitting him hard enough to leave a red mark, but she stepped up the intensity a notch.

He was right—she *was* getting into it. She'd been wet before, but was nearing the Niagara Falls level now—her pussy juice soaking her inner thighs. Still, his enjoyment was what aroused her. Causing him pain had nothing to do with it.

Despite having ejaculated only a few minutes prior, his cock was already beginning to stiffen, alleviating any doubt that he was enjoying every lash of the whip. When she swung it with a bit more force, he let out a satisfied grunt.

"Yes. Just like that."

Not planning to go beyond the requisite twenty-eight, Leslie had actually been counting the strokes. None of that mattered now. She had every intention of continuing until his cock fired off another round or he told her to stop.

She took care not to concentrate in one spot, but scattered the lashes over a wide area. Finally, creativity took over, prompting her to leave the mark of Zorro on his ass.

His entire butt was pink before he spoke again, his voice tight and strained. "Leslie... I'm gonna blow."

All thoughts of breast cancer and dying before her time had fled, replaced with a need for him that shook her to the core. "Come in my mouth."

Spinning toward her, he aimed his engorged cock at her face. She pressed her lips to his slit and reached behind him, spanking him with her hand until warm, tangy semen spewed from his cock. Part of it she swallowed; the rest ran down her cheek.

Speechless and panting, she collapsed on the step. "Well, I'm impressed," she declared after catching her breath. "Not only can you ejaculate from being whipped, but you can do it right after a hand job."

Robin sat perched on the edge of the tub, his laughter almost as breathless as her speech had been. "My claim to fame—or yours. Having my beautiful, sexy, naked Leslie flailing me with a horse whip has more to do with the outcome than you might think."

"Sweet talker. It's not often I hear sexy and beautiful and my name used in the same sentence."

"Then I should say it more, because it's true. You make me feel like no one else ever has." His eyelids drifted downward, shuttering the heat of his gaze. "And you have no idea how fabulously wild you look standing there with that whip in your hand."

Actually, she did. Robin might not have noticed their reflection in the huge mirror opposite the whirlpool, but she certainly had. Tangled blonde locks trailed over her face and her nipples stood out from her breasts like the nipple on a baby bottle.

"You look pretty wild yourself—I mean, anyone who requires a collar, leash, and a whip must be untamable." She nodded toward the tub. "Think your sore buns can stand water that hot?"

"They can if you'll wash them for me." His lip curled suggestively. "I haven't had my bath yet."

"You're right. And now that you've been whipped into submission, I suppose it's safe to get naked in a hot tub with you."

Rising from the step, she turned toward him and cupped his balls in her hand. She kissed his cock, which was only medium hard by that time. In its softened state, she discovered she could actually get the whole thing in her mouth at one time. When she swallowed, Robin yelped like she'd bitten him.

"Holy shit," he gasped. "It feels like you're pulling it out by the roots."

She slid her tongue all over the underside of his shaft before reluctantly letting go of him. "Sorry. Didn't mean to hurt you, but it sure felt good on my end."

"It didn't actually hurt—it was more of a surprise than anything." He shuddered slightly. "Damn. I'd better get hard again and fuck you before you eat me alive."

"You'll get no arguments from me." Her pussy ached with more need than ever before—and she had no one but herself to blame for the softness of his cock. "Come on—let's wash that sweet little bod of yours. Once it's clean and dry, I'm going to cover you with massage oil and give you the most sensual birthday treat of your life."

"Sounds fabulous."

Picking up the leash, she pulled him away from the tub.

Time to play dominatrix again.

"Let me get in first, slave boy." She climbed into the tub, giving him a good view of her ass as she swung her leg over the side. The hot, foaming water made the rest of her body feel as wild and sexy as the more erogenous zones. Her breasts bobbed toward the surface as she settled into the seat on the opposite side and tugged on the leash. "Hurry up. Your mistress is waiting for you. You've been lying on the floor naked. You're dirty and need to be washed."

"Yes, ma'am." His cocky smirk displayed his appreciation for her attitude.

If only I can keep a straight face.

"When you're all clean and oiled, I might allow you to fuck me," she said. "Would you like that?"

He nodded. "Yes, ma'am, I would."

"You may wash me first." She handed him the soap. "I'll do you afterward." She left what else she intended to do unsaid, but massaging his soapy cock and balls was sure to be in there somewhere.

"Yes, ma'am. May I begin?"

With a nod, Leslie drifted back in the water, closing her eyes as Robin's warm hands spread creamy lather all over her body. While she floated in a sensual haze, he teased her nipples to a fever pitch before moving down her abdomen to her legs. Her entire body felt caressed, cherished, desired, and loved. Turning her over, he eased her upper body over the side as he pulled her bottom up out of the water. His strong fingers massaged her skin, then delved into the cleft to tease her anus.

His other hand found her clitoris. Sliding his warm fingertips over the lubricated nub was reminiscent of what he'd done the night he'd used the anal plug, only much, much better. With no penetration whatsoever, he had her cross-eyed and moaning in no time at all. Her breasts were suspended just beneath the foam, the jets of water teasing her nipples to peak sensitivity. If she didn't climax soon, she would go completely insane.

Robin's touch was slow and deliberate, yet delicate. As he slipped his thumb inside her, the groan she heard came not from her own throat but from his.

"Does that feel good, Leslie? Do you like what I'm doing to you?"

Her affirmative reply was scarcely more than a whimper.

"I love making you come even more than I love watching you suck my dick. You turn me on so hard, I can't help but want to fuck you. I want my cock inside you, fucking you over and over, pumping in and out of your sweet, wet pussy." He paused for a moment, swirling his fingertips over her anus. "You like it when I talk that way, don't you?"

A nod was the only response she was capable of as he began to massage her G-spot with the pad of his thumb. A moment later, the speed of his feathery touches on her anus and clitoris increased, pushing her closer to paradise.

After scattering kisses everywhere his mouth could reach, he raised his head, his intense gaze locking with hers in the mirror. "I love doing you, looking at you, feeling you, and tasting you. You drive me fucking *wild*."

Her mouth dropped open as his head dipped again, his mirrored image alerting her to his next move. His hot tongue teased her tailbone before embarking on a slow downward journey.

The tip of his tongue had almost reached her anus when she went soaring into orgasm. Gripping the edge of the tub, she cried out in ecstasy—a cry that became a scream as he pulled her down into the water and into his arms. The heat on her engorged clitoris triggered even more uncontrollable paroxysms, and she turned toward him, clutching at his neck, hanging on for dear life.

She lay in his embrace for what seemed like hours before her mind finally reset itself. Her body took longer to recover, and she was still enmeshed in the lingering lassitude of her climax when he lowered his head for a kiss.

But not just any kiss.

Spearing his fingers through her hair, he devoured her mouth. His tongue fought a battle with hers and won, and his teeth nipped the fullness of her lower lip. Thrill after thrill spiraled through her until, at last, he broke the kiss. His hands framed her face as he gazed down at her with eyes grown soft, the water's turbulence the only disruption of the stillness.

"But above all that," he whispered. "I love *you*."

Chapter 29

"I love you too." Leslie's gaze was as loving as her smile, and no caress could've been sweeter than the touch of her fingertips on his cheek. "It scares me how much."

"I know what you mean," Robin said. "I feel the same way." He'd never loved anyone like this before. The possibility of losing her was terrifying—a prospect he was determined not to have to face.

Not for another thirty years or so, anyway.

She shook her head as though trying to rid herself of a pesky insect. "We shouldn't let it frighten us. Not when we should be celebrating." She glanced at the clock. "We have about an hour of your birthday left. We shouldn't waste it." Sitting up, she reached for the soap. "Close your eyes, babe. It's your turn to relax and enjoy."

She might have been talking about his birthday, but he knew she was thinking the same thing he was—that their time together might be much shorter than either of them wished. Moments ago, she'd spanked those thoughts from his mind, but they were difficult to keep at bay.

With a past as rocky as his had been, Robin had always believed that the best was yet to come. He'd never recognized the fact that the present moment was all anyone could count on, and that this moment *was* the best. Nothing that came before or after could surpass its perfection.

I'm in a hot tub with Leslie, and her soapy hands are all over me.

He leaned back, stretching his arms out along the edge of the tub. A sigh escaped him as his muscles relaxed—a function of the foaming water and Leslie's hands. His penis was flaccid at first, but as she came closer to it in her efforts to bathe him, it stiffened as though begging for her touch. She seemed to be ignoring it—perhaps wanting to give it a rest so he could fuck her later on.

Taking his hand, she pulled him forward, getting behind him to soap and massage his back. The buoyancy of the water enabled him to sit in her lap, and she slid the bar of soap down over his butt.

Time to put at least some of that past to rest.

Surging forward, he grasped the opposite edge of the tub, allowing his body to float on the surface. His outstretched legs floated on either side of her.

She took the hint and lathered up his buttocks before progressing to a deep massage.

As she moved down to wash his legs, he murmured, "You missed a spot."

"Impossible," she protested. "I've covered every inch of you."

"You didn't do my butt crack. I'm sure it needs washing."

"I doubt it. With all the time you've been soaking in this tub, there couldn't possibly be a speck of dirt or a single germ left anywhere on your entire body, let alone your ass. Besides, I didn't think you liked anyone touching you there."

"I've, um, changed my mind."

A glance over his shoulder revealed her arched brow. "You aren't expecting me to use my tongue, are you?"

"No. Your fingers will be fine." He sighed. "I shouldn't have stopped you the last time. You wouldn't have hurt me."

"This from a guy whose ass I just whipped until it glowed." With a quiet chuckle, she slid the soap between his cheeks, seeming hesitant to delve too deeply.

"That's different. I still should have trusted you."

"I dunno… You let me suck your balls. I'd say that takes a fair amount of trust."

It was his turn to laugh. "I hadn't thought of that, but you're right. That isn't something I'd trust just anyone to do." He drew his knees up under him, spreading his cheeks apart. "Go ahead, Leslie. Finish what you started."

"You're sure?"

"Absolutely. Go for it."

She lathered up her hands and soaped him from the top of his crack clear down to his balls, spending a fair amount of time at the most sensitive spot along the way.

Only then did he realize he hadn't known what he was talking about when he'd told her how good it would feel. Her gentle touch erased the memories of pain and humiliation, eliciting only pleasure. He let out a moan.

"Okay?"

He nodded. "More than okay. It's hard to believe, but that feels fabulous."

She smacked him on the butt. "You seemed pretty darn sure I'd like it when you talked me into it, bucko. How on earth would you know if no one's ever done it to you?"

"Hearsay," he admitted. "That girl I bought that anal plug for was really into the anal stuff. Would you believe she actually asked me to lick her asshole?"

"You came damn close to licking mine a while ago—which I will *not* do for you, by the way." She hesitated. "So did you?"

Yet another confession he was reluctant to make. "Yeah. I did everything she wanted me to do. Too bad she wouldn't return the favor."

"You astonish me," she drawled. "But I can't say I'm sorry. I mean, if she'd done the stuff you liked, I wouldn't be here."

"True." He probably could've left it at that, but there was another issue that needed to be brought out into the open—one that had made a much more lasting impression. He turned to face her. "Before you ask, that episode with my mother's boyfriend... If I remember correctly, I was seven years old at the time."

The soap hit the water with a splash. "That son of a bitch should've been taken out and shot—no blindfold, no last meal, no making peace with God or anyone else. Just a bullet to send him to hell. No one should be allowed to live after doing such a thing to a child—of *any* age. No one."

Her ferocity surprised him—although it shouldn't have. If Gabriel had been raped, he had no doubt that Leslie would've killed the bastard with her bare hands. His own mother hadn't known anything about it—and might not have cared if she had.

That's unfair.

She'd broken up with the creep after that.

Perhaps she *had* known, and that was why she ditched him. Robin might never know the truth—unless Nick or Laura knew something he didn't.

Funny how Laura hadn't said a word after Nick's outburst. She'd seemed as shocked any of the others. But Nick knew things even Robin had forgotten. He probably knew about that, too.

Sooner or later, the two of them would have to talk about it. But not now. Leslie hadn't finished yet.

"No wonder Nick feels guilty," she snapped. "How anyone could stand by and let that happen is beyond me." She looked him right in the eye. "You heard what he said. He was *there*. He might not have been an eyewitness, but he was close enough to hear you scream. Close enough to intervene—or at least call the police."

He nodded. "That explains a lot. Seems like he's been trying to correct that mistake ever since—and he hasn't done a very good job of it."

She blew out a derisive snort. "No shit—especially not today. I can't imagine how he'll ever be able to face either of us again—or anyone else who was there, for that matter."

"If he remembers it." Robin had never been one to use alcohol to wipe out a memory, but he suspected his brother did—or at least tried to.

"You think he won't?"

"No, he probably will," he said after a moment's reflection. "I've seen him worse off than that. We should rub his nose in it for a while, though."

"I'm game. Any ideas?"

He paused as a truly diabolical plan began to take shape in his mind. "Did you say you were off on Christmas Day?"

"Yeah. I work seven to seven Christmas Eve, but I'm off Christmas Day. Why?"

"I think we should have Christmas dinner at *my* house this year. We could decorate the hell out of this place and put up a humongous tree—a *real* one—and you could fix dinner. You're a damn sight better cook than Trish or Laura—your Thanksgiving leftovers were better than anything I've had in a long time. *That* would teach him."

"I'm not sure I understand," she said with a bemused frown. "How would that change anything?"

"Trust me, he'll get the message." *Loud and clear.*

"What about Gabe?"

"He can come too," Robin said. "The two of you could spend the night here on Christmas Eve—that is, if he wouldn't mind. I've got two extra bedrooms that no one ever sleeps in."

"I'll ask him." She still seemed cautious, but the more Robin thought about it, the better he liked the idea. "A real tree, huh?"

"Oh, yeah. We could even take a drive out to one of the tree farms and cut it ourselves if we can't find what we want here in town."

Her eyes lit up. "That sounds wonderful. Gabe and I haven't had a real tree since before my father died."

"I've never had a tree of any kind." He had her hooked on the idea. Now all he had to do was reel her in.

"Yeah. Gabe couldn't believe it when I told him that." She hesitated, chewing her lower lip. "I could cook everything here?"

"Absolutely. Bring over every pot and pan you have—or I can buy new ones if you like."

"What about using my grandmother's china?"

He chuckled. "Beats the hell out of Teenage Mutant Ninja Turtle plates, don't you think?"

"Okay," she said with a decisive nod. "You're on."

 ₮ℛ

Since Robin didn't have so much as a single piece of tinsel to his name, he and Leslie collected his truck from Laura's house the next morning and went shopping. After some debate about decorating the huge pines that grew around his house, they decided on pre-lit wire trees for the yard, which he thought would look very nice from the highway. The tree in the house—a twelve-foot Scotch pine—would be visible through the front window.

Robin grinned wickedly as they put the finishing touches on the tree. "Nick will definitely get the point. He's always going on about how his poor little brother has no wife, no family, no Christmas tree, and has to come over to dinner at his house or be all alone and depressed during the holidays."

She gaped at him in disbelief. "You've got to be kidding."

"Oh, no," he assured her. "He tells our construction crew that every year. The guys always tell me about it afterward—it's sort of a yearly ritual. They all think it's funny, but he won't be able to say it this time. I can hardly wait to see him tomorrow. I want to see his jaw drop when I invite him and Trish over for Christmas dinner."

"You're a better man than I am, Gunga Din," she muttered. "I wouldn't blame you if you called in sick for the rest of the month."

He shot her a wink. "Demons must be faced or they'll take over your life."

"Oh, you're facing them, all right—unless this is about revenge."

"Nope. This is about asserting my independence." *At long last.*

"Glad to hear it." She hung the last icicle and heaved a sigh. "That's it for the tree. I dunno about you, but I'm beat—and you have to work tomorrow."

"When do you work this week?"

"Tuesday, Wednesday, and Thursday," she replied. "Which means I probably won't make it up this way again until Friday."

"No worries. We can do the rest of the decorating next weekend." He gave her a hug. "Wouldn't want to wear you out."

"Oh, I get it," she teased. "You just want me to save my strength for the Saturday night spanking."

He shrugged. "I won't hold you to that—unless you really want to."

"You're asking *me* that?" She took a step back and fixed an incredulous gaze on his face. "Who are you and what have you done with my Robin?"

They'd had a fabulous time in the Jacuzzi the night before, but his fondest memory of the evening was after they'd gone to bed.

Slow, easy loving.

No pain whatsoever and highly satisfying. He reminded himself that they'd pulled out all the stops on the kinky stuff earlier, but he wasn't sure that was the entire reason.

Maybe it's because we're settling into a relationship.

Long-term relationships couldn't possibly involve fireworks with every encounter. The gentler aspects of life and love would always be there to be explored and enjoyed.

"I'm your Robin, all right—but with a slightly different perspective."

"Oh?" She still seemed wary. "Does this different perspective include a place for an old broad like me?"

"Of course it does." A chilling thought struck him. If he were to grow up, would she still love him? Was his immaturity what attracted her to him? Most women had seen his childish nature as a flaw—perhaps she considered it an attribute. "I love you, Leslie. Don't ever doubt that."

She nodded as though she believed him, but the tiny crease between her brows suggested otherwise.

Demons must be faced. "What about you? Does my declaration of independence turn you off?"

"No. But I can't help wondering if you'll still need me."

"You think I've been using you as a crutch?"

"Maybe. I'm not sure." Her shoulders sagged as her voice dropped to a whisper. "I hope not."

He pulled her into his arms and pressed a kiss to her cheek. "Need has nothing to do with it. This is about want—and I want you. I'm not like Gabriel. I won't grow up and leave home. You aren't my mother. You're my lover—and probably my best friend."

A tiny smile tweaked her lips, but he could still see uncertainty in her eyes.

"I mean it," he said. "Nobody else stood up for me when Nick went off on his little rant—not like you did. You were the only one with the courage to confront him."

"Courage, hell. I was shocked and horrified."

"Of course you were. But isn't that what courage is? Being afraid and doing the right thing anyway?"

"I suppose so." Lowering her head, she closed her eyes. "I certainly didn't feel courageous at the time. Honestly, so much has happened in the past three weeks, I'm a little overwhelmed."

He didn't have to ask why she felt that way or to what she was referring. "Believe it or not, this is the longest relationship I've ever been in. I'm not going to use you up and ditch you. What we have is too important." Smiling, he raised her face to his with a finger beneath her chin. "I'm keeping you, so you'd better get used to it."

"I'll try, but my 'relationships' have been practically nonexistent. I never told you my nickname at the hospital, did I?"

"Nope." *This ought to be good.*

She grimaced. "One Date Leslie—the reason for which is self-explanatory. We're both virgins when it comes to long-term commitments. I don't want to screw this up."

"Then don't try too hard," he said. "I think—well, that's not the only reason I've failed—but it's a big one. Take that girl I was telling you about last night. I didn't want to do half the things she wanted me to. But I did all of it, hoping she would stick around. Needless to say, it didn't work."

"Seems like I'm taking the same approach with you, don't you think?"

"Not at all. You're not doing anything you aren't comfortable with. Believe me, I can tell the difference."

A tiny giggle broke the tension in her. "You mean you've brought out the latent dominatrix in me?"

"Sure have. You're a natural—which reminds me, what are your measurements?"

She arched a brow. "And *why* would you need to know that?"

"So I can order a bustier for you for Christmas."

"Oh, God. Here we go again…"

"You love it. You know you do—and don't forget you're the one who bought whips and collars for my birthday."

"One of the more shining moments in my gift-giving career, I'm sure," she drawled.

"You'll get no arguments from me on that score. I'm just returning the favor."

"Yes, but you *wanted* a collar. I'm not the bustier type."

Robin laughed so hard he nearly choked on his own spit. "I've never seen anyone who could wear one better."

"Madonna?" she suggested. "I'm not in her league."

"That's your opinion. Her tits are nothing compared to yours."

It was Leslie's turn to laugh. "I'd like to see you put that on a T-shirt."

"I would if you'd wear it."

For a moment, he thought he might've had her convinced, but she shook her head and held up a hand. "Let's hold off on either of those things for a while, shall we? Something tells me it'd be bad luck."

"There's no such thing as luck—not at this point anyway. You already have a cyst or a tumor. What I get you for Christmas isn't going to change that."

"My fate is sealed?"

"Yeah. So you might as well tell me your measurements."

"I would if I could, but I have absolutely no idea."

He gave her a wink. "Good thing I've got a tape measure."

Chapter 30

On Monday morning, Robin wished he'd had his tape measure—or a camera—handy when he met Nick at the construction site. Either way, it was a jaw drop of truly epic proportions.

"You want me to *what?*" Nick exclaimed.

"Christmas dinner is at my place this year," Robin repeated. "Are you coming or not?"

"Look, I'm sorry about what I said at your birthday party," Nick said. "I was drunk."

"No shit?" Robin scoffed. "I hadn't noticed."

"I don't blame you for being pissed, but dinner? With *Leslie* doing the cooking?"

"What do you think she's gonna do? Put arsenic in your dessert?" Not that Robin would blame her if she did—although the courts probably wouldn't consider it justifiable.

"I just think it would be… awkward."

Robin stared at his brother, not quite believing what he'd heard. "We went way past awkward a long time ago."

"I don't think—" Nick was obviously gearing up to refuse, but Robin wasn't about to let him off the hook that easily.

"I get it, okay? You're embarrassed and so am I, but it's time we faced up to that—along with a few other issues between us. I love Leslie, and her son is a great guy. I'm gonna marry her if she'll have me, but you and Laura are still my family. We want you to have Christmas dinner with us. Just don't go on a binge before you get there."

"I won't—and believe me, Trish isn't looking forward to celebrating at our house." Pausing, he looked down until the bill of his cap hid his eyes. "I think you might have some idea of what my binges are all about."

"I believe I do." Robin tried to smile, and was surprised that it came as easily as it did. "I'm not blaming you, Nick. I just wish you'd stop blaming yourself."

"It's become something of a habit. I kept thinking if I just found you a nice girl and you got married, I'd—"

"Quit feeling so guilty? You don't *need* to feel guilty. Maybe you didn't do anything to stop the abuse, but it wasn't your fault it happened. Someone else deserves that blame." He hesitated. "Mom broke up with him after that. Any idea why?"

Nick was silent for a long moment. "I wish I could say it was something I'd done, but I think Laura suspected there was a problem. I walked in on an argument between her and Mom. I'm still not sure what it was about—God knows I never asked—but he was gone after that, so I never said anything." He drew in a slow, difficult breath and finally met Robin's gaze. "How come we've never had this conversation before?"

"Because we were both too damn chicken. But I've learned something in the past few days. In the long run, it's easier to face shit head-on than it is to worry about it—or try to pretend it isn't there. This has been the barrier between us for years. But guess what, Nick? I forgive you. Now all you have to do is forgive yourself."

Robin waited for his words to sink in, hoping that for once Nick wouldn't let his temper get the better of him.

"When did you get to be so damned smart?"

Robin knew the precise moment the change in him had begun. "When I figured out Leslie was the one who bought me that drink. Meeting her changed my life—and I believe I've changed hers. Neither of us has ever been in love before. But we are now, and we're gonna stay that way."

"I hope you aren't making a mistake," Nick said.

"If I am, it's *my* mistake. But I don't believe it'll turn out that way. And even if it does—" He paused, taking a deep breath. *Now or never.* "It's none of your damn business."

ഇറ

For once in her life, Leslie actually had a date to Miranda's annual Christmas party. She even had the day off.

"Can you believe it?" Miranda's son, Levi, exclaimed when he opened the door. "It's less than two weeks until Christmas!"

There were plenty of things Leslie had trouble believing—not the least of which that Robin was there with her. The fact that Nick and Laura had actually agreed to spend Christmas Day at Robin's house was even more unbelievable. In another week, Gabriel would be home from Purdue, and he was tickled to death with the change of plans.

"I can't wait to see the tree," he'd said when Leslie called him with the news. "Twelve feet? Seriously?"

"You bet. For once, the tree will be taller than you!"

"Gee, thanks, Mom," he grumbled. "I'm not the abominable snow monster, you know."

That Gabe and Robin got along was perhaps the most amazing thing of all—although it shouldn't have come as a surprise. She loved them both; therefore, they should at least like each other a little.

If it wasn't for this damned lump, my life would be freakin' perfect.

In her mind, that level of perfection was all that was needed to assure her that the lump wasn't simply a cyst. Nothing was ever *that* perfect. Life was cyclic—good times were always followed by bad, and they were usually proportional.

"Come on, cheer up," Robin urged her as Levi took their coats. "You know... smile?"

"I *am* smiling," she insisted. "I'm happy, excited, and... You're right. I'm still waiting for the other shoe to drop."

"Live in the moment," he said. "It's all we have."

"No shit—although plenty of people are banking on the future. The unit has been incredibly busy—I can't remember ever doing so many heart caths. Guess everyone's getting their ticker fixed for the holidays."

"I think the docs scheduled them like that so they won't be bothered on Christmas," Miranda said as she approached. After giving Leslie a hug, she gave Robin a quick, appraising glance. "Yup. He's still cute."

Leslie bit back a laugh. "Did you think I would've turned him into an old geezer in a month?"

"No. Just an observation."

A quick check of Miranda's husband, Travis, proved he was still a looker. Blue eyes, dimples, sandy blond hair…

Gorgeous.

It struck her then that, like Travis, Robin would never sire any children if he stuck with her. Miranda's childbearing days had ended with a partial hysterectomy after Levi was born. Menopause had ended Leslie's, but not until recently—for all the good it had done her since she'd given birth to Gabriel. There were other similarities between the two women—they each had one child and were both older than their men—but somehow Leslie doubted that Travis liked to be spanked.

Although I could be wrong…

She and Robin each got a cup of wassail and headed out to the living room. Leslie introduced him to everyone they passed by…

Until they got to Suzie.

Robin winked and held out a hand. "We met on the phone."

"Uh huh." Suzie shook his hand, then aimed a scowl at Leslie. "Still together, I see."

"Haven't murdered her yet." Robin's grin should've made Ebenezer Scrooge smile.

Suzie, however, merely rolled her eyes. "Sorry. It was a natural assumption."

Leslie spotted Angela and nodded in her direction. "If he'd bumped me off, Angie could've told the police where to look for my body."

"What?"

One of the hazards of twelve-hour shifts was that even the work schedules of best friends didn't always coincide. Leslie hadn't seen Angela since the night of her birthday, and her blank look spoke volumes.

"Didn't you get my message telling you where I went after we left the bookstore?" Leslie asked.

Angela shook her head. "Not that I know of."

Suzie snickered. "That was your insurance? You should've called me."

"I had my reasons," Leslie muttered. She glanced at Robin. "Looks like you missed your chance at becoming a serial killer."

"Life is filled with missed opportunities." He took a sip of wassail. "Hey, this is great stuff. Think you could make some for our Christmas dinner?"

Grateful for the change of topic, Leslie nodded. "If Miranda will share her recipe. I've never made it before."

"Travis made it this year," Miranda said as she joined them. "I'm not sure what he put in it. I'm guessing rum, but I'm not sure which—"

Travis looked up from his seat on the couch and pressed a finger to his lips. "Secret ingredient."

Robin took another sip. "Captain Morgan?"

"Guess it isn't so secret after all," Travis grumbled.

Leslie introduced the two men and took a seat on the sofa against the opposite wall. Miranda's house was always so cozy and comfortable—a perfect example of a farmhouse in the country, and there certainly weren't any Norfolk pines to hide behind—not that she needed one. She doubted Robin would, either—although he had to feel as out of place as she had at Laura's house. Thankfully, no one appeared to be quite as drunk as Nick had been. Leslie's only fear was that someone would mention the lump in her breast.

Damn. I can't even get through a party without thinking about it.

She would see Dr. Edlin in two weeks. If only she could forget it until then.

Not gonna happen.

Robin settled in beside her. "Doing okay?"

"The other shoe hasn't dropped yet, if that's what you mean. Probably won't for a while."

"We'll get through this, Leslie. Stop worrying."

"Can't help it. Worrying is one of the things I do best."

At least she hadn't succumbed to another panic attack.

Two weeks.

She had Christmas to look forward to. Her first, and maybe last, Christmas with Robin.

No. The first of many.

She was actually glad they'd been busy in the unit, and she had a fairly full schedule right up until Christmas Day. Robin kept her occupied most nights, but there were times when nothing distracted her.

Like now.

"So… what do you want to do this weekend?" he asked.

"Honestly, I don't care—as long as it involves whips and chains."

"I think that can be arranged."

"Thanks." Chuckling, she took a sip of her drink. "I picked a great time to find a kinky boyfriend, didn't I?"

"Sure did." He leaned closer, his breath tickling her ear. "Wait'll you see what I got you for Christmas."

"I'm guessing it's one of those 'not safe for family' presents, huh?"

He'd taken her measurements—at least, she thought he had. Somewhere along the line they'd gotten distracted by the alternative uses for a tape measure.

"Maybe, maybe not," he said with an air of mystery. "You'll see."

"Something else to worry about?"

He shook his head. "Something to look forward to."

80C3

Leslie made it through her shift on Christmas Eve, which was relatively calm—for once.

"Better than last year," Suzie said as they clocked out. "Kinda boring, actually."

Lola, who was working the night shift, let out a groan. "You just had to say the B-word and jinx us, didn't you?"

"Glad you didn't say that when we were clocking in," Miranda said with a chuckle. "We would've been forced to murder you."

"Sorry, Lola," Suzie said. "I figured it was safe now."

Leslie certainly hadn't been bored. She'd been kept busy, not by her patients, but by Robin and Gabriel. She'd sent them to the grocery with a list of last-minute items, and they'd called her at least four times. Since Leslie rarely received personal phone calls during her shift, she'd had to endure plenty of ribbing. Calls for respiratory treatments in the ER had kept Angela hopping, so she'd missed most of them, but since the other two filled her in on her return, the teasing didn't stop for long.

No one said anything about the lump, but Leslie suspected the teasing was intended to take her mind off it.

My friends know me all too well…

By the time she got to her car, she was in no mood to do anything but suck Robin's dick dry and go to sleep. Unfortunately, she had to make a pumpkin pie and a chocolate cheesecake. Robin had wanted her to make the best desserts possible, and since the mere mention of chocolate cheesecake made Gabe dreamy-eyed, she'd offered to make it. Pumpkin pie was a cinch, but the cheesecake required more effort.

She arrived at Robin's house only to find her son and her boyfriend, having done all the Christmas preparations they intended to do, engaged in a rousing game of Super Smash Brothers Melee down in the basement. She kissed them both and went back to the kitchen and got to work, only then realizing that with two ovens, she could actually bake both desserts at the same time.

Thank God…

After that, she took a shower and went to bed, knowing she needed to get an early start the next morning. The turkey they'd bought was the biggest bird she'd ever baked, and as such, was bound to take forever to cook.

Her exhausted body was willing, but her brain wouldn't cooperate. Despite having brought half the contents of her kitchen over to Robin's house for the event, she was sure she'd forgotten something. About the only thing that would've shut her brain up was sucking Robin's dick, but since the guys were still down in the basement playing video games, she doubted she would get any cocksucking done.

She drifted off at last, but she couldn't have been asleep for more than a few minutes when she was awakened by the smell of a freshly struck match. Candlelight gleamed from the nightstand as she felt the mattress dip behind her. Rolling over, she bumped into Robin's fully erect penis.

"Merry Christmas, Leslie."

She gave his cock a kiss. "Merry Christmas to you too, sweetie."

He chuckled. "Ever wonder why the British say 'Happy Christmas' instead of 'Merry Christmas' the way we do?"

She scowled up at him. "You woke me up for trivia questions? Here I thought you just wanted your cock sucked." She gave his dick another kiss and lay back on the pillow. "No, Robin. I can honestly say I've never wondered about that."

"They say *happy* because they actually know what it means to make merry—or what it used to mean anyway."

"And that would be...?"

"To have sex," he replied. "You know...'Eat, drink and be merry, for tomorrow we may die,' or however that saying goes. Think about it. If you were a soldier and knew you'd probably die in battle the next day, what would you want to do? Dance around the campfire with the other men? Nope, you'd want to eat a feast, get roaring drunk, and then fuck some slutty little wench senseless before you died."

"Possibly," she conceded. "But you'll have to admit, that's about as obscure as the origin of kissing you were telling me about. I doubt it's in the dictionary that way. Where do you get this stuff?"

"I don't know—TV probably. Makes sense, though, doesn't it?"

"Maybe. I just wish you'd come in here a little sooner. I have to get up early to get that bird in the oven."

"Sorry. Gabe and I were having a blast. He's a great guy."

"Yes, he is," she agreed, warming to the subject. "He's been my best buddy for a long time." She paused, frowning. "Wait a minute. You're trying to butter me up, aren't you?"

He chuckled. "That's another one I've thought about. I don't know if it's true or not, but I believe the expression to 'butter you up' refers to anal sex. Back in the old days, they used butter as the lubricant—so, if you were buttering someone up, it meant you were gonna fuck 'em in the ass."

"I'll never be able to keep a straight face when someone says that again, whether it's true or not. You're just a fountain of obscure knowledge, aren't you?"

He shrugged. "Or a cesspool of useless information."

"You *do* seem to remember the oddest things."

"Yeah." He trailed his fingertips over her hip. "Like how you can't resist my dick—especially when it's drooling all over your face."

Leslie's response was more of a choke than a nod.

"Or that, either—you slutty little wench. You like it when I talk dirty, don't you?"

"That's no sluttier than getting off from being spanked," she countered. "Speaking of which, I should smack your hairy little ass for not coming to bed sooner."

He flipped over onto his hands and knees with his butt aimed right at her. "Go for it."

"No can do. It's not Saturday."

"Picky, picky, picky. Just smack me a few times and then I'll fuck your brains out—unless you want to suck me first."

"Wouldn't want to miss out on the best part."

He wiggled his butt. "If you slap my ass, my dick will really be hard and juicy for you."

"Will you please keep your voice down?" she hissed. "I don't want my son to hear any of this."

"He's still in the basement—at least he was ten minutes ago." Tossing a devilish grin over his shoulder, he waggled his eyebrows. "Just don't scream and he won't hear anything."

"I'll try to contain my enthusiasm," she drawled.

"No need for that. Just be *quietly* enthusiastic."

Sitting up, she pulled off her nightgown and gave him a slap hard enough to make her palm sting.

"Hurt your hand, didn't you?" he teased. "That'll teach you."

"You forget, there's a whip around here somewhere, and I know how to use it."

"Promises, promises…"

Deciding to forgo the whip, she opted for a different style, ending each smack with a squeeze of his buns. He might not have liked it as well, but she certainly enjoyed it more. After a few squeezes, she slid her hand down to fondle his balls, then reached further to wrap her fingers around his cock.

Huge, hot, and dripping wet.

"Put that succulent dick in my mouth, slave boy."

Robin rolled onto his back and pushed her face down on his cock. "Suck my fuckin' dick, you slutty wench."

She opened her mouth and he thrust inside, fucking her lips while intoxicating her with his salty slickness. In a few short weeks, Robin had learned exactly which buttons to push. She was so wet, she could've played slutty wench to an entire company of soldiers without even bothering to break for tea.

She kept it up until her pussy ached for his attention. Pulling away, she mounted him backward, using all of her weight to drive him home. Although stretched to the point of pain, it was a good kind of hurt—one she couldn't get enough of. Robin thrust up into her like a piston, hard and fast, and she climaxed with a bang, clapping a hand over her mouth to keep from screaming.

Leslie's orgasm was Robin's cue. Rolling her onto her back, he dove into her with renewed vigor, pushing her into the yielding foam mattress with a deep, steady rhythm that had her groaning with each thrust. Totally helpless against the onslaught of his passion, she lay with her feet in the air and her arms sprawled out on the sheets above her head—the most beautiful and seductive sight imaginable.

Sweat beaded up on his face and dripped from the tips of his hair and onto her chest. His rhythm became more erratic as he edged closer to his own climax. Fucking her savagely, he grunted with the effort as he drove into her with all his strength.

Moments later, her slick inner muscles gripped him like a vise. With a gasp, he lurched forward, pushing down on the back of her legs as he shot his seed into her with a force she could probably feel.

He lay over her, sucking in great gulps of air until he realized her legs had to be popping out of their sockets. Rising up, he lifted her into his arms and kissed her wildly, invading her mouth with his tongue while devouring her lips with his own.

"I love you," he whispered between desperate kisses. "So much... so very, very much. I can't live without you now. I wasn't even alive before, but I am now, and I *like* being alive."

"So do I." Her voice was barely a breath. "You've done the same for me. I'll do my best to be here with you... always."

Reaching for the box on the nightstand, he opened it. "I can't wait until morning. I have to give you this now."

She stared at the diamond, flashing fire from the candle he'd lit.

He didn't even have to ask. She held up her hand, and he slipped the ring on her finger.

Chapter 31

Leslie eyes flew open.

Gotta get that bird in the oven.

She lay there, blinking in the darkness. She'd gone to bed early. Had she dreamed what came after?

Of course she had. Men didn't give engagement rings to women after only knowing them for a month.

Maybe it wasn't an engagement ring. Maybe it was just a pre-engagement or a friendship ring.

A quick check of her fingers proved it was on her left hand and the stone was way too big to be anything but the real McCoy. Robin hadn't asked her to marry him—not in so many words—but the implication was clear. They were engaged.

I'm fifty years old, and I'm engaged to marry a man of twenty-eight.

Fixing Christmas dinner for Robin's family was nothing compared to that. She'd been nervous enough before. Now, she had a diamond to flash around. She toyed briefly with taking it off, but dismissed the idea as not only cowardly, but inconsiderate. Robin's feelings would be hurt if she didn't wear it.

What on earth would Gabe say?

He and Robin obviously got along well, but was that enough?

The things Nick had said at Robin's birthday party still haunted her—especially the part about Robin only liking her because she had big boobs and was old enough to be his mother. Nick may have promised to be on his best behavior, but the thought of another scene like that—in front of Gabriel, no less—made her want to hide the rum, or at least leave it out of the wassail. Robin might notice the omission, but she was fairly certain he'd understand why she'd done it.

Robin... His breathing was deep and even, proving he was still asleep. She glanced at the clock.

Seven fifteen. No need to wake him yet.

She eased out of bed and headed for the kitchen. Unwrapping the turkey, she dug out the giblets and put them in a pan of water to boil for broth. Chopping onions and celery for the stuffing was strange with the diamond sparkling on her finger. She tried not to look at it as she sautéed the vegetables in what always seemed like an inordinate amount of butter.

She went on with the preparations—mixing the stuffing, packing it into the turkey—a ritual she'd performed on so many holidays in the past. She tried to recall the first time and couldn't—it was too long ago to remember whether she'd done it at her parents' home, her grandmother's, or her apartment. One thing was certain— she'd never done anything of the kind at Robin's house.

Was this the first and last time?

The ring on her finger seemed to chastise her for allowing such thoughts to exist. The sparkling facets spoke of life, love, and joy— and of many wonderful Christmases yet to come. Christmases with Gabriel and his wife and children—her grandchildren. So much living left to do. So many gifts left to give...

She'd had a sweatshirt made for Gabe that said "IU Sucks Big Hairy Donkey Balls" in big, bold letters, the donkey balls reference being a popular expression among Gabriel and his friends. Figuring that the local shops would have flatly refused to make it, she'd ordered it online—long before she and Robin had even met. Now she had a house full of IU fans to consider—although if Robin could wear a "PUCK FURDUE" T-shirt, she didn't think he had any room to talk.

Robin's present was comparatively tame—certainly nothing like the one he'd given her the night before. An engagement ring was a tough act to follow for any woman, but knowing that his family would be there, she'd opted against the kinky stuff. Instead, she'd purchased a set of hunter green ceramic mugs that matched the décor of his home—if not his other glassware.

The turkey was already in the oven, and she was putting together a green bean casserole when Robin came into the kitchen. Sidling up behind her, he put his arms around her waist and gave her a squeeze. "Merry Christmas, Leslie."

His breath on her neck set off a wave of tingles, and his kiss drew a sigh. "Merry Christmas, sweetie. Did you sleep well?"

"Like a rock," he replied. "You should've gotten me up sooner. I could've helped you with the turkey."

"Thanks, but I kinda like going one on one with the bird." She put the lid on the casserole. "I'm caught up for now. Want some breakfast?"

"Sure, whatcha got?"

"The usual—bacon, eggs, and toast—although I suppose I could make French toast or something equally festive if you like."

"Nah, eggs will be fine," he said "No point in eating a huge meal now. Gotta save room for the turkey and cheesecake."

"I used to make Christmas pancakes for Gabe when he was little. I have this set of metal cookie cutters that made great kid-sized pancakes—trees, ornaments, stars, even Santa. I haven't done that in years. Guess he outgrew them."

Suddenly, her throat tightened up and her eyes filled with tears. Pressing a hand to her lips, she fought back a sob.

"Leslie?"

She turned in his embrace and flung her arms around his neck as she began crying in earnest.

Holding her close, Robin patted her back and stroked her hair. "Don't cry," he said with a gentle tone. "Everything's gonna be all right. You'll see. Nick will behave himself, and that lump in your breast will turn out to be nothing."

His assurances only made her cry harder, and several moments passed before she was able to speak. "Promise me something?"

"Anything."

"Will you look after Gabriel when I'm gone? He doesn't have anyone but me. He'll be so lost. I know he's almost grown, but he has to finish college and he needs somewhere to come home to."

"I promise. But you're not going to die—not until you're old and gray and can't chase me around the nursing home anymore." He raised her head with his fist beneath her chin. "No more of that talk. You won't die. I won't let you."

She had news for him. People died all the time—despite the wishes and prayers of their loved ones. She'd seen it happen often enough during the course of her career—and several times with her own family.

Her mother had succumbed to one of the nastier forms of cancer. "Most of them are gone in a year," the doctor had said. "And all of them are gone in two."

That was thirty years ago, and he'd been absolutely correct. She'd lasted eighteen months after her diagnosis. Granted, her cancer had already metastasized to her lymph nodes when they found it. Leslie didn't think hers had, but that was something only a biopsy could determine. Great strides had been made in cancer treatment, but people still died from it—every single day.

Robin pressed a kiss to her forehead. "You'll see the doctor, and we'll do whatever it takes. I'll be with you every step of the way. You won't have to face anything alone—ever again."

"So stop crying and fix my breakfast, woman?" Her attempt at humor sounded pathetic, even to her own ears. She dried her eyes on the corner of her apron, although the "WILL GRILL FOR SEX" line emblazoned on it didn't seem quite so funny anymore.

"I wasn't going to say that." He smiled, pushing an errant lock of hair back from her face. "Actually, I was thinking about fixing my own breakfast for a change." His smile faded into a more serious expression. "I meant what I said, Leslie. We'll go through this together, and if it turns out bad, we'll make the most of the time we have left. But we don't know anything yet. Don't be writing your obituary too soon."

"Okay, just... bear with me for a while. I'm not as strong as I used to be. I've had to face so many awful things alone. I got through them—but I'm so very glad I have you now."

"That's my girl." He gave her another squeeze. "So, now we just have to 'eat, drink, and be merry, for tomorrow we may die.' Right?"

"Right." She squared her shoulders as if that action might shake off her melancholy mood. "And if we're ever going to eat this feast, I have to cook it."

Leslie went on with the dinner preparations while Robin fried bacon and scrambled eggs like he'd done it every morning of his life.

Yet another thing I've learned in the past month.

Cooking breakfast might not seem like much of an accomplishment to anyone else, but Robin considered it a milestone of major proportions.

Gabriel shuffled in, wiping the sleep from his eyes as he sniffed the air. "Mmm… turkey, dressing, and bacon. Christmas is off to a great start."

"I take it you're hungry," Robin said, chuckling.

"You bet. Think you could throw in a few eggs for me?"

"Sure thing." In a quieter tone for Leslie's ears only, he added, "I think I'm getting the hang of this."

Gabe must've heard him anyway. "What, are ye a rotten cook, then? Is me breakfast gonna suck big, hairy donkey balls?"

Leslie tossed a withering glance over her shoulder. "No, it is *not* gonna suck big, hairy donkey balls. So just sit down and be quiet. Robin's a good cook. By the way, Merry Christmas, Gabe."

"Merry Christmas, Mom—and to you too, Robin. Wow. We're here in the most awesome house ever, and me Mum and me little Dad are in the kitchen cooking. What could be better than that?"

"Not much," Robin said. "Unless, of course, *Junior* wants to go put some wood on the fire while *Dad* finishes fixing breakfast."

"Sure. Any secret to that?"

"Just open the dampers and let the smoke clear before you open the door to the stove. Then rake the coals down to a nice, flat bed and fill it up with wood. Close the door, wait for a while until the fire's going good, and then choke back the dampers to where they were when you started." Robin grinned at him. "Hey, it's easier than cooking."

Gabriel looked doubtful, but headed over to the stove anyway.

Robin had given Leslie the same instructions, and she'd been able to follow through—despite the fact that he'd been naked at the time. Gabe couldn't claim to have had that level of distraction.

"Did you hear that?" Robin whispered when Gabe was out of earshot. "He called me his little Dad. Guess we'll *have* to get married now that the secret's out."

She was smiling, but tears swam in her eyes. The "little Dad" comment had obviously affected her as much as it had him. "What secret is that?"

"That I knocked you up when I was ten years old—precocious little devil, wasn't I?"

Those same tears ran down her cheeks when she laughed. "Actually, I think you'd have been about eight or nine. Gabe is nineteen, and you have to allow some time for gestation."

"Damn. I should be in the *Guinness Book of World Records*."

"Probably so," she agreed. "You be sure and tell Nick that."

It was Robin's turn to laugh. "Oh, God. He'd have a cow."

"Then he'd be in the book too," she pointed out.

"Well, shit. I won't tell him then." He dumped the eggs and bacon onto a pair of Ninja Turtle plates. "Yo, Gabe. Breakfast is ready. Got that fire going yet?"

"Just about," Gabe called back. "How long does it take to heat up?"

"You've got time to eat. Check it again when you're done."

Gabe came back to the table. "That stove is so awesome. I don't suppose we have any chestnuts, do we?"

Robin raised an eyebrow. "You mean as in 'chestnuts roasting on an open fire'? Nope. Don't have any."

"Oh, ye of little faith," Leslie mocked. "Did you really think I wouldn't bring some?" She dug into the stack of provisions she'd brought over from her apartment and held up a large bag. "This'll be the first time we've ever had the chance to roast them over a real fire."

"Sometimes they explode in the oven." If the way his eyes lit up was anything to go by, Gabe preferred the firecracker effect to the flavor. "I bet they'd make some serious noise inside that stove."

"We'll have to wait until later to do that," Robin said. "You can't cook in the stove until the fire burns down to coals again."

Gabe's enthusiasm dimmed momentarily, but he dug into his breakfast with gusto.

"You were right, Mom," he said after a bite or two. "Robin really *can* cook."

"Damn right he can cook. He can do anything." Leslie's smile broadened. "He's perfect."

"Oh, please, don't get all mushy," Gabe begged. "At least not before I've finished breakfast."

"Hey, you were the one talking about Mom and Dad in the kitchen and roasting chestnuts," she reminded her son. "I'd say that was pretty sentimental, but what do I know?"

She set the bag of chestnuts on the table. Only then did Robin realize she'd been holding it in her left hand.

Gabe must've spotted the diamond at the same moment. After nearly aspirating his toast, he pointed to her ring and gasped, "Is that what I think it is?"

Leslie held out her hand, wiggling her fingers as though admiring the stone's cut and clarity. "I'm not sure. Robin put this on my finger late last night, but he never said what it was for." She aimed a questioning look at Robin. "Care to enlighten us?"

Should've known it wouldn't be that easy.

"It's an engagement ring," he replied. "Engaging *you* to be my wife—" Pausing, he turned toward Gabe. "And *you* to be my stepson." He waited the space of two beats of his pounding heart. "Any takers?"

"I'm all for it," Gabe said. "But isn't this a little sudden?"

Robin glanced at Leslie. If she didn't know why he'd done it when he had, she ought to.

"There are extenuating circumstances," she said. "I wasn't

going to tell you this until after I knew something more...
definitive."

"But?"

"I have a lump in my breast." Her words had seemed slow
before, but these came out in a rush.

Gabe stared at her in silence as though seeing his entire life—
and hers—pass before his eyes.

"I have an appointment on Friday with Dr. Edlin." Her voice
had steadied and gained strength as she continued. "If anything
happens to me, Robin—"

"Nothing is going to happen to you," Gabe said fiercely. "It
can't. It just *can't*." Dropping his fork, he leaned back in his chair.
"Not after everything else you've had to deal with. No way."

Leslie's fingertips were white where she gripped the edge of the
table. "You know as well as I do that this sort of thing is never fair. I
didn't want to tell you before I knew for sure. Maybe I was wrong to
keep it from you, but I thought if we could just get through
Christmas—"

Gabe raised a hand for silence. "Mom. We've gotten through
everything else together. We'll get through this, too. I know we
will." His gaze shifted toward Robin. "You, sir, are one totally
awesome dude. I can't think of anyone I'd rather have as my
stepdad."

Robin took the hand Gabe held out to him and gave it a firm
shake. "And I couldn't have fathered a better son."

By this time, Leslie was openly sobbing.

"Now, Mum," Gabe began. "No need ta be cryin'. 'Tis a happy
occasion we be havin' here."

Robin got to his feet and gathered Leslie into his embrace.
"You got that right—and between the three of us, we'll make sure it
stays that way."

Chapter 32

Any misgivings that Leslie might've had for going slightly overboard on the decorations and the dinner dissipated when Robin's nieces and nephews got their first glimpse of the wonderland that his house had become. Ranging in age from five to sixteen, the kids—each family had three—were all round-eyed with awe. The adults also seemed impressed.

With Gabriel's help, she and Robin had literally decked the halls with boughs of holly and pine, adding white lights, mistletoe, and sparkling garland to the greenery they'd hung from the beams in the vaulted ceiling. The cloudy weather didn't compete with the candles burning throughout the house, and as evening fell, their golden glow grew richer, the soft light augmenting the scents of turkey, pine, and spicy wassail.

"This is what I imagined when I first set foot in here," she said to Robin in an aside. "A crackling fire, the laughter of children, and that beautiful tree…"

He slipped an arm around her, pulling her close. "We'll have a tough time topping this next year."

If there is a next year.

"If we can equal it, that'll be enough."

"I dunno." Pausing, he directed a scrutinizing gaze toward the tree. "That star doesn't quite touch the ceiling. Might need a taller tree."

"Any bigger and it wouldn't fit through the door."

They'd had enough trouble with this one—yet another memory to cherish. The two of them wrestling that enormous pine into submission, laughing when it toppled over, cheering when it finally stood upright.

Wish we had a video of that.

If this was indeed her last Christmas, it was certainly one of the best. Nick didn't even get pissed when he saw Gabe's sweatshirt, although Leslie's engagement ring caused quite a stir.

Nick apologized to Leslie the moment he entered the house. She'd accepted his apology with the best grace she could muster, despite wondering why it was necessary—why he hadn't intervened when he could've spared his younger brother that terrifying ordeal. She never questioned his failure to act—after all, not everyone responded to disaster with heroism—but understanding it was difficult.

Nevertheless, if fate allowed her own life to continue, she wanted it to do so without the burden of carrying a grudge against her husband's brother.

Husband. No wedding date had been set or even discussed. If Nick objected to their union, he had the good sense to keep quiet. Everyone else seemed delighted that she and Robin intended to marry, but none of them knew the secret behind it.

Only she and Gabe understood the timing of his proposal.

Dear, sweet Robin. He meant what he'd said about standing by her, and he'd backed up that commitment with a diamond ring.

Robin had already related his conversation with Nick. Someday she might ask Laura the details of the argument with her mother, but not today. Not when happiness and contentment filled the house and everyone in it.

That night, she fell asleep in Robin's arms with visions of sugar plums dancing in her head, wishing that someday she might be able to look back on this special day and remember it as her first—and certainly not her last—Christmas in paradise.

Two days later, the payback for her time in paradise began when Dr. Edlin recommended a breast biopsy.

൫ൕ

Leslie had known it was coming, but the words still struck her like a blow.

"It's only a precaution," Dr. Edlin assured her. "I seriously doubt that we're dealing with a malignancy, but only a biopsy can give us that peace of mind."

His smile was reassuring, but she wasn't fooled. She could see the concern in his eyes.

His physical examination had detected no palpable lymph nodes, which was encouraging—something to hold onto during the ten days until her surgery.

They discussed all the options, chose a surgeon Dr. Edlin trusted, and decided to go with a lumpectomy and radiation should the lump prove to be cancerous with no metastasis. Radical mastectomy was mentioned as a possibility. With any luck, it would prove unnecessary.

Robin was optimistic, but still insisted that she would look incredibly sexy in a bustier with a swath of black satin to cover any scars. Fortunately, he didn't mention that to Dr Edlin.

The next ten days passed by in a blur. Surrounded by supportive friends, Leslie worked her regular schedule, and she saw the New Year in with Robin and Gabe. Beyond that, she felt more numb than fearful.

The day finally arrived, and as she lost consciousness, Dr. Edlin held her hand, just as he had prior to the last surgery she'd undergone.

ॐ

I'm awake.

As her awareness grew, she tried to focus on the pain in the left side of her chest—how severe it was, where it was located. Did it seem bad enough for a mastectomy?

I should be able to tell.

It stung in more than one place—which could have been due to any number of reasons—none of them good.

Oh, no, not good at all...

Robin and Gabe were talking, but she still wasn't awake enough to join in the conversation.

"Seriously?" Gabe said.

Robin chuckled. "Leslie slapped the shit out of him and I finished him off for her. He's been a lot different since then—although he did give me some crap about taking this week off. He didn't seem to think Leslie would need me since you were still on vacation from Purdue."

"You should have told him to suck some big, hairy donkey balls," Gabe advised.

"Actually, I did," Robin admitted. "That should shut him up for a while."

"If he gives you any more trouble, I'll beat the crap out of him—or at least threaten to. That's all it took with Mom's old boyfriends. I only slugged *one* of them."

Leslie tried to smile, but her mouth wasn't working yet.

Gabe's laughter was loud enough that she heard one of the nurses tell him to keep it down.

Someone squeezed her hand.

"When's she gonna wake up?" Gabe sounded nervous, impatient. "Seems like we've been sitting here for hours."

"More like twenty minutes," Robin replied. "Be patient."

"But I want to tell her it's gone," Gabe insisted.

"Go ahead and tell her."

Robin sounded reasonable and unperturbed—which was a good sign. But what was gone? Her breast or the lump?

Be specific.

"I don't think she can hear us," Gabe said.

"Oh, yes she can," Robin said. "Hearing is the last sense to go and the first to come back. I watch lots of medical shows, so I know it's true. She can probably hear every word we're saying."

Then for heaven's sake, tell me something useful. Don't just sit there babbling on about whether I can hear you or not.

"Really?" Gabe asked. "Will she remember it?"

"Now, that, I *don't* know," Robin replied. "Probably."

"You tell her, then," Gabe urged. "I don't want to have to tell her when she's wide awake and looking at us. I know I'll end up bawling."

Oh, definitely not good.

"Shit."

"What did you say, Mom?"

Nothing. I didn't say anything. I'm still asleep, remember?

"She said something," Gabe announced. He sounded pleased.

Experimentally, she attempted to shift her left shoulder, which was a bad move because it hurt like hell. She heard a moan, then realized it had come from her.

"Does it hurt, baby?"

Was that *Robin* talking?

It couldn't be. He *never* called her baby—except maybe once or twice when she was sick.

No, it was after my panic attack when he found the lump.

She remembered now. He was so good to her. She heard a grateful sigh.

That was me.

"Are you gonna tell her or not?" Gabe demanded.

"Yes, I'll tell her."

Definitely Robin...

His breath tickled her ear. "It was only a cyst. Nothing nasty at all." With a quiet chuckle, he added, "No need for you to wear black satin with your bustier."

"I tried to find one on the Internet," Leslie said, regaining the power of speech at last. "What you were describing is actually a cupless leather corset rather than a bustier. Goes great with a whip."

"I wish I hadn't heard that," Gabe mumbled.

"You're such a prude," she said. "Or is it an act? I mean, anyone who goes around talking about sucking big, hairy donkey balls..."

"Me own Mum in a bloomin' bustier—and with a whip, no less! Me poor little Dad," Gabe lamented. "Don't tell me I'll have to protect him from you, too."

Robin cleared his throat. "Gabe has been referring to me as his 'little Dad' to every one of the nurses who asks who we are. Said he didn't want them to think I was his brother. You'll *have* to marry me now."

Taking a deep breath, she forced her eyes to open. Gabe stood beside the stretcher, towering above her. Robin was closer.

Must be sitting down.

She scowled at her son. "Why would *anyone* think you were brothers? You're nearly twice his size." She aimed a puzzled frown at Robin. "And I thought I *was* going to marry you. You did ask me... Gave me a ring and everything... I'm *sure* you did."

"Yes, and I'm holding you to it," Robin said. "No backing out."

"We'll see," she mumbled. "Not sure I want to marry a man who thinks I won't marry him without coercion. Makes me feel cheap."

"You're not cheap," Robin insisted. "You're absolutely priceless. I'm just making sure nobody steals you away from me."

"As if anybody could—or would want to."

"I have to be here to look after you," he said, seeming to ignore her remark. "Believe me, if there's a lump the size of a grain of sand, I'll find it—just like I found this one."

"Shh... Don't say that. You'll embarrass Gabe."

Gabe's gasp was right on cue. "You mean *he* found it? What were you— No, don't tell me. I don't want to know."

"Hmm..." She pretended to search for the answer trapped inside her partially-anesthetized brain. "What *were* we doing, Robin? I know it involved whipped cream, but other than that..."

"Me own Mum!" Gabriel wailed.

"Oh, pipe down, Junior," Robin admonished. "Mom needs her rest." Any assumptions that he might actually be concerned for her welfare were dispelled when he added, "'Little Dad' has *plans* for when she gets better."

It seemed as though he would leave it at that, but when he suggested that Gabe go out to the vending machine for a Coke, she knew there was more to it.

Leaning closer, he whispered, "You're right about the bustier. It wasn't what I had in mind at all. I got you something better."

"Oh, really?"

"Yeah," he replied. "I forget what it's called, but it's made out leather straps and comes with matching boots. You'll look absolutely fabulous in it."

"You really think so?"

"I *know* so. As far as I'm concerned, you'd look good in anything—or nothing at all."

"Then why do I need to wear that–that *harness* thing? I'd feel like an idiot."

"No worries." He smoothed a hand over her forehead. "You only have to wear it on Saturdays."

"And why is that?"

His grin was simultaneously sweet and diabolical. "Because it has a hook for your whip."

"Oh, my…"

"And just in case you need any encouragement, I'm pretty sure I left the milk out."

"Boy, are you gonna get it when we get home…"

He kissed her cheek. "Sounds *fabulous*."

About the Author

A native of Louisville, Kentucky, Cheryl Brooks is a former critical care nurse who resides in rural Indiana with her husband, two sons, two horses, four cats, and one dog. Her **Cat Star Chronicles** series was first published by Sourcebooks Casablanca in 2008, and includes *Slave, Warrior, Rogue, Outcast, Fugitive, Hero, Virgin, Stud,* and *Wildcat.* Look for book 10, *Rebel,* in 2014. She has one self-published e-book, *Sex, Love, and a Purple Bikini,* and one erotic short story, *Midnight in Reno.* She has also published *If You Could Read My Mind* writing as Samantha R. Michaels. As a member of *The Sextet,* she has written several erotic novellas published by Siren/Bookstrand. Her **Unlikely Lovers** series includes *Unbridled, Uninhibited, Undeniable,* and *Unrivaled.* Her other interests include cooking, gardening, singing, and guitar playing. Cheryl is a member of RWA and IRWA.

You can visit her online at www.cherylbrooksonline.com or email her at cheryl.brooks52@yahoo.com.

www.ingramcontent.com/pod-product-compliance
Lightning Source LLC
Chambersburg PA
CBHW072235190626
46809CB00018B/2075